Epitaph

Full Circle

THE AWEN CHRONICLES:
BOOK 3

J. A. GIBBENS

 FriesenPress

One Printers Way
Altona, MB R0G 0B0
Canada

www.friesenpress.com

ISBN
978-1-03-917243-2 (Hardcover)
978-1-03-917242-5 (Paperback)
978-1-03-917244-9 (eBook)

1. FICTION, THRILLERS, CRIME

Distributed to the trade by The Ingram Book Company

AUTHOR'S NOTE

I invite readers to visit with me at www.gibbensauthor.ca, on Facebook as J. A. Gibbens (https:www.facebook.com/gibbensauthor), Twitter (@gibbensauthor), Instagram (gibbensauthor), and LinkedIn (J. A. Gibbens).

Readers are urged to refer to the *Partial Cast of Characters—Some Returning and Some New* for additional information. I have provided this list to assist those who may have read Book 1 and/or Book 2 of the trilogy rather long ago and might need a quick refresher.

If you have read a beta copy or ARC of Book 2, *Cow on the Ice*, please note that two characters have been provided new names. Astrid von Euler has been renamed Lilly von Euler and Elsa Carlsson has become Astrid Carlsson. (They are quite content with their new names.)

The glossary will provide help with foreign terms and clarify which terms and places are purely fictitious, where that may otherwise not be obvious.

With the powers vested in me, I have permitted jet traffic at Billy Bishop Airport. At the time of writing, this is merely a proposed change, and there has been mention of it but no more than that. I have exercised these same powers previously, moving the bluffs from east of Toronto to west of the city, where they have remained for Book 3 of *The Awen Chronicles*.

Many thanks to M. Nancy Tatham, MD, for her medical insight, and to Joyce McCombe and Patrick Gibbens who took the time to read an early manuscript and provide me with feedback. Many thanks to Sue Ratcliffe and her anything-but-red pencil. Thanks as well to Donal Carey for linguistic assistance and Greg Gibbens for IT help and much more. Your efforts are much appreciated.

DEDICATION

For Greg, in appreciation of your honesty. I would spend
another lifetime with you, if only I could.

*The fact that this person exists in the world at all, this alone
makes this world, and a life in it, meaningful.*

— Viktor Frankl (1905–1997)

TABLE OF CONTENTS

PARTIAL CAST OF CHARACTERS— SOME RETURNING AND SOME NEW

Agafya Orlov (Book 2)	Grigori's wife
Albin Tyrchniewicz (Book 1 & 2)	works for Kent; ex-military; lives with Eve
Aleksandra Orlov (new)	also known as Sandra, Sandy, Blomma, Zayka; Grigori's granddaughter; student at University of Toronto
Alexei Orlov (Book 2, deceased)	Grigori's youngest son; Aleksandra's father
Annie Hogan Sarto (Book 1, deceased)	Lucy's grandmother by birth
Astrid Carlsson (Book 2)	widow; brilliant scientist; dementia success story
Awen (Book 1 & 2)	allonym used by Lucy on her paintings
Bernardo "Bernie" Concha (new)	real estate broker
Bijou (new)	Serge's tricolour Cavalier King Charles spaniel

Blomma (new)	code name for Aleksandra
Calogero (new)	alias used by Langston Garner's crime syndi-cate contact
Carmine Gallo (Book 2, deceased)	Matteo Gallo's nephew; Gina's son
Carlo (new)	Tommaso's cousin; criminal
Charles "Chuck" Dickens (new)	Eve's former English tutor
Chernyye Volosy (Book 2, deceased)	Chloé's Russian alias
Chloé Corbin (Book 2, deceased)	Nathan's model and partner in crime
Clarence Garner (Book 1, deceased)	lawyer at Garner & Garner; the first Garner Janus; accom-plice of Jozsef Szabo
Connor Doyle (Book 1, deceased)	Irish stonemason employed by Gianni
Cookie (Book 2)	Eve's golden retriever
Croesus (Book 2)	Grigori's billion-dollar private yacht
Darri Fournier (Book 1, deceased)	French stonemason employed by Gianni
Darrin Fournier (new)	employee at Doyle's in Port L'Orté
Derwood Garner (Book 1, deceased)	Gianni Sarto's lawyer; Clarence's brother
Donald "Donny" Gallagher (Book 1 & 2)	Yoichi's boyfriend; a linguist

Elinor (Book 1 & 2)	Helen's partner; employed by the Gillespies
Emmy (new)	one of Aleksandra's university friends
Eve: Euphrosyne Vighild Ek (Book 1 & 2)	widow; Gillespies' neighbour; Lucy's friend; retired choreographer/dancer; Albin's partner
Fortunato Russo (book 2, deceased)	Criminal; Vincenzo Rizzo's friend
Frank Gies (new)	fire inspection officer
Giovanni "Gianni" Sarto (Book 1, deceased)	Lucy's grandfather by birth; associate of Garners
Gina Rizzo Gallo (Book 2)	Carmine's mother; Vincenzo Rizzo's sister; Matteo Gallo's sister-in-law
George Birch (new)	Maddie's father
Gracie Hogan Szabo (Book 1, deceased)	Annie's sister; Lucy's grand-aunt by blood and step-grandmother by adoption
Grigori "Grisha" Orlov (Book 2)	Aleksandra's grandfather; a multi-billionaire
Guilio/Julius Roman (Book 1 & 2, deceased)	Lucy's nemesis; Vincenzo Rizzo's friend
Helen Tyrchniewicz (Book 1 & 2)	Albin's sister; Gillespies' estate manager
Ilya Orlov (new)	Grigori's second son; Aleksandra's uncle
Jean-Pierre Allard (Book 2, deceased)	Serge's partner, both personally and professionally

Jozsef Szabo (Book 1, deceased)	Lucy's grandfather by adoption; accomplice of Clarence Garner
Juji Abebe (Book 2)	Nanovo corporate lawyer; Astrid's personal attorney
Juliette Garner (Book 1 & 2)	lawyer; works with Interpol in Lyon; former partner at Garner & Garner
Julius/Guilio Roman (Book 1 & 2, deceased)	Lucy's nemesis; Vincenzo Rizzo's friend
Kent Gillespie (Book 1 & 2)	Lucy's husband; architect and lawyer by training; works as a property developer
Kyle Garner (Book 1)	lawyer; senior partner at Garner & Garner
Langston Garner (Book 1)	lawyer; partner at Garner & Garner; current Janus
Lars (Book 1, deceased)	was Eve's husband sixteen years ago
Leo (Book 2)	Astrid's nurse
Lilly von Euler, Dr. (Book 2)	president of Astrid's pharmaceutical company, Nanovo
Luc Anouilh (Book 2)	Interpol
Lucy Gillespie (Book 1 & 2)	artist and central character
Lukas Carlsson (Book 2)	Astrid's son
Maddie Birch (new)	one of Aleksandra's university friends
Marge Birch (new)	Maddie's mother

Mark Witherspoon (Book 2, deceased)	billionaire friend of the Gillespies
Matteo Gallo (Book 2)	previously with Interpol
Matthew Gilbert Espie (Book 2, deceased)	Astrid's husband; Lukas' father; failed architect
Maxim Orlov (new)	Grigori's eldest son; one of Aleksandra's two uncles
Merlot (new)	Serge's Blenheim Cavalier King Charles spaniel
Mike "Killer" Kilpatrick (new)	Murray's friend
Murray McKelvie (new)	financial advisor; Mike's friend
Nathan "Nate" Bellamy (Book 2)	art forger and thief; Yoichi's former boyfriend
Nanovo (Book 2)	Astrid's pharmaceutical firm
O—Oko and Ebo Owusu (Book 2)	twins; security specialists and bodyguards
Patrick Brennan (Book 2)	police detective inspector
Peter Szabo (Book 1, deceased)	a previous owner of L'Orté Island and much of L'Orté Point; Lucy's great-grandfather by adoption
Petra Szucs (new)	President, University of Toronto
Preston Garner (new)	lawyer at Garner & Garner; Langston's son
Rashid Darwish (Book 2)	police detective
Roberto	criminal
Rojas (new)	lieutenant in El Viruñas drug cartel

Rufina (Book 2)	Grigori's name for Lucy, meaning "red-haired woman"
Sarah (new)	receptionist at Garner & Garner
Serge Proulx (Book 2)	retired Parisian architect having specialized in the restoration of historical buildings; friend of the Gillespies
Smith—Charles "Smith" Ponzi (new)	Aleksandra's boyfriend; university student
Sophie Dubois (new)	*juriste* hired by Nathan
Spencer Worms (new)	private investigator hired by Langston
Theia Witherspoon (Book 2, deceased)	Mark's wife; art collector; killed in Nice, France terrorist attack on Promenade des Anglais
Theia (Book 2)	Mark Witherspoon's yacht
Tommaso Camminatore (new)	Nathan's cellmate
Vincenzo Rizzo (Book 2, deceased)	Gina's brother; criminal; restauranteur; Carmine's uncle; killed in a confrontation with Kent
Yoichi Song (Book 1 & 2)	Lucy's art agent and long-time friend

CHAPTER 1
END OF THE BEGINNING

Southern Ontario, 1933 . . .

"Now what do we do?" Clarence asked, directing his question more to the Fates than to his protégé, Jozsef. "This is the second time, thanks to you, that I've needed to consider how to dispose of a body."

"He wasn't going to tell us anything anyway," Jozsef replied. "What makes you think Gianni's will is around here anyway?" He continued his search, attacking the shelves of books in the manor house library in pursuit of hidden treasure. "You said he didn't have one."

"I said that *I thought* he didn't have one. It appears that young Derwood may have written one for him. I just caught a bit of his conversation with Father. The details were unclear, but I'm sure I heard Derwood mention Gianni, a will, and Doyle."

"Whether your brother arranged for Gianni's will, or not, will be your problem to sort out at your end. If you do, great; if not, then it's been good working with you, but I'll be moving on to bigger and better things on my own. Remember, my own father died as well, so now I've got full control over all the Szabo business interests."

"Yes, yes, Mr. Big Businessman." Clarence said, deriding him. "You haven't come across any keys have you? This desk takes a cabinet barrel key, like the one for my office desk."

"No. No keys, no nothing," Jozsef replied. "Try your key if you have it. It's time we had some luck." Jozsef continued to flip through the pages of a large journal, searching for the missing paperwork.

Clarence removed his own desk key from the pocket of his wool herringbone jacket, but it didn't fit the keyhole in Gianni's desk. Increasingly frustrated by a task that had so far proved hopeless, he used a letter opener to pry open the drawer, only to discover it contained nothing of interest to him.

Time passed, and the two men became progressively more tired and agitated.

"I'm done. It doesn't appear to be here. Let's go." Clarence pushed his arms into the armholes of a crudely-made tarpaulin greatcoat found during his search of the house. *This should keep me more comfortable*, he thought, now considering the well-oiled leather coat in a more positive light. He turned for the door then remembered his office desk key. He grabbed the key and dropped it into a deep pocket of the coat.

"There's a dinghy tied at the dock. We could float the body out in the boat, then sink it where it gets weedy. I'm not digging a grave, not with all the rocks and tree roots."

"You just had to get carried away yet again, didn't you, Jozsef. How do you propose we carry his body to the boat without getting blood on ourselves? Your burns are not yet healed, so you're not moving well, and I'm not going to pick up your slack."

"We'll wrap him in that big coat you found and drag him. I saw a hatchet back near the hod box." Then Jozsef proposed a simple solution. "If I butcher him here, we'll have a smaller bundle to drag."

"Sounds bloody simple." It was going to be a disgusting task; nevertheless, Clarence agreed. "Do it and be quick about it then." He reluctantly donated the tarpaulin greatcoat to the task. *Damn, but I'll be cold getting back to Port Myer.*

In short order, the dinghy was loaded with the leather-bound package containing Doyle's body parts, and they made their way back to Clarence's mahogany launch. Once aboard, Clarence looked back to see Jozsef drinking slivovitz from one of the bottles he had secreted aboard the launch.

"Hand that over here," he called out. Jozsef passed the bottle to Clarence, who drank deeply from it. "Hopefully, that'll keep me warmer. I hate this damp cold; I so look forward to leaving here. Did I tell you? I've an invitation to visit with some important business people in Europe, so I thought I'd take them up on that sometime soon. France, Monaco, Italy . . . just as soon as I've cleared up this Gianni mess." He drank deeply once more then returned the bottle to Jozsef.

Jozsef took a quick swallow, corked the bottle, then started the motor and cast the lines. The waves were increasing in size; an autumn storm on Lake Erie was rapidly approaching. The launch struggled to pull the load as the dinghy began to take on water, sinking earlier than they had planned.

There was little choice but to sever the tow lines, letting the dinghy containing Doyle's body parts sink to the bottom. Jozsef took a celebratory swig of slivovitz and offered some to Clarence. While Clarence imbibed, Jozsef removed something from his pocket: a medallion on a chain. He dangled it in front of Clarence.

"You realize that's not gold, don't you?" Clarence said. "You got Gianni's gold pocket watch, the watch my uncle and father gave him. That's gold; this isn't. It's just brass."

Jozsef grunted with displeasure then threw his worthless find toward the sunken dinghy. Clarence returned the slivovitz, and now quite drunk and rapidly becoming angry, Jozsef stood and drank deeply. He threw the empty bottle toward the dinghy then bent to retrieve a second he had stored on board.

"Enough!" Clarence hollered, putting the boat in gear for the return trip. The launch jerked forward, and the bottle of slivovitz slipped from Jozsef's grasp and into the water, where it sank beneath the waves.

CHAPTER 2
NETWORKING

France, present day . . .

Nathan Bellamy completed a final flourish on the serving plate he had been assigned and grabbed a quick glance at the wall clock. It was nearly quitting time. He secured the tops on the paints he had been using for the project and washed his brushes in solvent. The serving plate itself was placed on its own shelf in the rack assigned to him.

While Nathan and the other inmates, who worked at the porcelain factory near Limoges, soon would be leaving to return to the prison, a skeleton crew of regular employees, working on a staggered shift, would place the items in the large kiln room for firing and set out the supplies for the next workday.

Nathan found the work uninspiring and tedious, but at least it provided a break from the daily routine of life at Aubry Prison. He hoped that a willingness to work might help ensure him parole, but he had also hoped that work might be found closer to Paris. He considered it most unfortunate that there was a porcelain factory so very near the town in which Aubry Prison was situated.

Being near Paris would have been inspiring; being nearly five hours from Paris was mind-numbing. His *avocat* had smiled and seemed to pat himself on the back upon hearing that Nathan was to be incarcerated at Aubry. Apparently, it was the most modern facility of its type in France, and he should consider himself fortunate. While his *avocat* considered this a good placement, Nathan didn't see it that way.

Five years! The prison counsellor had suggested that he celebrate the fact that his job involved painting, even though his skill level far exceeded that required for the job. At least he wasn't working in a mechanical or electrical shop or, worse yet, on a farm. He found the very idea abhorrent.

"Bellamy," he mumbled, completing his boring day with more of the boring routine.

The guard checked off his name on the list affixed to a clipboard he carried and smiled cordially despite the rote work. Nathan stepped up and into the transport vehicle and took the seat beside Tommaso Camminatore, his most recent cellmate.

Tommaso was a younger man but more knowledgeable about prison life than Nathan. Whereas this was Nathan's first incarceration, Tommaso claimed to have already experienced prison in several countries. Nathan and Tommaso often spoke of his experiences within the system—not that Nathan understood all of it. Tommaso spoke Italian and French, while Nathan spoke English and French. Although Nathan had tried to learn Italian, he found it too difficult and soon gave up on the idea. Fortunately, Tommaso's English was improving rapidly. Soon they would be able to speak to one another solely in English—providing greater privacy to their shared communication within the confines of prison walls. Nathan held high hopes of his affiliation with Tommaso.

Nathan grabbed at the back of his neck and rotated his fingertips about an area, all the while exerting pressure on that same spot. He cracked his neck to one side and then to the other. Finally, he rotated his head: down, left, up, right. He repeated the action five times. Tommaso had counted.

"Why you do this?" Tommaso asked, demonstrating his newly-acquired ability in English.

"Loosening up my neck," Nathan said. "My muscles get tight, painting like that all day. I'm used to keeping to my own schedule and taking a break whenever I choose."

"*Postura* no good," commented Tommaso. "You know yoga?"

Nathan shook his head in reply. He'd never been one to exercise, and now in his mid-forties, he wasn't inclined to begin. But the discomfort he felt in his neck and upper shoulders had increased over the years, and clearly his own attempts to massage-away the pain and stiffness weren't being effective. He began to consider Tommaso's assessment of his problem.

The return trip to the prison was both brief and dreary. Yet chilled by what seemed a particularly long winter, the air remained too cool for other than the hardiest of spring flowers. The April sky was grey, and a breeze carried the threat of winter's return, rather than the promise of a milder season. The guards claimed it was the worst spring weather in twenty years. Soon their bus was turning into the driveway and entering the compound through the first set of gates and, a short time later, disgorging its passengers within the medium security sector Nathan was forced to call home.

Nathan had operated an art gallery in Montmartre, but due to a set of what he deemed "unfortunate circumstances," he had lost everything when Interpol focused on his lucrative side hustle. Last he heard, his partner and model, Chloé, had disappeared after joining her paramour in Toronto. *Lucky girl.* As the sole available target, his dissatisfied customers had focused their considerable ire upon him, and Nathan suspected it was the reason his sentence had been particularly harsh. Be that as it may, Nathan rejoiced in the knowledge that he alone retained access to all the offshore accounts into which the profits had been funnelled. He had been savvy enough to isolate her from the financial details. While his official books displayed a record of each transaction, the offshore details were in his head. As a result, millions in euros awaited Nathan upon his release.

Nathan tried to remain focused on his release. He created a pleasant and cooperative façade for the prison staff in an effort to gain parole—or perhaps full release—at the earliest possible date.

Nathan had shared his story with each new cellmate; it was a bonding ritual of sorts. Yoichi Song, a Canadian girlfriend from his university days, had somehow learned about his side hustle and notified Interpol. He had offered to make her his partner once it became necessary to replace Chloé, but the owner of the Song Gallery in Toronto had involved an artist friend of hers, Lucy Gillespie, and Nathan's side hustle had been brought to an abrupt halt.

It hadn't helped his case that he had burglarized a client's penthouse apartment in Paris and replaced a priceless painting with a forgery, or that he had attempted to remove the original from the premises. It also hadn't helped his case that he had attempted to fight the man who had caught him, even though he himself had suffered injury in the exchange and not the man he'd tried to fight. Nathan tended to keep that part of his story to himself.

The most serious charge against Nathan hadn't been the forgery but rather the tax fraud he had perpetrated by not paying tax on the income generated by the side hustle. Nathan remembered that Al Capone had been brought down in the same manner. He considered himself in fine company.

"This is—how you say in English—upward-facing dog," Tommaso explained, demonstrating the pose. "Very good for *postura*. Even *asma*. And, this called *ustrasana*, or camel pose;

also for *postura*. And for down here, try half cow face pose," he said, touching his lower back before demonstrating the pose himself.

Nathan tried the poses on several occasions, adding his own variations. Remaining seated was his preferred position for executing his version of an upward-facing dog pose, and he found it easier to accomplish a camel pose by letting his head fall back, rather than maintaining a forward-facing position. Attempts by Tommaso to correct Nathan's form were futile; apparently, Nathan knew best.

CHAPTER 3
REMEMBRANCE OF A CRIME

Southern Ontario . . .

As their limousine pulled into the traffic on Lakeshore Boulevard, and away from Billy Bishop Toronto City Airport, Astrid Carlsson looked back toward the CN Tower, just over a kilometre away, and remembered her last visit to Toronto. She didn't remember everything, but her deceased husband's girlfriend had given her a coffee laced with chloral hydrate and attempted to kill her—that she remembered. She hadn't remembered immediately; instead, the memories had returned gradually, over months and years. Their return was encouraged by the Mnimi treatments she received from the current head of Nanovo Pharmaceuticals. The blight of dementia, which had driven Astrid from the very company she had founded, was being lifted by Mnimi, a drug she herself had designed.

"Astrid, how are you feeling?" Leo asked, already accessing his medical pouch. "Here's a potassium tablet for you, and some water."

Astrid smiled at him, took hold of the uncapped bottle he proffered, and downed the pill. Leo returned the pill container to his medical kit. He had been Astrid's nurse through the worst of her dementia events as her Alzheimer's had increased its hold, and he now had the pleasant task of making a detailed record of her recovery. The plan was to have Astrid co-author a book with Leo, sharing the complex story of her recovery with others going through the challenges of dealing with similar forms of dementia. Leo's notes would provide an objective view, while Astrid's would be subjective. His notes were also part of a formal assessment of Mnimi for the research team back home in Gothenburg, Sweden.

Juji, Astrid's lawyer and friend, sat beside Leo and across from Astrid in the limousine. "Flying in a private jet is certainly preferable to flying commercial, isn't it Leo?" she said. "I didn't have an opportunity earlier to tell you, Astrid. When we went to visit my family in Addis Ababa . . . the connections for our flights to Ethiopia were terrible."

"Yes, I was intending to ask you to share details of your trip, but we've all been so busy recently," said Astrid, "How do you mean 'terrible'? What happened?"

"I let an acquaintance—someone I'd met at the gym—make the arrangements. She works in the travel industry and found a flight for us that required two stops. We later discovered that we could have reduced the duration of our travel time by fifty percent with a non-stop flight on Ethiopian Airlines. Instead of taking merely eight hours, our trip took sixteen."

"Was your acquaintance incompetent or simply new to the industry?" Astrid inquired.

"New. So, it was my fault. We could have done better on our own," Juji explained. "Apparently, one of the airlines she placed us with had a rep visit the agency where she works, and she was more interested in impressing him with a sale than in doing her job for us. Silly girl."

"You could have asked a staff member at Nanovo to make the arrangements for you. I don't know who's currently handling such work, but I'm sure that Lilly would have okayed the assignment," Astrid added, referring to Dr. Lilly von Euler, the head of Nanovo since Astrid's departure from that position. "Even so, your trip was a success if the photos I've seen are any indication."

Juji looked over at Leo, and the recently-weds smiled at one another and nodded in affirmation of Astrid's statement. It warmed Astrid's heart to see two of her most favourite people happy at having found one another.

"When would you like to go to the police station, Astrid?" Juji asked.

"Give me a couple of days, so I can get reacquainted with my son, and then I'd like to see Detective Inspector Brennan. What do you think, Juji? I'm not creating some problem by not seeing him immediately upon arriving in Canada, am I?" Astrid queried.

"No, not at all. Are you certain that two days is sufficient time to catch up with Lukas? It's been nearly six months since you've seen him."

"I am."

"Then I'll make our appointment with the detective inspector for as soon as possible after that."

Three days later, Astrid, Juji, and Leo returned to Toronto's city centre. While Astrid and Juji went off to locate the office of the detective inspector, Leo did some sightseeing, all the while prepared with his cellphone and medical kit in case there was a need to return and treat Astrid. She had a genetic heart condition, which was potentially aggravated by strong emotions, so Leo was prepared with her potassium tablets, just in case they were required. Juji had described Detective Inspector Patrick

Brennan as having "intelligent brown eyes," and Leo hoped that this intelligence had penetrated well beyond his eyes. They were said to be the windows of the soul; Leo hoped this was true. It would be important for Brennan to listen, to see, and to hear Astrid with his soul.

Before the women entered the building, Juji turned to Astrid. "I'm going to ask you one last time: Astrid, are you certain you want to do this?"

Astrid's lips were pursed, and while she merely nodded, her pale-blue eyes held Juji's gaze, and it was apparent that she was resolute in her decision.

A young constable escorted Astrid and Juji to the office of Detective Inspector Patrick Brennan. The inspector's office was small and cluttered; the detective inspector himself was stocky and bald. The April day was unseasonably warm, and as the central heating was yet turned on, the atmosphere in the office was something between warm and suffocating.

Once greetings and introductions were exchanged, Brennan, who was pressed for time, asked, "And what is it I can do for you?"

Juji provided the answer to his question. "When I was last here, the matter at hand was the murder of Astrid's husband, Matthew Gilbert Espie. The matter we are here to present today is both separate from that and inextricably linked to it." She pulled several files from her business bag and placed them in front of Brennan.

"We understand that in September of 2019, the body of a slender, young female with long black hair was found in the house being constructed by Astrid's husband. Astrid now has much to tell you about that, if you have time to listen."

Brennan found himself thinking about that case even now, years later. The press had called her the Blue Angel when it was revealed that most of her possessions were either blue or grey.

She had been identified and characterized, but they had never determined how she had come to die, locked in the panic room of the unfinished house.

"Back in 2019, as my dementia was being treated with an experimental drug, I overheard portions of Juji's half of the conversation she was having with you when you phoned to inform us that my husband had been shot and killed at the Gillespie residence here in Toronto. I somehow got it into my head that I had to go to Toronto. My memory has improved during treatment, and now I'm able to retrieve recent and long-term memories, though some are less clear than others.

"I took a flight to Toronto—without any luggage—and a taxi to the house my husband was building. I don't know what I was thinking. Was the irrationality due to Alzheimer's or to the shock of hearing that my husband had been shot dead in Toronto? I really can't say.

"A young woman with long black hair and dressed in blue and grey came to the door and claimed to be me. She claimed to be Mrs. Espie. I explained to her, as best I could, that I was the registered owner of the house: Astrid Carlsson from Gothenburg, Sweden, and that *I* was Mrs. Espie. At that point, she invited me inside. Her actions were much like those of a naughty and petulant pre-teen faced with no other choice in the matter.

"She offered me a coffee, which I foolishly accepted. We chatted, as I remember, but I don't recall what we chatted about. Then I identified the distinctive taste of the drug she had given me in the coffee she served, and realized I was in trouble."

"How had you become familiar with this drug?" Brennan asked.

"We're talking about chloral hydrate, Inspector. I was familiar with it for several reasons. Firstly, I'm a chemist—or I used to be—and I was the head of a pharmaceutical firm; secondly, when I was a child, chloral hydrate was sometimes used as an anaesthetic for children, and finally, my father was also an MD with degrees in chemistry, a lab in his cellar, and a very curious daughter who adored him, namely me."

"So, this woman gave you a Mickey Finn but with coffee instead of alcohol?"

"Yes, and as a result, the rest of the story becomes even more fuzzy in areas because the treatment drug was affected by the chloral hydrate she had put into the coffee.

"I eventually collapsed, and I have a sense of having been dragged. She wasn't very strong. There was lots of jerking and adjustments in where and how she grabbed me. Then I recall she became agitated and started to bang on the keypad. But the chloral hydrate kicked in thoroughly at that point, and I drifted off in a weird dreamlike state.

"In due course, I awoke, feeling like I'd had too much alcohol to drink . . . hungover is the word I'm looking for, I guess. I saw her across from me. She appeared to be asleep. I thought nothing of it. Instinctively, I moved toward the wall at the far end of the room and entered a code on the second keypad I located there. Matthew tended to use the same four-letter code for all such things. Furthermore, I had occasion to see the plans for the house when Matthew was drawing them. A hatch opened in the floor, and—there's a gap my memory here—the next thing I remember is walking toward the Gillespie residence. I called for a car to drive me to the airport, and from there I texted my team: Juji," Astrid said, nodding toward her lawyer, "Leo, who is my nurse, and Lilly, my physician. They were looking for me and had just arrived in Toronto from Gothenburg. My memories of my time in Canada were mostly gone by then, and those that remained were fragmented and didn't seem real.

"You know, to this day I don't know who that woman was, but her identity is no longer important to me."

Brennan read from the electronic file on his computer screen, looking for specific information. "Dr. Carlsson, you need to hear this. That woman was Chloé Corbin, a French citizen. She also went by the name Chernyye Volosy. She was wanted for crimes related to art theft and art forgery. I have absolutely no difficulty believing you when you say that she claimed to be you. That's precisely what she told our officers when we began investigating your husband's murder. She was forced to vacate the Gillespie house because the Gillespies had authorized access only for your husband. It seems that she just moved a short distance down the street, into your unfinished house.

"By the time we wanted to talk to her again, well, it appears that you'd come and gone. It was months later that her body was found. By that time she had an active file with Interpol, so we were readily able to identify her.

"Now, all this has been very interesting, but why are you telling me?" a confused Brennan asked, his gaze panning between Astrid and Juji. "This case is closed. So what's really going on here? Explain, please." His eyebrows were raised, and his gaze intent upon Astrid. "Dr. Carlsson?"

"Call me Astrid, please, Inspector. My progress in response to the Mnimi treatment of my dementia is starting to plateau. My theory as to the cause of this plateau is that, as things become apparent to me, I have need to share these new revelations with a relevant authority, someone who is in a better position to assess the accuracy, the truth of the memory. In this case, that would be you. In the absence of such affirmation, I can't trust everything I seem to remember. This mistrust is very deep-seated and results in confusion. If I am to be able to function with confidence about who I am and what I have—or haven't—done, then the foundation must be built on truths. But I don't know where that truth lies.

"In this case the memories are factually dramatic, and, if true, I would have expected some emotional response within myself, yet I have very little. I would have expected to feel guilt, yet I have none. Therefore, the memories are questionable in my opinion, and I don't know if the Mnimi has created memory artifacts which I am entertaining or is revealing actual events to me. I need reality, not fiction. It is not an exaggeration when I say that I am desperate for reality. As a result, I am providing you with this information so that I can move forward. Do what you must do, whatever it is that you should do."

Brennan glanced toward Juji, who was sitting poker-straight and staring straight ahead, her eyes moist, before turning his attention once again to Astrid. He looked toward her, unable to find the right words. As his head dropped, and he readied himself to speak, Astrid explained further. "It's not the guilt, but the *lack* of it that makes this necessary," she said before he could utter a word.

"And you think that by having this information revealed in this manner that you will ultimately experience the guilt you seem to be looking for? Do you need to *feel* guilty or actually *be* guilty?"

"To feel, Inspector. If I cannot feel, then I am naught. I might as well not exist."

"And you think that if you put this information into the system, so to speak, that this will reaffirm your memory concerning these events? It's as if you can't decide whether it actually happened, is that it?"

"Yes, Inspector, that's part of it. The other is that if I am technically, legally guilty of having committed a crime, then well, I guess I deserve to be punished accordingly. Can you . . . will you help me? I am not at peace with these events."

"Well, Astrid, you have delivered this information into the hands of the authorities. In this particular case, that would be me. I'll look over the material and think about what you've said; however, from where I stand, there is no crime that was committed by you in the course of these events. The death of Chloé Corbin has been deemed a death by misadventure. For there to be any other resolution to this would itself be a crime, and then it is I who would feel guilty. That is the truth of the matter. I can present this to the Crown attorney's office if you like, but they'll just tell me not to waste their time. If you do want me to, just say so, and I will, but I'm a busy man, and there are actual criminals out there I need to concentrate on.

"I'm no psychologist, but my guess is that you don't feel guilty because you aren't guilty. Simple as that. If you're looking for an emotion to connect with these events, I'd consider one of triumph and joy at your survival. The victim's actions brought about her death, not you. Had things been reversed, had she walked away and you had been left to die, I seriously doubt she would have become overwhelmed by guilt and come to me with a confession. Given her history, I sense that she would have felt no such guilt. But she no longer exists, and I for one am very glad that you do. Please continue to do so."

Once they had exited the building, Juji sent a text message to Leo and the three met at a nearby coffeehouse. Leo arrived first and nervously awaited the return of Juji and Astrid. His fears evaporated when he saw Juji's smiling face as she entered. Both she and Astrid looked as if a burden had been lifted from their shoulders. He raised his hand to get their attention in the crowd and rose to greet them as they approached his table.

There was clearly no need to ask, but he wanted to hear the news anyway. "So, how did it go?"

"Well, very well," they answered in unison.

Leo put aside his medical bag. In the absence of stress, Astrid didn't require a potassium tablet.

"Now we will enjoy a celebratory *fika*!" Astrid announced. Over espresso and pastries, they planned out the remainder of their stay in Toronto.

CHAPTER 4
THE BALL STARTS ROLLING

France . . .

As the days wore on and an exhausted April gave way to a more promising May, Nathan shared many of his frustrations with Tommaso. The exchange provided material for the improvement of each other's language skills. Nathan discovered that Tommaso was a keen student of art, a willing protégé Nathan was happy to inspire.

"I know people," Tommaso said one day after listening to Nathan's frustrated rantings, which punctuated their discussion of art. "If you have the money to pay, you can give me the names, and your losses can be avenged."

This is what Nathan had been hoping for since Tommaso, a low-level crime syndicate enforcer, had become his cellmate. "I can give you their names and some information about each one. It needs to be done while I'm still in here, before I'm released. Let me know the price; I'll arrange for payment."

"I need the names, their occupations and location."

"How much for five?" Nathan asked.

"Five . . . that will be very costly," Tommaso replied. "It depends. I need their occupations and location."

Nathan gave the matter additional thought but couldn't identify any among them he would remove from such a list. Each in their own way had been instrumental in his downfall. He had the funds available, and to spend it in this fashion would bring him great pleasure. He provided his list to Tommaso.

" . . . and third, Kent Gillespie. He's an architect and lives in Toronto. You might want to tell someone that he's also a martial arts expert. Fourth is Yoichi Song. She owns an art gallery in Toronto, the Song Gallery. And lastly, my old partner, Chloé Corbin. She also goes by the name *Chernyye Volosy* when she's got a Russian mark. You should find her in Toronto as well, maybe with an architect by the name of Matthew Gilbert Espie. If you take care of him too, fine, but I'm not paying. Collateral damage would be nice."

"So, two locations, two men who are architects, two women who are artists, and then your partner," Tommaso said in summarizing. "If you're not paying for this other architect, Espie, then I won't mention it. I will let you know when I hear from my people."

"How will you contact someone and communicate this to them?" Nathan asked.

"Not your concern. There is a way, but for now, I must concentrate to memorize the information you have given me."

That night, Nathan executed his versions of the few yoga poses he had learned from Tommaso then fell into a deep and restful sleep. He was entertained by dreams in which he enjoyed a luxurious lifestyle in an exotic locale, surrounded by scantily-clad young females eager to tend his every need. As such a master, he would become the envy of all who would make his acquaintance. Starting again with such a clean slate would make it all possible.

CHAPTER 5
A TALE OF TWO WOMEN

Southern Ontario . . .

Although it was officially spring, a cold front had moved into the region. The early morning air was cool, nearly cold, and it was crisp. Had it been damp, it would have been uncomfortable, but the humidity was low. Since Astrid was well bundled and sported good footwear, she found it delightful. The few lingering stars disappeared one by one as night gradually transitioned into dawn. Within this silence, she generated the only sound, as her feet crunched the debris left by the side of the roadway. She walked past the entrance to the Gillespie estate and continued further along the road toward Eve's gate, just as Eve and Cookie approached from the other side.

"We couldn't have timed that any better!" enthused Astrid.

"I might have been late, but Cookie was so eager, she wouldn't let me dawdle," Eve explained, while she struggled to control her enthusiastic golden retriever.

The two friends spoke Swedish to one another primarily for the benefit of Eve, who wanted to maintain her familiarity and fluency with the language of her youth. Astrid bent down and acknowledged Cookie by scratching the exuberant dog's muzzle and ears.

When will you be able to remove your fancy footwear," Astrid inquired, looking down at the thermoplastic boot that secured Eve's injured left ankle.

"Soon, or so I am promised. They say I am healing well—for my age. Why must they always make such a comment? Someone makes a positive statement, then they spoil it. For my age! I dislike that so much—that, and becoming invisible when I turned fifty." Eve's feelings appeared more injured than her ankle, and she adopted a haughty posture.

"Do you want me to take hold of Cookie's leash so you're not struggling with it as well as with your crutches, Eve?" Astrid asked. "You've just had your previous cast removed, and I wouldn't want you to hurt that ankle yet again."

"Well, perhaps," Eve answered before handing Cookie's leash to her. "You're right; I don't want to re-injure myself. Be careful, though. Cookie's a good girl, but she can become very single-minded if she takes notice of a rabbit or a squirrel. I don't want you to end up with a broken ankle like I have."

"You know, you've not told me how your accident happened."

"It was all so stupid.

"This past winter the weather was very changeable. It would be very cold, and then we'd have a little bit of spring-like weather, followed by another deep freeze. As a result the roadway and shoulders became very pitted. And there's a buildup of ice as the accumulation of ploughed snow begins to melt, then freezes again. It's such a quiet neighbourhood; I think the municipality forgets us sometimes. We were experiencing one of the thaws, and I took Cookie for a walk. I think she must have seen a squirrel or a rabbit. I wasn't prepared, so when she jerked the leash, down I went. I thought I'd just sprained my ankle, twisting it awkwardly, but no, I broke it. They said it's a trimalleolar fracture," Eve explained, sounding frustrated with herself even still. "It required surgery, and I needed to be well behaved for . . . it must have been nearly eight weeks with the first cast."

"Well, take your time. You certainly don't want to complicate things."

"I think I may keep this boot cast and wear it periodically even after I'm told it's not required. I don't want to damage the tendons and ligaments supporting my ankle. And I do want to be able to return to my exercise schedule as soon as my energy level is back up. I know I need to be careful, or it will take even longer for things to return to normal. That is why I especially appreciate these early-morning walks, when the world is quiet—and so does Cookie."

"Will you come sit with me after our walk?" Astrid asked. "We can have *fika*; I have some special treats: *punschrulle, kardemummabulle, chokladbiskvi, arraksboll . . .*"

"I would enjoy that, Astrid. Now, you're not going to tell me that you are an accomplished baker as well as a pianist and scientist, are you?"

"Oh, no. Lukas located a Swedish bakery, and their pastries taste much like home."

"I really enjoy being able to speak Swedish with you, Astrid. It awakens memories of my early days in Stockholm. Lucy has good language skills, and she's been working on her Swedish—which I appreciate—but this is different." They paused while Eve adjusted her crutches, then Cookie led them up the wooded path through the conservation area.

"I feel much the same; I enjoy our talks, too. It's actually relaxing for me to be able to speak Swedish. English remains a bit of a chore for me. Lukas is much better than I am. He says my English is good, but I am frequently self-conscious, and that makes it awkward.

"I don't recall how I came to be speaking English," Astrid continued "I'm told that my husband was Canadian, so I guess I've been speaking it for a long time."

"It must be odd when you lack an awareness of your own past experiences. I'm sorry," Eve said, sincerely saddened by the thought of just how much Astrid had lost due to her dementia and the subsequent complications to the drug treatments.

"Thank you, but I've been advised that I'm not missing much in having little memory of him, and I'll trust those who have told me. I wish I hadn't lost as much of my knowledge of pharmacology," Astrid mused. "I have a PhD and an MD, but I now have no more knowledge of my field than many others who read broadly. It's as if I climbed a challenging mountain only to find myself back at basecamp without any recollection of the achievement. I have no urge to regain what I've lost; at this age, I lack the energy required. At least I have my music, so I concentrate on it, not the science.

"How did you come to learn English; you speak it so well, I think?" Astrid asked. "I think it would be difficult without constant reinforcement."

"My husband, Lars, was actually English, but I knew the language before I met him."

"I wasn't aware that you had been married, Eve."

"It was many years ago. He died sixteen years ago, but we'd been married for only four. I guess this year would have been our twentieth wedding anniversary, had he survived. Cancer," she added.

"Sorry."

"Charles Dickens taught me to speak English," declared Eve, smiling at the memory. "I struggled to learn the language as any immigrant does, so I hired a tutor. His name was Charles Dickens—well, actually, it was Chuck Dickens. Anyway, that was the start of me reading the old Dickens novels. It was quite a struggle and a far cry from conversational English, but I enjoyed it."

"Your favourite?"

"Ah, that's easy: *A Tale of Two Cities.*"

"Why?"

"One day, I found myself on the final page of my book. For the first time I had completed an entire classic English novel, and I was so proud of myself. It was *A Tale of Two Cities* by Charles Dickens, and I just loved the last line of the story," Eve explained. "That was a turning point for me. From then on, I spoke English and be damned if every so often I make an error. Lucy and I have our laughs because of my errors and blending of Swedish with English, but I manage to communicate."

"I had an experience similar to yours but with a French novella when I was learning that language," Astrid said. "The novella was *Le Petit Prince* by Antoine de Saint-Exupéry, and at one point near the end of the story the Prince says, 'And now here is my secret, a very simple secret: It is only with the heart that one can see rightly; what is essential is invisible to the eye.' It convinced me that it would be worthwhile for me to learn French, else I'd be missing such gems or, at the very least, find myself dependent upon others for a translation."

Suddenly Eve pitched forward, and Astrid grabbed hold of her until Eve was steady on her feet. "The trail is so uneven, it's easy to stumble. Be very careful. It's a long way down for you when you fall. I am closer to the ground," Astrid said, "but you are taller than most men I know."

"And when I am able to exercise, I feel stronger than most of them as well. It's the freedom I feel when I dance that I miss the most," Eve said, punctuating her statement with a sigh. "Oh well, I must be on my best behaviour. That is very difficult for me, it seems. They tell me it could take as long as two years for things to be as they were before—if ever."

CHAPTER 6
THE PRICE TO BE PAID

France . . .

The May air was becoming stifling and heavy with humidity. Nathan paced in his cell, the one he shared with Tommaso. Soon Tommaso would return from his visit and, he hoped, have good news for him. Nathan needed him to provide the information before Nathan's own visit could occur, else there would be delay in the implementation of the plan.

While Aubry was a rather new French prison, it was still a prison in every way that mattered, and the hollow, echoed, industrial-sounding noises were damaging to Nathan's psyche. The smells of the prison alternated between nauseating organics and that of disinfectants and industrial air fresheners intended to cover the offensive odours of bodily functions. Nathan longed for the smell of turpentine, linseed oil, and oil paints—and the day when he could finally return to them.

The locking mechanism sounded in the hall door. The door clanged as it was opened and again as it was shut. Soon a guard arrived with Tommaso, and the prisoner was directed to enter his cell, the room he shared with Nathan. They didn't speak until the hall door was heard clanging shut again.

"Well?" Nathan asked.

"Fifty-thousand euros each, plus expenses."

"Each? Plus expenses? Well, how much do you, do they, expect those expenses to be—or do I pay that after you've completed the job?"

"Expect the expenses to be fifty-thousand euros each as well. You pay upfront, and then there's a final tabulation when the job is done, just in case."

"Just in case of *what*?"

"If you don't like it, fine. If you want the job done, then transfer the money. Simple. And they want to know what to do if you die before the job is completed."

"Wha-what do you mean?"

"I mean exactly what I said. Do you want the job completed if you die before the job is done? If you do, then there's a bonus hundred thousand euros to be paid upfront at the same time. The whole job would cost you six-hundred-thousand euros."

"Well, I don't feel that my life's in jeopardy here, so you can just forget the hundred thousand for this bonus. I'm not paying that. You'll complete the job at a hundred thousand each, all-in. How do they want the money transferred?"

CHAPTER 7
WHO'S THIS?

Southern Ontario . . .

Aleksandra was stunned. *How could he have done this? And why would he?* She closed her laptop computer and sat staring off into space, numbed by what she had discovered. *What to do?* Thoughts swirled about in her pretty little head, but none of them provided her with insight, let alone a solution.

She had elected to attend the University of Toronto, and she didn't want to make the phone call to her grandfather to tell him of her problem. *He might make me come home!*

Her father had been a selfish child. He had lived the life of a selfish child. And he had died doing something selfish. Aleksandra didn't want her grandfather to think she was like her father. And she didn't want him to think that she was like her mother either, though Aleksandra—if not her grandfather—knew that her father's failings had far out-weighed her mother's.

She walked into her small, well-appointed kitchen with the intention of making her evening meal but found herself so distracted that when she opened the refrigerator door, she forgot for a moment what it was she had wanted to do. She merely stood in the light of the refrigerator, staring into its interior.

"Arragghh!" she growled in frustration while trying to refocus her thoughts and devise an appropriate plan to resolve the problem. She shook her head, her blonde hair taking on an increasingly dishevelled appearance. She grabbed her hair and withdrew a scrunchy from her pocket to secure it in a messy bun.

From the refrigerator, Aleksandra selected borscht soup, some mushroom piroshki, and a small container of sour cream. The food was from the Russian restaurant just down the block from her condominium apartment, and it reminded her of home. She hoped it would calm her, allowing her to think and devise a plan.

While she ate, she tried to consider the situation more logically. The first decision she made was that their relationship was over. The fellow student, who had been her boyfriend for the past several months, had demonstrated that he was not trustworthy. She wanted nothing more to do with him, except to deliver such news to him.

By the time she finished her tea, generously laced with cherry jam, she was feeling strong and determined. She decided that she didn't want him in her apartment ever again. Instead, she would connect with him by phone to deliver the news. Aleksandra positioned herself comfortably in her reading chair and made the call.

Her hand trembled as she positioned her phone for the conversation. "Hi, it's me," she said, wondering if he could detect any tremor in her voice.

"Heh, you calling cuz you want me to come over, eh?" he said in reply, his tone an awkward attempt at being sexy. But *sexy* doesn't communicate well through a mouthful of tortilla chips.

She could hear him munching on chips, one after the other. "No, nothing like that. There's something I need to discuss with you . . ." And then she added, "Over the phone."

"Whoa, Babe, sounds serious. What'd ya do, break a nail?"
He laughed. Aleksandra didn't join in.

"I've learned something today that I find very upsetting,
and I'd like to hear your explanation."

"Okay, which class you talking about? Can't be any of the
few we take together, so it must be your poetry class or one of
those other ones you got that I don't."

"Actually, I'm talking about your extracurricular activities."

"Extracurricular activities? You think I'm *cheating* on you?"
His voice was louder than it needed to be. It seemed both con-
trived and defensive.

"No, that's not it."

"Well, what then? Cuz I don't got no extracurricular activities, other than you, Sandy." Her fellow students knew her as
Sandra, and he alone called her Sandy. She realized that she no
longer liked to hear his voice saying her name.

"You looked me up on Who's This? and I want to know why."

"Oh, that—that was just for fun. I looked up lots of people
I know just to see what the site had on 'em, if anything. I was
just being curious."

"And you provided my photo, and now it's out there, associated with whatever information you provided about me. I
need to know exactly what information you shared."

"You're awfully touchy, Sandy; that time of the month?
You're fully clothed in the photo, so don't worry. Besides, it's
just a shot of your face, so even if you'd been starkers, the
photo wouldn't be showing your bits to the world. No probs,
eh?" He rattled off the words as if there were no significance to
the action he had taken.

"Make a list of everything you shared about me. Copy the
information and send it to me. Best if you can send me a complete copy of what you submitted. Now! And I want it *all*."
Agitated, she found herself standing, pacing.

"Okay, okay, just simmer down, all right. Are you sure you don't want me to come over to discuss this, Sandy . . . Babe?"

"Send it *now*." She continued to pace the uncluttered floor of her minimalist-styled apartment, her agitation building. Eventually, she took a seat at her piano.

"Just give me a sec, okay?" he replied. She detected a change in his tone. She'd finally gotten his attention.

She loved her clear piano. Unlike her cousins, she preferred it to jewels. It was transparent and outfitted with LED lights; it was stunning. Her calm increased, and she began to contemplate what she might play after her conversation with him was concluded.

Finally, the information arrived, accompanied by a copy of the photo he had used. She looked it over and gave the matter some thought before returning to the conversation.

"Sandy? Babe, you still there?" He seemed worried.

"I am." She thought for a moment, breathed in deeply, and announced, "I never want to see you again. Do you understand? I want absolutely nothing more to do with you, ever again."

"I'm sorry, Babe. I didn't realize you could be so touchy. You got your woman ears on or somethin'? I mean, I was going to find out about you, eventually."

"And what is it you think you've found out about me?" Aleksandra winced, realizing that it might have been better to have held off a bit in telling him that their relationship was over.

"Other than the fact that your grandfather is a fucking Russian oligarch, and he's your legal guardian? You hadn't even told me that your parents were both dead. I told you about my family and even told you how my dad lost his business and now drives an Uber and how my mom is trying to make some money doing multi-level sales of crystals and essential oils." It sounded as if he was becoming annoyed. That in itself annoyed Aleksandra.

"I didn't go poking around behind your back. You did! You didn't ask more questions of me—probably because you've generally done most of the talking—and you didn't ask my permission before posting my personal information. Like I said, we're through!"

"Bitch," he snarled, revealing more of himself in that one word than he had since she had first met him. "Don't think you can treat me like this and get away with it. And when the guys hear about this—and they will, I guarantee—you'll be ghosted so much, you'll think you're haunted. I'll ruin you, bitch! Remember, I'm a fuckin' computer genius! Being with you has been one long negaton, and I don't need it. Damn Russian princess—"

Aleksandra she ended the call. She had little choice now but to contact her grandfather, Grisha. Grigori Orlov, Grisha to his friends and family, was Russian by birth, an oligarch by association—and one of the wealthiest people in the world. His massive yacht, the *Croesus*, was testament to that wealth. This was the man who could protect her from harm. She didn't want to speak with her grandmother, Agafya, for fear that she might declare that Aleksandra should return home. That was something she did not want to do.

Other than this unfortunate situation with her idiot boyfriend, Aleksandra had been enjoying her time in Toronto. She was happy with her courses in psychology, English literature, and creative writing and had no plans to leave Toronto until she graduated—and perhaps not even then. She enjoyed her small, modern apartment and the pace of life in her new neighbourhood, convenient to the subway that delivered her to the university campus.

She readied herself once again in her reading chair and selected the number. "*Dedushka*, I have a problem," she blurted out as soon as he answered. "I don't know if it's a big problem or a small problem, but I need your help."

"Aleksandra, wonderful to hear from you," her grandfather, Grisha, declared. "What is this problem, *Zayka*?"

Just hearing his warm, rich baritone voice and the familiar term of endearment he always used toward her—bunny—comforted her. She told him about her boyfriend and shared with Grisha all the details that she could remember about her boyfriend's personal life. She provided a full accounting of what he had done using Who's This?

"I'll have O look into this." Grisha's head of security was called O, and though Aleksandra had talked to him only once years before she retained a positive opinion of the striking German ex-military man. "Tell me, how did you come to learn of this indiscretion, *Zayka*?"

Aleksandra breathed in deeply and started to reveal the most upsetting part of her tale. "I received a message from someone I don't know. They sent me photos of myself. One was the photo submitted to Who's This? That's how I knew who was responsible. But there were other photos—taken recently, but not here in Toronto, but from shortly before I left to come here. The person listed members of our family, and they claimed that they were friends of yours. They even listed my class schedule." She breathed in deeply yet again and continued, "I'm afraid, *Dedushka*." Aware that she was on the verge of tears, she was now angry with herself for such a weakness and nearly deaf to Grisha's next question.

"Did you contact the local authorities—the police, someone at the university?"

"Ah . . . no, I called my boyfriend—or, my ex-boyfriend—and you but no one else."

"Good. Now, what is the name of this boyfriend?"

"Smith," she answered.

"Is that his given name or family name?"

"I don't know. Sorry. Now I feel so stupid. He just wanted to be called Smith. He said he was trying to make a name for himself, to establish his brand, so he wanted everyone to call him Smith. Really, I don't actually know that he didn't just pull that name out of thin air. I've never seen his official identification, so I don't know." Aleksandra felt foolish and she couldn't bear to have her grandfather think of her as being foolish. "I have a photo though; I'll send it to you. And he said that his parents lived on Bridge Street in Niagara Falls. I'll send you a text with as much detail as I can recall."

"Hm-m. Do you have the plate number for his car?"

"No, I've never seen his car, and I don't know if he has one. In Toronto, we usually just take the bus or subway."

"I'll handle it and get back to you. Would you be comfortable talking with O, or would you prefer to have me relay information for you?"

"For a little while at least, can you please be the one? Maybe later I'll talk directly with O, but I think I need to hear your voice, *Dedushka*."

"Okay, take a deep breath, *Zayka*. Play your piano and allow yourself to relax. I shall contact you each day at least once. Call me whenever you want to, and especially if you need to. Don't hesitate! It is good that you have responded as you have. Be aware and don't venture far—at least until we have this matter sorted."

"What about my examinations? The final evaluation period has begun, and I have many exams scheduled over the coming weeks. What should I do? I have completed my assignments, but—"

"Leave that with me," he said. "I'll make special arrangements and let you know. I don't think it is wise to return to the campus. I want you to stay in your apartment if at all possible. Do not contact anyone. Try to think of this as a little vacation from school."

"But—"

"I'll see what might be possible. Already I have something in mind. It is something that will be a bit different for you—interesting but safe and secure as well. I'll see to that. You can be assured. Leave it all with me."

"Thank you, *Dedushka*. I'm sorry, I haven't asked how you and *Babushka* are, and what you have been doing. Please, tell me."

"Your grandmother has been kept busy with worries about your cousins, your uncle Maxim's children. Now that their mother is gone, she thinks they need her more. But they are too old for this, I think. Even at your age, it is necessary to spread your wings, not hide in some sadness. She reads too much Dostoevsky, I think," he concluded with a forced chuckle. "It darkens her mood too much."

"And you? All business, or are you taking some time to enjoy yourself?"

"Business *is* enjoyable, *Zayka*, but Maxim has encouraged me to try tennis and golf again. I dislike both." As he said this, Grisha massaged his left shoulder and winced in pain. The balance of their conversation was pleasant, and by the time they said their goodbyes, Aleksandra was feeling much better about the situation. As she returned to her kitchen for a cherry piroshki and more tea, she wondered what Grisha, her dear *dedushka*, might suggest.

CHAPTER 8
A VOICE FROM THE PAST

Bbrrinngg . . .

The morning light that filled her studio was perfect, and Lucy was optimistic that she would complete the current painting soon, within the week perhaps. Reluctantly, she descended from the platform that she had been using to access the uppermost regions of her massive canvas. She disliked interruptions which interfered with her productivity. They were annoying.

Bbrrinngg . . .

She always expected the wall phone to stop ringing before she could reach it. This time, it didn't.

Bbrrinngg . . .

"Hello, Gillespie residence," she answered as brightly as she could muster.

"Lucy, is that really you?" The voice sounded vaguely familiar.

"Yes. Who is this, please?"

"Juliette. Juliette Garner."

"Juliette! Oh, my goodness! I thought we'd never hear from you again, especially after your email when we had that situation in France." The last time they had communicated, an Interpol agent had delivered a message from Juliette to Lucy and her husband, Kent. In it, Juliette had instructed them to sever all ties with her and consider her dead to them. *For everyone's safety*, she had said.

"How are you, Juliette?" Lucy asked, flooding the caller with questions. "What's changed that you can now communicate with me? Are you back in Toronto?"

"I'm well, and I'm still in Lyon actually. That's where the headquarters of Interpol are located, but I expect to be leaving soon. It's a long story—it always is, so it seems. I need a place to hide while at the same time remain connected and able to communicate. Eventually, I'll be returning to Canada, but I've a few things to take care of here first."

"What do you mean 'need a place to hide'?" Lucy asked, genuinely confused about what she could do to help the former lawyer, who had been working with Interpol since 2016. "What happened?"

"I'm still with the organization here in Lyon, but I need to disappear without Interpol dictating the means. There's been a breach of security here, and I fear that my life is in danger. If mine is, then given how things have played out in the past—"

"Kent's and mine are too," Lucy said, completing Juliette's thought. "What would you like me to do?"

"You and Kent seem to have some very well-placed friends, and I know it's asking a lot, but is there someone, some place rather near to where I currently am, who could help me lie low awhile, until I can return to Canada?"

Lucy could detect the worry in Juliette's voice. Except for a fleeting moment years before when she just happened upon Juliette in a crowd of people in Menton, France, she had last seen the Toronto lawyer in 2015 when Juliette was still a senior partner in the prestigious law firm of Garner & Garner and destined to take the reins at the firm. "I have an idea, but I just need to bounce it off Kent first, and then I'll get back to you. Can I give you a call tonight?"

"I'd rather that I call you. Should I call this number or your cell?"

"I'll keep my cell with me at all times, so that's the number to call. I'll need some time though—can you call me back tonight? I should know something by six, so call between seven and nine—I guess that's between one and three in the morning your time, assuming you're still in France then."

"I should be. That would be great. Thanks so much." Already she sounded relieved. They chatted briefly, but it was apparent that light banter was the farthest thing from Juliette's mind at this time. Their conversation soon came to an end.

When she had disconnected from the call with Juliette, Lucy returned to her bedroom to retrieve her cellphone, and while there she placed a call. Kent, her husband, was in Quebec, overseeing a construction project he was spear-heading for Grigori Orlov. The project involved the construction of a ski resort with ski village, condo development, and a full complement of warm weather activities as well. As an architect and property developer, Kent was in his element, and he and his firm had designed most sectors of the resort.

"Hey there, sweetheart, how are you doing?" Kent said upon answering her call.

"Everything is fine here. I've joined Eve, Astrid, and Cookie on some of their early-morning walks into the conservation area, all the way to the pond and back. Eve is wondering when you'll be returning Albin to her. She's really not herself at the moment."

"You can tell Eve that Albin will be returned to her very soon. He's still in one piece last I checked, despite the skiing. But I sense that's not the reason for your call. What's up?"

Lucy described the call she had received from Juliette. "I was wondering if Serge might host Juliette for a time. Yoichi is already there, working to catalogue and pack his art collection, so I think one more person wouldn't actually be an imposition. Well, it is, of course, but I think she'd be less conspicuous as a result of the activity created in the apartment due to the work Yoichi is doing."

"Do you want to talk with Serge, or do you want me to? Your French is better than mine, so it might be less awkward," Kent acknowledged.

"If you agree that this is appropriate for us to do, then I'll speak with both Serge and Yoichi," Lucy said.

"There might be something happening here too in the near future," Kent said. "Grisha is scheduled to visit the site sometime this week. He phoned last night and said that he needs to talk to me about a personal matter but in person rather than over the phone. So I don't know what that'll be about, but it certainly does seem unusual, given my usual communications with him.

"How's your painting for Grisha coming?" Kent inquired.

"Well, but it's a very long process. I'm still working on the one I started before you left for Quebec. I think I'm beginning to channel Klimt, given all the metallic gold I'm using. I thought I'd save the smaller one for when we go to L'Orté Island later in the spring," Lucy explained. "Remind me about all the fun I'm *not* having the next time Grisha wants to commission a painting from me." They chatted for a short time, then ended the call.

She continued to give thought to how she might best approach Serge with a request to have Juliette, a stranger to him, remain in his home, a lavish Parisian apartment in the 16th arrondissement. She left her bedroom in the master suite and made her way to the kitchen where she found Helen at work. "Kent says that Albin has been doing some skiing," she reported to Helen, Albin's sister.

"Coffee?" the ever-prescient Helen asked, already beginning to assemble things. Lucy nodded and smiled. "That man fails to count the years he's been on this earth," Helen exclaimed, shaking her head. "That's wonderful—as long as he doesn't get hurt. Eve is bound to kill him if he gets himself injured. Elinor is rearranging the pantry room, so I'd better go and check on how things are going before she's made too many changes."

As Lucy sipped her coffee, she considered various avenues by which she might broach the topic of Juliette with Serge. Time passed, and her cup was emptied of coffee, but no idea had materialized. Having failed to devise a plan, she decided to lay her cards on the table with Serge. In typical Lucy-fashion, she would be forthright with her request.

"Bonjour," Serge said in answering the phone.

"Bonjour, Serge! Lucy Gillespie from Toronto. How are you?" Lucy inquired, planning to keep the rest of the conversation in French since Serge's English wasn't particularly good, and the matter required that he fully understand the seriousness of the situation.

"I am very well, Lucy. It is nice to hear your voice. Yoichi is in one of the back rooms, still working hard. I appreciate all that you have done for me in arranging for her to deal with my art collection. I had done nothing about it since you and Kent were here. Tell me, how is the young man?" Serge inquired.

"Not quite as young. He is still in Quebec, building a ski resort. It's beautiful. As you ski some of the runs, it's as if you're going to ski right into the St. Lawrence River. You should see it."

"I think I am too old for skiing. My dogs keep me as active as is possible."

"When did you get dogs, Serge? What kind?" Lucy asked, wondering how Yoichi was dealing with the presence of pets, especially ones that could claim a greater right to be present than she could.

"I acquired brother and sister Cavalier King Charles spaniels the year after I last saw you. Merlot is a male Blenheim, and Bijou is a tricolour. They have developed quite an affection toward Yoichi, but I am not certain their enthusiasm for her is matched by hers toward them. Let's just say, she tolerates them well." Serge chuckled.

"Serge, I have a situation to discuss with you and, if you are willing, a favour to ask of you on behalf of a third party." Lucy went on to outline Juliette's situation to Serge.

As an afterthought, she added, "Truly, I don't feel that I know her all that well, Serge. It's not as if we were ever close friends or intimate confidantes. I met her because she was my grandaunt's lawyer and helped in the transfer of that estate to me after my grandaunt was murdered. She discovered some unsettling things about a colleague and relative of hers, which caused her to leave the family law firm and offer her services and insight to Interpol in Lyon. Now she is in danger as a result of some security breach at Interpol. I don't know if this will put you and Yoichi in danger, or not, and that worries me."

"Don't worry, Lucy. Of course, Juliette may stay here. I shall ready one of the bedrooms for her. She can join Yoichi, Merlot and Bijou, and me. Perhaps all the activity here will help to take your friend's mind off her troubles. We mustn't let the villains win. As well, Yoichi is more than half-finished with the work here, but I have so much—perhaps she can be of some assistance to her.

"The invasion of my home by that thief, Bellamy, years ago has made me feel invincible." He paused. "Surprised? It might seem logical that I would become afraid of the world, but in fact, since we neutralized—I think that's the word they use— since we neutralized that threat, I feel more confident. I have been tested. Jean-Pierre would be proud of me—proud and much surprised, I think."

And so it was arranged that Juliette would take up temporary residence in Serge's penthouse apartment near *Jardin du Ranelagh* in Paris, amid his vast collection of artworks and collectible furnishings. While Lucy was pleased that she had succeeded in securing a place for Juliette, she was a bit worried about Serge. Certainly, the elderly gentleman was confident and claimed success over the villainous Nathan Bellamy, but Serge had merely phoned the police and gone to get cording to secure Bellamy. It had been Kent who had discovered, accosted, fought with, and ultimately secured Nathan.

Her conversation with Serge having concluded, Lucy placed a telephone call to Yoichi.

"Hello, stranger; what's up?" Yoichi asked as she put aside the spreadsheet she'd been working on and got comfortable in a side chair.

"How are things going?" Lucy asked.

"Very well. It's a slow process, but I'm getting there. Serge has some very interesting pieces, and sometimes I get a bit sidetracked and find myself just appreciating them. But I've got a system in place, so we are definitely making progress. Catalogue and pack, catalogue and pack . . . I had collected a lot of useful information regarding packing and necessary documentation out of France when I arranged transport for the Theia Witherspoon collection for you. That was just a warm-up for Serge's collection, I think. Fortunately, nothing much in the documentation requirements has changed over the intervening years. This apartment is larger than I expected, and it is also more crowded with treasures than I expected. Nevertheless, as much as the workload is significant, I'm having a great time, Lucy. And Serge is a dear," she added. "Every once in a while we deal with something that was particularly significant to Jean-Pierre and he experiences a flood of emotion, but he pushes through. Even old stationery engraved with Proulx-Allard and this address triggers the response, so I have some idea how difficult this is for him."

"I recall Serge saying that the collection was largely within Jean-Pierre's purview. Every couple shares responsibilities, so it must be emotionally difficult to deal with such things when that partner is gone."

"How are things back in Toronto?"

"Just fine. Busy painting. I called to discuss something with you, Yoichi. Remember the lawyer, Juliette Garner, whom I dealt with when I learned about Grandaunt Gracie?" When Yoichi acknowledged that she vaguely remembered hearing about her at the time but that they had never met, Lucy inundated her with information about Juliette, the activity of the law firm, Garner & Garner, and how it related to Lucy's forebears, as well as a summary of the involvement of Interpol.

"So, Serge is prepared to have Juliette join you at the apartment, but I wanted to hear from you on this. I don't know if there's any danger that I'm bringing to you and Serge by arranging for Juliette to join you, but it also doesn't feel right to give her the brush off." Lucy found herself pacing, too agitated to have a relaxed chat while remaining seated. "I'll respect your veto if that is your decision, Yoichi. I know what it's like to be stalked and literally fight for your life, and I sure don't want any of you to have that sort of experience. If you say no, then I'll just tell Serge that Juliette made other arrangements, and I'll go back to the drawing board to see if I can come up with another idea."

"I may not have been present when you dealt with your stalker or those other times either, but I was present when we found that body. I'm tougher than I look, Lucy. Don't let the manicures, facials, and wardrobe mislead you. Running an art gallery such as mine is a tough business, and I've been doing this since we graduated from uni. Don't write me off just because I'm less inclined to enjoy all that nature stuff—Eve with her bird-watching and Helen with her plant surveys or whatever. I'm tough, Lucy. You and Juliette can count on me."

Lucy was pleased that Yoichi wasn't inclined to veto the arrangement she had made with Serge. She appreciated her enthusiasm and confidence. At seven o'clock, she would be able to give Juliette Garner the good news.

CHAPTER 9
A FRIEND IN NEED

Quebec . . .

Kent read Grisha's text message yet again, trying to read between the lines, but the short message provided no insight.

"Will arrive shortly. Must speak in private, just two of us."

No matter how he wracked his brain, he failed to develop even an inkling of what favour Grisha might require of him, or what private information he might wish to convey. He had acquired no additional information since mentioning to Lucy that there was something up with Grisha.

Kent looked out across the vast property, dotted with the various structures that formed the new-build ski resort Grisha had named *Aurores Boréales* or Northern Lights. The luxury hotel, nearly as important as the ski hill itself, was in the final stages of having various amenities installed. A special occupancy certificate listing various exceptions had been issued for a section of the hotel. That was where Kent had moved his office and where he and his right-hand man, Albin, were in residence. Where Grisha would stay was anybody's guess—wherever he wanted, most likely.

The view was glorious; the hills stretched to the St. Lawrence, and the dramatic scene took his breath away, yet again. Kent left the warmth of the suite and stood on the balcony, breathing in the fresh air, cool and invigorating. In the spring, construction sites tended to be messy with machinery churning the soil and residual snow into mounds of mud. Instead, a cold front and the unexpected arrival of a significant amount of new snow the previous night had made the scene especially attractive, just in time for Grisha's arrival. *Typical.*

Kent detected the sound of an approaching helicopter and left the suite to meet Grisha at the landing pad located on the roof of the hotel. The Russian multi-billionaire was a jovial sort with a booming voice and high expectations of those in his employ. As Grisha stepped from the helicopter, Kent noticed that he appeared somewhat distracted and obviously quite intense. *Whatever it is, it must be serious.*

They shook hands, and Grisha embraced the younger man in a bear hug conveying genuine warmth and friendship. Grisha said nothing as Kent led him back to the suite being used as both his residence and office. Members of the entourage had apparently received their assignments and moved off to deal with whatever had been designated their responsibilities. As per his request, Grisha would be able to have a private conversation with Kent. His personal bodyguard, O, remained in the hallway, securing the door. The tall, muscular, ebony-skinned German was an imposing presence.

"Is there anyone else in this suite, Kent? Anyone at all?" Grisha asked.

"No, just the two of us," Kent assured him. "This suite is soundproof as well. Please sit. Can I get you anything? A coffee perhaps."

"I'll take a coffee—double espresso. I find that caffeine helps clear my head, so I can think." He brought his fist beneath his rib cage, grimaced, and massaged the region momentarily.

Kent crossed into the kitchen, the unfinished area providing access to water, a refrigerator, a microwave, and a Nespresso machine, and set about preparing Grisha's coffee.

"Then again, perhaps I drink too much. Agafya says I should cut back, but Agafya says many, many things.

"You know, I rather like the stark simplicity of raw concrete, but it is not practical for this sort of project. It is unfortunate." Grisha accepted the cup from Kent, took a sip, leaned forward toward him, and began, all the while avoiding locking eyes with him.

"I need to share with you some personal information concerning my family. As a rule, I do not do this. But, you and I, we have a history—granted, a relatively short one so far—but a history of sharing our souls with one another. It is true. For example, you have told me about Rufina's tragic past and your own challenges." (Rufina, or red-haired woman, was what Grisha called Lucy, Kent's wife and Grisha's art tsar.)

"What is it, Grisha? How can I be of assistance?"

"Do you remember my youngest son, Alexei? You would have met him at the party on the *Croesus* back in 2019, in Antibes." Kent nodded, and Grisha continued, "Alexei was quite the daredevil—"

"Was?"

"My dear boy was run off the road between Eze and Monaco. We have lost him."

"I'm so sorry, Grisha." There was no need to inquire about his injuries. Not only had Alexei been a daredevil, but he had been a fool as well. He had a need for speed and a willingness to drive well beyond the speed limit, especially on his specialty motorcycle, which was capable of three-hundred-fifty kilometres per hour. He had once said that he was planning to ride from Antibes to Monaco in under fifteen minutes. *Zoom indeed*, Kent thought, remembering the conversation aboard the *Croesus* that night.

"He died doing something he enjoyed. Both the motorcycle and my Alexei were broken into a million pieces. I suspect it was a planned attack—whether it was intended to have such a devastating result, I do not know, and I do not care. Whoever it was who did this, I will find them." Grisha clasped his hands together and squeezed until his hands appeared mottled by the constriction of blood flow. Whoever they were, they had poked the bear.

Kent still didn't know how he fit into the story Grisha was weaving but thought he would just let the distraught father find his own way through the information.

"Alexei had a bit of a drug problem. We tried to help him deal with this, but nothing worked. Several times, he appeared to have conquered his demons, but then he would relapse. I hadn't realized that he had relapsed yet again—not until the autopsy results revealed that drugs were present in his system. The police have conveniently decided that his death was due to this combination of drugs and high speed on his motorcycle, but I know for a fact that he was intentionally run off the road. The question is: who and, perhaps, why? O is working on this, but his investigation appears to have hit a dead end."

"How can I help, Grisha?"

"About twenty years ago, when he was merely a young teenager, Alexei fathered a child, a daughter. The young mother, who was Alexei's age, died from a drug overdose when the little girl, Aleksandra, was about eight years old, so her care fell in its entirety to Alexei. He was, of course, totally ill-prepared to act as a father to her, so Agafya and I have provided for her. She is now studying at the University of Toronto. My *zayka* is a good, hard-working girl and prefers a simple life. Now her life is threatened, and I fear it is by the same people who harmed her father. I could demand that she return home to us; that is what Agafya would prefer. But Aleksandra intends to continue her studies into the summer term, and I don't want to restrict her more than is absolutely necessary.

"In his great novel *Crime and Punishment*, Fyodor Dostoevsky writes, 'Pain and suffering are always inevitable for a large intelligence and a deep heart. The really great men must, I think, have great sadness on earth.' I think that Aleksandra, my *zayka*, is in the process of becoming truly great, and I fear her sadness on earth may as yet be incomplete."

Grisha went on to describe the situation created by Smith and the complications due to Aleksandra's upcoming examinations. "I would like Aleksandra to leave her apartment and stay with you and your dear wife until we have this sorted out. This will give Aleksandra a little vacation from school, the opportunity to do some reading and writing, and perhaps to learn something from Lucy—or you," he said, and Kent thought he detected a particular warmth in Grisha's gaze. "It will broaden her experience in a good way and distract her from her concerns."

"Grisha, I will need to discuss this with Lucy of course, but I'm confident that we can provide some assistance to you and your granddaughter. I'll call her right now. While I do that, I recommend the view from the balcony." Kent left Grisha and headed into the bedroom to place his call more privately to Lucy back in Toronto.

"Hi there, handsome, how ya' doin'?" Lucy answered brightly. "What's up?"

Kent outlined the situation to Lucy, and they discussed their concerns and the logistics involved.

"We'll pitch in and do what we can to help. I hope she's not like her father or the women he attracted, because that will make the task all the more difficult," Lucy said, thinking aloud.

"Grisha assures me that she is a bright and diligent student."

"What about O? How does he fit into this?"

"Grisha says that O will be involved—"

"But we likely won't see him, right?" Lucy interjected. "Okay, so they're doing something to discover who killed Alexei, and who—possibly the same party—is threatening Aleksandra while we just keep her occupied, happy, and safe."

"Yes, that's it in a nutshell," Kent said, in response to Lucy's summation.

"So when will you be returning home?"

"Soon. My team will stay here, but most of what remains is finishing work, and that's all done according to a well laid out plan, so I should be home soon. I'll let you know when I know.

"By the way, I've been reading the book of poetry that Serge sent me. It's taking me considerable time because it's in French, but there's one line I came across just last night in *La Nuit de Mai* by Alfred de Musset: '*Partons, dans un baiser, pour un monde inconnu,*' which translates as—"

"'With a kiss, let us set out for an unknown world.'" They whispered in unison.

"Consider yourself kissed, Lucy."

When Kent returned to the living room, he found Grisha and O engaged in a heated conversation. He kept well back until he was invited by Grisha to join in the discussion.

"We are discussing the potential for danger to be brought upon you as a result of me laying this matter at your feet, Kent. Were you able to discuss the matter with Lucy?" Grisha asked.

"Yes, she's both willing and able."

"Thank you," Grisha said. "Do you have any questions, Kent? Whatever they may be, I'll try to answer them."

Kent thought for a moment then said, "You may consider this too delicate, Grisha, but I think it's pertinent. How did you manage to avoid the sanctions, confiscations, and all the other steps taken against the many Russian oligarchs?" Then he added, "I wouldn't normally pry, but this is now my business as well as yours."

Grisha took a deep breath, sighed, and began. "This is difficult for me because I prefer my privacy. It is also essential to my business interests. Information in the wrong hands can be very destructive, but I guess that's what I am already experiencing.

"If by 'oligarch' you are referring to a powerful and wealthy person supporting a despot, then know that I am not now and never have been such a person. There are many tales told about me: that I am ex-KGB being perhaps the most popular one. For many years such misunderstandings served me well, then suddenly they did not. I was able to clear up the misunderstanding with the various governmental bodies around the world, so my assets remained, and continue to be, untouched. You see, though I am an ethnic Russian and proud of my culture, I have never been particularly politically active—no more than the average citizen. Business appeals to me, but politics does not. Actually, the frequent overlap of the two is profoundly irritating to me. Privately, my family enjoys the citizenship of other countries. Some view this as a citizenship of convenience, like choosing a flag to fly under for one's yacht. Let's just say, that to have had Russian citizenship thrust front and centre suddenly became a very great liability, and it was convenient that we were not involved in that liability."

"What else should I know?" Kent asked, making eye contact with O when he could think of no further questions to pose.

"I think that's everything," Grisha said in closing the topic.

"Assuming that you have continued your physical training, I have a good idea of the skills you and Lucy have regarding self-defence. Do you have any staff that will be present and able to assist? You and Lucy have proven your abilities, but is there anyone else who has?" O asked.

"Yes, quite a few surprisingly enough. You've met Albin; he's ex-military and provided us with training for years before you, O. He lives next door to us. His partner, Eve, is a retired professional dancer. She's very fit and the opposite of Lucy if you focus solely on stature. She's a tall and strong Swede and was one of the people who helped take down Lucy's stalker, but that was years ago. Eve and Lucy exercise together quite often. And then there's Helen, Albin's sister. She, like Albin, is ex-military and works as our household manager, so she's either at the house in Toronto or the summer house on the island."

"Do you have any guard dogs?" O asked.

"No. The only dog in the neighbourhood is Eve's golden retriever, Cookie. She's a sweet dog and likely to be of no assistance whatsoever. Maybe she'd bark and create some mayhem, which might confuse an intruder, but then it's even more likely she'd just get in the way as she tried to help us. So, no, we don't have any dogs to attack an intruder."

"Is there anyone else on the property?" O asked.

"There's Elinor, Helen's partner. They both live in an apartment on the estate. Elinor works under Helen's guidance, but I've no idea whether she could defend herself, let alone assist anyone else. I suspect not."

"I think it is excellent that so many have training. I also think that what will serve you best is that these same people, yourself included, not only have the skills, but you have all been in situations requiring the use of your training. You know that you did not freeze or fail to follow through, so you will have confidence when under pressure. You are all—or nearly all—well-tempered. That is the sort of strength which will serve you well if there is a problem. We suspect a kidnapping attempt," O said in conclusion.

The private flight from Quebec City to Billy Bishop Airport in Toronto presented an opportunity to Albin. While Grisha and O were discussing the matter concerning Aleksandra at the far end of the plane, Albin turned to Kent and asked, "How did you know it was time to ask Lucy to marry you?"

The highly personal question came as quite a surprise to Kent, but the two men had known each other seemingly forever and had shared both joys and hardships, so he endeavoured to answer. "I really don't recall. Clearly some sanity and good sense overtook me to finally pop the question. We'd both been dancing around the idea awhile, but the formal proposal seemed so daunting. I don't know what drove me finally to broach the topic. Sorry." Kent looked over toward his friend, who seemed somewhat troubled. "What's up? Planning to ask Eve?"

"Yeah, but if she says no, then that may be the end of a wonderful friendship. In so very many ways we already consider ourselves to be married—for years now actually—but I think I'd like her to know yet again how committed I am to our relationship. I think she needs reminding. She's had a tough time of late, with surgery on her ankle and then me being away."

"I'm really sorry; I can't help you there, Albin. Once you've sorted it out for yourself, the only other person who matters is Eve. Courage, old man—I wish you well, truly. Although I'm certain that Lucy would agree, I won't be telling her—that's your privilege. Besides, since she and Eve spend so much time together, I wouldn't want to be instrumental in having your proposal leaked ahead of time. Accidents can happen; the wrong word innocently spoken . . ."

"I've already got the ring," Albin said *sotto voce,* but Kent had already disengaged from their conversation. Albin groaned softly and adjusted his seat for a brief nap.

CHAPTER 10
HOULALA

France . . .

"Bellamy, you've got a visitor," the guard announced as he drew open the cell door, permitting Nathan to exit. "You seem pretty excited about something. I understand; I saw her too, *houlala!*" It was an accurate assessment of the physical attributes of Nathan's legal representative. Because it was a meeting with his *juriste*, they would be using a private room, not the common meeting area. He was uncertain where Tommaso's meeting might have occurred—likely in a private room as well, if the person he'd met was his legal counsel.

As the guard accompanied him through the halls and toward the private meeting rooms, Nathan adjusted his attitude, adopting an appropriate facial expression and body language—something that appeared open, warm, and desirable. He felt a bit out of practice, once again becoming a charming ladies' man on cue. He used to be so good at this, yet now he had to dig deep to rediscover his skills. He had done all he could regarding his personal hygiene. It was unfortunate that there were such limitations regarding what could be achieved within the confines of the prison. Instead he focused on acquiring a sparkling visage and tried to reassert his confidence.

"Madame Dubois, how wonderful to see you again—and as lovely as ever. Are you getting younger, perhaps? Your presence has made my day, verily, my week!"

"Monsieur Bellamy, please call me Sophie."

"Sophie, it is," he responded, taking care to caress her name as he spoke it. "And please, call me Nathan."

Nathan guided the conversation through a variety of inconsequential matters in an attempt to smokescreen Sophie regarding the actual purpose of this visit. He had not seen her often, and he now regretted this. Greater familiarity might have helped. However, he found many opportunities to exercise his powers of persuasion, primarily involving blatant flattery of the woman.

"I will be out of this hellhole within months, I know, but this payment cannot be postponed without bringing irreparable harm to innocents. I have taken care of them for many years, and I wish them to remain ignorant of my present hardship." He piled lie atop lie, having learned years before that if you're going to lie, best to tell a whopper and stick to it. "I fear I cannot share more information with you; it is best that I don't. I do hope you understand. This is not to cast aspersions upon you but to lessen your burden. The emotional impact of dealing with the recipients of these funds might be quite overwhelming for you, dear."

Of course, it was all nonsense, but it employed every trick of a common scam artist—and it worked. Sophie Dubois was so taken with Nathan's charms that she had disengaged her rather formidable intellect from their discussion and fallen under the distinctly dubious spell he had woven. She was but a tiny insect caught in his spider's web of deceit, and she acquiesced to his every request of her. The funds—kept separate and safe from European authorities—would be transferred promptly, as per his request. Nathan focused on the results of the venture; his revenge would be great. Indeed, this would be a fine week.

That night his yoga routine again brought him a deep and rewarding sleep. And again Nathan dreamt of scantily-clad nubile women satisfying his every whim. Such dreams helped compensate for the dreary work that continued to fill his days. Soon there would be other things to amuse him, real world things.

CHAPTER 11
ASSAULT

Southern Ontario . . .

The day presented with unsettled weather as an occluded front moved into the region. Astrid paused to consider whether her shoes and coat were the best choice, given the variability in the spring weather. "No matter, whatever I pick, it'll be the wrong thing. The weather will change," she muttered to herself.

She locked the front door behind herself and exited the property through the main gate. From there, she walked down the street in the wooded enclave, toward the Tudor-styled residence where Eve lived. She expected to see Eve and Cookie approaching, as they usually did, but today there was no one at Eve's gate. Astrid waited, but there was no movement apparent from anyone inside the grand residence. Concerned, she activated the intercom at the gate.

Eve answered. "Come to the house, Astrid. I'll meet you at the front door." She sounded tired.

The gate opened. Astrid entered and made her way up the cobblestone driveway. The house had been the original structure on the large estate whose land had been developed for the more modern dwellings, which now were its neighbours. The years, though many, had been kind to the Tudor-styled residence. There was an abundance of half-timber work, and the roof was complex in its accommodation of numerous gables. The brickwork itself was rather fanciful, as were the chimney treatments. It reminded Astrid somewhat of her own home in Sweden. The massive oak door opened, and Eve welcomed her to enter. Astrid noticed Cookie peeking around a corner, but she could not be enticed to come forward.

The interior did not appear to have been significantly modernized since the house's original construction nearly a century earlier. Polished, dark wood strap carving and panelling covered the walls, and large wooden beams intersected on the ceilings of the largest rooms, forming geometric patterns. In others, the ceilings featured moulded decorative plasterwork and cornices. Many of the rooms appeared to be on different levels, just a step or two, up or down, as one passed from room to room. It was rather quirky in that way.

"Come, sit by the fireplace. I have a small *fika* prepared for us," Eve said.

Astrid had come prepared to walk, not sit by a fire for *fika*. It wasn't particularly chilly, certainly not enough to warrant a fire, but she said nothing about the matter. "Are you not well, Eve?" she finally asked.

"I'm in an odd mood today. I don't know how to describe it to you. And . . . and . . . " Eve began to weep.

Astrid moved to sit beside Eve and turned to face her, clasping her about the shoulders and giving her a reassuring hug. "What's wrong?" she asked.

"I really don't know. I am very emotional. Up, down—all over the place. And . . . and . . . " Eve began to weep, yet again.

"And . . . and . . . *what?*" Astrid pressed, encouraging Eve to complete her thought.

"I hit Cookie!" Eve blurted, clearly horrified by her own actions.

Astrid said nothing.

Eve stood and crossed the room to fetch a box of tissues. As she bent to pick up the box, she appeared to lose her balance and allowed herself to fall sideways into a nearby chair.

Concerned, Astrid moved to a chair nearby. "Dizzy?" she asked.

"Yes, just a bit. It comes and goes. At least I'm not nauseated this time. Sorry."

"Pregnant?" Astrid asked, in jest.

Eve stopped and looked at her, then broke into a smile and guffawed. "No, for two good reasons: first, this is highly unlikely at my age; and second, Albin has not been home enough to have caused such a thing.

"I mentioned it to my doctor and he made a joke that the air was thinner up here. Stupid. No one would say such a thing to a tall man, but when a woman is over six feet tall, suddenly the 'air is thinner up there' is what we hear."

"I've never had a dog, Eve, but I'm told that they live very much in the moment. I know you feel bad about hitting Cookie, but I bet she knows that you still love her. And she'd probably be more than willing to forgive you if you took her for a little walk. We could take a very slow walk. It needn't be long—just something to help provide a break from how you've been feeling. Perhaps throw her ball around in the backyard if you're not up for a walk on the trail."

Eve managed to pull herself together; there were no more tears. Since she had prepared *fika*, they decided to take a short walk after enjoying the pastries and strong coffee. Cookie appeared to be more than willing to forgive Eve's assault, cautiously approaching Eve and placing her head on Eve's thigh while she enjoyed *fika*. Eve rewarded her with a cookie.

CHAPTER 12
HOW MANY ZEROS?

"Hey, guys, wassup?" Smith called out as he approached a few classmates standing outside the computer science library.

"Just talkin' about the game last night. Montreal Canadiens just steamrolled Boston. Did ya' see it?" asked a lanky young man, his dark hair cut into a Caesar with an undercut.

"Nah, I had better things to do," Smith answered before tossing his empty can of caffeinated energy drink in the general direction of the trash can. He missed.

A tall, athletic-looking blond sniggered, "What? Sandra come crawling back to you?" He polished off his electrolyte beverage and made a basket into the same trash can.

"Nah, she knows there's no point in trying," Smith said, without any hint of emotion. "Been workin' on one of my deals. I got *beaucoup* bucks comin' my way soon, bruhs."

"Yeah, sure man," a third commented, "whatever."

"Might not even bother to write the rest of the exams when this deal comes through. Maybe, maybe not."

The small group broke up shortly thereafter with individuals heading off to various parts of the campus. Smith turned away from them and made his way off campus.

Smith waited at the corner, as he had been instructed. Eventually, a black Jeep Grand Wagoneer with darkly tinted windows pulled up to the curb. A passenger exited the front seat then opened the door behind. Smith clambered in and took his seat beside another passenger already seated directly behind the driver. The front seat passenger crowded into the seat beside Smith, effectively book-ending him. The seat beside the driver was left unoccupied. Smith took a furtive glance backward to check the row of seats behind him, but they were empty. He felt relief.

"Where're we going?" Smith asked.

"You'll see," the driver replied as they entered the flow of traffic.

All Smith could think of was how many zeros there might be in their offer. He should have thought more broadly.

Smith's heart fluttered. He interpreted this as a response to Aleksandra's absence. Maybe he did love her, though he doubted it. But his heart fluttered again. This had been happening since their big blow up over the information he had submitted to the Who's This? website weeks ago, and he found it unsettling.

The men in the vehicle refused to answer his questions. The big one seated to Smith's right said something about a lieutenant by the name of Rojas who would explain. If this was the reality of venture funding in high tech, he told himself, he was going to need to get used to it, calm down considerably, and quite possibly learn Spanish. He shifted in his seat and adjusted his seat belt. It was something to do.

In due course the vehicle left the city, and as the trip continued Smith concentrated on how he would answer the questions he expected would be asked. He wondered how many zeros they would be talking about. He hoped there would be six, but he would settle for five. Truth be told, he'd settle for four, which would be four more than he had currently. Smith was flat broke.

He'd promised his pals a yacht vacation in the Caribbean during the next spring break, but he was already unable to pay his rent. All the money he'd had, all the student loans he'd obtained—it was all gone. In marketing, he'd learned that you must play the part, look successful, in order to attract investors. He'd heard that success breeds success, so Smith had spent his money, entertaining like successful people in the tabloid articles do and publicizing his participation with an abundance of social media posts.

All that had led to this—a long trip northward in an SUV with heavily tinted windows and three big guys playing babysitter. Smith was unable to get comfortable. He bit at the skin around a fingernail, nipping and tearing the cuticle toward the quick—it was a nervous habit. Again he shifted in his seat and adjusted his seat belt. It failed to help. There was some blood, so he sucked at his finger. Doing so gave him comfort, though not much.

"You'll be blindfolded now; it's the lieutenant's orders," the big guy seated beside Smith said as he took a black cloth from his jacket pocket. Smith focused on the zeros and complied. He could tell he was getting excited because his heart rate had increased. He could feel his heart jumping in his chest.

He thought it was fortunate that they had picked him up and given him a ride. Smith lacked personal transport and the money to acquire a vehicle even for the day. Their offer of a ride was a perquisite he could not refuse. He hoped there would be a number of such advantages.

With the blindfold secured, Smith had no idea where they now were or where he was being taken. His heart fluttered again in the excitement of it all. He wondered how much it cost to rent a flashy yacht in the Caribbean. He hoped the zeros were few.

The SUV came to a stop, and he could hear a large door grinding open. The vehicle moved forward a short distance then stopped. The car door opened, and the passengers exited—Smith being guided by someone he couldn't see. The man smelled of cologne heavy with musk, and when Smith bumped into him, he detected suiting material, not some fabric indicating casual attire. Smith wondered if he too might be wearing such apparel very soon. Smith began to remove his blindfold, but someone grabbed hold of him and secured his hands behind his back.

"When the time comes, *we'll* remove the blindfold, not you. And, since you can't behave yourself, we'll need to tie your hands now." And someone did, a might too tightly.

"Sit," someone commanded. The voice was without an accent. Smith sat. Eventually, his blindfold was removed, and his hands were untied.

The room was furnished as an office, but the decor was non-descript, the lighting poor, and the equipment dated. Smith tried to utter a few words in comment, but instead he emitted a wheezing sound.

"Ah, this is all too much for you, is it?" said a rather large man whose voice was the same as one Smith had heard earlier. The large man had curly dark hair and wore a dark suit.

The desk chair swivelled to face Smith. In it sat a middle-aged man with a short haircut and a bit of facial hair trimmed in a current style. The man spoke with a slight accent, perhaps Italian, or French, or Spanish . . . Smith was unable to identify the accent; his personal experience of other cultures was very limited.

"Mr. Smith," the man behind the desk began.

"Just Smith," Smith corrected him.

"Mr. Just Smith," the man continued, unfazed by the correction of his apparent error. "Where is Aleksandra Orlov?"

"I don't know. We broke up a couple of weeks ago. Heh, what's this about? I thought you said you had some money for me, that you were an investor."

"I am, Mr. Just Smith, an investor—just not in this computer thing you are peddling. I invest in information. What do you have for me?"

"I don't know where Sandy is. She got—" He gasped for air and found his shortness of breath alarming. "I don't know where she is. She cut off all ties with me. Like I said, I don't know where she is."

"Well, that is too bad then, Mr. Just Smith. What information *do* you have concerning Aleksandra Orlov? Remember, I invest in information, and so far you have disappointed me because you have no information."

As quickly as his unexplained wheezing would permit, Smith offered whatever details he could regarding his former girlfriend. He had little to offer—merely her class schedule, her friends, and her habits.

"Now, that information's got to be worth something to you, eh? I'm not even asking why you want it. It doesn't matter to me." His heart did a little flutter, and he paused to catch his breath.

"Hm-m," the man behind the desk said, "If she's not communicating with you, who do you think she might communicate with, Mr. Just Smith?"

"You could try Maddie Birch; she's a psych major, and Sandy has psych as a minor. Maddie's a former girlfriend of mine, but I think Sandy still considers her a friend. You could try her; I've got her number."

One of the men grabbed a pen and pad and handed them to Smith.

"Ah . . . I'll need to check my phone for the number; I don't know it by heart."

Smith was permitted to examine his phone for the number, but once he found it, the same man removed the phone from his grasp. He watched as the man copied the information to a pad. He was still watching as the man pocketed his phone, all the while staring straight at him. Smith was unnerved; he felt faint.

"Get him some water," the man behind the desk commanded. In short order a bottle of water was thrust into Smith's hand.

He tried to drink but aspirated the water while trying at the same time to catch his breath. He began to cough. His eyes suddenly opened wide as if he had seen something surprising. He wheezed once then went silent and slumped in his chair, shortly thereafter falling to the concrete floor.

The man who had sat to Smith's right in the SUV checked him for a pulse. Speaking in Spanish, he said, "Yeah, he's gone. His heart's stopped. I hate when that happens. There's nothing more you expected from him, is there boss?"

"No, you can dispose of the body but not around here. Take him back to Toronto and dump him in that lake. It'll attract less attention."

"The scrawny little thing'll fit inside a garbage bag. And he's so light we won't even need to use a heavy-duty one," the same man said with a derisive chuckle. "The guy's a zero, boss. No one'll miss him."

"Now find me this Maddie Birch," Rojas commanded, stroking his well-trimmed stubble.

CHAPTER 13
ARRIVAL OF THE SAMOVAR

The message from O stated that they would be arriving shortly. Lucy read the message a second time, resigned to the fact that she had agreed to care for Grisha's granddaughter, Aleksandra, for some indeterminate period. Those who needed to be informed had been informed, and issues of safety and security had been discussed and resolved. They were as ready as they were ever going to be.

Albin remained near the gate and busied himself by tending the shrubs in the vicinity, all the while keeping an eye out for anything unusual. Unlike Lucy and Kent, he'd never met the man, but when the SUV approached the gate, it was obvious to Albin that the driver was O. Lucy's description had been accurate. Moreover, Albin could sense a kinship with the ex-military O. There was just something in his bearing, an attentiveness and sense of confidence to which Albin related.

Once the gate was secured, and the SUV parked under the portico had disgorged its occupants, Albin entered the house to discuss security with O.

"Welcome, Aleksandra. I'm Lucy, and this is your new home, for a while at least. Please come in." The young woman hesitated momentarily, then she followed Lucy through the anteroom and into the foyer. "Albin and O will bring your things from the car and take them to your room," Lucy explained.

Aleksandra was quiet and seemed shy. Lucy suspected that Aleksandra's shyness would disappear over time, as she became more accustomed to her new surroundings.

"Please, call me Sandra," the young woman said, offering her hand and bending forward ever-so slightly.

"Sandra, it is then," Lucy said, taking her hand and air-kissing her on each cheek in the French style. "I'll show you to your room, then give you a quick tour of the house."

"O, just leave the samovar here for now," Aleksandra said, addressing her bodyguard. Next she accompanied Lucy up the open staircase, which encircled the small glass elevator. "Oh, I see you have a piano," she said upon noticing the highly polished black grand piano in a corner of the living room.

"Do you play?" Lucy inquired.

"Yes, a bit. I find it relaxing."

"Well, feel free to use the piano, Sandra. You might find a few other things here to help you relax as well. We'll see what we can find that interests you as I give you a tour."

"On this upper floor we have the guest suites and the games room as well as my private studio. The door at this end of the hallway leads to the upper level of my husband's office, specifically his library. That's a private area. At the far end of the hall, there is access to Helen and Elinor's apartment, their private area.

"And here's your room," Lucy said as she opened the door to the guest suite she had selected for Aleksandra. "It's not so grand as anything on board the *Croesus*—"

"Oh, it's lovely. Thank you," Aleksandra said. Lucy wondered about her sincerity, but the smile that accompanied those words came from the young woman's eyes, so she accepted the statement as being truthful.

"Well, I'll leave it to you to get settled. Elinor will remove the suitcases and boxes to storage, so just leave them out in the hallway when you're done."

Lucy returned to the main floor, eager to speak with O. "Welcome, O! It's so nice to see you again." They embraced, touched cheeks, and kissed the air, then changed sides and did it all again.

"It is nice to see you again as well. It has been far too long," O replied. "Too bad we must meet under such unfortunate circumstances."

"Indeed. You're staying here as well, aren't you?"

"Yes, if you'll have me."

"But of course! How about the room across the hall from Sandra? That'll put you facing the front while she faces the back. I thought it might be safer that way, in case someone tries to spy on the house from the street. Not that there's much traffic in this area since it's not a through street, but still . . ."

O grabbed his bag and followed Lucy as she led him to a guest room. "Sandra insisted on bringing her samovar and that is still in the foyer," he said. "Where should it be put?"

"That's for making tea, right?" Lucy considered for a moment, then remarked, "Either in the kitchen or in the games room. I'll ask Sandra once she joins us. For now, we'll just leave it where it is. It's probably good that she brought it. It'll help provide some comfort to her, something familiar amid all this upheaval."

"Yes, that is what I thought as well, so I didn't try to dissuade her. It's a modern version of a traditional Russian samovar, but I was still surprised that she would bother with such a thing. She insisted upon it quite strongly."

"When you're ready, please join us on the main floor for a casual lunch. We'll eat in the great room where the kitchen is located, and both of you will have the opportunity to meet everyone."

Helen and Elinor had prepared an extensive lunch, and it was set on the kitchen island as a buffet. O found his way to the great room ahead of Aleksandra, then he and Albin set off to collect Eve and Cookie from Eve's home next door.

"You could have just phoned," Eve said when Albin and O arrived.

"Yes, but I thought O should see this property as well in order to ensure security next door."

"I like the bridge you constructed over the wall. You can move from one property to the other without anyone on the street being the wiser. I really like that," O opined. "It doesn't look new."

"It's not," replied Albin. "I built it some years back when Lucy and Kent were travelling, and the Espie fellow was staying there. I guess you've heard about all that." O nodded his head. "I've been responsible for general maintenance and security for many years now. I actually used to live in the apartment with my sister, until Eve invited me to live with her here full time."

While Albin gave O a tour of Eve's property, Eve took Cookie across the wall bridge and into the Gillespies' property. She and Cookie arrived for lunch at the same time as Aleksandra made her way downstairs and into the great room. Cookie was obviously focused on Aleksandra, and both Lucy and Eve smiled in acknowledgement. Aleksandra appeared to enjoy Cookie's attention and relaxed further. So far, things were going well, but there was a long way to go.

"We weren't certain how long you'd be, so we started without you," Eve said, directing her antagonizing comment to Albin once he and O had returned from the neighbouring residence.

"After I gave O a tour of your property, I did the same here, so he knows how things are set up outside," Albin explained. And then he returned his attention to O, "You should talk to my sister, Helen, about tactics, O. Actually, after lunch, why don't the three of us meet in the security office in her apartment?" Helen nodded in acknowledgement.

Lucy was pleased to see Albin taking the initiative to inform O about the properties. It was important that everyone know all there was to know about the area so that they might devise effective tactics for dealing with whatever might come their way.

Once people were busy eating and interacting, Lucy gave Kent a quick call. "Where are you?" she inquired as soon as he answered his cellphone.

"I should be on my way shortly. Grisha had more he wanted to discuss, so I'm at Aleksandra's apartment with him and O. They'll be staying here. We're just finishing up, so I should be home shortly."

"Will both your O and Grisha be joining us for dinner?"

"No, they've got something to take care of, as I understand. Grisha thinks that if he actually meets with Aleksandra, she'll cave and end up returning with him. He doesn't want to be instrumental in weakening her resolve, so he won't be meeting with her until this is all cleared up. But he does phone her every day apparently."

"Well, in that case, it'll be Sandra, my O, and Eve and Albin . . . eight of us, counting Elinor and Helen. O thinks the

Carlssons should be involved in this, but I'm not convinced. We can discuss it tonight."

"Do you have Ebo or Oko?" Kent asked.

"You know, I've not even tried to determine that. Perhaps during the intervening years they've changed just enough that I wouldn't be able to tell who's who like I used to. Best to abide by their wishes and say nothing to distinguish them from one another. I've not acknowledged that there's two of them, not even in my most private conversations with O. I wonder if Sandra is even aware. Well, I'll see you shortly. We can talk about it more then."

CHAPTER 14
A LITTLE BIT OF KNOWLEDGE

France . . .

Several days had passed since Nathan had directed his *juriste* to forward the funds. He had just completed executing his yoga poses when Tommaso returned to their cell.

"Payment has been received, and the work will now begin," Tommaso said, informing Nathan of the status of the contract he had entered into.

"How long?" asked Nathan.

"Probably longer than you'd like, but it will be as rapidly as possible. There is no need to discuss it further," he said, immediately becoming irritated by what he predicted would become Nathan's incessant prodding.

"I paid a lot of money, Tom, and as a result I expect to receive good service on this. I think it's fair of me to expect that. I'd like to know what the plans are."

"No matter, the answer is no. It is not done."

"What about after? Can you tell me then? You'll have all the details, won't you?

"No matter, the answer is no. It is not done."

"So, for all that money, all I get is the five executions?"

Tommaso looked at him. "You want six instead?"

"No need to get churlish, Tom. I just wanted to get some details about the five. Is that really asking too much?"

"Yes."

CHAPTER 15

MARY JANES AS WEAPONRY

Southern Ontario . . .

"O is a very attractive man, isn't he?" Eve commented, surprising Lucy with her frankness. "I admire his apparent fitness and his attitude. There's such a sense of professionalism. And he dresses well too."

"What's going on, Eve?" Lucy asked when they found themselves alone in Lucy's suite in the master wing of her home. "Are you and Albin having problems?"

Eve cast her eyes downward and shuffled her feet like a naughty child.

"Not really. It's just that he was away in Quebec with Kent, and now the focus is on Sandra and her security. And, I mean, I understand the importance of it, most definitely. I just need to spend some time with my Albin, just the two of us. I guess I missed him more than usual for some reason. You don't think I'm getting needy in my old age, do you?"

"You've always been such an independent woman, Eve. I'm sure it's not that at all. I think you just missed Albin, and maybe you're a little angry with him because of that, even though you know that doesn't make sense. How about we treat you to a workout session with O? By the time you're finished, you'll be too exhausted to be upset with Albin. Believe me, O's quite demanding. I learned that when he trained me on board the *Theia*, where he was in charge of security before moving to the *Croesus*. So, we'll see you in the gym, four o'clock, got it?"

"So, this is where Mark Witherspoon got the idea for the LED wall on board the *Theia*," O exclaimed upon seeing the gym wall covered with integrated LED polycarbonate panels. Kent referred to the self-luminous installation as "animated architecture."

"Yes," Lucy confirmed. "Unlike Mark, we tend to use this to provide light therapy during some workouts. We've also watched the odd blockbuster film down here when Kent thought a huge screen better suited the subject matter. But Mark had cameras that captured all the action under the waves, and that was more exciting than just looking out over our backyard."

"So, you're saying that you have outside surveillance that can be viewed on this wall?"

"Yes. What are you thinking, O?" Lucy asked.

"I think that Albin and I should arrange all the cameras to feed into this installation. We can get on that in the morning.

"Right now, we've got a warm-up to do. I don't want anyone straining anything because they're not limber."

His final comment had been made with an eye to Eve, and it caused Lucy to smile to herself. Though Eve was every bit as tall as O, with her foot size matching his as well, O was under-estimating her and perhaps displaying a bit of ageism. He should have seen from her bearing alone that this ex-dancer and choreographer was far more capable than he assumed.

"Okay, so we've got Lucy, Eve, and Sandra. Before we get started, does anyone have any medical issues I should know about?"

"I broke my ankle about eight weeks ago and was told to refrain from using my foot as a weapon for at least another month. Personally, I think it's nonsense, but now you know." Eve shrugged, still indignant about being so cautioned by her physician.

"Your doctor actually specifically mentioned you're not to use your foot as a weapon? Those words?" O looked at Eve.

She sent him a crooked grin, raised her eyebrows and tilted her head toward an uplifted shoulder.

"Why?" he queried. "Why would that be something he felt he had to say? Do you usually use your foot as a weapon?"

"Well, a few years ago I did some *fouettés en tournant* while wearing my Mary Janes, and whacked a man in the head numerous times and, I might add, rather thoroughly. But it was Lucy who took him out with a flying kick to his groin and popped his nuts."

"I sense it was done on purpose," O said, wincing.

"Oh, most definitely," Eve and Lucy answered in unison, nodding their heads in synchrony.

"And well deserved too!" Lucy added. She looked toward Aleksandra, who appeared quite horrified by the revelation. She realized then just how much the young woman needed protecting. Despite her personal hardships and challenges, Aleksandra was still very naive.

O focused much of the training on defensive moves, including how to extricate oneself from a hold and, in the process, deliver a damaging blow to the attacker. This wasn't merely a workout, but a preparation session for Aleksandra.

"The first step is to not allow yourself to become captured. Know the territory—where the rooms are in which you might conceal yourself, the various ways to move through the house: where the halls go, what doors have locks, windows, and so on. Your knowledge of this is better than that of the intruder. But, if that fails, you use the techniques I've shown you today to get free, which again puts you at the first step, avoidance. Don't think it's over just because you've gotten away once. Keep your guard up.

"Clearly Lucy and Eve will understand what I'm about to say next, Sandra. Whoever is after you isn't trying to hand deliver a party invitation. They are going to be here to do you harm, which begins with your capture. Don't wait until they have inflicted harm before you really start to fight back. Think of your attacker as the most vicious person you might ever encounter, and protect yourself without care for your attacker. This won't be a random attack, but something well planned by professionals. Chances are they'll be very well trained, geared up, around one hundred and ninety centimetres in height, and about a hundred kilo, largely muscle. And there won't be just one. You're what? Less than one hundred and seventy centimetres and probably no more than fifty, perhaps a bit more, kilograms dripping wet." He left it there, not offering further explanation.

Lucy looked at Aleksandra, and the expression on Aleksandra's face revealed that O's little speech had hit home. "I think we should review these moves every day. If this time is good for everyone, then let's meet here daily for a refresher, okay?" The others agreed. "I'll suggest to Helen and Elinor that they join us as well," Lucy added.

Lucy, Eve, and Aleksandra remained behind when the lesson was concluded, while O left the gym to discuss with Albin his idea of directing the security feed to the LED wall. Lucy and Eve began their ballet barre routine to work on their flexibility and encouraged Aleksandra to join them.

"Don't force the stretch; just ease into it," Eve advised Aleksandra. "You certainly don't want to chance injuring yourself. You know, I might just start wearing my boot even during our training. Now is not the time for me to do something stupid and injure my foot again." Eve stood away from the barre and lifted her leg, essentially doing the splits while standing on one leg. Then she transferred the potential energy into an axe kick and forcefully brought her leg downward.

Aleksandra watched in amazement. She tried to mimic Eve's movements but failed to sustain a one-legged stand while trying to bring her leg up. She seemed to realize that she had something to learn from Eve, who wasn't simply the older woman who lived next door.

"Anyone want a hot tub, sauna, or swim? I'm just going to get myself ready for dinner, but you've had the grand tour, Sandra, so you know where those things are. You're welcome to use them, though perhaps you should have someone within sight of you, just in case. I'll check; Elinor should be available." Lucy reminded Eve that Astrid Carlsson and her son, Lukas, would be coming for dinner and Eve brightened at the news. Then Lucy left to speak with Elinor and ready herself for dinner.

CHAPTER 16
POLYESTER, PENSIONS
AND PATHOLOGY

Detective Inspector Patrick Brennan signed off on yet another report and added it to the stack on his cluttered desk. While glancing up at the old wall clock above the door opposite his desk, he yawned and stretched. It had been a long day, and he wasn't getting any younger. He took hold of his coffee cup and paused to consider a walk down to the break room for a refill. Then he considered how excess caffeine had begun to affect his sleep. With a growl of frustration and disgust, he pushed the cup away and continued with the paperwork.

At the appointed hour, Brennan grabbed a file folder, exited his office, and headed to the floor that housed the Human Resources Department. The previous week he had attended a pre-retirement seminar arranged by the department and had scheduled the meeting that he was now on his way to attend.

He was about to knock on the door of the private office when it was opened by a fresh-faced young man wearing a cheap suit and sporting a garish polyester tie.

"Oh! Sorry!" both men exclaimed as they avoided bumping into one another in the doorway.

"Patrick Brennan?" the young man queried.

"Detective Inspector, if you please," Brennan responded.

The young man smiled and directed Brennan to the guest chair on the opposite side of a small desk in the small office. There was a small window to the side, but no view. The office smelled of stale coffee and body odour combined with an industrial floral air-freshener. Ventilation was less than adequate.

"I was just coming to find you," the young man said. "Murray McKelvie." He proffered his hand, and Brennan seized the limp appendage. It was slightly damp.

"I see that your retirement is coming up, and you've requested a financial consultation," Murray stated. "Do you have any specific questions?"

"Well, yeah, actually. I've been focused on my work all these years, and haven't given any thought to preparing for retirement. Suddenly, I'm here, and I really have no idea how this all works or how much I'm to receive each month as my pension . . ." Brennan shifted in his chair. Clearly, this was not familiar territory for him.

"Your sources of funding after your retirement will be Old Age Security and the Canada Pension Plan—both of which are government plans with certain characteristics we can discuss later. Then there's your pension through work, with police services. Each month, you've paid into the pension and your contribution has been matched by your employer then invested for growth. There are some options available to you regarding how best to access those funds once you're retired. We definitely need to talk about that. Then we can discuss things like TFSAs, RRSPs, and RRIFs, and LIFs and annuities. Later, we can take a look at GICs and mutual funds as well as individual stock purchases . . ."

Brennan listened until his eyes glazed over, and he distractedly massaged his temples with his fingertips. "It might be easier just to continue working," he mumbled.

The meeting with the financial advisor lasted for an hour, though it seemed much longer, and by the end of the session, Brennan was considerably more confused than he had been when he first arrived. With a tired and very small smile on his face, he again took hold of Murray's limp, damp hand and gave it a tentative shake. Although he had scheduled a second meeting, he was unimpressed with Murray McKelvie and thought he might very well cancel. He'd have a week to think about it.

As soon as Brennan was out of his office, Murray McKelvie returned to his small desk and placed a telephone call. "Heh, Killer m'man, how ya doin'?"

"Makin' a killing," his old school chum, Mike Kilpatrick, replied. "Got somethin' for me?"

"Yeah, definitely. Heh, you sure you can't go forty-sixty on the split, man?"

"Nope, no can do. I got the licences—well, some of 'em," he sniggered. "And the overhead . . . Hell, I deserve more than seventy just to compensate me for the damn paperwork. You should be grateful for the thirty points you get; others only get twenty-five from me, and I'm planning to offer only twenty in the future."

"Okay, don't get all upset about it; it was just a question."

"What's the situation?" Mike asked.

Murray outlined the salient points of Patrick Brennan's file for Mike. If the lead panned out for Mike as he expected, thirty percent of Mike's commission on the sales would find its way into Murray's clammy hands. Mike was a real magician at *churning* a profit.

Brennan returned to his desk to drop off the file folder he had taken with him for his meeting with the financial advisor. He was about to depart for home when a colleague stopped him in the hallway.

"That body they found in Ashbridges Bay earlier this week, the one in the garbage bag—still don't know who it is, but pathology found something on it they think we'll find interesting. I'm heading down there now."

"Okay, keep me posted, Rashid," Brennan replied before continuing out the door and heading home.

CHAPTER 17

IN NEED OF CHAMPAGNE

France . . .

When her cellphone trilled, Yoichi was in the process of trying to read hallmarks on silver, a task which she found distinctly tedious. With a sigh combining both irritation and relief, she abandoned her work to answer the call. It was her long-time boyfriend, Donald.

"Well now, Mr. Gallagher, what is it I can do for you?" Yoichi said in her most sultry voice.

"Hello, dearest, I've missed you." His words and tone were soothing reminders to her.

Yoichi paused and, struggling to control her emotions, answered, "I miss you too. What are you doing?"

"I'm talking to the woman I love, just passing the time."

"Oh, Donald, what have you been up to? It's been so long, or so it seems. We used to see each other regularly and talk every day, but recently I've not heard from you. It's been ages! Is anything wrong?"

"Nothing's wrong, Yoichi. I've just had lots of annoying little things to take care of, some of it work-related, much not. It just didn't put me in the mood for a chat; I'm sorry about that. Time just sort of got away from me, but I think I've got it worked out now, save for the participation of other interested parties."

"What on earth are you going on about?"

The doorbell sounded. "There's someone at the door, Donny, so I've got to go—unless you want to hang on—I've got to run. It might be Serge. He might have forgotten his keys."

"I'll hold—" he began, and then he lost the signal. "Dammit! The entire month has gone like this." He had one more inquiry to make, and then there would be more time available. *Tomorrow. Things would be settled tomorrow.*

Yoichi quickly made her way to the door of Serge's apartment, confident that Serge would be at the other end of the intercom, but she was mistaken. A mature, distinctly feminine voice greeted her.

"I'm looking for Serge Proulx and Yoichi Song. I'm a friend of Lucy and Kent Gillespie," the voice declared.

"We've been expecting you; please enter and follow the stairs to the uppermost level. It's probably faster than using the elevator."

At about the same time, Serge, Merlot, and Bijou returned home and made their way up the gracefully sculpted limestone staircase to the penthouse suite. The expected visitor was too exhausted to climb the stairs, opting instead to ride the brass open-cage elevator, however slow it might be. To their mutual surprise, the visitor and Serge arrived at the uppermost floor simultaneously. They were met at the apartment door by Yoichi, who ushered them inside.

"You must be Juliette," Yoichi and Serge said simultaneously, though Serge said it in French and Yoichi in English.

"Yes, I'm so very pleased to make your acquaintance," Juliette replied, greeting them in the French style, with an exchange of air kisses on each cheek. They noted that she was visibly exhausted, likely stressed by her recent security challenges. She was somewhat dishevelled, as happens when you've been travelling constantly, and her skin had taken on an unhealthy pale shade, as might be caused by improper nutrition and inadequate sleep.

Yoichi showed Juliette to her room while Serge delivered his few recent grocery purchases to the kitchen and opened a bottle of champagne. Soon the women joined him.

"*J'ai besoin de champagne!*" Serge declared, announcing his need for champagne. "We must celebrate even the smallest success. Today, I cheated death itself!" He provided elaboration of his claim without waiting for anyone to encourage him to do so. "I was crossing *Boulevard de Beauséjour* and an eastbound car nearly hit me. The idiot was taking a shortcut and decided to travel the wrong way on a one-way street. People have no respect for rules, it appears." Champagne in hand, Serge led Juliette through a quick tour of the apartment and its treasures.

"Cataloguing this collection must be keeping you very busy, Yoichi," Juliette said.

Yoichi raised her eyebrows at the understatement.

"Serge, your collection is magnificent. I read about the court case concerning the attempted theft of your Portnoy. Do you still have it?" asked Juliette.

Serge guided her further along the hallway. He stopped in front of a dark painting of a woman carrying an injured child and screaming as she runs from a fiery scene. "Here's the Portnoy, *Siege of Sevastopol*. It is my least loved painting, so I don't know why I've had it for so very long."

"I quite like it, Serge," countered Yoichi. "I mean, it's troubling and very dramatic, but it depicts a strong woman expressing her reason for hating war—the death of innocents. Great stuff!"

Simultaneously, they refocused their attention from the painting to Juliette. "Don't look at me!" Juliette exclaimed, holding up her hands in mock defence. "I'm no art critic; I just interpret for myself. I knew of the Portnoy solely because of the court case. I understand that the perpetrator remains incarcerated, though he's due for release within a year or two, as I recall."

They retired to the living room for a chat. They felt pressured by circumstances to get to know one another, understand the situation, and formulate some response if the apartment and its residents might come under attack. In the end, they came up with nothing but determination and bravado. Among the three of them, there was no tactician to be found.

CHAPTER 18

FLIRTATIONS

Southern Ontario . . .

"I see there's work being done out front, on the street. Do you happen to know what they're doing? I couldn't tell from the little equipment they had," Lukas said, as he and Astrid entered the living room, and Astrid took a seat at the piano. "There's a cherry picker, so perhaps they're looking for tree pests—but it seems too early in the season for that—or, maybe they're planning to trim the trees. But then they would just mark the trees until the arborists are available, wouldn't they?"

"I think this warrants an investigation," announced O, getting up from the sofa. Soon he was joined by Albin. The two men accompanied Lukas back out to the road.

Helen had been in the living room replenishing beverages but quickly excused herself and disappeared into another room.

"They've gone," announced Lukas upon returning from the gate. Albin and O remained deep in discussion in the anteroom.

"Actually, they were never here," corrected Helen. "I just spoke with the city's works department, and there was no work scheduled to be done on this street by any city department or utility operating in this area." The comment drew the attention of both Albin and O, and they moved toward the living room, pausing in the foyer.

"That was fast," said O, perplexed. "I wonder how they managed to find us here. I doubt they would have been able to confirm Sandra's presence, but they seem to know that she is connected with the house, and I can't figure out how. I may have an idea; excuse me while I return to my room to flesh out my plan a bit more before sharing it with you." With that, O turned and made his way upstairs.

"How can he be so sure that this is connected with Sandra? Perhaps the city's works crew just went to the wrong address," Lukas ventured.

"Trust me," said Albin. "He knows, and he knows he's right too. They were surveillance. That was well spotted, Lukas."

Upon O's departure from the room, Albin turned to Kent and quietly commented, "O was on the plane with us and at the apartment with Grisha, and you said they're staying there. But here's O, and it seems he's been in Toronto awhile already. So I'm confused, but I didn't want to say anything in front of everyone."

"My office," Kent replied. The two men left the others in order to continue their discussion in Kent's office, behind locked doors. Kent sat behind his desk, tilting his chair as if he might yet be undecided about what to say. Albin sat across from him in a guest chair, visibly eager to hear an explanation for this puzzle he'd identified. "What I'm about to tell you is highly confidential, Albin, but I can't see any way forward except to let you in on this. Besides, I know you can be trusted. . . ."

O returned just before the evening meal was served, but he said nothing about his deliberations, though his appetite appeared tempered by his more serious concerns.

As Elinor served the dessert, Lukas began, "Excuse me, but I find myself thinking about what steps I might have taken, had I been so inclined in the manner of this individual, Smith. It occurs to me that a tracker on your cellphone would seem useful." He had directed his statement more to Aleksandra and O than to the others at the dining table.

"I got rid of the tracker app before we left Sandra's apartment, and there was no evidence we were followed from the apartment," O said, then paused, apparently deep in thought. "No, we weren't followed. I just can't see that having happened." He shook his head and looked downward at his untouched trifle. "Yes, I checked immediately upon my arrival and removed the app that I assume was installed by Smith at some point prior to this blowing up," O explained, much to Aleksandra's horror.

"You mean that Smith was tracking me?"

"Well, he certainly had the means to do so if he wished to use the app that was installed. We have no way of knowing if he actually used it at any time, nor of confirming that he was the individual who installed it," explained O.

"You're welcome to come and visit with us at anytime, Sandra. We're just down the street, the next house, just around the bend, at the cul-de-sac. Give me a call, and I'll walk up here to accompany you. I don't think you should just set out on your own. And, of course, you should clear it with O first," Lukas added.

The manner in which Lukas looked at Aleksandra and spoke to her made Lucy think that the young man was attracted to her house guest. Lucy's eyes met Astrid's across the table, and they both smiled. Clearly, his mother held the same opinion.

Aleksandra was incredulous. "I was being tracked . . ."

"As O said, the app was there, so yes you were being tracked, but Smith might not actually have accessed it to find you. What is his area of study?" Lukas asked.

"He's into computers, specifically setting up an online mall, which he called Abizmall. I think he already had the name registered or whatever. Some of his courses were in aspects of entrepreneurship. His first project was a collection of T-shirts under the name: Psyche Shirts," Aleksandra explained.

"What was that about?" Kent asked.

"The slogans were all uplifting and encouraging but written in mirror-image so the person who wore the shirt would read the message each time they saw themselves in a reflective surface. His girlfriend at the time, Maddie, is a psych major, so she helped him with the slogans. But I guess having a product is merely the first step, so Smith became more interested in the marketing of it, which led to him applying his interest in e-marketing and networking, and developing a strong online presence on a variety of platforms to help him build his brand," Aleksandra explained. "He figured that his future lay in marketing, and that he could market any product whatsoever through Abizmall."

Lukas appeared to give the matter some thought before he elaborated. "I guess our business is just so different, it's a bit difficult for me to grasp the journey he might be trying to map out for himself. I spent my time at university working to acquire knowledge in the areas of medicine, pharmacology, and business, which led to a collection of letters that I hope demonstrate my acquired knowledge and ability in the subject matter. I am now working here in Canada as president of the Canadian arm of Nanovo Pharmaceuticals. I guess this is an old-fashioned career path, but it's one that suits our industry, I think. We have products that are not readily adaptable to e-commerce, certainly not at the retail level."

"Unlike you, it sounds as if Smith is more interested in the marketing structure than in the product being marketed," opined Kent. "That too has its place, of course, but I would find it difficult to accept the job of building something that I didn't think was fundamentally a good idea, and I'm pretty certain I'd feel the same if I were in retail."

"But Smith is building a marketing system, not the product being marketed," Lucy chimed in. "You and Lukas are each involved in businesses that do both steps. You make the product and market the product, though, in your case, you market it first, then produce it. And as Lukas said, this venture of Smith's is a different sort of business and less traditional."

"However, Abizmall sounds to me a lot like many other popular sales platforms, so it, too, is already part of our tradition, isn't it?" Albin said. "Pretty much everything builds upon something that existed previously, and in the case of Abizmall, perhaps those tweaks are more significant to Smith and people with interests such as his than they are to those of us who are more traditionally traditional."

Eve guffawed and shook her head. "You actually said 'traditionally traditional,' didn't you?"

"Well, I really don't care about his great—or not so great—ideas," Astrid interjected. "He seems like a very egotistical individual who cared more about himself than Sandra when he put her personal information online. If he were smart and well-versed in this area of study, then surely he would have realized the downside to his actions. It's unconscionable."

A chime sounded, and Elinor responded, opening the gate to permit entry.

Kent greeted the new guests at the front door. "Welcome, Juji, Leo," Kent said. "It's been a long time."

"I hear you two dined at Flirtations tonight," he said as he ushered them toward the living room. "You'll have to tell us all about it. I understand they've got a backlog of reservations, as they're currently en vogue for dining in Toronto." As the others made their way into the room, Kent introduced them to Albin, O, and Aleksandra, who were the only guests they didn't already know.

Astrid took a seat at the piano while the others enjoyed their after-dinner drinks. She found it relaxing to play and preferred it to an after-dinner liqueur. Aleksandra declined an after-dinner beverage and considered the room: its fossil-laden rock wall installation, the black piano gleaming in the corner, the view across the water marked by the twinkling lights of small and large shoreline communities. She listened as Astrid played a few bars of *I'm Always Chasing Rainbows*, and just as she stood and took a step toward the piano herself, Astrid began to play Ravel's *Bolero*. After pausing for a moment, Aleksandra continued toward the piano and was enthusiastically welcomed by Astrid. Together they they played the selection as a four-hand duet. The two seemed to have a natural compatibility, which was further evident with their next selection: a Mozart sonata for four hands.

"That was most enjoyable!" enthused Astrid when the piece was concluded. Aleksandra smiled, as did Astrid while she retreated to the sofa, leaving Aleksandra to a solo performance of Chopin's *Torrent*.

At its conclusion, there was a round of applause. "I can just imagine you playing the Rimsky-Korsakov piano concerto, Opus 30, while accompanied by a full orchestra," Astrid declared, marvelling at the younger woman's ability to have delivered such an exquisite performance.

"Actually, I have already done so. It was an experience gift from my *dedushka*—I mean, my grandfather—for my sixteenth birthday. I've never done so on merit alone."

"Well, dear, I think everyone here would agree that it was indeed a well-merited gift. Your playing is lovely. If you wish, come and visit with us anytime you would like to play a duet or share some ideas. Lukas keeps a piano at his house—just for me when I visit, I think. He is not particularly musically inclined, wouldn't you agree?" Astrid concluded, garnering a nod and a smile from Lukas.

"But in my defence, I have been known to sing a bit," Lukas declared.

"So, Juji, Leo, tell us about Flirtations," Kent coaxed, after only a brief pause in the conversation.

"It was a lovely gift from Astrid and Lukas for our second anniversary, but a shame that our reservation conflicted with tonight," Juji answered, nodding to both in acknowledgement.

"They tend to be fully-booked but had a cancellation we were able to snag for you," Lukas explained.

"The food, the service, the ambience were all so wonderful. Its reputation is well deserved. They refer to the appetizers as 'teasers,' the mains as 'temptations,' and the desserts as 'jealousies,' which I thought was fun," enthused Juji.

"How long are you staying?" asked Eve.

"Well, that's something we have yet to discuss," Leo said. "Juji feels she should return, so I thought I might pop back and forth until Astrid decides to return to Gothenburg. I'll be flying economy. Will that still qualify me as a jet-setter?" Juji merely shook her head and smiled lovingly at him.

"Since we're all together—Helen, Elinor, please stay—I have a plan of sorts that I'll be discussing with certain of you as needed, but there is a very simple thing that concerns all of us in our endeavour to keep Sandra safe—that is, Sandra needs a code name. Suggestions?" O prompted.

"Blomma," Lukas stated confidently. "It's Swedish and means flower, so it could be a girl's name."

"I like that," O said. "It's not so unusual as to be an obvious code. And it does sound like a girl's name."

"What do you think, Blomma?" he asked, directing his question to Aleksandra. "Or, would you prefer to be referred to as bunny? I understand that your grandfather calls you bunny or in Russian, *zayka*."

"My name is now Blomma, as Lukas suggested," she answered, shyly glancing toward Lukas. "How did you think of this name?" she asked him.

"My guess is that you were thinking of the flower in your favourite book," Astrid said, her eyes soft on Lukas.

He nodded and smiled at his mother. "*The Little Prince*," he clarified, without further comment.

"And I would now like to introduce you to our new Sandra," O announced, encouraging Elinor to come forward. "Elinor has volunteered to be identified as Sandra or Aleksandra, and she will wear a blonde wig."

"Won't this be dangerous for her, O?" inquired Aleksandra. "I mean, you're protecting me, but if Elinor pretends to be me, then you now have two people to protect: me and Elinor."

"Clearly, they want you, Blomma, not me. If there's a problem, then I can just whip off the wig, and when I reappear, they won't realize what's happened," Elinor explained. "No one is making me do this, Blomma; I volunteered. I can't fight, but perhaps I can confuse."

"Yes, you should be able to provide confusion very effectively," proclaimed Helen. "After all these years, there are still times you confuse me."

Elinor looked at Helen and shrugged. "I'm a natural."

"Elinor will temporarily move from the apartment and take a guest bedroom across the hall from Blomma and beside me. If anyone is watching, as I suspect they recently tried to do, they might see Sandra-Elinor in a front bedroom, and, as they then have no need to attempt to see into the back bedrooms, they won't see Blomma. If you increase the duration the lights are turned on in your studio, Lucy, then that may lessen their awareness of any bedrooms facing the back," O explained. "I have some other ideas as well, but I'll speak privately with the parties more directly involved in those."

CHAPTER 19
A GREY DAY

France . . .

It was raining and had been for several days. Paris became grey, as if the entire city existed within a cloud. The dampness was penetrating and unpleasant. Serge considered confining the spaniels to the terrace, then decided that a short walk— even in the mist—would be beneficial for all three of them.

While he was gone, Yoichi continued her work with Juliette's assistance. For the most part they worked in silence and followed Yoichi's well-established plan.

"How long have you been working on this?" inquired Juliette when she and Yoichi stopped to take a short break.

"Much too long. I was overwhelmed by the sheer enormity of the task. I saw photos and some lists, but nothing prepared me for this. We're nearing the end now, so the pace will pick up. There's a lot that has already been removed from here; you just can't tell since there's so much that remains."

"What's the next step?"

"Well, some things have been pre-sold, or promised to local dealers, and others will be transported to auction houses. There are quite a few that are coming back with me and will be displayed at Canadian museums or transferred into private

Canadian collections. Given the variety and quantity, there are many venues vying for the opportunity to acquire them. What has slowed me down a bit is that I'm not just cataloguing, I also deal with these other individuals and companies and that's a bit distracting, though necessary and highly desirable from a sales perspective."

"From what I've seen during my years with Interpol, isn't the security of this collection rather precarious?"

"Yes, you're right. And that's yet another concern. I've got to get this done already; besides, I've got a gallery back home to run. Hopefully, we've done this rather quietly, so perhaps we've not drawn too much attention to the task and aren't on the radar of any art thieves."

"Don't count on it. There's always someone out there looking for a quick buck, Yoichi. Art thefts aren't merely art thefts these days. You're looking at money laundering on a grand scale, and art plays a role in that. And money laundering is what funds all other sorts of nefarious activity."

They returned to their work and were deeply engrossed when they heard a key turning in the lock and the apartment door opening. This was followed by the scampering of eight little feet and the stomping of one much larger pair. Merlot, Bijou, and Serge had returned home.

Serge left the women to continue their work while he set about preparing lunch for them. Periodically, he poked his head into the room in which they were currently occupied, but he didn't disturb them. It was quite obvious that Serge had something to discuss with them, but he would wait.

When they finally broke for the midday meal, Serge presented a terrine served with a cube of aspic on a bed of endive as an appetizer. The main course consisted of quail, stuffed with wild rice and truffles and glazed with a Seville marmalade laced with ginger. Dessert was always a special surprise.

"Serge, sometimes I think this work is taking me so long because subconsciously, I just can't deny myself such wonderful food," Yoichi said. "But you should know that we are definitely closing in on the end, and I should be out of here inside of a week or two. Shortly, we'll have most of the items gone from here, and I can concentrate on the items going to Toronto."

"I've been giving that some thought, Yoichi. Given the quantity to be transported and considering that both you and Juliette need to return to Toronto, I thought I might rent a plane for us." His guests appeared stunned into silence by the announcement. "Yes, *us*. Perhaps I should take this opportunity to visit Lucy and Kent in Toronto. I can even take Merlot and Bijou with me. If you would please look into that for me, I would appreciate it."

Yoichi slumped. It was yet another task to consider. Would it simplify or complicate things? At this stage, she couldn't predict.

"I should let both of you know that I had an odd interaction with a rather robust-looking gentleman toward the end of my walk today. The encounter would not have concerned me under usual circumstances, but today it just felt odd."

"Perhaps we should hear all the details, Serge," Juliette suggested.

"The path I followed is one I regularly use. I mention this because I have never before seen this man. While we spoke only toward the end of the walk, I became aware of him about midway. He just made me feel a bit uncomfortable.

"He followed more closely as we approached home, then tried to start a conversation. He claimed that he was looking for an apartment to purchase and asked if I could recommend anything. I just said '*non*' and acted the part of a doddering simpleton. That was easy to do because he had so completely unnerved me. Generally, I'm eager to speak with new people, to sit and discuss something—but not in this case. As well, neither Merlot nor Bijou was fond of the man, and usually they love everyone."

"I shouldn't have come here," Juliette declared. "I've put you in danger, both of you."

"Nonsense!" Serge exclaimed. "Your arrival could be completely coincidental. I've been the subject of surveillance and robbery and attempted fraud—all before you came into my life, Juliette. Remember, even yesterday someone nearly ran into me with their vehicle! No matter. It is the three of us against this element. As before, we shall prevail!"

Serge was defiant and appeared confident, but the women were worried, both for themselves and for him. It wasn't the incident with the vehicle—that was likely to have been simply a matter of poor driving resulting in a near-accident; no, it was something far more sinister that worried them: malice.

"Martin and Mansfield, the art movers, will be here on Wednesday to begin packing the items going to Canada. I'll speak with them this afternoon regarding the rental of a plane for all of us to be with the consignment. And I'll contact those who have been tardy in picking up the items they've selected. I don't know what they're playing at with such unnecessary delays."

As Serge brought espresso to the table after their meal, the doorbell chimed. It wasn't the bell for the outer door to the apartment building, but rather the bell for Serge's penthouse unit. Therefore, it was either a neighbouring apartment dweller or someone who had gained access to the building through deception.

Yoichi and Juliette looked at one another and armed themselves as best they could. Juliette took a tenderizer mallet from a kitchen drawer, and Yoichi retrieved a Japanese katana she had just recently catalogued. Serge grabbed a roll of packing tape and approached the door.

Serge glanced through the peep-hole in the door. The situation was confusing. The individual may have been a fellow resident unknown to him, and he did not wish to appear rude. Keeping the security latch in place—and regretting that he had failed to upgrade to a modern video system after Nathan Bellamy's attempted theft—Serge cautiously unlocked the door and drew it open, just enough.

The well-dressed man at the door was of average height and quite bald. He didn't look like a thief or troublemaker; moreover, his accent was refined as he spoke in French. "Another resident held the door for me to enter," he explained. "I am sorry to have disturbed you, but I'm looking for a woman by the name of Yoichi Song. She's Canadian and speaks French quite dreadfully."

"Quite dreadfully? Donald, is that really you?" Yoichi said, clearly surprised, yet delighted. "Serge, it's okay; he's with me."

There was some slight confusion while Serge disengaged the remaining security latches and stepped aside to welcome Donald Gallagher into his home.

"Why don't Juliette and I go elsewhere while the two of you have a chat," Serge suggested, moving toward the hallway and pausing just long enough for Juliette to join him. Merlot and Bijou refused to follow.

"Sorry if this is awkward for you, Yoichi. I couldn't be patient and wait until you returned." And then, as if his mere presence wasn't surprise enough, he added, "Will you marry me?"

"Marry? Us? Donald! Yes!"

They kissed and laughed, and then Donald paused and sighed.

"This is the point at which I present you with a ring, which I don't have presently." Donald looked rather defeated for a man who had just had his marriage proposal accepted. "We're always busy, but we've never been apart so completely for so long. You've been holed up here working, and I've been flying hither and yon, and it's been one so-called work emergency after the other. I realized I was miserable without you." Donald paused to take a breath. "I just couldn't let that continue any longer."

Yoichi appeared to be without words—certainly not finding any to use under the current circumstances.

"I thought we could get married here," Donald continued, "then have a reception back in Toronto. Unfortunately, that's not doable. The legal marriage is a civic affair in France, and we're not eligible. We could have a church wedding, but that's merely ceremonial. I tried everything I could think of, and I came up with no alternative. However, I thought at the very least, I could propose in Paris. I could give you that. We can always return for our honeymoon—if you'd like, that is."

She kissed him again—long and hard. "It's the thought that counts, and I've been thinking about this too!" Barking and general mayhem ensued from Merlot and Bijou.

CHAPTER 20
OHIO

Southern Ontario . . .

Aleksandra felt isolated and overwhelmed; she needed to connect with her friends. As upset as she was about Smith's actions, she nevertheless experienced a sense of loss. His absence from her life had left a void. The sensation left her feeling insecure, as if she were adrift on a tiny raft in choppy seas—no matter that she had contacted her grandfather and no matter that O was there, entrusted to keep her safe from harm.

She decided to make just one quick call.

"Hi, Sandra, what's up?"

"Hi, Maddie," Aleksandra said, "just wondering what's been happening."

"Well, I haven't seen you in the library recently, and there are lots of rumours going around about you."

"Like what?"

"Well, the wildest one was that you were like this Russian princess or something, but even I know that's ridiculous. Most are things like you just decided to drop out—but that doesn't really sound like you. Another I heard was that your life was in danger so you were in hiding—but obvs, that's probably started by someone who consumes wa-a-ay too much crime fiction and the like, so my psych senses tell me that's another fake story. Oh, another was that you were preggers. That seemed like a possible explanation because Smith disappeared about the same time. Which is it?"

"None of those. . . . Smith disappeared? What do you mean?"

"Oh, the guys saw him a few days ago. He was talking about a big deal and how he might blow off exams if the deal came through. Maybe it did. They said he didn't write the next exam, and none of them have seen him on campus since."

"Well, the next time you see Smith, you can mention that there's someone else in my life now, and I'm doing just fine, no thanks to him," Aleksandra said, carefully choosing her words. She was a poor liar, but what she had said was technically accurate; there were many other people in her life now.

"Where have you been?" Maddie asked.

"I don't want to run into Smith, so I've just been working at home." Aleksandra didn't share any classes with Maddie, so there was no exam they had in common. "Later, I may be going to an island . . . with some friends," she added. "Or, maybe I'll stay here. I need a break, but I haven't decided. What about you?"

"Haven't decided. Smith said he had a great idea and was making plans for everyone. I'm hoping he's treating us to tickets for Lizard Brain. Did you hear? They've just announced new concert dates, so now there's one some place in Southern Ontario; I'm thinking probably Toronto. I didn't catch the details, and he hasn't shown up for a while, so who knows what's going on. Really, Sandra, just think—Lizard Brain—it'd be a crazy night!"

Aleksandra was unable to reach Maddie's level of enthusiasm for Lizard Brain, yet such an experience sounded appealing, particularly given her current circumstances.

"Actually, I don't think anyone in our group has bothered to make any firm plans yet. I'll probably end up working a till somewhere. I may have left it too late to get a better job for the summer. My dad's always saying things like, 'When you fail to plan, you plan to fail.' I probably should have just enrolled for the summer term like you did. Oh well."

"Where do you think he is?" Aleksandra pursed her lips and squeezed her eyes shut, annoyed with herself for being concerned about Smith.

"Smith? Oh, he's probably heard from one of his potential investors, and is off somewhere working on his big deal as we speak, making connections. Maybe it'll result in something for me too, you know like a snowball effect, where you get caught up in something that just keeps getting bigger and bigger.

"Say, you don't mind that him and me are on again—I think . . . maybe."

"No," Aleksandra quickly replied.

"I'm kinda hoping that when he does return, he'll whisk me away to some exotic place, maybe even on a yacht in the Caribbean, and it won't matter that I didn't get a summer job," Maddie blabbered. "He already got some money from an investor, so I hear. He was telling us that he's going with crypto; by the time he needs to access it, it'll be worth even more."

"Hm-m, I think that was what he was planning to do, but don't hold your breath," Aleksandra advised, less impressed by the yacht in the Caribbean and Smith's claim of financial acumen than Maddie could ever imagine. A knock sounded at her bedroom door. "Sorry, Maddie, gotta go. Bye. Take care."

"Okay, bye then—"

But Aleksandra had already disconnected from the call, placed her cellphone onto the recharger, and readied herself to answer the door.

"Oh, hi, O! Sounds like a place . . . Ohio. Get it?" Aleksandra appeared to be nervous; she was babbling.

"I want to talk to you about something, Blomma. This is what I am proposing, but I want your feedback in order to deal with any concerns you may have. . . ." He outlined the plan, telling Aleksandra only what she absolutely needed to know and nothing more.

CHAPTER 21
BREAKTHROUGH

The following morning, Brennan bumped into Rashid exiting his office. "I just put the report on your desk, but I think it would be better if I could explain it to you," the younger detective said.

"Well, good morning to you too. I can read," Brennan replied, glancing toward the break room and coffee.

"It has to do with computers. How about I get you a coffee while you read, and then if you have any questions . . ." He was gone before Brennan could reply.

The report concerned a tattoo found on the body in the bag. It consisted only of numbers: 077 097 100 100 105 101. Brennan had questions. He was still staring at the numbers when Rashid returned with his coffee.

"So what do we think this is then? It's too long for a phone number. And crypto wallets employ both upper and lowercase letters as well as numbers. Seems a bit long for a bank account number or other such ID number, but might be. You said 'computers,' so enlighten me."

"I think it's an ASCII code," Rashid replied.

"And what's that?" asked Brennan. "Sounds like something only a computer nerd would know anything about."

"ASCII is short for American Standard Code for Information Interchange. It's a numerical representation of text. Ultimately, computers rely upon a binary code of ones and zeroes, but specific patterns of those ones and zeroes correspond to specific numbers. And specific groupings of numbers then correspond to specific letters and symbols. It was bugging me last night, but now I'm completely confident; I know what that says," Rashid declared.

"You seem awfully smug about it; are you going to let me in on your great discovery?" Brennan said, taking a sip of his coffee while it was still hot.

"It's a name: Maddie."

"And that leads us where, exactly?"

"The guy's got to be a computer nerd if he's going to get a tattoo of his girlfriend's name using ASCII code. And the body is that of a young male; forensics peg the age at about twenty years. Seems kinda young to die from a heart problem, but the pathologist says it happens not as infrequently as you'd think. And there's something else. I happened to be down in Missing Persons—"

"Ah, yes, visiting your girlfriend again? Just get married already; you'd see less of her then, and we just might get some work done around here."

"My point is, I was there when a new report came in. The missing person is a nineteen-year-old female by the name of Maddie Birch. She's a psychology major at the University of Toronto. There could be another garbage bag out there."

"Might be worth considering. I'll look into us running this as a joint operation with Missing Persons. In the meantime, without stepping on anyone's toes, see if you can identify our body. Talk to Maddie Birch's family and friends; show them the facial photo we've got. Use the one that tech's modified to look alive," Brennan instructed. "And get back to me as soon you've got something definite."

It was late afternoon when Rashid reported back to Brennan. "It's the ex-boyfriend of Maddie Birch. According to her family and some friends of hers, he called himself Smith."

"Just Smith?" Brennan replied. "Who did he think he was, Elvis?"

"Yeah, well, University Administration recognized him, both from the photo and because he'd often tried to have his records modified to Smith. Our body appears to be that of Charles Ponzi. I've got a home address for him in Niagara Falls and his address here in Toronto as a student. He was in second year and taking courses in computing, marketing, and entrepreneurship. We'll get the parents in for a formal ID."

"Well, the missing girl is either a suspect in Ponzi's death or a victim herself. Continue with the investigation into Ponzi's death, and I'll have a chat with Missing Persons. Good work, Rashid."

When Brennan arrived at work the following day, he came upon a new stack of files on his desk—information to date gathered on the Smith case as well as the Birch case. He distributed them to his team, and everyone went to work.

A public appeal was scheduled for late morning. The time was chosen to coincide with the noon news report. As nervous and emotional as they were, Maddie's parents would speak, supported by police personnel.

CHAPTER 22
RACHMANINOFF AND AKVAVIT

"I'm home, Mom," Lukas announced as he swung the front door shut with his elbow. "Where are you?"

"We're in the living room, dear. Blomma is visiting," Astrid called out.

"How long have you been here?"

"Lukas!" exclaimed Astrid.

"Perhaps it's time for me to leave," said Aleksandra.

Both women spoke at the same time, and all Lukas knew was that quite clearly, he had said the wrong thing.

"Please, don't leave, Blomma. It's good to see you again. Stay and have dinner with us. I only asked because there are linesmen working just down the road, and I was wondering if they were there when you left the Gillespie residence."

"Linesmen?" the women queried.

"Yes, people who work on the utility poles. I didn't notice if they were from the electrical power company or one of the communications companies. It might be nothing to be concerned about, but given Blomma's precarious position, I think I should let O know about it." Lukas located O among his contacts and phoned him, explaining about the workers he had seen. They spoke for only a short time before signing off.

"O thinks it is a good idea for you to visit with us and stay for dinner, Blomma. He'll look into this business with the linesmen and then get back to us when he thinks it's okay for you to return to the Gillespies'. So, now that's out of the way, greetings to you both. Did you have a good day?"

"Oh yes, we shared stories, had a lovely *fika*, and played our favourite pieces on piano. Blomma plays so beautifully. We've been taking turns playing pieces we think are the most beautiful. I, of course, have my favourite Chopin, and not unexpectedly, Sandra appears to prefer Rachmaninoff. Oops, I mean Blomma. I must remember to be more careful about that!"

"I'm just going to check on dinner," Astrid said, before leaving the two young people.

"Subtle." Lukas chuckled while looking at Aleksandra, who appeared to be smiling, though somewhat shyly. "Would you like an aperitif, perhaps akvavit?"

"I've never had akvavit, but sure, thanks," she answered enthusiastically. While Lukas crossed the room to prepare their drinks, Aleksandra filled the silence with an observation. "Your house rather reminds me of the Gillespie residence. I can't quite put my finger on it. The rooms are located differently, and some of the materials are quite different, yet somehow the two houses feel similar. Is that just my imagination?"

"My father designed and oversaw the original construction, but after he died, Kent reworked the plans considerably before completing the project. Initially, it was to be sold, but with our company expanding, we decided that we'd open a subsidiary here, and I would use the house as my residence. I quite like it; how about you?"

"It's lovely. That explains why it reminds me so much of the Gillespie house. Both are ultimately Kent's designs.

"O said that I should ask if you've got a panic room, so that I could use it in case . . ."

Epitaph

"Yes, let me give you a tour and show you how our panic room works. It's one of those things you want to have very well designed, and well equipped—and then never use. It's rather like an insurance policy."

CHAPTER 23
NEWS AT NOON

It was lunchtime, and those currently at the Gillespie residence congregated in the great room for their meal. It was informal; the food was set out on the centre island as a buffet. Someone turned on the television to catch the local news.

With the obscuring blinds closed in the games room upstairs, Aleksandra had spent the greater part of the morning by herself, playing video games and refreshing herself with caffeinated energy drinks, a habit established during her time with Smith. Neither the games nor the beverage provided sufficient distraction. Hours before, she had retreated to the games room to catch a bit of local news, and it was then that she had first heard the report. It had left her feeling somehow responsible. She was deeply troubled by it, but there was no way she could run to O or Lucy with the details. She only revealed to them that she knew the victim.

She was uncertain if her nervousness was due to the situation, or merely a reaction to the large quantity of caffeine she'd imbibed. Suddenly aware of her hunger, she took note of the time then made her way downstairs to the buffet in the great room.

Astrid had been invited to join them, and she, Lucy, O, and Elinor wearing a blonde wig were already seated, eating. "Blomma, Sandra, Astrid—there's one piece of chicken left. If you don't want it, I'll take it," O said, noticing that Lucy was already into dessert.

"This is about Maddie, isn't it?" Aleksandra said, her eyes intent upon the screen.

"Shush, everyone," Lucy instructed as she increased the volume.

The appeal to the public for information regarding the disappearance of Maddie Birch was, not unexpectedly, an emotional one. Maddie's father was a slight man, well-groomed and with a receding hairline. He wore a custom tailored suit and appeared pale and tense. His appeal was well delivered, though he paused several times to compose himself before continuing. It was clear that Maddie's mother was overwrought. She was accompanied by a police officer as she left the area on the point of collapse. Mr. Birch continued without her, accompanied by Detective Inspector Brennan and another police spokesperson.

"Perhaps we should contact the police so I can tell them what I know," Aleksandra suggested when the appeal came to an end.

"No," O replied decisively. "I don't know anything about the policeman who's in charge, this Detective Inspector Brennan. If he goes about it the wrong way, he could ultimately capture those responsible, but your safety could be severely compromised. At this stage, it's merely that a University of Toronto student is missing. There is no reason to assume this is connected to you; nothing you've told me indicates that."

"I know something about Detective Inspector Brennan," Astrid interjected. "He's the one who Juji dealt with when my husband, Matthew, was murdered."

"And I think he's the one who investigated the body we found at the house Matthew was building," Lucy added. "I would have thought him retired by now."

"Juji and I went to see him when I arrived in Toronto some weeks ago. I had a matter to discuss with him, and I found him to be very open and empathetic. A reasonable person and very respectful," concluded Astrid.

"What do you think, O?" Lucy asked.

"I'll give it some thought and get back to you. Please, no one do anything about this until I get back to you with a decision. We've all got to be on the same page," O replied, looking straight at Aleksandra.

O had been unable to connect directly with the detective inspector. Unwilling to speak with a subordinate, he identified himself as an associate of Dr. Astrid Carlsson, Juji Abebe, and the Gillespies and requested that a message to that effect be passed along to Brennan. His call was returned within the hour.

CHAPTER 24
NATHAN'S CONTRACT HAS AN IMPACT

France . . .

Days had passed, but there was nothing to report to Nathan, nothing that would satisfy him. Contrary to information provided by him, Yoichi Song was not in Toronto. However, it appeared that both Lucy and Kent Gillespie were there, or in the area. The individual contracted for the job, Roberto, decided that his first target would be local: Serge Proulx, the old man living near Ranelagh Gardens in Paris.

The surveillance of Serge Proulx revealed little about the man that was of any use. He had small dogs that he took for walks, and there were a few shops he patronized, but there was little else that he seemed to do. Surprisingly, he had a heightened sense of the things around him; most people didn't.

Roberto was irritated that Serge possessed such an awareness. It was difficult to devise a method which would be declared accidental rather than intentional, so intentional it would be.

He watched as Serge and his two small spaniels exited the imposing residence near Ranelagh. A robust man, Roberto followed at a distance and kept to the opposite side of the broad boulevard. At some opportune time, he planned to move quickly to take position behind Serge and inflict a mortal knife wound, so quickly as not to alarm even the dogs. Done right, it would appear that Serge, being elderly, had collapsed due to natural causes. Done right, the blood revealing the wound would not become apparent immediately, as it would be absorbed by the clothing Serge wore. That was the plan. And it was a good one.

Serge was walking with his dogs, travelling west on Avenue Mozart. Roberto was familiar with this route and waited for him to fall into position. The streets in this area intersected at various angles and were a combination of one-way and two-way traffic flow. There was so much to look out for, he expected that Serge would be somewhat distracted and unable to segregate the new threat posed by Roberto's presence from the distinctly mundane threat posed by vehicular traffic. That was the plan.

Roberto carried a blade in his right hand, hidden from view within his right pocket. The pocket of his outer coat held merely a slit—much like that of the arm hole of a cape—through which his hand, holding the blade, was secreted within his deeper pant pocket. This arrangement provided concealment of his weapon while guaranteeing him easy access to it.

He saw Serge with the dogs. Serge's attention was focused on the traffic. Roberto planned to cross the boulevard while Serge was yet distracted. Then he planned to withdraw his blade quickly, plunge it upward into his target, and finish him off by giving it a twist. One of several significant arteries would be severed, and the old man would die, succumbing rapidly due to the excessive loss of blood. As his target crumpled to the pavement, Roberto could position him to hide the blood. He decided to donate his outer coat to the cause in order to cover the old man, guaranteeing that no one could stop the flow of blood from a wound they would not realize existed. Roberto planned to call out for assistance as if the old man had taken a sudden stroke or heart attack, then he would disappear amid the onlookers left waiting for an ambulance that would fail to arrive on time. It was a good plan.

But the plan fell apart as soon as Roberto stepped from the curb. He didn't see the vehicle that hit him. It was a one-way street, and the vehicle shouldn't have been there, but there it was. The front end of the vehicle struck him, knocking him against an A-frame sign positioned on the sidewalk in front of a bistro. The sign advertised the daily special: oysters on the half shell, steak tartare, and Grand Marnier soufflé. Onlookers thought the hapless victim was fortunate. Although the whole matter was quite shocking, they expected the victim to be able to pick himself up—though it was always possible he had broken something. But the accident victim didn't move.

His hand was still on his blade, deep in the pocket of his trousers. It was a sharp blade being firmly held very near the crease at his groin. During the process of being thrown against the sign, the tip of the blade had severed Roberto's femoral artery when he landed, and the bleed had produced a torrent of blood. Much of the blood was obscured by his apparel, and onlookers were unaware of the blood gushing forth from his body at a tremendous rate. There was no time to call for an ambulance, let alone for one to arrive on time. No, there wasn't time. Exsanguination occurred rapidly, and the formerly robust man was soon dead by his own hand. This had not been part of Roberto's plan.

"I saw an accident today," Serge announced when he returned home with Merlot and Bijou. "I don't know how badly the victim was injured. I suspect he didn't look both ways before attempting to cross the street. I always tell people that you've got to look both ways, even on a one-way street like Mozart. If someone is already driving the wrong direction, I doubt that they are otherwise a very attentive driver and would avoid hitting you. It's a bad habit some people have developed. They go the wrong way for some metres just to catch another street in order to shorten their trip, rather than taking the time to drive around the block.

Word of the Serge-related incident eventually filtered back to the bosses. They regretted losing the robust Roberto. Fresh eyes were called upon to evaluate the surveillance, and a new plan was implemented.

CHAPTER 25
NATHAN GETS JUSTICE

"Any news?" Nathan asked when Tommaso returned after meeting with his visitor.

"Yes, quite a bit. It'll be over very soon."

"Everyone?"

"Yes, the entire contract will be complete."

Nathan was thrilled. So easy—just pay and play. And, given the state of his finances, he might consider employing Tommaso's help in the future as well. "I've got a few ideas we should discuss before our time as roommates here is up, Tom. We'll talk later, when we're not likely to be disturbed." Nathan's time during incarceration was providing the means by which he could achieve greatness upon his release. He relished the thought. A short nap before dinner . . . Nathan nodded off contentedly, musing how he might make further use of Tommaso.

Shortly after the evening meal was concluded, the prisoners returned to their assigned sections, where socializing could continue for a time. Whenever an opportunity presented itself,

Tommaso preferred not to socialize with Nathan. The man had no morals, or so it seemed to him. Eventually, it was time to return to their own cells, and Tommaso had no other choice but to endure Nathan's incessant yammering.

"You said *soon*, yet I've heard nothing substantial about the fulfilment of the contract, Tom."

"I was expecting to hear today, but I did not get my visitor," Tommaso answered.

Nathan began his yoga poses, employing the variations he had devised to make them easier. He stayed seated for a downward-facing dog pose and disregarded Tommaso's reminders concerning the importance of proper form.

Tommaso rose from his bed, where he had been reading, and began his own stretching exercises, loosening his rather substantial arm muscles. Tommaso enjoyed working on his upper body. His legs were scrawny and his glutes pretty much non-existent, but he possessed admirable development in his shoulders and arms. He wasn't what some people might refer to as muscle-bound. Indeed, when required, Tommaso could look good in a suit, but there would be no opportunity for him to display such a look, not for a very long time.

Nathan closed his eyes and relaxed into a camel pose, with his head dropped backward, again demonstrating improper form.

Suddenly, Tommaso raised his formidable right arm and delivered a quick and devastatingly powerful blow, targeted successfully just a couple of centimetres below Nathan's Adam's apple. The clout destroyed the cricoid cartilage of his larynx. Nathan was beyond hoarse; his vocalizations were desperate but feeble.

"You really shouldn't call me *Tom*," Tommaso hissed.

Nathan was startled and confused, and very soon he became thoroughly terrified. The damage to his larynx was severe and quickly produced significant internal swelling. Rather than making its way into his lungs, air was now escaping into Nathan's neck and chest. His breathing rapidly became compromised, and he began to suffocate. Gasping for breath, a desperate Nathan looked beseechingly into Tommaso's eyes, but they weren't welcoming. Nathan had never felt so alone, so vulnerable, so close to death. He didn't like the feeling. He began to choke as he aspirated his saliva and was further horrified to see frothy blood bubbling from his mouth. It all happened so quickly. There was little time for much thrashing about in an attempt to get air, but that was how Nathan chose to spend the last moments of his life. There was no contemplation by him of the damage he had caused others throughout his life, merely panic that he had no future. None.

Tommaso lifted Nathan's limp body onto his bed and covered it with a blanket, concealing any evidence of the trauma. He used Nathan's pillow to wipe up the wet spot he'd left on the floor and pressed the pillow against his face, just to be certain he was dead. Then he tucked himself into bed and fell into a deep and peaceful sleep.

Tommaso was delighted. The contract was now fulfilled. The funding received was secure. Nathan was dead, and there was no contractual requirement to proceed against his proposed victims. He had failed to pay the bonus one hundred thousand, which would have secured their deaths in the event of Nathan's own demise. The pretty boy from Canada had been Tommaso's easiest and most lucrative source of funding in many years. He trusted that his bosses would forward his share to him. He never trusted Nathan—not someone who would put a contract out on a former partner as Nathan had done with Chloé Corbin. *That was despicable.*

In the morning, during the general rush to get ready for breakfast and work detail, none of the guards noticed Nathan's absence—until it was already far too late. In the confusion, they lost track of Tommaso, nicknamed Tommaso Tocco by the Italians and Tommy Touch by American and British authorities. He had the benefit of excellent attorneys and a worldwide support network. The money obtained in the contract with Nathan had funded Tommaso's escape, as well as having added to his retirement fund. The authorities would be more concerned with the involvement of Sophie Dubois than the death of Nathan Bellamy. They would follow the money.

CHAPTER 26
BRENNAN VISITS THE GILLESPIES

Southern Ontario . . .

It was mid-morning, and the weather was yet unsettled when DI Brennan arrived at the Gillespie residence to meet with O, Aleksandra, Lucy, and Kent. Elinor met him at the door and ushered him through the anteroom. He paused just for a moment at the spot where Astrid's husband, Matthew, had died. Following Elinor, he continued through to the foyer, turning left into the short hallway and ultimately arriving at the door at the end of the hallway, just beyond the cloakroom. Kent met them at the door and welcomed Brennan into his office.

There was seating for the five of them congregated about a low table. A comfortable chair sat vacant, and Brennan was urged to take a seat, placing him in an appropriate position for a conversation with everyone who was present. Kent introduced Brennan to Aleksandra and O, who had requested that at this juncture there should be no mention of Grisha.

"Just so I have this straight—your name is O, and you are this young woman's bodyguard."

"Yes."

He next addressed Aleksandra saying, "And you are Aleksandra Orlov, a student at the U of T. And you were also the girlfriend of another university student who went by the name Smith. As well, you are the friend of a fellow student, Maddie Birch, who is the former girlfriend of Smith, and who is now missing. Have I got all that correct?"

They confirmed that his understanding was accurate and began to offer additional details, but Brennan interrupted.

"Now, just hold on here a minute. It'll be in the news today anyway—I'm sorry to have to tell you this—your boyfriend, Smith . . . his body has been found."

Aleksandra was rendered speechless. She had considered herself in danger, and yet the danger had been to Smith and now to Maddie, and Smith was dead.

"How?" she asked, her body suddenly shaking uncontrollably. Lucy moved to crouch down beside her, and she put her arms around Aleksandra's shoulders to comfort her.

"The coroner determined that death was due to natural causes, cardiac arrest. However, given the details surrounding his death, it is being treated as suspicious. I'm sorry, but I can't share anything more with you at this time. But I do have a few questions for you, Aleksandra. Have you ever heard mention of Ashbridges Bay?"

Aleksandra shook her head, and while Brennan had several other questions, her answers remained the same. She merely shook her head. With that out of the way, they returned to providing Brennan with further details. He learned about Smith's business venture and financial desperation, and the reason why Aleksandra was his *former* girlfriend.

"I'm still a bit confused about why you, Aleksandra, found it necessary to call upon a bodyguard just because your boyfriend posted your photo on this website. I mean, it most definitely was inappropriate for him to have done that, but your reaction seems a bit over-the-top to me."

There seemed to be no choice in the matter. Aleksandra looked at O, her eyes imploring him to explain further. He would know what more could and should be shared, and what needn't be mentioned.

"This is all in strictest confidence, Detective Inspector. We wouldn't normally share such information, but Aleksandra is concerned about Maddie, so we are breaking from the usual this time," O said as a prelude to the explanation he was about to provide.

"I am in the employ of Aleksandra's grandfather. I was assigned to protect her after her grandfather learned of Smith's inappropriate posting to the website. This was considered a serious threat to Aleksandra's safety because of the identity of her grandfather. He is Grigori Orlov. If you are unfamiliar with that name, let me explain by saying that he is one of the wealthiest men on the planet and the owner of the *Croesus*, a personal yacht valued at a billion dollars. Mr. Orlov's youngest son, that's Aleksandra's father, Alexei, was recently killed in what police in France have deemed a vehicular accident, but which our own investigation has revealed to have been an intentional action by unknown actors in which he was forced off the road as he tried to escape at high speed."

Brennan had not taken his eyes from O since he had begun to unravel the tale. When O finished Brennan was silent then he closed his eyes, pursed his lips, and hung his head. "Well, you folks do come up with the most creative problems. First, the Espie murder, then Corbin, and now this. But this time we're trying to keep someone alive as well as catch the culprits responsible for her abduction." He breathed deeply, then continued. "There are a few things I think we can agree need to be done here. We need Maddie recovered alive and those responsible for her abduction, apprehended. I'm going out on a limb here and assume that these are the same people involved in Smith's death. And, if this isn't resolved, we might be looking at continuing threats to Aleksandra here and likely to an even greater number of those close to her, right?"

O nodded.

"All right, leave it with me. I'll contact you when I've got something in mind. Keep me posted if anything comes up, or changes, or if you have an idea to share. You're quite certain that Aleksandra is the focus of all this?"

Again, O nodded.

The visit to the Gillespies' had taken Brennan's mind off his retirement and financial concerns. He found it an intriguing puzzle, and one he wanted to solve before he retired. The report he now planned to file would not provide all the details he had learned from O. His team would continue their tracking of the evidence as it was discovered, but he would focus on this new angle.

Perhaps work done to solve Smith's demise might lead to solving Maddie's disappearance and prevent her murder. It wouldn't be a bad way to bring an end to a long career—preventing a murder instead of solving one. Already he had ideas to consider. He hoped that the situation would remain somewhat static so he might implement a plan—as soon as he could come up with one.

CHAPTER 27
LUCY'S ARTISTRY

Lucy needed some time to herself; her home was in turmoil. Immediately after breakfast, she retreated to her studio to continue working on the painting for Grisha. It was to be a gift for Agafya on their wedding anniversary. Actually, there were three paintings; the project was a triptych.

She had focused her efforts on the central and largest piece, whose theme was today. It would express the current life of the Orlovs: Grisha, Agafya, and their immediate family. A smaller painting, depicting their ancestry, would hang to the left and a second smaller painting, to the right. This second smaller painting would depict the future, and the concept perplexed Lucy. Nevertheless, she loved the challenge it presented.

The first of the two smaller paintings had gone smoothly. Grisha had provided photos and a written account of his and Agafya's ancestry, which she used as inspiration. Being the past, she'd selected tones and shades of the selected hues: green, blue, red, and orange. She had used an array of colourful minerals, including many gemstones in her creation of the pigments. There was little metallic gold in this first painting. The muted hues signified health, loyalty, strength, and love. Her use of shades produced a rather dull product, one whose elements were identifiable but becoming increasingly masked.

The other smaller painting—the one to depict the future of the family—would feature tones as in the first painting, but instead of shades she planned to make use of tints of violet, orange, and red to signify mystery, optimism, action, and energy. These were all necessary attributes for the future of the family. In this third painting, Lucy planned to use more metallic gold than the first, but less than the second painting. With tints rather than shades, this painting would be delicate and its elements somewhat concealed. No one knew what the future would bring . . .

The largest of the grouping was her current concern. This was the most significant of the three, both in size and subject matter. It would reflect the current family, its achievements, and values.

When the three were hung side-by-side, the central panel would dominate, but not merely by size. Lucy had employed an effect similar to that of a soft-focus lens. The further from the centre of the composition, the greater the blurring. Borrowing from Kent, she used the idea of fractals to great advantage in the composition. At a distance, the triptych gave an overall impression of being an homage to the Orlov family, which indeed it was. However, as one got nearer to the painting, the detail was increasingly revealed and the elements of the composition were found to consist of even greater detail, and so on. In that way, the composition created intrigue and necessitated that the viewer continue to approach the canvas. And metallic gold was used to great advantage in this, the largest of the panels. She had been informed where on the *Croesus* her painting would hang, and she kept that in mind as well as she planned the triptych. It gave her information regarding proportion.

Lucy had already worked on the canvas for several months, but the end always seemed just out of reach. She considered it fortunate that Yoichi was otherwise occupied, else the gallery owner would have hounded her for an additional lot of paintings to be sold through her gallery in Toronto. But now, even without pressure from Yoichi, Lucy no longer had the time she had expected to have available for the completion of the project. The situation with Aleksandra had seen to that.

Having worked for most of the day, Lucy brought the session to an end and made herself a double espresso to celebrate, a party for one. She took her cup and went to sit in her favourite chair to relax and let the day wind down. A knock at the studio door interrupted her tranquility. It wasn't any of the usual participants in her life; they knew not to disturb her while there was yet sunlight.

"Enter," Lucy called out, choosing to remain seated.

Gradually the door opened, revealing Aleksandra. "I apologize for disturbing you, Lucy."

"It's all right—this time—I'm done for the day and was just taking a break before getting ready for the workout with O. What's up? If you want a coffee, go and make one for yourself. The coffee maker, cups, and pods are on the counter near the sink."

"No, thanks. Caffeine will keep me awake, and I'm sufficiently wired as it is," Aleksandra explained.

The large canvas at the far end of the room caught Aleksandra's attention, and she stood before it, transfixed. At that distance, the image appeared as a portrait of Grisha and Agafya, her grandparents. As Aleksandra approached the canvas, Lucy knew she could now make out the depictions of her uncles, Maxim, Ilya, and her late father, Alexei—all three of them found within the faces of their parents. If she got closer, she would discover much more detail hidden within the brushstrokes.

"I'm really not happy with people seeing my work before it's complete," Lucy said, annoyed by the intrusion yet trying to be understanding about the situation. "I find it quite stressful actually. Since you're not going to have a coffee, why don't I just lock up here, and we can get ready to join O in the gym, okay?"

Aleksandra was insistent. "I really need to talk to you, Lucy."

Lucy stifled a sigh. She knew she wasn't at her best today and should make a greater effort to be sociable. "Okay, come and sit. What's going on?"

"What is it that allows, or perhaps I should say *causes* you to continue living your life, Lucy?"

Lucy wasn't at all certain what Aleksandra meant. "I don't understand. Can you ask that another way perhaps?"

"I'm getting depressed. I've lost my boyfriend. I know he was an idiot, but still . . ."

When Lucy said nothing, Aleksandra filled the void. "I can't attend my classes or see my friends. Granted, that too is largely because of my boyfriend . . ."

Again, Lucy said nothing.

Aleksandra sniffled and tried to explain. "This situation just seems to continue into infinity. I have no sense of whether we're closer to resolving it, or not. I can't get a sense of it from anything O or *Dedushka* tell me. We talk every day, *Dedushka* and I; surely he would have mentioned something! What have you heard? Anything at all?"

"Before we met with Brennan, I'd only heard that they had not been able to locate your friend, Smith, that he seemed to have disappeared. He hadn't been at school, and he hadn't been seen by his friends or family since about the time you came to stay with us. We now know why, I guess."

"Yes, I'd talked to Maddie, and she told me that Smith was missing. That troubled me, but there was nothing I could do." Aleksandra paused, took a breath, threw back her shoulders, and assumed a stern facial expression. "Please don't call him my *friend*," she snipped.

"How should we refer to Smith then?"

Aleksandra appeared confused. "I don't know. It's just that a true friend wouldn't have treated me like that."

"Does that really matter at this point, Blomma?" Lucy waited for a response, and when none was forthcoming, she asked, "Did you tell Grisha or O about Smith having gone missing?"

"No."

"Why not?"

"Because I didn't want them to know that I had called Maddie."

"That's what I thought. Who exactly is Maddie? Tell me more about her."

"She's in one of my classes. She's the psych major I mentioned when I told everyone about Smith marketing his Psyche Shirts. You already know that she was Smith's girlfriend for a while, before he met me. Now, she's just one of the group I used to hang around with, though I think she wanted to get back together with him."

"I'm disappointed and frustrated with you right now, Blomma. I might even be angry. There are many people who have put their lives on hold in an effort to protect you from harm. They might have placed their lives in jeopardy, not merely on hold. We don't know yet. You were told to refrain from contacting anyone. When did you call?"

"The day that Lukas first called me Blomma."

"I think O might have found that information useful. I don't know if you found out Smith was missing before O did or not, but in the future, you must tell him everything. You owe that to him."

Aleksandra began to protest, but Lucy would have none of it. "Yes, it is his job to protect you, but you needn't make it more difficult for him to do that—and perhaps even more dangerous for all of us," she said, admonishing Aleksandra.

"Wouldn't it just make things easier for everyone if I . . . ?" she sniffled. "Lucy, have you ever been drawn to do something dangerous, and then regretted that you survived?" Aleksandra shuffled about, staring at her feet.

"My father used to say that," she explained. "That, and similar things. I never felt an understanding of him. Now I think I'm starting to."

"So what makes you keep going when things seem so bad?"

"Curiosity, I guess," Lucy answered. "I want to see what's served tomorrow, what's on the agenda, around the corner, on the next page, in the next episode—"

"Not love?"

"No. That's not what propels me through life, not consciously. Love provides a sweet complexity to life, but not everyone finds someone special, someone . . ."

"Their soulmate?" offered Aleksandra.

"I guess that's the term, though I do dislike it; it's so very *cliché*. Many people live full and happy lives without ever having found someone with whom they want to have such a close relationship. I'm quite certain that there's tremendous variety among all the relationships you see. It's very personal and just between those people as regarding how they define or construct or live their lives. And the timing varies among people as well. So, if you think you should have found someone by now, you should probably shake that thought right out of your head. Just live your life as best as you can, and be curious about what lies ahead. You've got today; use it well.

"If you are depressed and wish to talk with a psychologist, I can arrange that for you. I'm not trained in such things, and my good intentions can only go so far in helping, I'm afraid. So, we can talk in general, but if you need a counsellor, then that's what I'll arrange for you, okay?"

Aleksandra nodded.

"You've met Leo, Juji's husband. Well, he's got the appropriate credentials, I think. You could ask him yourself, or I could approach him on your behalf. Just let me know, okay?"

CHAPTER 28

ALEKSANDRA MAKES CONTACT

Lucy had phoned DI Brennan and left a message, requesting that he return her call. He hoped it was good news. His plan was coming together, but if it could be made simpler by Lucy's news, it would be a good day.

"Detective Inspector Brennan here, Mrs. Gillespie. What have you got for me?"

"I'm afraid I may have a further complication for you, Detective Inspector."

Brennan's optimism tanked. "What's the complication?"

"It's a separate matter, but the complication is that the two will be hitting us at the same time." Only identifying Juliette by her first name, Lucy conveyed the seriousness of the situation to Brennan without breaching Juliette's privacy.

"Is O available? I'd like to speak with him," he asked.

"Shall I have him phone you, or do you want to phone him?" Lucy asked.

"I just thought he might be handy to you. I've got his number; I'll give him a call now."

"I don't know this Juliette," O explained. "From what I was told, she was using a residence in Paris as a safe house but had to vacate when her security was compromised. As a result, she is returning to Toronto, but she has no secure location here either, so she'll be dependent upon the Gillespies and their friends for shelter until her situation is resolved."

"Yeah, that's what I understand as well," Brennan said. "Hopefully it won't be something we'll need to deal with in addition to the Birch kidnapping.

"About that . . . Listen, I've got a plan, but I don't think you're going to like a lot of it. In the end, it'll get both of us what we want: Maddie, alive, and the kidnappers, apprehended." He outlined the plan to O. It was a good plan; he hoped.

"Hi, Emmy, Sandra here. How are you?"

"Omigod, Sandra! How are you? Did you hear about Maddie? Oh, and I'm sorry about Smith. I know you guys had broken up, but still . . ."

They spoke for a short time, then Aleksandra brought the call to an end.

Subsequently, she made additional calls, connecting with all her friends from university as well as some of her professors. All the calls followed a similar pattern.

There was one final call to be made. As expected, no one answered, so she left a message. "Hi, Maddie, Sandra here. I haven't heard from you in ages. I've been away, and would you believe, there was no cell service! It was horrible. Now that I'm back, I was wondering if we could get together sometime soon. Give me a call, okay?"

J. A. Gibbens

Upon concluding her final call, Aleksandra took a deep breath and then accepted a glass of Massandra offered to her by O. She found the sweet wine, served on ice, a welcome distraction from the serious nature of the calls she had just made.

"You did well. Now we wait to see if the fish nibble. I'll let Brennan know that you've completed your part of his plan."

CHAPTER 29
L'ORTÉ ISLAND

Lucy had discussed Aleksandra's apparent depressive mood with Kent and O, and it was decided that a few select individuals would accompany Aleksandra to L'Orté Island and remain there with her for some indeterminate period. The healing power of nature would be put to good advantage. Aleksandra seemed quite keen on the idea, but Lucy wondered what her expectations of the island might be. This was no Caribbean hideaway.

Tear-drop shaped L'Orté Island was located in Lake Erie, at the approximate midpoint between Port L'Orté—formerly called Port Myer—situated on the lake's northern shore, and L'Orté Point, a property purchased by Lucy's grandfather a century ago and eventually inherited by Lucy. She had donated the Point to the Province of Ontario nearly ten years earlier. In time, the Province would become beneficiary of the island as well. For now, the private island featured the ruins of the old manor house as well as a new eco-residence complex designed by Kent. It was used as the Gillespies' summer house and often welcomed select groups of naturalists and artists. The island was accessible by boat, but on this occasion, their little party would travel by helicopter.

The Sikorsky S-92 was a frequent rental by the Gillespies, who were by now well-known to both the air and ground crews. Initially, Lucy had wondered if Aleksandra might be uncomfortable in the helicopter, as some of her own friends had been when they first began to visit the island. She needn't have been concerned.

Aleksandra was familiar with helicopter travel and able to relax, even in the older aircraft. The *Croesus*, her grandfather's massive yacht, carried two helicopters—in addition to a submarine—as tenders. It was easy to forget that Aleksandra hadn't lived an ordinary life. Her *naiveté* in certain matters was astounding, yet she was well-versed in other matters—matters in which her university mates would have been completely out of their depth.

The flight path of the Sikorsky, as usual, would sweep over L'Orté Point before approaching the island.

"You can see that there are no roads established on the property. It was logged by a previous owner, whose name was Szabo and who, coincidentally, was my father's adoptive father's father. Got all that?" She smiled at Aleksandra, knowing that the statement was confusing, though accurate.

"Huh? Please explain that again, Lucy."

"Well, my grandfather, Giovanni Sarto, purchased the property from a man by the name of Peter Szabo. Gianni developed a fishing and hunting lodge on L'Orté Point and lived for a time in the manor house he had built on the island. There was a fire at the lodge and Gianni was killed. There's a lot more to tell, but ultimately, my grandmother died giving birth to my father and he was subsequently adopted and raised by Jozsef Szabo—that's Peter's son—and his wife."

"Oh, I understand . . . I think . . ."

"If you look carefully, you can see the remnants of the lodge. At one time, this area was heavily forested, which is why

Peter Szabo had acquired it and logged it extensively. There are still a few stands of black maple and black walnut, but most of the trees are now cottonwood. Those would be the trees that appear silvery, with heart-shaped leaves. In time, the area may again give way to maple and walnut but not yet. It takes time . . . lots of time. Helen knows all about the plants in this region, so if you've got any questions, you now know who to ask."

Helen smiled from across the cabin and gave a little finger wave to Aleksandra.

"There's no sand beach on the island, and the west-facing shore is rocky, while the east-facing one is quite reedy. Lake Erie is shallow, so it tends to be quite warm as compared with the other Great Lakes, but it's still early in the season, so it's likely too cold for me—certainly without a wetsuit. I'll let you decide for yourself. We haven't yet launched the floating dock off the east shore for swimming and sunbathing; however, I think you'll find plenty to do."

The pilot flew over the entire island before setting down in the meadow located just south of the central portion of the island. As the helicopter looped over the property, Lucy pointed out the location of the summer house, the docks, and the manor house, all hidden amid the trees and shrubbery.

"You forgot to mention the glass-bottomed boat, Lucy," Helen said.

"Ah, yes, you're right. There's a small glass-bottomed boat with a tiny outboard motor you can use if you want to watch the fish when you're on the water. Helen will instruct you on its use. I haven't used it much, but it is fun, especially in the weedier areas, where the fish shelter to hide from one another.

Aleksandra appeared eager to begin her adventure; Lucy was pleased. The three women exited the helicopter and loaded their supplies onto the trailer of the ATV stored in a nearby shed. The helicopter departed and the little group made their way across the meadow to the summer house.

While Helen busied herself with opening the residence and its facilities, checking the power source and water, and storing the supplies, Lucy and Aleksandra inspected the area in general—Lucy out of concern for the condition of her property and Aleksandra out of curiosity about the place. Would it have something that might inspire her?

Nothing appeared amiss. Lucy installed Aleksandra in one of the bedrooms and showed her the various common areas available to her. Then she spent time arranging art supplies in her summer studio.

Lucy's bedroom was directly beside her summer studio. Here there was less chance of anyone walking into the studio to disturb her. They couldn't enter the studio without first traversing her bedroom. She hoped she could make some progress on the third and final panel of the triptych she was painting for Grisha.

"By the way, each person on the island wears a GPS tag so we can find you more easily in case there's a problem. That information made O quite happy, as well you can imagine," Lucy announced.

"This is an aerial view of the entire island," Lucy explained, drawing Aleksandra's attention to a large photograph mounted on a wall near the main entrance. "It's rather like one of those 'You Are Here' signs."

"Oh, this is great, Lucy. It even indicates the different terrain."

"Yes, Helen thought it would be helpful to guests if we provided that information, so she maintains the accuracy of it, updating whenever something new and significant is found. We could probably do it far more efficiently by hiring a team to assess the property, but this is more fun, don't you think? As the saying goes, 'Life is a journey, not a destination,' or something to that effect."

"Lucy, I've got an idea," Aleksandra declared. "I've been thinking about it ever since the detective inspector had me make those telephone calls. If these people want money, then perhaps they should just be given the money. I mean, if it'll save Maddie, why not? Right now, they probably think that the only way they can get the money is to kidnap me, so they're just using Maddie to get to me. That's inefficient, and it's put Maddie in danger. I don't think they've thought it through very well. Smith's death might very well have been an accident on their part. I'm not excusing or forgiving them, just saying."

"What are you proposing?" queried Lucy.

"I think I should return to your estate, and we should attempt to contact them—or *Dedushka* should—and get them to state the amount they want. But, instead of paying for me, *Dedushka* would be paying for Maddie. It also takes Elinor out of danger as well, doesn't it?

"I mean, right now, we're just waiting for someone to attempt to kidnap Elinor, thinking that she's actually me, and I think that's pretty dumb. All the focus is on catching them, not rescuing Maddie. And, if they do succeed with Elinor, then we'll need to rescue both her and Maddie. I know Elinor said that she'd just whip-off the wig, and *voilà* Sandra is gone, but perhaps she won't be given such an opportunity. Maybe they'll get a bag over her head before she can. Maybe they'll take her and then get so pissed off that they hurt her. Lucy, I couldn't bear the guilt for something like that—"

"Okay, okay; I hear you, I do. I'll talk to O and whoever else is making these decisions, and I'll explain your idea and relay your concerns. I understand what you've said, except I don't think you need to leave here in order to do it. I think Elinor is a good failsafe to your security. If we remove her, it's possible they'll continue their search for you, and that might lead them here. But, I think you do make some good points, so leave it with me. And just as O would remind you: don't do anything on your own—nothing."

CHAPTER 30
AU REVOIR

France . . .

Tommaso's cousin, Carlo, kept an eye on the Ranelagh apartment. Surveillance photographs had revealed the presence of Juliette Garner, someone the bosses were very keen to destroy. The interest in Juliette Garner came from on high, and though Carlo wasn't certain about the details, he understood the action he was about to take. Further, he had been told that while the others were no longer targets, they were of no consequence and could readily be removed as mere collateral damage. Juliette was now the focus.

There was action at the front of the building, and Carlo observed the old man with his dogs, a younger man who was bald, and two women with straight, long, black hair exit the building. He thought the women might be Asian. Carlo wasn't certain if the group represented a single party or if they were separate. Recently, there had been much activity involving moving companies—Martin and Mansfield appeared to be a favourite—and he had concluded that there were new residents, so other than Serge, the other three might be such new residents. Perhaps. He continued to watch as the men went in opposite directions, and the women remained together. In short order, the women were met by a vehicle—possibly an Uber—that whisked them away.

Carlo didn't see Juliette Garner, his target. He approached the building and entered the security code. The key code was changed periodically, but a good pair of binoculars had helped reveal the current one. He quickly made his way up the stairs to the uppermost landing. He paused to determine whether it would be best to enter through the main door or to exit through the window onto the terrace and, from there, enter the apartment. He decided to use the terrace. He crept to the first set of French doors and peered through the glazing, into the large living room. It was devoid of furnishings. Confused, Carlo continued along the terrace until he arrived at the next room, likely the old man's main suite. Carlo shaded his eyes to get a better look inside, but all he could do was confirm that this room was empty as well. He continued to creep along the broad terrace to the next room and was not at all surprised to confirm that it too was empty, but for an old landline phone.

Carefully and with a need to collect complete information yet leave no clue to his identity, Carlo removed a pane of glass from the door and unlatched it from the inside. Upon entering, he was struck by the emptiness of the residence. It echoed, seemingly shouting to him: *They've gone! They've eluded you!* Carlo was made uneasy by this. All he could do was inform the bosses—and hope that they wouldn't conclude it was his fault for waiting too long. It wasn't good to make the bosses unhappy.

Serge, Merlot and Bijou, Juliette, Yoichi, and Donald caught up with one another at the air terminal used by the rental company Yoichi had found through Martin and Mansfield. Serge's collection was already carefully stowed away. Aircraft personnel showed him how things were set up to keep the dogs safe. He was pleased that they would be in the cabin with him, rather than treated like luggage and left in the hold. Serge seemed more concerned about them than about his impressive array of collectibles. Juliette was eager to remove her wig but decided to wear it unless and until immigration officials required that it be removed. Yoichi and Donald just wanted to get home.

Juliette was the first to phone Lucy. "Hi, Lucy, Juliette here. I won't take long. I just wanted to let you know that all is well. There were no snags. I'm coming home with Yoichi and Donald, and Serge and his pups. We've got a private flight and expect to be in Toronto in the morning."

"Okay, sounds good. Let me discuss things with Yoichi and Donald, and then let's talk again, okay?" After concluding her call with Juliette, Lucy phoned Yoichi.

"So, I hear you're heading home."

"Juliette called you, I take it. Yes, and I've got to take care of Serge's collection, so I'll be tied up for several days. Donald showed up and got dumped in the middle of all this intrigue, though I get the impression he relishes it. Donny Gallagher, double-O-seven . . ."

"Can you take care of Serge? He invited himself, and he's brought Merlot and Bijou along as well. It's more than I think I can handle at this point."

Lucy detected stress in Yoichi's voice. "Yes, I'll arrange for someone to pick up Serge and bring him here," Lucy assured her.

"Before I let you go, I have something more to share with you, Yoichi." Lucy provided her with a summary of the situation regarding Aleksandra, and she heard Yoichi groan. She had attempted to stifle it—that was clear—but so was her dismay. "So it's important that you don't mention to anyone at all, anything about any of us: what we're doing, where we are, or were—absolutely nothing. We'll make some adjustments here, and we'll be okay."

CHAPTER 31
A BOAT NAMED *GRACIE*

Southern Ontario . . .

"Would it be okay for me to take out the glass-bottomed boat today? I think I would find it really relaxing, just watching the fish. Perhaps it might inspire me to write some poetry. My productivity lately has been dismal, and what I have written is simply depressing and uninspired," Aleksandra explained.

"Sure, but perhaps you should have someone with you; talk to Helen. Sorry, but I really don't want you out there, exposed and by yourself," Lucy replied, being cautious. If it weren't Helen, then she herself would accompany Aleksandra. Lucy wasn't going to let her be on the water alone, even though that appeared to be her young charge's preference.

Breakfast on L'Orté Island was casual since, by and large, everyone tended to have their own schedule. Aleksandra had insisted upon bringing her samovar with her, but other than that single item and the tea it provided, breakfast was the usual offering of yoghurt, granola, coffee, fruit, and whatever else a guest might have mentioned when indicating their preferences to Helen the previous day, subject to availability.

The chalkboard in the kitchen displayed the lunchtime menu: chicken fajitas. If someone wanted to opt out, they were welcome to prepare their own meal from the kitchen pantry. Lucy was surprised that Helen had continued this practice since there were just the three of them, but then she noticed Aleksandra reading the board.

"I'll find Helen and ask her to show me how to put up the canopy for shade on the boat. And, I'll ask her to please accompany me," Aleksandra added begrudgingly, or so it appeared to Lucy. "I noticed that the light is best just before and just after noon, when it strikes the water at a bit of an angle, so we'll be back for fajitas at high noon and perhaps go out again in the afternoon."

Later in the morning, Lucy watched as Helen accompanied Aleksandra to the dock. She had no sense of the danger in which Aleksandra might be, but Grisha, Maxim, and O considered the threat to her safety significant and ongoing. At the same time, days had passed, yet nothing had changed. There had been no indication—at least none apparent to Lucy—that Aleksandra's life was threatened. However, she respected those who advised that security must be maintained.

The glass-bottomed boat, christened *Gracie* after Lucy's grand-aunt, the previous owner of L'Orté Island, was built with function rather than style in mind. The boat was approximately four metres in length, moulded of fibreglass, and made highly buoyant by its foam core. It was flat at the stern, where a small outboard motor was attached to the transom plate. Supplies were sparse, save for safety items such as life preservers and paddles. The boat was too wide for oars to be used as one might in a row boat. A canopy covered a tubular frame and provided shade from the direct rays of the sun. A short funnel featured in the centre of the boat, and at the bottom of it there was a clear window of polycarbonate plastic. Bench seating was fixed around the funnel, and at the stern for the driver operating the outboard motor.

"Where did you want to go?" Helen asked.

"I'm not really sure; the map is great for the island, but it doesn't indicate much about the surrounding water."

"Did you want to take some fishing gear and throw in a line?" Helen asked.

"No, I think I just want to watch fish. I know that sounds crazy, but I heard that some types are rather stealthy hunters, so I think it could be interesting."

"I think you're referring to the pike; they'll be in the long weeds just up that way," Helen said, pointing toward the water at the north end of the island. "They're aggressive hunters, but then again, their prey aren't the brightest, I guess."

"If you want to do some fishing, that's certainly okay with me," Aleksandra said. "Perhaps your bait will attract even more fish. I dunno; I really haven't done this sort of thing before."

"Okay, it's settled. We'll head just offshore at the north end of the island," Helen said. "There are some tall weeds in the area, and the pike should like to hang out there.

"I'll bring the gear, even though I may not use it. It's frustrating not to have it since that's usually when I'm sure to come across a school of large perch, or a solitary small-mouth bass that's even bigger than the last one that got away on me."

"Yeah, I understand. Better to have it, just in case." Aleksandra waited patiently while Helen obtained the fishing gear and placed it in the boat.

Gracie's small motor was used only if they were going to be staying very close to the island. The motor was far too weak to propel the heavy fibreglass vessel through the waves that might be found farther out from shore. Whenever guests decided to venture further out, they'd been towed by one of the launches, then anchored to float about and watch the fish while the launch continued elsewhere and caught them on its return, bringing them back to the dock.

When they reached their destination, Helen quietly dropped the bow anchor, so as not to disturb the fish. While Aleksandra enjoyed the view through the funnel and watched fish interacting, Helen set about to catch sunfish. They both enjoyed the fresh air, the warm breeze, and the silence, broken only by periodic squeals of delight by Aleksandra at the antics of predatory fish, or the "gotcha's" expressed by Helen whenever she celebrated her own predatory success as she reeled in a sunfish, the fish spinning in the water as if corkscrewing to the surface. Little was said, though much was enjoyed.

The breeze picked up and shifted the angle of the boat. It moved off the weedy area and onto a relatively sandy patch, a glade within the weedy freshwater forest, sheltered by a scattering of rocks likely delivered into position during construction of the original manor house.

"What's that?" Aleksandra suddenly said, startling Helen.

"What's what?"

"The breeze shifted us again. It's just a bit off in that direction," Aleksandra explained, pointing a bit further northward. "It looks like maybe it's a little boat, a rowboat perhaps. Kinda spooky the way it just suddenly shows up through the glass in the funnel."

Helen switched on the underwater lighting and handed Aleksandra a large adjustable float on a long line to which she had secured a large brass sinker. "When we're close again, toss the sinker onto the spot. Then we'll adjust the position of the float so it's at the surface but not too distant from your target. We can return here after lunch. I'll bring gear, and we'll examine close-up what it is you've found. Your choice of bathing suit, wetsuit, or drysuit—we have them all. Personally, I'd go with a wetsuit for you; it'll keep you warmer, yet able to swim comfortably. Sound good?"

"Sure thing!" As they again drifted nearer to the underwater glade, Aleksandra tossed the sinker into the water.

"That does look interesting! You get a much better look at it with the lights on now that these clouds have rolled in. I bet Lucy'll want to come with us as well once you tell her what you've discovered," Helen said.

After Aleksandra adjusted the length of the line to properly position the float, Helen started the motor and withdrew the anchor. They putt-putted back to the dock, eager to share their news—and fish catch—with Lucy.

"Why don't you come out with us this afternoon, Lucy?" Aleksandra asked while enjoying her fajita lunch.

"I think I will. My work has progressed well this morning, but I think it's time for a break. Besides, there are many secrets we're still uncovering here on the island." Lucy went on to explain a bit of the history of L'Orté Island and its significance to her life.

"May I poke around the manor house sometime, Lucy? It sounds so very mysterious. You mentioned something called an awen. I know you sign as Awen on your paintings, but is it also some sort of *thing*?"

"It's a Neo-druid, some say Celtic, symbol with three dots inside a triple circle. From each dot there's a ray extending downward, like this," Lucy explained, sketching the symbol for Aleksandra. "It originated sometime in the eighteenth century and symbolizes mind, body, and spirit, or earth, sea, and sky, or the balance between male and female energy. I remember my father using the word as his mantra for meditation, and he also used the symbol to mark places where he hid important things."

"So if I poke around the manor house, I should look for this symbol?"

"Yes, that's right. But, I don't think it's a good idea to poke around the manor house by yourself. It's well-made, and we think it's stable, but you never know. It's nearly one hundred years old and was occupied for only a very brief period of time before being left to the elements. I don't want to be the one to tell your grandfather that you got hurt. So for my sake if not for your own, I'd rather you didn't go inside the building unaccompanied. But now that I know you're interested, you can accompany me when I go, okay?"

"I'd like that. When can we return to investigate what I saw in the water?"

"Dessert first!" announced Helen. "I made strawberry-rhubarb pie this morning."

After lunch, the three women loaded their gear into *Gracie*, then motored the glass-bottomed boat out to the underwater glade discovered by Aleksandra. This time, Helen dropped the stern anchor as well as the bow anchor in order to prevent the boat from drifting with the wind. Finally, she switched on the underwater lights. Through the funnel, the shape of a small boat was visible, just as Aleksandra had said, though it was largely obscured by sand, mud, and debris. Helen planned to remain in the *Gracie* while Lucy and Aleksandra carried out their investigation.

Aleksandra noticed a modest-size cabin cruiser off in the near-distance. "I've seen that boat before, that one over there," she said, nodding toward the vessel. "It's not always in that particular location, but close by around the island. Should we be worried?"

Lucy withdrew her phone and made a quick call. "Hi. Someone has just noticed you lurking offshore. We're investigating what looks like a small sunken row boat or dinghy. Why don't you come for dinner tonight?"

"That's O, isn't it?" Aleksandra shook her head at the inevitability of O always being close by—whether you could see him or not.

"It is. Yes, O is impressive. You know, he saved my life a few years ago, so I trust his ability to provide you with protection, Blomma.

"You're comfortable using a re-breather face mask, aren't you?"

In response, Aleksandra nodded energetically.

"I presumed you'd done some diving off the *Croesus*. And you've not had any problems, or have you?" Lucy asked.

"No worries, Lucy. Piece o' cake!" Aleksandra answered enthusiastically. "These are much like the ones I've used from the *Croesus*. Does the communication system work on them?"

"It did the last time I used it, but if not, we'll just rely on hand signals. Now, don't touch anything without checking with me first, please. If it is a little boat, we'll need to get a licensed marine archeologist to come out and do a survey.

We'll just take photos so we can show them what we've found." She handed Aleksandra one of the cameras.

Shortly thereafter, Aleksandra and Lucy entered the water to investigate the wreck. As they approached, Aleksandra noticed something embedded in the lakebed, quite apart from the small boat. She pointed it out to Lucy, then took a few photos of the corked glass bottle containing a liquid. Lucy marked the spot with a sinker and float on a line and photographed it yet again. After a brief examination of the boat itself, they returned to the surface with additional photos but no artifacts.

"Something glinted in the sunlight just back there, Lucy," Helen said when they were back aboard. The item in question was a short distance from the little boat, so Lucy returned to the water to examine it. Again, she marked the spot with a brass sinker and float on a short line then took an array of photos.

Eager to learn more about what they had discovered, they briefly examined the photos before returning to the dock.

"There's nothing more we should do, though I admit I'm tempted. Very tempted," Lucy said. "But I remember when we had the survey done prior to constructing the docks. I heard it from officials more than once: 'The *Ontario Heritage Act* forbids anyone altering or removing artifacts or any physical evidence of past human use,' blah, blah, blah . . .

"Let's see if we can get more out of these photos with a larger screen," Lucy suggested.

The three of them congregated in front of the largest video screen available in the summer house. The photos of the bottle found by Aleksandra revealed that it was topped with a cork and contained a liquid, but that had already been quite evident.

There appeared to be no label or marking of any kind on the bottle. The photos of the little boat were even less revealing. Clearly, there was a boat, but it was filled with sand and debris and would require the attention of professionals to convince it to give up its secrets. There appeared to be some yellowish metal objects, perhaps brass fittings. What the other lumps and bumps might be, they could only speculate.

The photos Lucy had taken of the glinting object detected by Helen were particularly intriguing. It appeared to be a medallion on a chain. There was lettering on the medallion, but it was unclear until Lucy enlarged the detail and manipulated the photo with an editing program. They thought they could make out a C, then an O followed by an N, but the next little bit was obscured, though the final letter was clearly an R.

"That was so hard to leave behind!" declared Lucy. "I hope the markers don't move before we can get someone out to do a formal investigation of the site."

Lucy called Kent to share news of the find and to request follow-up. It wouldn't take long—it never did with Kent, the master of making arrangements and getting the people and gear necessary to perform any specialized task.

CHAPTER 32
BIENVENUE AU CANADA

Kent met their plane at Billy Bishop Airport. "Welcome! How was your flight?" he inquired, focusing his attention on Serge, who was looking toward the CN Tower and appeared somewhat curious about it.

"Very good, but always tiring for me. It is good to see you again, my friend. Where is your lovely wife?" Serge responded as the two men shook hands. "And what exactly is that tower?"

"Lucy is away currently, but I'm confident that I can be of some use. We'll make a visit to the CN Tower while you're here since you're interested and I was also thinking the Welland Canal and the power stations at Niagara Falls as well." His comments had been directed at Serge, and he now turned his attention to other members of the party.

"Welcome home, Yoichi." Kent kissed her on the cheek. "I see you've got your work cut out for you with all those crates."

"Fortunately, Martin and Mansfield are quite capable of taking care of most of this, but I do need to check on things. Sorry, Kent, I don't wish to appear rude, but let me tend to this, and I'll get back to you and Lucy as soon as I come up for air, okay?" Then she was off, making her way to the security truck that had arrived from Martin and Mansfield.

For a moment, Kent and Donald just looked at one another, then shook hands. "Donald! Good to see you, chap. We haven't seen much of you these past months. I was wondering what was keeping you so busy."

"It has been hectic and continues to be so. Look, I really want to sit down and have a chat with you, but I think I should see if I can be of any assistance to Yoichi. I think this project has thoroughly exhausted her. As she said, we'll get back to you and Lucy soon, as soon as the dust settles. I really hate to rush off on you . . . ah, just tell Lucy that we have some news to share. And if you've got a suggestion for a very special restaurant for a little gathering, I'd appreciate it. I've been out of touch about such things recently."

"Consider Flirtations," Kent said. "It's top-notch."

"Knew I could count on you, Kent. Thanks." With a smile and a wave, Donald turned to follow Yoichi.

"Lucy mentioned that you have dogs, Serge. Where are they?"

"The veterinarian wanted to see them. A spot check, I presume. Everything is in order; they each have their EU Pet Passport. Ah, here they come now," Serge explained, just as an airport official came forward with the two Cavalier King Charles Spaniels and documentation to be returned to Serge.

"And Juliette, welcome home! I wish it were under different circumstances," Kent said as they shook hands. He reached for her suitcase.

"No, thanks; I'll take that," she said as she regained control of her sole piece of luggage. "Everything I value is in there. It's become my security blanket."

Kent didn't press the matter. "Well, Donald and Yoichi are on their own, so why don't we load your things into the vehicle and get you out of here," he said as he began to walk to his

Escalade. "Juliette, Serge, this is Albin. Albin, perhaps you remember Juliette, but you haven't met Serge, and . . ."

"Ah," Serge explained, "Merlot is the Blenheim, and Bijou, the tri-colour." Kent paused and crouched down to stroke the small dogs, much to their delight and his. "I knew they would like you," Serge commented, smiling fondly.

"We actually met at Gold Farm, I believe," Juliette said, greeting Albin with a handshake. She watched as he placed her precious bag in the vehicle.

"Yes, I recall. Welcome back."

"I'm afraid you'll find things a bit tense here right now, specifically in our neighbourhood and involving our friends," Kent began.

"Yes, I'm sorry to have involved all of you in my problems," Juliette said.

"Oh, no, Juliette. We've been in the thick of something for quite a while already. Although, when I said 'friends,' you were most definitely included.

"Consider the entire neighbourhood under siege. Lucy is currently at our summer house on L'Orté Island with Helen. She's Albin's sister. A young woman, Blomma, is there as well. We think it would be wise for you to be taken there, Juliette. Blomma, like you, is being sheltered from threats to her safety. Actually, it's been more than mere threats, but you needn't be troubled with the details of her situation. You'll have Wi-Fi access and be isolated from . . . well, from pretty much everything while you're on the island.

"Serge, we think you, Merlot, and Bijou would be best accommodated with Albin and Eve, who live next door to us, *us* being Lucy and me. Cookie is a golden retriever and part of their family. Serge, do you think Merlot and Bijou will get along with a larger dog such as that?"

Kent needed to translate and reword his information before Serge understood, but the answer was a resounding yes.

"The Carlssons live at the end of the street, at the cul-de-sac just around the bend. Astrid, the mother, is visiting from Sweden but her son, Lukas, lives there full time. A couple, Juji and Leo, also from Sweden, may be visiting with them as well—they travel back and forth rather frequently. You'll probably see them periodically.

"I'm at home with yet another young woman, Sandra, and then there's her bodyguard, O. O keeps a low profile, so you might not even see him, but she too requires our protection."

Not everything that Kent told them was the complete truth, but it was close enough.

"Once you get a sense of the place, just keep an eye open for anything or anyone you consider suspicious, and let one of us know, okay?" Kent didn't expect either Juliette or Serge to embrace the idea of having entered such a situation, but it was important that they avoid complacency. They needed to be aware at all times. "Recently, we've formed our own rather tightly-knit little community, these three residences. People intermingle and continue to socialize, including at meal times. The threats to safety aren't welcome of course, but we've banded together, and it's quite a cohesive little society we've developed. That part, that pulling together, has been quite rewarding. Admittedly, we're all getting tired of being under some threat, but at least it's a shared threat, and we're prepared to face it. If at anytime it ends up becoming too stressful an experience for you, then please know that no one would think less of you if you decided to leave for a situation that's more suited to your needs.

"Serge, we've already explained much of this to Yoichi, so I'm sure she'll share the information with Donald. Either Albin or I, or perhaps Lukas, can take you into the city centre whenever you want. And I've got the challenge of putting together something architecturally interesting for you, though I'm afraid it won't be possible to rival the tour of Nôtre Dame de Paris you arranged for Lucy and me. Yoichi lives right downtown, near her art gallery, and it's likely she'll be busy with your collection for quite a while.

"I understand that dinner tonight will be at Eve's, so we can introduce you to everyone then. Any questions?"

"No, not now, perhaps later," Serge replied.

"Same with me. I'm overwhelmed just being back. Until I get more settled . . . No, I can't think of anything right now," Juliette chimed in.

A short time later, Albin pulled the Escalade off the highway and entered the wooded enclave that he called home. "There's a trail through the woods where we can walk the dogs, Serge. Juliette, if you're available, you're welcome to join us. I'm just going to drive all the way down the street first to give you a quick tour. The house at the end here is the Carlsson residence. There's just an empty lot next to it." Albin rounded the end of the cul-de-sac and continued back up the street. "Here's the Gillespies' on the right. Then, next is this Tudor, which I call home." He paused to activate the gate, then passed through onto the cobblestone driveway. When the gate closed securely behind them, Albin continued up the drive to the house.

"I'll unload Serge's luggage. Juliette, did you want to take yours, or should I?" Albin asked.

"Actually, I'm getting comfortable rather more quickly than I'd expected. It's good to be home. If you could take care of it for me, that would be great—but I thought Kent said I should go to the island?"

"We'll get you to the island tomorrow, if that's all right with you, Juliette," Kent explained. "For tonight, you have your choice of residences. While Albin takes your suitcase, let me show you and Serge something you may find convenient."

While Albin took care of the luggage and the vehicle, Kent walked with Juliette and Serge, accompanied by his dogs, to the little bridge connecting the two properties. "You can move from this yard into ours without going out on the street. It's well hidden."

"Nice idea," Juliette said.

"Albin installed it when Lucy and I were away on our year-long travels. It was for convenience back then, and now it's for security. I'm glad we didn't remove it when we returned from our travels. But just remember that it's here; if the dogs are off-leash and seem to disappear, Serge, you might find them next door."

"I think I should stay in your house tonight, if you don't mind, Kent. Albin and Eve will have enough on their hands with dinner and Serge and the dogs. Share the burden—you get me!"

"Now, cut that out, Juliette. You're no burden. You present a bit of a logistical challenge, yes, but not a burden," Kent explained, hoping to encourage her to relax.

Eventually, everyone was settled. Serge and his dogs took up residence with Eve and Albin, while Juliette set her suitcase in a room at the Gillespies'.

CHAPTER 33
ALEKSANDRA, THE EXPLORER

"You mentioned the awen symbol yesterday, Lucy. I was reading the pages of the little book that you have mounted in frames along the upper hallway near that big painting, and the awen is mentioned as the footprint of this red cat—"

"Well, that little story certainly shouldn't be taken literally. It's more an allegory with symbolism, and I think it's to inform, to get the reader thinking."

"Where is the book from?" Aleksandra asked.

"We found that book here, at the manor house, about eight years ago. I think it was written in the early 1980s and placed in the box by my father, who then buried it. It was addressed to me, but I was just a baby back then. I don't remember anything about it from when I was a child."

"Do you know who wrote it?"

"Gracie Hogan, my grandaunt. She was both my father's aunt because she was the sister of Annie, his birth mother, and his stepmother because Gracie married his adoptive father after he became a widower. At the time she sent it, she had moved from Canada and was living in Ireland."

"Lucy, if you recall the name she gave to the red cat in the story, would you please spell it aloud."

Lucy was a bit confused. Aleksandra's request made little sense to her. "C-O-N—oh my goodness, Connor!

"I really hope that the marine archeologist can complete his work promptly. I can't help but wonder what else they might find in and near that wreck. I'll give Kent a call, and we'll see if he can give someone a little push to make this a priority."

"Well, you did tell me that your curiosity kept you going, didn't you?" Aleksandra smirked. "So, when do we leave for the manor house?" Aleksandra appeared keen, and Lucy was pleased. It seemed that spending time on her isolated little island was enjoyable for her charge after all.

Lucy and Aleksandra geared up and set out for the manor house about mid-morning. Dressed in cargo pants, a T-shirt under a long-sleeve shirt, and light-weight hiking boots, they carried water, snacks, and sundries in backpacks.

"You've got your GPS transponder, right?"

"Yep," quipped Aleksandra. "But, I've got no intention of wandering off, Lucy."

A smile crept across Lucy's face.

"Yeah, okay—O insisted, right?" remarked Aleksandra.

Lucy nodded her head.

The path to the manor house was well worn. It wandered through stands of sugar maple; tapped by Helen in the early spring, their sap was boiled down to make maple syrup for L'Orté Island guests. Among the sugar maples, there were some very old ash trees, the odd walnut tree, and clusters of honey locust. The sunlight filtered through the developing leafy canopy, and a variety of wildflowers thrived on the forest floor.

A massive oak tree marked the point on the trail where the path to the manor house veered off toward the shoreline.

"This thicket has lots of thorny shrubbery," Aleksandra complained, though the tone of her complaint was mild. "Have you considered hacking it down? It'd be easier to get to the manor house, wouldn't it?"

"The honey locust gets damaged during the winter and tends to grow more shrub-like here. It would probably be an easier trek if we did as you suggest, but for now I'd rather discourage others. Besides, most of the offending canes are wild raspberry, and the birds love them. I enjoy nibbling on them as well. I'm using the thorny plants as a bit of a deterrent. Once I'm satisfied that I've poked around in there enough, then perhaps we'll clear a better path, but it's too soon for that."

When they arrived at the manor house, Aleksandra appeared perplexed.

"It's not what you were expecting, is it?" Lucy said.

"No, you're right. It's not. How old is it?"

"It was likely built in 1930. I started calling it Mishmash Manor because it's such a combination of conflicting architectural styles, but that's a modern conceit, I guess. Clearly, it was built for function. It was occupied for no more than five years, if that. Despite having no maintenance, it has survived. It's suffered through harsh winter winds, snow and ice, fallen trees, insect invasions, larger animals using it as their home . . . Yet, it's still here, for the most part.

"Here's where the little book was discovered, back in this area. You can see various awen carved into stones and into some of the wooden beams," Lucy explained.

"This scene looks much like the scene in that big painting back at the summer house," Aleksandra said. "Is the furniture still inside?"

"Yes, and dishes and all the other things you need to run a household. My grandfather planned to return, but then he was killed in that fire at the Point. My grandmother remained until it was time for my father's birth, at which point she moved into a convent infirmary. But since she died giving birth, there was no one left to return to the manor house. There was much confusion, and many years passed before ownership of the properties was clarified. The events themselves aren't completely clear, but I do have a greater sense of the situation now."

Aleksandra listened, somewhat comforted in the knowledge that other people's family situations were also complex and somewhat unpleasant, not just her own. This wasn't *schadenfreude* on her part; rather, it made her feel more connected and less alone, less a social oddity with a family that defied the recognizable characteristics of the average family. Sure, there were books written about unique families, but it meant so very much more to her to meet someone whose personal experiences were somewhat similar to her own.

While they wandered about the interior of the large stone house, looking for awen markings and hiding places, Aleksandra and Lucy compared notes. Aleksandra was surprised to learn that Lucy's mother died when she was the same age that Aleksandra had been when her own mother died, though the cause of death differed. And Lucy had been orphaned just prior to starting university, just as Aleksandra had been.

Suddenly, Aleksandra asked, "Did you work through some of your family baggage with the help of your art?"

"Probably, though I've not been conscious of doing that. When I look back at the growth of my work, I can see certain issues being addressed by some of the work. And . . ." Lucy's voice trailed off into a mumble.

"What is it that you were going to say, Lucy?" The look on Aleksandra's face demanded an answer, an openness.

Lucy took a deep breath before furnishing Aleksandra with further details. "When I first began to learn about my birth grandparents and L'Orté Island and L'Orté Point, it was like stirring up a pot of vague memories. I actually began to sleep-walk. I somehow managed to complete two huge paintings in my sleep."

"No way!" exclaimed Aleksandra.

"I'll show them to you when we return. I've got one of them here, on the island. You've seen it. It's the large painting in the upper hall. The building in the painting turned out to be a portion of the manor house."

"I thought it looked familiar. Remember, I said so," Aleksandra interjected.

"The other painting is in storage back at the estate. I can't bear to part with either of them. Four years after that second episode, I again did some painting while sleepwalking. You can ask O about it. He's the owner of that painting, so I think it's aboard the *Croesus*."

"You gave him the painting?"

"I did. It was the least I could do to thank him for saving my life. Like I said, ask O. He was the one who was awake during the entire episode, not me."

"I think I'd like to spend some time out here on my own, Lucy. Would that be okay with you?"

"You want to hang out around the manor house? That's fine with me, dear, but I think we're going to need to bounce the idea off O. He'll have final say. We should be able to accommodate any concern he has for your safety."

"Perhaps *Dedushka* has overreacted, and my safety is not in jeopardy at all. I mean, there's been no threat identified by O. Not as far as I know."

"No, not as far as you or I know, but I doubt that Grisha and O would tell you everything. They wouldn't want to worry you.

I don't want to worry you either. Worry is useless. However, I think you need to continue to be very aware. Problems can arise quickly, and I haven't heard that your situation is resolved. I understand that your uncle Maxim is increasing his involvement and may be taking charge, although I suspect that he'll be doing things much as Grisha would."

"Maxim is much like Agafya, my *babushka*. His wife died of COVID during the pandemic, and he now fills his heart with those of us he considers to be vulnerable. It is different for *Dedushka*. He has a hunger that cannot be satisfied, so he focuses on business and more business. *Babushka* surrounds herself with her grandchildren and—it sounds terrible of me to say this—but since my father died, she tries to have too great a control of me. I think she is using me to plug the hole left in her heart when he died."

"Was your father, Alexei, her favourite, do you think?"

"Definitely. He was her baby, and she treated him as such. She indulged him. He didn't have much in common with my uncles, Maxim and Ilya. They were both attending university when he was born. Perhaps *Babushka* also feels a bit guilty that she was so indulgent. Had she been stricter, perhaps he might not have gotten himself into so much trouble. I don't really know, but I wonder about it sometimes."

"It's futile to wonder about such things, Blomma. If it really concerns you, then ask her. Talk to her about it. And if you plan to do that, then do it sooner than later. Eventually, time runs out and you can no longer ask. It's just another lost opportunity, and all that you reap is regret.

"I think it's time to return for lunch. If I can connect with O, we'll get his opinion of you being at the manor house on your own, and hopefully, you can return this afternoon, okay?"

Once Lucy informed Aleksandra that her wandering about the island in the vicinity of the manor house was acceptable to O—as long as she carried her GPS transponder and phone—Aleksandra wolfed down the last of her lunch, putting aside a few items to be carried in her backpack with bottles of water, and ventured out.

Aleksandra followed the same path she had taken earlier with Lucy, and eventually she arrived at the large oak tree that marked the fork in the trail. Instead of following the path to the manor house, she took the less travelled path into the woods.

The scurrying of garter snakes across the path no longer startled Aleksandra, but she failed to share Helen's fondness for the striped reptiles. The many spiders continued to alarm her. "Sneaky, creepy things!" she declared, speaking aloud but to herself. She picked her way through the woods, trying to avoid any patches of dense shrubbery. Eve had been very enthusiastic about the birds on the island, and Aleksandra was pleased to notice that some of them seemed to be quite willing to feed on the juicy arachnids.

A short distance ahead, Aleksandra spotted a glade, just off to the left side of the path. Dead trees, rocks, and thickets were scattered about the area. She struggled to access the most appealing parts of the glade. She stumbled and grabbed for a dry branch as she went down, but the brittle branch broke. "Well, you weren't much help," she said as she picked herself up and brushed away dirt and bits of plant debris from her clothing.

As she entered deeper into the small glade, Aleksandra stopped to consider the area, then she removed her backpack and accessed her notebook, sketchpad, and water. A tree trunk rooted nearby was all that remained of a once-large hardwood, and it was that trunk she selected to provide her seating. The trunk had been left with a large splinter along one side, and that splinter now formed a natural back to her arboreal chair. The sun filtered through the leafy canopy, and Aleksandra smiled at the simple beauty before her. She turned over a piece of wood with her foot, exposing a salamander, and carefully replaced the wood before the amphibian could react and move away.

It had been a long time since she last put her thoughts into words on a page. Seated in her rustic throne, she passed the time: seeing, writing, dreaming . . . She was so very still for long periods of time that young rabbits confidently emerged from the woods to nibble on the tender shoots in the glade.

A cluster of rocks near the centre of the glade was covered in mosses and lichens. As the direction of the sunlight changed, the organization of the stones became increasingly apparent, and it was there that Aleksandra's attention was drawn. The stones appeared to have been skillfully stacked, and though a few of the stones had fallen from what might have been their original position, the pile was largely undisturbed. Aleksandra examined it from several directions and took photos to share with Lucy.

As the glade began to darken with the advance of the day, Aleksandra packed her belongings into her backpack, retraced her steps back to the big oak tree, and followed the main path to return to the summer house.

When Aleksandra arrived back at the main house, Lucy was nowhere to be seen. However, she was able to locate Helen, who was searching through the foodstuff on a shelf in the large pantry.

"What do you make of this, Helen?"

"That looks like a cairn to me," Helen declared when Aleksandra showed her a photo of the pile of stones in the glade.

"What's a cairn?"

"Well, the word is Gaelic and refers to a pile of stones, assembled to mark something. Hard to say what might be marked way out where you found this," commented Helen. "Right now, I wish there was one in this pantry to mark what it is I'm looking for—aha, gotcha!" With that, Helen reached deep into the storage cupboard and withdrew a can containing hominy. "I knew there was one here—now to make the salad. Would you please grab a bell pepper and a Spanish onion for me, Blomma?"

Helen selected her favourite stainless steel chef's knife—the one with a six-inch blade—and continued with her food preparation, appearing to ignore her. A short time later, she turned to Aleksandra and, while gesturing with the knife, asked, "Why don't we see if we can get Lucy to go back out there with us? She can decide how much of it she's willing to have pulled apart for a more thorough investigation. First the boat you found with the bottle and the medallion, and now this cairn. Is your island vacation unfolding as you expected?"

CHAPTER 34

COMMUNICATING WITH CASH

Kent was eager to show Serge a good time; he had so appreciated his time spent with Serge in Paris. However, he was finding it difficult to compete with the behind-the-scenes visits Serge had arranged for him at Nôtre Dame Cathedral, the Louvre, and the Eiffel Tower.

Kent was involved with the Faculty of Architecture, Landscape and Design at the University of Toronto and a strong supporter of their work in Urbanism. He and Lucy frequently socialized with Petra Szucs, the university's president. Their sizeable donations had been formally acknowledged by President Szucs, who was also impressed by the gift of L'Orté Point to the Province of Ontario, which had been made by Lucy some years earlier. So, when he called to request a favour, he received a positive response. Happily, they were able to provide a francophone history major to serve as docent for a tour of the campus and surrounding area. Kent was pleased that she was also well-informed regarding campus lore.

An architecture professor invited himself, joining them for the entire tour. Apparently, he was an admirer of the work done by Proulx-Allard, the Parisian firm headed by Serge and his now-deceased partner, Jean-Pierre, in restoration and revitalization of historic properties in France. While this had not been expected, Kent was pleased. Serge was simply delighted.

Kent was beginning to feel rather superfluous, but that soon changed when the university's president herself eventually joined their little group.

"I hear that the Rachitsky Tower that was erected on your island is working well. We're all very excited that our engineers have brought the project to this stage so quickly," President Szucs said, referencing a beta version communications tower designed to boost cellphone access for remote locations. The offer of the tower had been an opportunity Kent could not resist—neither was the presence of President Szucs. They chatted awhile about things in general and then more specifically about Lucy and her work as Awen.

"A friend of mine has a concern you might be able to address more effectively than anyone else, Petra."

"Oh, what might that be, Kent?"

"I'll need to be a bit cryptic since he's not asked me to do this. His granddaughter is one of your foreign undergraduate students. Her boyfriend's death is currently being investigated by the police, and she herself has been threatened. As you are well aware, exams have recently begun, but it is considered unsafe for her to expose her location. Might you be able to make special accommodation for her under these circumstances, to postpone or otherwise work around any need for her to be bodily present or reveal her location in order to complete her requirements?"

President Szucs smiled—a bit of a sly smile, it seemed. "Oh, he probably should have spoken with you about this, but we're glad he didn't."

Kent's confusion became clearly evident in his facial expression.

"Mr. Orlov has decided to sponsor the enhanced Russian Studies program here, as well as the complete refurbishment of the building in which Russian Studies has been housed. It's currently in a less-than-ideal state of repair. The building will take on his name as well."

"Oh, that's interesting."

"Yes, I thought you might find it so.

"And after matters pertaining to the sponsorship were settled, he requested, and we agreed to, such accommodation as you have just mentioned." President Szucs looked at Kent, anticipating his response.

"Well, Grisha might have mentioned that to me."

"All he needed to do was to have outlined the situation as you have, and we would have agreed. It's quite reasonable under the circumstances."

"I know."

"But we're happy to have received the funding."

"You could have gotten more."

"You don't know how much we've received." She smiled, and her eyes twinkled.

"No matter. You could have gotten more."

CHAPTER 35

ELLIE CALOGERO

"Garner and Garner, how may I direct your call?" the receptionist inquired.

"Langston Garner, please." The voice was gruff, and the tone was somewhat aggressive.

"May I say who's calling?"

"I'd rather surprise him. Just tell Mr. L that it's to his advantage."

"Yes, sir, please hold," the receptionist replied, connecting with Langston Garner's office. Clearly, the caller knew to refer to the senior partner as Mr. L, rather than Mr. Garner. There were many Garners at the firm, and all the partners, or potential partners, were family members: siblings, cousins, parents, children. The most senior and currently active partner was Kyle Garner, and Langston was next in line. Behind him were Marcus, Nelson, Ogden, and Preston. In her five years with the firm, no one had ever told her why there were no women in line. It was an old law firm, and she didn't question its traditions. One eccentricity of which she was aware, and which she thought rather amusing, was that you could always determine relative ages of the partners and potential partners: their first names descended the alphabet. (Andrew and Bennett Garner, his brother, had founded the firm over a century ago.) There was considerable prestige associated with this law firm, and she valued her job.

Langston Garner was exhausted. It wasn't an exhaustion borne of physical exertion, but rather one of extreme mental fatigue. He felt old beyond his years as he stared at the edge of his desk where the small brass plates affixed across the surface were testament to its history. His was the third, and he hadn't as yet decided who he would select to follow in his footsteps—likely his only son, Preston, or perhaps Quenton, who was a favourite nephew. Langston fingered the antique decorative hardware at the midpoint. The brass keyhole escutcheon was constructed with a split cover depicting the Roman god Janus. A decorative panel inlaid with marquetry could be flipped up to cover the brass name plates and the keyhole. The key had been missing for a couple generations already. He suspected it might have been a joke arranged by Clarence: a kneehole with a keyhole—but without a key. Intriguing. When his office phone indicated an incoming call, he grunted, repositioned the panel, and answered.

"Yes, Sarah?"

"Sir, there's a gentleman on the line who says he wishes to surprise you. He referred to you as Mr. L and said that it is to your advantage."

Langston's body tensed, his lips pursed, and his eyes narrowed. "Okay, put him through. No one else, you hear? And I mean no one," he stressed.

"Yes, sir."

"L here."

"Ellie, you haven't been answering your phone."

"Don't call me that!" Langston hissed into the receiver. "Who is this?"

"A friend of Calogero."

"Call me at the other number." Langston ended the call and rooted in his drawer for his other phone, locating it just in time to turn it on and answer a second call. "I'm here."

"Look, you've got to keep yourself available at this number at all times, Ellie; you know that. We might need something. In this case, the matter is a mutual concern."

"You mentioned Calogero. Last I heard the apartment in Paris was empty, and your people had no information about where Juliette might be. Has that changed?"

"It might have, Ellie."

"I said not to call me that! So what's changed?"

"She might be in your area, *Ellie*." Calogero's friend emphasized the nickname, as if poking and taunting Langston. "It's not definite, but it's worth you checking it out. An informant of ours overheard a conversation between an old man and a younger man. He recognized both of them from some target photos we'd distributed. The old man was the one from the Paris apartment; Serge Proulx is his name. The younger one was another target we were considering for the same job, an architect by the name of Kent Gillespie. Gillespie lives just outside Toronto. Your cousin, Juliette, was staying at the old man's apartment. Both the old man and Gillespie were targets before their contract was pulled, so they're all connected."

"Juliette and this Serge person could have gone their separate ways. She might not even be connected with Gillespie."

"Maybe, maybe not. But the informant overheard the old man refer to someone by the name of Juliette. You should look into it, Ellie. You find her; we'll take care of the rest."

"If it is her, I want to be there when you take care of her, hear me? She's caused us a lot of trouble over the years: G and now me. So I need to see her gone for good." Langston ran his finger along the small, brass nameplates mounted on the edge of his desk: Clarence Garner, Grantham Garner, Langston Garner. "This time, I don't want her to go running off to Europe. Leave it with me. I'll have someone look into it further."

When the call was concluded, Langston placed the phone in an outside pocket of his attaché case and looked through a desk drawer, on the hunt for a specific file. He grunted with delight when he located it. He withdrew a series of photographs from a large envelope and began to examine them. The photos were portraits of Juliette, aged appropriately and sporting a variety of hairstyles in various colours. He hoped she'd not taken the time to have plastic surgery. He doubted it. It wasn't her style, though the need to consider her own survival might have provided her the necessary push in that direction. His cousin had tendered her resignation from the firm and disappeared from their lives in 2016. She and her Interpol colleagues had been inflicting pain upon his clients, the friends of Calogero, ever since.

Kyle Garner knocked, then quickly opened the door to his cousin Langston's office, catching him unaware. Surprised, Langston jerked his hand, spilling a small quantity of single-malt Scotch in the process. "Oh, sorry about that, L, I was just leaving and couldn't recall whether you'd accepted my invitation for tonight. Are you on?"

"I doubt I'll be able to make it tonight, K," Langston answered, wiping the spill with his handkerchief until the burled walnut surface was dry once again. The desk, an antique, had originally belonged to Clarence Garner. Langston treasured it; it anchored him. Clarence had been the first Garner Janus, and Langston was now the third—not that Kyle or anyone else at the firm was aware of this, of course.

When he was confident that Kyle had gone for the day, Langston ventured out of his office and down the hall to the storage room. The oldest files, concerning matters that had closed, were archived at a secure location off-site, but Kyle had been careful to have certain of the old files remain on-site. Those were the ones he now sought.

He entered the master key code and was granted access to the room. Juliette's old files were found in the back, separate from the others. It would have been easier to do an initial search on the computer for the information he wanted, but he wasn't certain how to cover his tracks. Not that it was wrong for him to obtain such information—he was a senior partner after all—nevertheless, this low-tech search was preferable.

The name provided by Calogero's friend was Kent Gillespie. Langston located the Gs but could find no such person. However, there was a "Gillespie, Lucy" and that particular file was cross-referenced with one for a "Hogan, Grace." He removed both files and placed them on the only table in the room.

It didn't take long for him to appreciate the connection. Gracie Hogan had been the wife of Jozsef Szabo, an early associate of Clarence Garner back in the 1930s. She was the grandaunt of Lucy Gillespie, who had ultimately inherited the balance of the Szabo trust as well as the L'Orté trust. The Gillespie file contained references to the massive property known as L'Orté Point, now a conservation area. And, unless the Gillespies had moved since 2015, the year Gracie died, Langston now had the address.

He made a copy of the files and returned the originals to the storage cabinets. As he re-entered his office, he felt both satisfied and anxious. He'd need to see this resolved promptly, else he thought he'd go mad. Using his special phone, he contacted the independent contractor he had used on previous occasions.

CHAPTER 36
A TORRENT OF EMOTION

Aleksandra became noticeably more cheerful over time, and while that was good news, Lucy couldn't help but wonder as to the cause of this change. In due course, her curiosity was satisfied.

"Thank you for recommending that I speak with Leo, Lucy," she said during breakfast.

"I didn't know you had contacted him, but I guess that's how it should be, isn't it?" Lucy replied.

"Yes, though I guess it sometimes isn't. Immediately after my father died, *Dedushka* arranged for me to see a therapist he had vetted. I opened up to her, just as you're expected to if you really want help. I followed her advice, just as one should." Aleksandra became quiet.

"Did something happen?" Lucy asked, concerned that she might have ventured into unsettling territory during their previous discussion.

"It seems that my therapist was friends with my boyfriend's family. She revealed just enough that he was able to piece things together. He determined that I wasn't as serious about our relationship as he'd previously thought because I was becoming more open to meeting new people. He dumped me.

And I was just following her advice! She'd suggested that since my tendency was to cut myself off from people and rely upon only a very few friends and family, I should make an effort to broaden my associations."

"Well, that makes sense to me, though it's certainly not my field," Lucy said. "Was there any disciplinary action taken against her?"

"I don't think so. I was so traumatized that I didn't want anything more to do with her or that entire family or their friends. I did notice that she retired shortly after. I didn't think she was all that old, but perhaps she realized she was getting sloppy in managing sensitive information.

"Anyway, that messed me up awhile. I guess that's why the situation with Smith was so difficult for me, though I understand why anyone who didn't know the full story might have thought I was overreacting, like Detective Inspector Brennan seemed to earlier on," Aleksandra concluded.

"Well, I'm pleased that you followed up with Leo, and that he has been a help to you. It's good that you can continue the arrangement online, no matter where either of you happens to be at the time.

"What have you decided to do today?" Lucy asked.

"Helen and I are going for a walk across the meadow and down into the southern end of the island. She says there's a pond and some interesting plants. I've seen some of her sketches of them, and I think I'd like to try my hand at sketching. Besides, I'll be learning some botany. Perhaps I'll switch majors," Aleksandra declared. "Nah, that's unlikely. I'll stick with psych and English lit, but perhaps I'll add a bit of art.

"Have you given any thought to investigating the cairn, Lucy?"

"It hasn't slipped my mind, but I really haven't had the time to give it much thought. There's just so much going on right now. When we do it—and we will—it'll be done like an archeologist would. I may even bring in a professional to do it right. There's no point in messing things up. And now is not the time to have strangers invited here, is it?

"Careful around there, okay? There's some dense shrubbery and a rather steep cliff hiding behind it. Just check out that map again before you go."

Aleksandra nodded her head.

"Regarding the sunken boat—Kent has contacted the marine archeologists who performed a survey of the waters immediately around the island years ago," Lucy explained. "This was prior to our construction of the docks and boathouses. Given the history of the island, we were interested in anything that might be found, but there was nothing reported at the time. It would seem that for some reason, they missed this boat. He thinks they'll make this investigation a priority because of that, but they'll be bringing out their own equipment and remaining on their boat, just like O does."

"So, how long do you expect them to take before they report to you?"

"There's no way to know, Blomma. We'll just need to be patient. If your situation has been cleared up before their report is received, we'll make arrangements with you to get together with us and go over everything, if you'd like. Until then, you just go on your walks with Helen and enjoy nature.

"I'm going to continue my work on the final panel of the triptych for your grandparents. I've done the preparatory sketches, prepared the pigments, and roughed in some of the background, so I'm ready to start working with the finer oils and gold leaf."

"You managed to complete the big central piece?" Aleksandra asked.

"Yes, it's at home, drying in the studio. It's good I was able to complete it before coming to the island. It's not easy to travel with a still-wet oil canvas, especially one of such a size," Lucy said, reminded of the many long hours she had spent on the complex painting.

"Spring is particularly wonderful on the island, isn't it?" Helen asked, inhaling deeply and concluding with a sigh as she exhaled. "I love the colours of the new growth, and the flowers . . . just look at all this flowering dogwood!"

Helen and Aleksandra had just cleared the meadow and were on their way to the pond Helen had claimed she would find magical. Indeed, it was. The verdant area was abundant with species that didn't mind getting their feet wet so close to the reedy shore, as the elevation of the island dropped off gradually at its southernmost tip.

They located a few fallen trees and spread blankets on the ground, using the trees to support their backs. At first glance, the area seemed devoid of animal life, merely a vignette of vegetation.

"What do you say, time for a snack after that trek? I happen to have carrot cake." That got Aleksandra's attention.

While nibbling on cake, the women sat quietly and watched as the wildlife, previously unseen, accepted them and resumed their normal activities. Birds argued as they competed for nesting sites and materials. Early insects buzzed, making the most out of their brief existence. The pond was still but for the interruptions caused by insects and small fish breaking the surface of the water. Periodically, the chirping of small frogs and the bellow of bullfrogs would pierce the silence, then be stilled after an attack by a predatory bird.

"I am being very well fed," Aleksandra declared.

"That's good. Just let me know if there's anything in particular you want, and I'll try to prepare it for you—"

"No, that's not what I mean, Helen. You're a great cook and thanks for the wonderful meals, but I meant that my soul is being fed. By this," she explained, drawing her hand across the scene before them. "It's simple and simply beautiful. It appeals to me fundamentally as a human. It's nourishing. It's . . . enough." She sighed. "I can see why Lucy wanted this to be preserved, left to itself and not developed.

"If that large section, L'Orté Point, is anything like this, that's a wonderful gift to have given to future generations. Perhaps they should rename it after her. Gillespie Point or Lucy Point," she suggested with a giggle.

"Actually, it's already named after her grandfather, Giovanni Sarto," Helen said. Understandably, Aleksandra was confused.

"It's complicated and can't be verified, but we're all agreed that it's accurate," Helen explained. "Sarto means tailor in Italian. At some point—I forget the year, and it doesn't matter anyway—the family name was anglicized to Taylor. That's a phonetic reversal of L'Orté which is the name he gave to the property. Previously, it had no such name. There's a bit more to it, but that's the story in a nutshell."

"But I understood that the family name was Szabo."

"That was the name of the family that had adopted Lucy's father, not her birth grandfather's surname. Oddly enough, Szabo—I think it's Hungarian—also means tailor. There's more to the story, as there usually is with such things, but I don't suppose the details of the past matter at this point, eh? It's been nearly a century."

"Do you have boots and a small net back at the dock?" Aleksandra asked.

"We have some waders and a few minnow nets, if that's what you're considering. What have you got in mind?"

"I just thought I might bring them with me next time and investigate this area more thoroughly. Do you think just an older pair of runners would be better than the boots?"

"Well, I think you shouldn't venture out here on your own, is what I think. Certainly not without giving O a heads up so he can bring the boat to watch this end of the island. Promise?"

"Okay, I promise. Really, Helen, I do!"

"Today, she seems pretty much okay, but in general she's getting frustrated and increasingly concerned, Kent, and I can't say that I blame her. Even the smallest things are beginning to get to me as well. One can only take the tension for so long, I'm learning. For example, I thought Juliette was due here this morning, but she hasn't arrived. Is anything the matter? And why am I having to ask about it?" Lucy could hear the note of irritation in her own voice.

"Yeah, sorry about that; time got away from me—again. We were planning to leave this morning, but she needed to buy some clothes. She had very little of anything with her and certainly nothing suitable for the island. But we couldn't just have her go shopping now, could we? So, it was all done online as a special order that Albin picked up. I tell you, it was crazy," Kent explained. "And, I do understand. This is really getting to me too. There's only so much one can take, even with the best of intentions and greatest concern for others. I keep wondering when we'll get our lives back.

189

"And now there's something else I've just learned. Grisha's not doing well. I think it's the accumulation of personal stressors over the past couple of years. He seems fine dealing with business matters, but not personal, I guess. So, he's directed Maxim to take the lead on all matters related to Sandra. It's probably for the best, given his age."

"Do I tell her, or will someone else being doing that?" Lucy inquired, hoping that the task wouldn't fall to her.

"Grisha will, in his next phone call—tomorrow she'll be told that he's returning to France. I hope Maxim lets me know precisely what it is she's told, so we don't say the wrong thing. He's not always forthcoming with information, probably because he doesn't know me as well as Grisha does."

"And I'm rubbish at lying; remember that, please."

"You were great lying to Nathan Bellamy in Paris," Kent reminded her.

"Yeah, but that was quite different. I can't lie to someone I care about, someone I consider a good person. I couldn't even surprise you for your birthday.

"And has there been any decision made about Blomma's idea regarding payment for Maddie's release, assuming she isn't dead already?"

"I conveyed the information to O, and he's promised to pass it along to Grisha, though soon that will mean Maxim. Maxim's thinking is quite different from Grisha's, so I don't know where we stand. When Maxim eventually phones Blomma, she should try to sell him on that idea herself."

"Perhaps I should contact Brennan, considering that Maddie is his primary focus. Perhaps he can put some pressure on the Orlovs."

"Actually, Lucy, I already did that, though I'd never admit it to Maxim or Grisha because they'd consider it an end-run. I'm just a little cog in their big wheel, and though no one has come out to say it, I should know my place, my limitations. There may be some truth to it, but this is my—*our*—place and these are our friends . . ."

"Have you ever heard how all this came about? Is this some sort of vendetta against the Orlovs?"

"I just catch bits and pieces. From what I've gathered—O is far more forthcoming with me—Alexei wasn't just using drugs; he was giving them to his friends. You'll remember the drug use we witnessed when Alexei held that party in one of the rooms on the *Croesus* the night of the Grisha's big party in Antibes. Well, he wasn't paying for the drugs, so he ran up quite the bill. Then, to top it all off, he took charge of a large consignment of drugs—I don't know what, but that wouldn't mean much to me anyway—and promptly lost them. It sounds to me like they were stolen, perhaps by the competition, but I'm not sure about that. So, we're talking mega bucks, and these guys—whoever they are—are truly pissed. They want revenge.

"Now, I can't validate any of that, but it sounds about right, given how we'd pegged Alexei's personality back when we first met him. Perhaps you'll remember that old Russian saying, 'Intelligent thoughts have always followed him, but he was faster.' That was most definitely Alexei. I doubt he was killed intentionally; they probably just wanted to scare him into paying his bills. How the son of a multi-billionaire could get himself in such a situation is beyond my comprehension."

"I'm learning that it's not so much a matter of one's financial status, but one's personality and character." Lucy sighed. "Greed and poor judgement seem independent of social status."

"The Orlovs are really trying to isolate our function solely to keeping Sandra safe, and they're not letting us in on the bigger picture. Personally, I'm beginning to resent that. It puts others in jeopardy, quite clearly, and my trust in the Orlovs is rapidly diminishing," Kent concluded, his concern apparent to Lucy.

"Grisha is no Mark Witherspoon, is he?"

"No, he isn't. My father used to say that people were packages, so I should probably cut Grisha some slack. I don't understand his perspective, but we're learning more about him, and he's clearly a different package from Mark, that's for sure. I'm finding it difficult," Kent admitted.

"Because it could lead to more deaths—just collateral damage, I guess," Lucy added, wryly. "I don't want anyone to become collateral damage because the Orlovs, with all their money, couldn't be bothered to buy these people off. I'd find it beyond difficult if any of our friends were hurt as a result—and I can't begin to express how I'd feel . . . how I might react if something bad were to happen to you!"

Lucy lost control and could no longer contain her emotions. "Kent, I can't bear the thought of you being injured. I felt I'd lost you when Julius kidnapped you, and though that was years ago, I can recall that feeling as if it were all happening again, now. Promise me that you won't sacrifice yourself for the Orlovs. I need you to be there for me when this is all over." It sounded selfish even to her own ears, but she didn't care.

"I appreciate that, sweetie. I do. And know that there'd be hell to pay if anything were to happen to you. I'm pretty sure I could even take out O if it came to that, my motivation would be so great. So you take care of yourself, and I'll do my best here as well. We'll come through this. We always have.

"I've promised to take Serge on another outing, or I'd have hopped on the heli with Juliette just to see you for a moment. Albin loaded up the supplies Helen requested. They should be with you shortly."

"I'll be on the lookout, and I'll let Helen know. She's already at that end of the island. She and Blomma went to the pond. I'm not sure where the ATV has been left, but it's either at this end, or they rode it down to the other end. I'll say bye for now, and I'll talk to you later. I love you."

"I know you do. And I love you. Take good care of yourself."

"You too." They ended the call then. It was difficult to disconnect . . .

Lucy phoned Helen, advising her that the helicopter transporting Juliette and the supplies would arrive shortly, and that Albin was on board as well. She made her way to the shed which housed the ATV, re-attached the trailer, and set off for the south end of the island, arriving just as the sound of the incoming helicopter broke the stillness. Moments later, Helen and Aleksandra emerged from the thicket to the south of the meadow.

It didn't take long to unload the supplies and pile them into the utility trailer. Albin had barely enough time to reconnect with Helen and have a brief chat with Lucy. Aleksandra stood close by and assisted with the transfer of foodstuff from the aircraft to the trailer. She appeared to have regressed into shyness in the presence of their new guest, Juliette.

As the helicopter departed with Albin, the four women on the ATV made their way across the meadow to the summer house.

"You must be Blomma," Juliette said, extending her hand in greeting. Shyly, Aleksandra took her hand and smiled.

This simple greeting startled Lucy. Juliette had become the first person to use the name Blomma without knowing that it was the codename for Aleksandra Orlov. That made the moment significant. It served as a reminder to Lucy of the danger which lurked and threatened the young woman. And now there was the danger that seemed to follow Juliette as well. Suddenly Lucy was exhausted; an emotional fatigue engulfed her. Once again she needed time for herself, so she headed to her studio, announcing that she was not to be disturbed unless there was something serious in the offing.

While Lucy tended to the final Orlov painting, Helen used the ample time available to give Juliette a tour of the island, its facilities and the treasures that had been found, though treasures might seem a bit of a stretch. Aleksandra accompanied them.

"The last time I saw this island was . . . must be sometime prior to 2015. There was simply no reason to visit for a weekend back then. I'd come to get an idea of the condition of the manor house, and once I took a look, I was out of here. Now, however, it's quite different."

"What was your opinion of the manor house back then?" Helen asked.

"Well it was pretty much as I expected, being so old, open to the elements, and without any repair. I'll bet that having heard it referred to as a 'manor house,' you expected a bit more in the way of architectural elegance and expensive finishings, didn't you?"

"Well yes, actually. But it has provided many hours of interesting activity, poking about the place and investigating, that's for certain," Helen said. Behind her, Aleksandra nodded vigourously.

"Have you found anything particularly interesting?" inquired Juliette.

Helen provided a synopsis of the metal boxes they had found over the years as a result of following the awen markings. "This'll be a good opportunity for you to get caught up on all the things that were discovered after you disappeared."

If Helen had hoped to hear details about Juliette's departure from Garner & Garner, the family law firm, she was to be sorely disappointed. Juliette was not forthcoming.

"Don't forget the sunken boat and stuff," Aleksandra suggested.

"Why don't you tell Juliette all about that then?" Helen urged, noticing that Juliette's interest was piqued.

It didn't take long; there wasn't much to tell, but Aleksandra's enthusiasm in telling her story improved everyone's rather dreary mood. Odd that a sunken boat, a bottle, and a medallion should be able to do that, but they so needed a distraction from their personal troubles.

Lucy had invited O to join them for dinner and that provided an opportunity for Aleksandra and Juliette's security concerns to be aired. Lucy winced when O made it abundantly clear that his concern was Aleksandra's safety. It sounded as if he didn't care about the security of the others, and Lucy hoped that wasn't the case. She planned to speak with him later, in private.

"Blomma can't be secure unless and until we are *all* secure, O," Lucy said, as she and O moved from the dining room and into the study. She closed the door behind them. Recognizing that she was on edge, Lucy breathed deeply and took a moment to compose herself.

"Yes, of course, I understand your point of view, Lucy, but you must understand mine—"

"Understand this, O," Lucy abruptly said, cutting him off. "If your focus is so narrow, then I can narrow mine as well, and the two of you can seek refuge elsewhere. I understand that your job is to take care of Blomma, but if you are prepared to sacrifice others in order to do that, then you can just find some other sacrificial lambs because Juliette, Helen, and I are equally important. Actually, since I'm the one who agreed to this arrangement, I'd say I'm the least important of the three of us."

O tried to speak, but Lucy continued to tear into him. "You're being paid to do a job, I know, so do your job, but please understand this—this isn't *my* job. Actually, *my* job is being hindered by Blomma's situation. Our lives have been put on hold, and you appear to consider us pawns in some greater game. As much as I empathize with her, I won't have you express what amounts to a cavalier attitude toward the well-being of my other guests or employees. Do you understand?"

Lucy was livid. She was aware that her response was excessive, but it was the culmination of weeks of careful work, focused solely on the well-being of Aleksandra, that had put her on edge and frayed her nerves beyond easy repair. The more she said, the more irate she became. It was the product of constructive interference. Waves of emotion criss-crossed through her mind, adding together until she could no longer contain their energy.

O grabbed her by the shoulders and put her in a bear hug, as he had done that night aboard the *Theia*. "Shush, your nerves are shot, Lucy. I didn't mean it that way, not the way you have interpreted." He looked into her green eyes and was reminded of Colombian emeralds, flashing in the light. "I am aware of the imposition this must be on you and your friends, and that you feel your needs and concerns have no place in our considerations. Please know that for me to live with myself, you *all* must survive. Over my career I have witnessed the deaths of too many innocents and those who have taken on danger in order to assist others. I am trained and have chosen this profession. I see it as my responsibility to ensure that you all survive, so that you all have the opportunity to thrive."

Lucy was silent, still processing what he had said. She was sorry she had overreacted, but she was relieved that she had been straight with O and let him know precisely what was on her mind without suppressing her feelings. Having unloaded, she felt considerably better—somewhat embarrassed but overall, better. *Had the sound travelled? Had the others heard?* She didn't care.

"You're welcome to spend the night in the house, O, rather than return to your boat."

He considered her offer briefly. "Thank you, but it is best that I remain off-shore. I have a better view. And I have equipment on board which I lack here, but thank you." He placed his hands on her shoulders and imparted a gentle squeeze.

"Thanks, Oko," she said, startling him.

"I didn't think you could tell, not after all this time."

Lucy smiled. "You're hard to forget," she said.

When Lucy awoke the next morning, the sun was shining brightly through her bedroom windows. Her first thought was that she should take advantage of the wonderful light conditions and continue her work on the third painting. It was a difficult one, and she thought it might present an even greater challenge per square centimetre than the largest of the three, the centrepiece representing the present.

The future was an unknown, yet the third panel would anticipate subsequent generations of family members and their successes. Although Lucy had extrapolated from certain well-established characteristics found within the Orlov family, it seemed like tempting fate to make predictions. Nevertheless, she considered the hours of meticulous preparation she had already put into the panel. She anticipated the positivity she would feel, putting brush to canvas on this project.

Rather than take an early breakfast, she decided to work on the Orlov triptych awhile. She quickly showered and threw on some clothes. "I'm sure I closed you last night," she said, noticing that the door leading from her bedroom to the studio was slightly ajar. Lucy drew open the door, perhaps just a bit more slowly than she otherwise might have.

An easel was positioned in the centre of the studio. Sharp beams of morning sunlight illuminated the surface of the moderate-sized canvas mounted upon it. Startled by the sight before her, Lucy froze in her tracks. Overwhelmed, she dropped to the floor, her legs crumpling beneath herself. And she cried—tears of frustration, tears of longing, tears of confusion, tears just for the sake of tears . . . She pressed her face onto the cool floor and silently howled, pressured by circumstances to contain the immense emotion that engulfed her. She felt broken, and even in this time of need, she couldn't lessen her pain by sharing it with someone.

Her green eyes darkened with the reflection of the vibrant red canvas. Clearly, she had sleep-painted. The painting depicted flames, simply flames, and she had no indication of where this would occur, and who might become involved, or when it might happen. Nevertheless, she knew that it would;

she sensed the truth in it. She felt small, helpless, insignificant . . . and she didn't like it. She hadn't felt like that in many years, and she had no intention of going backward into that morass.

The first sleep-painting had been of the manor house; the second had depicted an assault upon her person when she was but a child, and the third had predicted the death of Mark Witherspoon. But this painting troubled her more than all the others combined. It set her heart ablaze with fear of an unknown.

CHAPTER 37
JULIETTE GOES MISSING

"Report?" Langston queried.

"You just gave me the file the other day. I haven't got anything to report right now." The independent contractor was obviously displeased with Langston pressuring him.

"I need to know,"Langston said. "I need the information yesterday, Spence," he emphasized.

"Looks like there's some kind of surveillance in that area, but it's hard to tell which house is the focus of attention. Might be the one you're interested in, might not. If you want me to give you a better answer, you'll need to give me more time."

There was nothing further Langston could say. It was true that he needed the information before Juliette could do any more damage to his enterprise or that of Calogero's friends, but it was also true that the information needed to be accurate. His life depended on it. He was to remain frustrated awhile longer.

Having encountered more than his fair share of Rottweilers, German shepherds, and Dobermans, Spencer wasn't fond of dogs, but now he found himself in need of a dog—something a woman would consider adorable. The animal shelter he visited had such a dog. They were, as usual, overcrowded, so there was no waiting period and no real vetting of applicants. Spencer liked desperation; it fed his business enterprise. His clients were pushed beyond their limit by situations that had suddenly gotten out of hand, leading to desperation for them and opportunity for him. And it was the shelter's desperation that resulted in him acquiring the dog. Her name was Lulu, and she was a senior, a Havanese cross according to the employee who arranged for the adoption. Spencer didn't care whether she was a cross or a purebred, young or old, Havanese or not—as long as the dog was cheap, could walk, and was cute.

Cookie enthusiastically investigated the undergrowth, alternating from one side of the trail to the other, sniffing the spring flowers. Astrid and Eve watched as she sashayed up the trail, her thick and feathery tail waving from side to side. She sniffed the moist earth and undergrowth, appearing to smile as she frequently returned to one or the other of them as if to consult with her human companions.

Spencer approached, following the woodland trail toward the cul-de-sac. Although his ears were tuned to their conversation, he failed to discern what it was they were saying. As the distance between Spencer and the women diminished, he remained uninformed. Astrid and Eve with her golden retriever were chatting away but in Swedish. It was a language Spencer neither spoke nor understood. He paused on the trail and bent down to adjust the collar of his canine prop.

Eve permitted Cookie to socialize, so she approached the little dog.

"What a lovely dog you have," he said, feigning an interest in the larger canine.

"Thank you," Eve replied, delighted that Cookie had garnered the well-deserved compliment. "Her name is Cookie. And what is *this* sweetie's name?" she asked as she crouched down and gently petted the elderly Havanese. Astrid stood by and kept an eye on Eve, readying herself to provide assistance should Eve experience one of her bouts of dizziness.

"Meet Juliette," Spencer announced, all the while looking into the faces of the women and searching for some indication that they had reacted to the name. "She's getting on in years, and we've just lost her Romeo, so she's not at her best, I'm afraid."

"Aw, poor thing," Astrid said. "It is terrible to lose a dear friend, whether one is a human or a dog." They exchanged a few additional comments before each party continued on its way.

Spencer turned around when he and Lulu reached the cul-de-sac and retraced their steps back toward his van. Again, their paths crossed with that of Astrid, Eve, and Cookie, and yet again he could not interpret their private conversation.

"I've nothing definite to report yet," he said in conversation with Langston upon returning to his vehicle. "However, I do get a sense that they recognize the name."

"Juliette?"

"Yeah, it was subtle, but I'm pretty certain it was there."

"Get me something more substantial, Spence," Langston demanded. "I mean it."

"I can only do so much. I can't actually get down to their road. It might as well be gated for all the security I've detected. If I don't get something tomorrow, I might need to do just that, though security will be all over me, I'm sure," Spencer explained.

"I mean it, Spence."

The next day, Spencer was in his van with his binoculars trained on the endpoint of the trail at the cul-de-sac. Lulu was confined, but she was ready and wearing her collar with the leash already attached.

"Ah-ha, this is a bit different. Today, there are three people and three dogs. Different is good," Spencer said to Lulu. "It opens up a whole new range of opportunities." He opened the van door and exited with the Havanese in tow.

Serge spoke French and a smattering of English. Eve spoke Swedish, English, and a smattering of dance-related French. Astrid spoke Swedish, English, and French. They settled on English as their common language and tried to help Serge improve his proficiency in the language.

"Ah," Astrid remarked when she noticed Spencer with Lulu in the distance. "Cookie's new friend is here again today. Let's see how good your English is now that you've been practising, Serge."

Astrid held a leash, at the end of which was Cookie. Serge kept hold of Bijou's leash, and Eve had chosen Merlot's—just the one dog, in case she had another bout of dizziness. She had a bit of a headache and even her face hurt, so she decided not to take any chances on her safety. One fall was quite sufficient; her ankle still didn't feel right.

"Good morning," the women called out in unison to Spencer.

Spencer waved in greeting, then said, "Good morning," when he was within easy hearing distance. By this time, the two groups had merged on the trail, resulting in a bit of mayhem as the four dogs interacted and leashes became entangled.

"I see we have two more today," Spencer said.

"Yes, we have a new visitor," Eve said, directing her comment to Spencer. "And Serge, this is Juliette," Eve continued, introducing the little Havanese.

Serge bent down to pet the old dog and offer a few words of comfort, given her obvious infirmity. "Juliette," he said, addressing her. "I know a Juliette and I would introduce you to her, but she is not here right now. Maybe another time when you walk, she might be back, and we can all visit together. I am certain she would like you."

Neither Serge nor either of the women saw this as anything other than a pleasant encounter among strangers. Talking to dogs seemed quite natural to them under the circumstances. When Cookie started to become agitated, and the attitude spread to Merlot and Bijou, the conversation ended. The two groups separated, and each continued on their way.

"Okay, I learned something today that might help you," Spencer said, while reporting his findings to Langston upon his return to the van. "Someone by the name of Juliette appears to be friends with these people, most definitely. I don't know which house, but that may not matter. She's not there right now. She's away some place but is expected to return."

"So she's off shopping perhaps?" Langston commented, merely thinking aloud.

"No, I think it's more than that. I think she's made some sort of side trip, but she'll return at some point."

"All right, stay on it, just in case there's more to learn," Langston said, and he ended the call before Spencer could share anything further.

Langston leaned back in his chair, clasped his hands behind his head, closed his eyes, and tried to focus his thoughts. He retrieved the copy he'd made of the two files and began to review them yet again.

He examined each page carefully for any clue to Juliette's whereabouts. Greedily, his eyes settled upon the transfer of Gracie Hogan's estate to Lucy Gillespie. Something had caught his attention. "Three-two-seven-eight," he said slowly. "That's one hell of a big piece of property, and she gave it all away. Fool. Well, not quite all of it, eh? What's this? L'Orté Island: a hundred hectares. I wonder . . ." He picked up his special phone and made a call.

"Spence, I've got some clerical work for you. Pause the surveillance for now and make a trip down to land registry. I want you to find out who currently owns L'Orté Island. I need the information immediately."

"Everything is always 'immediately' with you, isn't it?" Spencer grumbled as Langston disconnected.

Langston was already busy pouring himself a Scotch. He leaned back in his chair and stroked the marquetry panel across the front of his desk.

The following morning, Spencer returned Lulu to the animal shelter, claiming that his job was forcing him to move and it would be impossible to take her with him. He could have just let her loose, but Lulu was lucky—the shelter was on his way to the wooded parkland. He was early, so he sat in his van, peering through his binoculars toward the cul-de-sac, and he waited.

When he saw the little party of three humans with their dogs, he exited the van and began to walk toward them, all the while maintaining an energetic pace. As soon as he noticed that a member of the group appeared to have taken notice of him, he ran up toward them, waving his arms.

"Have you seen Juliette?" he asked, trying his best to act the part of a concerned dog owner. "Somehow she got out of her collar, and I can't find her!"

"How could that have happened?" asked Eve, puzzled by the claim.

"I guess it was too old; it broke. I should have gotten a new one for her, but—"

"No," Eve said in answer to Spencer's original question. "We haven't seen her," she said, looking at Serge, then Astrid. The three shook their heads and seemed concerned about the plight of Spencer and the missing Juliette.

"Perhaps she's wandered down to the cul-de-sac. It's been quite a while that I've been looking for her."

"Why don't I come look with you," offered Astrid. "You two continue the walk. Serge, here's Merlot's leash; I'll go help look for Juliette."

Eve and Serge continued to walk Cookie and the two spaniels while Astrid and Spencer quickly made their way toward the cul-de-sac. "We'll keep our eyes peeled for her, just in case," Eve shouted as they departed, and the distance between her and Astrid increased.

Just as Spencer expected, he was stopped by security personnel. A couple of men, casually dressed but with a bearing and attitude which he had correctly interpreted as security, approached him and inquired as to his purpose. If it hadn't been for Astrid, he likely would have been followed by one or more of them under the guise of providing assistance in the search for his lost dog. As it was, one of the men joined them on their search but appeared to be more accepting of his presence and actually making an effort to find the missing animal.

"What's with the security?" Spencer asked, sounding as innocent as possible.

"Oh, I think the trailer and the vehicles indicate they're finally going to be building on this lot. Perhaps it's some celebrity, though it makes no sense to me that they begin to take such precautions before the house is even built and in this case not even started."

"Oh, interesting, I guess," Spencer commented, staying in character. "I'll go to this house and ask," he said, indicating the Carlsson residence.

"That's where I live, so let me," Astrid volunteered.

Astrid left Spencer in the company of the security guard and activated the intercom at the gate. Leo answered. "Leo, I'm looking for a lost dog. She's a very old Havanese and seems to have wandered off. Perhaps you and Juji could search the property, just in case she was able to get in. I'm going to continue searching out here. Bye." And then she continued toward Spencer and the security guard.

By the time she reached where they had stood, the security guard was busy searching across the street from the Gillespies' and Spencer was trying to connect with a resident via the intercom at the Gillespies' gate. Astrid caught Spencer's eye and put a finger up to indicate she would deal with this household as well.

A distinctly feminine voice answered, "Yes?"

"Elinor, Astrid here."

"I'm sorry, there is no Elinor here," came the reply.

"Oh, yes, Sandra, this is Astrid. I'm helping someone search for a dog. She's an elderly Havanese. Would you please take a look around the property and see if perhaps she's found a way in?"

"Okay, I will. Bye," the voice said.

"So, there's just the Tudor next door, just the three houses on this road?" Spencer said.

"Yes, but I don't think anyone's home right now." A moment later, she added, "Don't worry. If no one is here, we can still enter the property to search for your little dog. I know how concerned you must be." She pressed the button for the intercom, but no one answered. "I thought perhaps Albin might be home—the tall woman you've met, that's her partner—but no, so . . ." She entered the code that Eve had previously shared with her, and the gate opened. Astrid, Spencer, and the security guard entered. "With the three of us, we should be able to search very quickly."

Spencer wasn't surprised that the security guard accompanied them. He was surprised that his ploy had worked so very well.

When the search again failed to reveal the presence of the animal, the three exited Eve's property, and Astrid secured the gate. Spencer considered the time and, after thanking Astrid and the security guard, ran back up the road and toward the van. When he again encountered Eve and Serge entering the cul-de-sac from the trail, he merely shook his head, thanked them for their help, and continued onward.

Although Kent, Albin, and O were in the Gillespie house, Elinor chose not to involve them in the search for the lost Havanese. As she walked the property as requested by Astrid, a thought increasingly niggled her. When she returned to the house, she immediately sought out Kent.

"Sir, something odd just occurred," she said and proceeded to describe the intercom conversation she'd had with Astrid. "It might be perfectly innocent, but I thought I should let you know. For some reason, it's bothering me."

Spencer drove over the speed limit on his way to the land registry office, hoping to arrive shortly after their opening. He was in a good mood, and though he would be a bit later than Langston might like, he was confident that his tardiness would be forgiven.

Spencer had just exited the Registry Office and was getting into his van when he made his call to Langston.

"Well?" Langston barked.

"L'Orté Island, all 101 hectares, is currently owned by Lucy Gillespie. Since coming into possession of it back in 2015, she's built a house on it. The house is winterized and self-contained, meaning there are no public utilities provided."

"Good, we're done—"

"Hold it Langston, there's something else you should know."

"What?" Langston curtly answered.

"The first house on the cul-de-sac, the Tudor, has a little bridge connecting that property to the Gillespie residence next door to it. It's hidden by trees, but it's there. And, I think that's where the old guy, Serge, is. I'd put money on it."

"So?"

"Do the names 'Sandra' or 'Elinor' mean anything to you?"

"The only name I'm interested in is 'Juliette.'"

"Fine, but there's something happening at the Gillespie residence; I can feel it."

"We're done here, Spence. I'll let you know if I have anything else for you."

Spencer had been prepared to offer his reasoning, but Langston made it clear that the job was done. That was just fine with Spencer. His concern was paying his bills, not enlightening his clients.

CHAPTER 38
QUADCOPTER AND CANDLES

"This has been a very interesting and enjoyable day for me, and I thank you, Kent," Serge said, in gracious acknowledgement of his Kent-guided tour of Niagara Falls. "The history of the construction of the Welland Canal is particularly interesting to me, though it is not the type of construction in which I was ever involved. The lives lost—that is the element with which I connect. The humanity at the root of this project—all such public works projects—should connect us all.

"The falls themselves are an especially powerful sight when viewed from below, in the boat.

"It is good that you advised me not to bring Merlot and Bijou. I don't think they would have enjoyed the tour of the power station as much as I did." He laughed.

"Now you're in for a bit of a long drive, Serge. I've got something to deliver to Lucy, and I need daylight." Kent turned south and followed the roads westward along the northern shore of Lake Erie until they arrived at Port L'Orté ninety minutes later.

Serge appeared bewildered. He watched as Kent readied a quadcopter drone and placed a package in the payload compartment. "You should hear the drone when it's nearby, Lucy,"

Kent informed her by phone. "I've got the controls set for autopilot, but when it gets to the island, I'll take over for the landing. I've attached a parcel for you containing two metal items and a letter of explanation. I think you'll find it interesting. It should arrive within ten minutes, depending upon the wind."

While Kent busied himself with the drone, Serge wandered off to examine the wares displayed for sale at the waterfront boutiques and managed to secure a quick purchase in the process. When he returned, Kent was again on the phone with Lucy.

"Got it? Great. Now make sure that the latch on the compartment is secure again and step out of the way. I'm not particularly skilled at this.

"Serge and I are at Doyle's in Port L'Orté, and we're going to grab some perch and chips—not exactly elegant Parisian cuisine but certainly tasty. Once we're done, we'll head home. I'll give you a call later tonight. Loves."

Kent returned the drone to its point of origin and then to the Escalade. When the task was complete, he and Serge selected a table on the patio of the rustic waterfront restaurant complex.

"I see you found something in one of the shops, Serge. Just let me know if there's anything specific you're looking for, and I'll take you to the best store I can find."

"I needed some candles, even such plain ones," Serge explained. "Our anniversary is very soon, and I always light candles for Jean-Pierre. These two will do very nicely. There is nothing else I need, but I thank you." He showed Kent two scented tealights.

"Blomma . . . Juliette . . . Helen," Lucy called out upon returning to the summer house. "I have something to share, if you're
interested." Curiosity brought them together as quickly as a call
to carrot cake might have, and the four women convened in
the great room. "Kent sent something by drone. It's a response
to our query about the boat wreck Blomma discovered. His
note reads:

> Archeologist at site for short time. Retrieved
> bottle, medallion, and wreck. Testing contents
> of bottle. Medallion enclosed. Testing contin-
> ues on wreck itself. Second of two items, key,
> found in wreck. They asked if we have info
> about it. I've signed for all items. They may
> want them returned, pending what's found in
> the wreck. Determination will be made when
> the evaluation is complete. I sense they'll release
> everything to us since not considered signifi-
> cant wreck, not likely part of any community's
> history other than L'Orté Island— that's us.
> Description follows:
>
> Item 1A—brass cable chain (24 in./61 cm)
> with a lobster clasp.
>
> Item 1B—brass medallion (2.5 cm diam-
> eter) bearing mass-produced imagery re: St.
> Christopher on the obverse, circa 1930, and
> the engraving CONNOR on the reverse.
>
> Item 2—brass barrel key, 7.6 cm length, given
> the decorative bow and relatively short shank,
> this may be a cabinet key, circa early 1900s.

"Here's the medallion and chain," Lucy said as she passed the items to Helen. "It's easy to read now that it's been cleaned. You were right about the engraving on the medallion, Aleksandra. Well spotted. . . . I wonder how all this fits into the story as we think we know it . . ."

"This key presents a new puzzle . . ." Lucy turned it over in her hand and tried to make out the details, something that might have meaning and require interpretation, but nothing came to mind. As she gave thought to the keyholes they had located at the manor house, she passed the key to Helen.

"I guess we'll need to look for some barrels, Lucy," Aleksandra suggested.

"Actually, a barrel key is just a style of key that's hollow and that hollow part, the barrel, fits over a pin inside the lock. No need to look for barrels," Helen informed her. "There's no identification of the type of decoration on the bow of the key?"

"No, there's no mention of that. Perhaps they couldn't make it out clearly, or they didn't think it was important enough to bother telling us. They call it a cabinet key, and it's certainly too big for the metal boxes we've found. Besides, I don't think the ones we've found have been that old. No, this is for a cupboard perhaps, or a piece of furniture, I guess."

"Fascinating," Juliette declared. "The date they've determined is certainly in keeping with the time during which there was considerable activity out here. Unfortunately, I'm not at all familiar with the contents of the manor house, so I can't help you. However, if you want us to search it with you, then count me in."

"I guess that's what we should do, just so that task is done and can be reported to the archeologist. Perhaps by the time we've completed a search, they'll have more information on the rest of the contents," Lucy said.

"May I please see that key again? I'd like to get a better look at the decoration on the bow. Let's see if I can make it out." Juliette took several photos, varying the lighting in each, then began to manipulate them by using an app she had downloaded.

"Eventually I'll put the medallion and chain into a museum case here so they can be displayed," Lucy said. "But I'll hold off doing that until after they've completed their assessment of the wreck, just in case there are more discoveries.

"You're all invited to join me. If you like, we can get started on a search of the manor house shortly after breakfast tomorrow, okay?" There was general agreement among them. Lucy packed up the various items and returned to her rooms to have a private conversation with Kent.

CHAPTER 39
THE SAFETY OF *CROESUS*

France . . .

The clouds thinned, and the late morning sky welcomed the sun, while an unspeakable blueness spread out beneath them. Grisha stared out over the scene, as if searching for an inspired solution amid the waves below. The flight attendant brought him another double espresso and placed it on the table before him with a selection of Russian pastries. No words were exchanged; Grisha may have nodded.

"So, in your expert opinion, O, what is the likelihood of these people ceasing this vendetta, or whatever it is, if I give them the forty million euros they have asked for?"

"I have no way of knowing. But it is clear that it will continue, and people will die—perhaps members of your own family—if you do not pay this. We know that the people at the head of this group are from South America, not Europe. That is why it has been so difficult for us to track them. If they were European, it is likely that it would have been quite different. But because of that, because they are not here, they may be content to receive this money. With Alexei now gone, they have no one in your family to continue this activity on their behalf, and may decide to return to their more familiar activities—those which would not involve you."

"Forty-million euros, O! And for what? This stuff they stick up the nose. It is crazy! What could Alexei have been thinking? Had he only been willing to learn the business as Maxim and Ilya have done, as some of their children have done and are doing, his income and his life would both have been much greater. Forty-million euros for nothing, O!"

"That is the value they have placed on it, and my research has indicated that it is a fair market value for the product, though it likely represents more than double their actual loss at that stage. I am told that Alexei lost control of a tonne of cocaine. I don't know how he expected to distribute that amount, and I don't think he gave any thought to securing it."

"And he sinks my submarine for this. If only he had separated the submarine from the cargo he had attached. If only he had come to me about this matter, we might have salvaged the submarine and returned the product, somehow. At least he was able to escape but only to delay his death. I'll never understand this."

"It was likely a harrowing experience for him, and he did well to escape. That would have been his concern above all else, I am sure."

"The police didn't know of him then. They wouldn't have suspected such a thing from a son of Grigori Orlov. He doesn't think to speak with the South Americans or with me in order to resolve the problem."

"I think he was justifiably afraid of the consequences. It was as if he thought it might go away if he just ignored it and treated it as a bad dream. But the South Americans wanted their money, and they followed him, probably just wanting to talk to him about resolving their mutual problem."

"And they ran my boy off the road, and now he has no life. I have lost my dear Alexei. They don't have their money, and the authorities have salvaged my submarine and confiscated the product. Alexei sullied my family name, and I am filled both with anger and a profound sadness. Agafya is losing her life to grief, and Aleksandra's life is threatened. This must end!"

"We are looking into someone by the name of Rojas. Our intel reveals that he is a lieutenant in one of the cartels, *El Viruñas,* and the one we need to negotiate through. We don't know how much power he has to make decisions—"

"There's a lot you don't know, O. Too much. It's time already that changed. Show some initiative. This girl they have taken is not my concern. Aleksandra is my only concern. We have committed significant funds to the University of Toronto for development and support of their Russian Studies Program. As a result, they agreed to provide accommodation so that my *zayka* may adjust her schedule as becomes necessary and is able to write her examinations at another time. And Maxim has taken other steps to keep Aleksandra safe."

O wondered what steps Maxim had initiated and if those steps might hinder their own in protecting Aleksandra. He was aware of the security guards housed in a trailer at the cul-de-sac. *What else might there be?*

At Côte d'Azur Airport in Nice, Grisha exited his private jet and walked across the tarmac to his waiting helicopter. Agafya claimed she needed him, and Maxim could handle the situation in Toronto. In a short time they would be landing on the deck of the *Croesus,* the vessel he had increasingly considered his home over the past several years.

As the helicopter gained altitude, the *Croesus* immediately came into view and might have been mistaken by others for a cruise ship. The vessel's eight decks and 230-metre length—nearly a quarter of a kilometre—guaranteed that it featured prominently on the water outside Port Vauban in nearby Antibes. The bright Mediterranean sun reflected off its polished surfaces. As had become the custom, the Sikorsky circled the *Croesus* before finally landing on one of its two helipads.

Agafya and several senior members of the crew of one hundred greeted him upon his arrival. If the paparazzi were viewing the scene, as they often did, they would have suspected that perhaps a significant government leader was arriving. They wouldn't be able to obtain a photograph of the event; security measures had been installed years ago to prevent that. Their photographs would always result in the *Croesus* appearing overexposed, merely a flare in the photo.

Grisha Orlov felt very secure here. It wasn't merely the missile-defence system of the *Croesus* that provided a sense of security, nor was it his bullet-proof suite. No, he actually didn't know why he felt secure here, but then he'd never asked himself that question. He dismissed O, despite protestations from the bodyguard, and shared a few words in private with his wife.

"The chef has prepared a celebration feast for you," Agafya explained. "We'll be eating early, so I suggest you do not take snacks before then."

His eyes narrowed as he teased her. "Not even a morsel of Almas? A bit of Beluga?" He cocked his head and pouted.

Agafya closed her eyes and shook her head. She had been married to him for over fifty years already. He was incorrigible and self-indulgent, and she loved him.

He gently touched her cheek. "I look forward to it," he replied. "Do not tell me what he has prepared; I want a surprise today."

"Yes, this business with Aleksandra has been difficult for you, for us. First Alexei, now Aleksandra—when will it end?"

Agafya said, once again shaking her head, her eyes closed to keep out the unwelcome world.

Grisha gently kissed his wife on the forehead. "We shall discuss this later. Now, I wish to take a walk."

It had become Grisha's custom to walk all the decks of the *Croesus* whenever he returned from one of his longer trips. He made his way to the nearest elevator and selected the uppermost level. Breathing in the fresh Mediterranean air, he considered the vast expanse of water and then focused on the port and the largest of the smaller vessels in their births. Specifically, he considered the *Theia*.

The *Theia* was half the length of the *Croesus* and sported only seven decks, but his friend Mark had loved that vessel. Or was it that Mark had loved his wife, Theia, after whom the vessel had been named? The *Theia* had been put up for sale shortly after Mark's death and was currently available for rent, lease or hire. It was nearly time for a complete refit of the *Croesus*, and Grisha considered the possibility of temporarily acquiring the *Theia* in order to bridge the time during which the *Croesus* would be unavailable to him. This was a common thing to do under such circumstances but presented its own problems. Mark hadn't been interested in acquiring all the newest features, and Grisha's family members would be disappointed in such a comparatively spartan vessel for an entire season.

Some of his friends maintained two vessels for that purpose. The secondary vessel would be maintained in a manner similar to the primary vessel and be available for rent or lease unless required by the owner, as in the event of the refit of the primary vessel. He considered purchasing the *Theia* to serve that purpose; once refitted, it could become the *Agafya*. He had intended to pursue that idea, but world events post 2020 were largely out of his control, so he had postponed the decision. Then again, choosing not to act is also a decision.

As it was approaching mealtime, an attendant arrived and presented Grisha with his usual aperitif: vodka, served frigid and neat, with an accompaniment of caviar. In this case, it was Almas. The serving tray also held blini and dark bread with butter, chopped onion, pickled tomatoes, quail eggs, sour cream, and tiny boiled potatoes flavoured with dill. Grisha made his selection, downed two shots of vodka, and continued his stroll. The attendant followed at a distance, just in case he might desire more.

Grisha stood still awhile and imagined Lucy's painting hanging in the *Croesus*. The wall on which it would hang was presently quite devoid of ornamentation, as if it were awaiting the installation of Lucy's work. He had merely outlined to her that he wanted it to honour his family, the Orlovs—past, present, and future. He and Agafya had often discussed this, and it was, after all, a gift to her as much as to himself.

Lucy had described her interpretation of it to him, and he thought it sounded wonderful. He especially liked the use of the triptych and the metallic gold. It was so very Russian. He had demanded that she send photos showing her progress, but she had failed to do so. This had not angered him, which surprised him. This Rufina had a strength he found most appealing. Aleksandra was in good hands.

Grisha's walk continued past the guest infirmary, and he thought he might drop in and ask the doctor to examine his shoulder. It was becoming a nuisance. The pain wasn't great, just annoying, and occurring only periodically. There would be no more golf or tennis. But the doctor didn't appear to be present, so he decided to continue his walk about the *Croesus* and have the doctor visit him in his stateroom later in the day, after the feast that Agafya and the chef had planned.

As he reached the beach club level, Grisha's heart fell upon seeing the empty storage spaces. Alexei's motorcycle was gone, and now miscellaneous items filled the storage cage which had once housed Alexei's most prized possession. As well, there was the space where once the submarine, now lying at the bottom of the Mediterranean, had been dry-docked.

Grisha considered returning to his stateroom and taking a quick shower; he was sweating and that disgusted him. But first, he would complete his walk and his survey of the *Croesus*. He ventured out onto the fan tail of the beach itself, essentially an expanse of deck at water level, one that could be made larger by the fanning out of the deck surface. A feeling of nausea suddenly swept over him, and though dizzy, he hurried to the water's edge in anticipation of vomiting. He wondered if there had been something wrong with . . . *surely not the caviar* . . . He found it difficult to catch his breath and, deep in a panic, grabbed for his tie, loosening it and stretching his neck in an effort to get air. But it was denied him. At the same time, he was cold—cold and damp from sweating. Horrified, he felt as if an invisible force were sitting on his chest; it felt heavy, it burned, it pinched . . . and then it was over. His body toppled into the Mediterranean.

The attendant watched the attack unfold, but it happened so quickly, there was no assistance she could have offered him. She dashed to a security panel and depressed the emergency button, summoning O and the doctor, and alerting the captain to a crisis situation. Panic-stricken, she tried in vain to reach Grisha. Ultimately she could only stand and watch as his body was taken up by the current and away from the *Croesus*.

When the crew's rescue team arrived, they quickly retrieved Grisha's body. His face was contorted in pain, and he looked surprised. He had been unable to utter any words during the event, so there was no final message to disclose, no profoundly insightful declaration to reveal. There was nothing to share.

CHAPTER 40
YA ZDES

Southern Ontario . . .

Having heard nothing in response to her idea about paying the ransom for Maddie, combined with not hearing as regularly from her uncle Maxim as she previously had been hearing from Grisha, Aleksandra ultimately took the initiative and arranged a three-way call among the key players, including O. Focusing on doing what she could to save Maddie helped her deal with the death of her dear grandfather.

The last to join the call was Maxim. "*Ya zdes*'," he said in greeting, offering merely an "I am here"—something that was quite obvious to Aleksandra. He looked haggard; she didn't care. Her *dedushka* was *dead*.

"I won't keep you long, Uncle Maxim. I know you must be extremely busy with very many matters now. I understand that the ransom amount—whether for me, or for Maddie—has been set at forty million euros. Why has this not been officially agreed to by you and payment made already?"

"Your grandfather did not agree to pay this ransom for your friend. He had been generous with you and spent several million dollars to have your examinations rearranged for your convenience, and on his behalf, I contracted a specialized squad of security experts to bolster your safety, rather than merely to rely upon this Gillespie couple and their friends. He did these things for you but was not willing to do this for your friend."

"My friend is where these people want me to be—in captivity. Better that payment is made for her life, rather than waiting until they eventually take me. I cannot live isolated on a small island forever. Besides, they will be waiting when I leave."

Aleksandra breathed deeply and dove headfirst into the argument. "But why am I explaining this yet again? I already had this same conversation with *Dedushka*, and he ultimately agreed with my reasoning, and said he was prepared to pay the forty million euros ransom for Maddie. He even told me he would think about taking it from my future inheritance, which he knew did not matter to me. He says this, yet there is no action!"

"I am unaware of any such decision on his part, Aleksandra."

"It is true, Maxim; before he began his walk of the *Croesus*, Grisha did indeed tell me that he would pay this ransom and to discover the details of how payment would be made. He said he would contact you once he had completed his walk. But, of course, that became impossible since he took his heart attack shortly after. With the turmoil in the aftermath of his death, I had forgotten the timing of his call to inform you, remembering only that the ransom was to be paid. This detail is my failing; I am sorry."

Aleksandra's heart fluttered with excitement. Her palms began to perspire. She held her breath in anticipation.

"He agreed to pay forty million euros in ransom? I would have expected him to demand to negotiate the amount down considerably." Maxim seemed unconvinced. "We had decided that the forty million was far too high."

"He said he would take it out of my future inheritance. I think he was joking, but perhaps not. Either way—it does not matter to me," Aleksandra repeated.

"I believe it is right to execute my father's final wishes, and O has corroborated this decision, so I'll have someone take care of that immediately. O, you can contact the police in Toronto to give them this news.

"I'll come to a decision later whether to announce this as an example of my father's generosity; perhaps it can be done at the same time as the university announcement. Neither of you will be involved in that anyway.

"This is inexcusable on your part, O; we'll be re-evaluating your position here, of course." With that, Maxim said, "*Do svidaniya*" to Aleksandra and left the conversation.

There was silence awhile during which O smiled at Aleksandra. "Grisha told me to show some initiative," he said. "I'll let Oko know what has been said here, and I'll inform Detective Inspector Brennan as well. Aleksandra, I sincerely hope we can contact the kidnappers in time to save your friend."

"Do you really think she's still alive—and unharmed?"

"Of course, I don't know. Realistically, it must be recognized that this cartel is, ultimately, a ruthless organization. However, no matter their funding, they must also know that forty million euros represents a significant win on their part, and pushed further, the Orlovs would declare war rather than be subjugated by them, without any possibility for resolution. This is very much to their advantage, and the only way it works is if they have Maddie in good health as evidence of their adherence to the agreement. Your father was not some cheap drug mule. I think they will be pragmatic."

CHAPTER 41
SOCIAL CLIMBER

Matteo Gallo hadn't climbed a tree since he was a child, and never before had he done so at night. Yet here he was, a full-grown adult scaling an old sugar maple growing in the publicly-owned verge at the corner of a gated, private property. He struggled to find toe-holds on the lower portion of the trunk, and more than once he considered abandoning his mission. When he reached the lowest of the large branches, he managed to swing himself up then move to the other side of the trunk where an even higher branch extended over the property that was his target. He hadn't really given his descent any thought, and now he was reminded that he was primarily a desk jockey and unsuited to skulking around as he was. The ground seemed even further down than it should have been.

He considered himself most fortunate to have discovered a collection of youngish spreading yews planted in a tight cluster inside that same corner. He hoped they would act like a spring and cushion the impact. He breathed in deeply and jumped—admittedly, a bit concerned that whoever had recently planted the young shrubs might not have removed all their tools from the site. The fall knocked the air out of him, but other than that, his mature frame remained intact. Given the absence of witnesses to the feat, so did his dignity.

Keeping low to the ground and close to the inside of the fence, he continued along the frontage of the large, landscaped property, trying to avoid the guide wires securing some recent plantings of other tree species, thereby ensuring their vertical growth to be perpendicular to the ground. He'd only been tripped once, though tripping wasn't as much a concern as decapitation. He changed his tactics and crept along at a slower pace. Eventually, he found himself at the edge of the driveway and used it as a guide to turn inward, deeper into the property. He remembered that what he sought was located just opposite the house, so he decided to use the structure as his next guidepost.

Just as he was getting ready to turn right, toward the neighbour's property, a side door to the house was opened by an unseen hand, and he heard conversation, though he couldn't make out what was being said. Matteo held himself frozen in position and waited for the door to be closed once again. There was more conversation, and just as the door appeared to be closing, a golden retriever exited the house and the door closed behind it. The dog wandered about near the house and seemed pre-occupied with sniffing—sniffing and, eventually, peeing.

Through the trees that surrounded him, Matteo thought he could make out the form of the wooden bridge, which spanned the property line. While the dog was distracted, Matteo moved rapidly toward the bridge, crossing into the neighbour's property—and was quickly followed by the golden retriever.

The evening workout session in the Gillespies' gym had just recently concluded. While Eve returned home to keep company with Serge and tend to Cookie, Albin remained behind with Kent and O. Elinor had joined them during the session; however, she was not naturally inclined to favour such exercise, so she had departed once the moves exceeded her slight capability, saying she had things to tend to.

"I suspect I underestimated Eve's ability, Albin. She would be quite capable of putting most anyone out of commission," O admitted, taking a mouthful of water fortified with electrolytes to aid recovery. "She strikes me as someone who could really put her heart into executing an effective defence."

Albin began to respond when his eyes suddenly detected movement within the scene presented on the security display on the LED wall. His attention was immediately drawn to an individual dressed in what appeared to be a camouflage tactical uniform. He was uncertain what gear the individual might possess; nothing was readily visible.

"We've got company," Albin said, then he grabbed something from a storage cabinet drawer before entering the tunnel to the swim spa in the backyard.

O seized his equipment and followed to join Albin in the pool house.

"You forgot communications, Albin," O said, shaking his head and handing a wireless microphone headset to Albin. "Kent will let us know what the cameras are picking up." O positioned his night-vision goggles, and they silently exited the pool house and began to approach the area in which the man had appeared onscreen.

"I don't think you're going to have a problem," Kent informed them. "Cookie is trying to play with the guy, and he keeps tripping. They appear to be by the old oak."

"Weapons?" Albin asked.

"No, nothing visible. He's not even being rough with Cookie."

"I'll get him," Albin said, before running across the lawn, toward the old oak. Upon his arrival, Cookie left the intruder and ran toward Albin while he quickly utilized his weapon of choice. The weighted net thrown by Albin effectively entangled the intruder, especially when Albin pulled the tether line, tightening the perimeter of the netting. The intruder flailed, tripped, and dropped to the ground. He groaned, but it was an expression of exhaustion and frustration and, finally, acquiescence.

O removed his goggles, and Kent turned on the outdoor lighting, illuminating the entire area. A quick scan of the area confirmed there was no other intruder present. While Albin took Cookie back home across the bridge, O secured the intruder and threw a hood over his head before taking him into an empty basement room and removing the hood. Kent released Elinor from the panic room to which he had sent her, then he returned to O and the intruder, entering the room behind his unwelcome guest.

"Right then," Kent said as he approached the intruder, "Who the hell are you?"

"Get these handcuffs off me first," the intruder demanded, turning to look at Kent then reversing his position to display his hands, cuffed behind him.

O unlocked a hand and brought it to the front, securing it once again.

"Come on-n-n," the man implored them.

"Hold it," Kent said. "I know you from somewhere." And then it came to him. "You're the Interpol agent who was following my wife and me in Antibes. I remember your body language as you sulked by the side of the road the last time O handcuffed you. What are you doing here?" As he posed his question, Kent removed the handcuffs, and O merely stood by, watching and listening.

"Yeah, Matteo Gallo."

"Long time, Agent Gallo."

"Not long enough," mumbled Matteo.

"So, what brings you all the way from France and into my backyard?"

"I work for Maxim."

Kent and O exchanged glances, clearly surprised by this information.

"In what capacity?" O inquired.

"I left Interpol not long after a matter concerning Mr. and Mrs. Gillespie concluded in Antibes some years ago, and I started my own security firm, Horus Security. Maxim Orlov contracted with us to provide security here. It's my men who are in the trailer around the cul-de-sac.

"You know," Matteo said, directing his comment to Kent, "I just realized that this fellow you call O, he doesn't recognize me, not even after you did, even though he's the one who supposedly cuffed me in Antibes. Not my best moment, I must admit. I guess what I've heard isn't just a story after all. There really *are* two of you."

"You would have encountered Oko. I am Ebo Owusu, and I am as yet uncertain if it is good to meet you, Matteo Gallo. I worked for Grigori Orlov until his passing. I guess I as well now work for Maxim, but I've never heard of you. What precisely *is* your assignment?"

"Under normal circumstances, I would have introduced myself and the entire team since we're all the same side in this matter; however, Maxim was most emphatic. He directed me not to engage with you, except in our professional capacity in maintaining security of the public area. It's simple—if we recognize you as someone who belongs here, then we don't engage with you. He actually purchased the property that serves as the location for our trailer, and as you've probably surmised, that's where we live and have our gear stored. I don't think he was happy with a bunch of amateurs providing security for his niece. Those were his words, not mine."

"A bunch of amateurs?" O repeated the phrase in disbelief. He wondered what skills Maxim might claim to possess and how he had come to this assessment concerning the capability of the Gillespies' friends, let alone his own. He wasn't insulted, and he was already planning a workaround for the Maxim problem.

Matteo watched as Kent and O had a brief, private conversation in a corner of the room.

"Is it your practice to accompany your men on such jobs? One can see that fieldwork of this type is not really your forte, Matteo," Kent commented.

Matteo sighed in agreement. "No, it's not, and yes, you're right. Might we perhaps sit somewhere more comfortable? This chair isn't conducive to a friendly conversation."

Rather than invite Matteo upstairs and into his more private space, Kent ushered the former Interpol agent into another basement room. It was the one O, Albin, Kent, and Helen had been using to discuss strategy and bits of intelligence they'd collected. They had a few white boards with dry erase markers and four comfortable chairs arranged about a round table. In a corner sat some tech: computer, printer, rechargers . . .

"Tea? Coffee? Water?" Kent asked.

As Albin entered the room, he directed a comment toward Kent. "I'm calling the Public Works Department in the morning. I want an arborist out here to remove the two lowest branches from that big maple on the verge. I told them last year but got nowhere with them. They just warned *me* not to cut a tree on city property." Albin was visibly annoyed by the ease with which Eve's security, and consequently the Gillespies', had been breached.

While Kent grabbed a beverage for himself and Matteo, O brought Albin up to speed on the situation. In short order they were ready to continue the discussion.

"All righty, now that we're all here, please explain your presence in my backyard."

"It's a long story, so please don't jump on me until you've heard everything, okay?"

"Agreed, for now."

"My nephew, Carmine, was the young and impressionable son of my brother and his wife, Gina. Carmine lost his life in the eruption of Etna on July 19, 2019. Gina wondered if perhaps you were somehow responsible for his demise."

Kent began to rise from his chair, shaking his head and muttering.

"Sit, please, and keep to what you agreed," Matteo reminded him. Kent sat but continued to be visibly agitated.

"Carmine worked at the border crossing into Menton, France, and was present when you and your wife passed through during your brief trip to Latte. I believe you were looking for your wife's Italian relatives. Anyway, it appears that my nephew is the individual who alerted Vincenzo Rizzo to your presence."

Upon hearing that name, Kent drew himself up in his chair.

"I see you recognize the name of the man who tried to kill you on the *Sentier Corbusier*. Gina is a sister of the late Vincenzo Rizzo, and Carmine was his favourite nephew.

"After the death of Vincenzo, Carmine had expected to inherit his uncle's restaurant in Naples, but Vincenzo's criminal activity came to light and the authorities seized his assets. Carmine was frustrated by this turn of events, and thus set out on his ill-fated trip to visit Etna 'to gain strength from the volcano,' or so I am told. Somewhere there must be a logic in that, but it escapes me; I myself am no longer an impressionable and foolish young man."

"This makes no sense whatsoever, Matteo. I don't know these people—any of them. Have you information about why Rizzo came after me? At the time, you and the other agent mentioned something about Julius Roman, though you called him Guilio Roman. Actually, I don't know why he wanted to kill me either, except perhaps so he could have access to Lucy. She was a relative of his as a result of some rather twisted and complicated genealogical accidents. The guy was clearly unhinged, so it hurts my brain, trying to make sense of his actions."

"I asked Gina what she remembers her brother and son discussing, something she may have overheard that was not intended for her ears. Remember, we already knew that this Julius Roman was the criminal partner of Vincenzo Rizzo. All that Gina remembered, or admitted to hearing, was that Guilio Roman hated you and blamed you for all that was wrong in his life—and apparently there was much that was wrong, so you were hated very much. When he died, Vincenzo and another criminal, Fortunato Russo, hatched a plan to take revenge upon you in Toronto. Roman had them all fired up, blaming you for all that was wrong in his life. When he died, they decided it was somehow your fault.

"We know the attempt on your life didn't go as they intended; they mistakenly killed your friend, and Russo died shortly after in a traffic accident in Toronto. Vincenzo probably blamed you for his death too. It seems that Vincenzo escaped injury and made his way back to Italy in time to share some version of this story with young Carmine and restart this revenge scenario upon you."

"All that may very well be the case, Matteo, but it still doesn't explain what the hell you were doing in my backyard."

"I promised Gina that I would investigate further. I've been trying, unsuccessfully, to get a sense of you and perhaps question you. However, my heart has not been in it. You have not been available for me to bump into for a casual conversation and to request an interview wouldn't have provided me with the information I wanted. Moreover, that would have been in direct contravention of Maxim Orlov's contract with Horus."

"You wanted to get a sense of the person, not merely answers to questions—am I right?" said O, interrupting.

"Yes. I have already confirmed that you, Kent, were aboard the *Theia* when Carmine met his demise, but I too am curious why you have been singled out by these people.

"So tonight I came up with this not-so-intelligent idea to be what you call a Peeping Tommaso, and here we are."

"You've said this is a favour to your sister-in-law, but how did you become attached to this detail?" asked Albin. "I understand you were an agent with Interpol when Kent first met you in France."

"I left Interpol under a bit of a cloud when it became known that my sister-in-law was the sister of a rather infamous criminal, a syndicate enforcer. I had not disclosed this because I did not know this at the time. It was a large family with many distractions, and Vincenzo was quite simply never mentioned with any significance. However, that was what brought about my move to the private sector. My firm has been quite successful, and we have operatives worldwide. They are highly skilled, and I am an effective administrator. When, by chance, this opportunity here in Toronto presented itself, I paid special attention and noticed your name in the notes concerning the file. That is when I decided to combine the Orlov case with my personal one, the favour for Gina. And that is why we are here, like this, at this time.

"And I would just like to say one final thing, Mr. Gillespie: I sincerely apologize for the aspersions cast upon your character throughout these matters."

Kent nodded his head in solemn acknowledgement of Matteo's heartfelt apology. "What has happened with the second Interpol agent we met back then?" he asked.

"That would have been Luc Anouilh. He comes from a fine family, a very long line of people in service of the French state, all in the area of law enforcement and judicial matters. He was promoted at about the same time as I was asked to resign, and he is now the section head dealing with Interpol cases originating in eastern France, including Paris.

"Don't feel embarrassed for me, please. It was upsetting to my pride initially, but I have learned that I am very good at the business side of this sort of venture and not the political gamesmanship necessary to advance within the organization itself. The traits necessary for that sort of success elude me; I just don't have it."

"Ah, packages."

"Pardon?" Matteo queried.

"No, sorry, nothing . . . just something my father used to say."

Having brought this matter to its logical conclusion, they returned to considering the situation regarding Aleksandra. O took a marker in hand and began to outline the situation on a white board.

"How about we go through everything on this again and try to get on the same page?" The question O asked was rhetorical, but everyone answered anyway, nodding their head in agreement.

"Not that there's much of the story sourced directly from the Orlovs, but we've managed to put some meat on the bones of the story Grisha threw our way.

"We know for a fact that Alexei Orlov assumed possession of a tonne of pure cocaine from *El Viruñas*, a South American drug cartel. Alexei's attempt to secure the load failed, and both the submarine and its payload were lost in the Mediterranean. Alexei escaped, only to die in a traffic accident trying to elude cartel soldiers.

"*El Viruñas* still expects to get paid—not merely compensated for their loss, but an additional amount you might consider punitive damages. Although we have discovered that the total amount is forty million euros, it has been argued that they might be content with ten million. Then again, to offer the lower amount may anger them, and they may demand fifty.

"In an attempt to pressure Grigori Orlov, they threatened to kidnap his granddaughter, Aleksandra. As a result, we now have the death of one male and the kidnapping of the female known as Maddie Birch.

"Kent, Matteo—independently, until now, you have been charged with keeping Aleksandra safe. Clearly, you have so far succeeded.

"Moving Aleksandra to your island was an excellent decision, Kent. Maxim suggested we follow and provide security there, but I managed to convince him that there was greater benefit in supporting the fiction that she was yet here, at your home," Matteo explained. "Sorry for interrupting, Ebo."

"Please, call me O, Matteo.

"My brother and I have tried to gather information on the representative of the cartel who may be the party with whom we should be discussing this payment. This person seems to be a cartel lieutenant by the name of Rojas. Detective Inspector Brennan is working on the kidnapping of Maddie Birch, and he has been provided with information concerning Rojas."

"Excuse me, O, how on earth did you make contact even to discover the amount of the ransom? Brennan wasn't able to make contact and is still hoping to be able to use Maddie and Sandra's phones to establish contact for the drop location," Kent asked.

"We had contact through the police dealing with the original sinking and the cocaine they recovered at the site. They determined the source of the drug and already had information—and very likely informants as well—concerning this group.

"Unfortunately, until we again make contact, we cannot pay a ransom. It is possible that they do not yet realize that the ransom will be paid for Maddie Birch and it is not necessary for them to kidnap Aleksandra in order to get their money. They have not provided instructions regarding the payment.

"While I don't know if Maddie Birch remains alive, we have been instructed that it is not our concern. It is Brennan's concern, and his investigation appears to be going nowhere. Contact was attempted by having Aleksandra leave a message on Maddie's phone, but there has been no reply. She's either dead, or they haven't checked for new messages, or can't for some reason.

"The Orlovs initially did not want to pay a ransom, citing that it sets a bad precedent, and they have a point there. But, as I see it, the only way out of this is to satisfy the cartel, to give them whatever they ask. I think that if they are low-balled, this type of vendetta will continue, and Aleksandra or other family members will continue to live under threat. Things may even escalate and there could be more deaths if Rojas and his associates become angrier. These people are known for being remarkably violent, and the restraint they have shown thus far may weaken. In their opinion, the Orlovs owe this money in exchange for the cocaine—it's simply business. I must say that I agree with their logic.

"Anyone have any additional information? Insight? Questions?" O asked, looking at the three seated at the table.

"Just an observation," Matteo began, "but the range in the ransom amount may be the difference between the actual cost to the cartel up to the point that the drug came into Alexei's possession and its street value, which is the high end that is more punitive. Regarding contact with them: I'll contact one of the few friends I have left back in Lyon and see if they can put word out to someone who may be able to get a message to them that they should look at Maddie's phone, or attempt to contact the Orlovs through some other channel. What might that be?"

"Grisha is gone," O said, thinking aloud. "Maxim is his father's successor, but perhaps Agafya, Grisha's wife and Maxim's mother, would be best. I can arrange for an account in her name, and they can deal through her. She has my contact information. Although she'll likely turn to Maxim for advice, I think she's our best bet. An attempt at direct contact with Maxim could get lost in all his business correspondence and the layers surrounding him. I'll do that after we're finished here and provide you with the information, Matteo—and share it with the rest of you as well, of course. No more secrets.

"Shall I let Brennan know about the situation with the ransom?" Kent asked.

"I think that would be a good idea, Kent," O replied.

"A thought occurs to me, O. If Brennan does by some chance manage to apprehend Maddie's kidnappers, do you think that will cause the threat against Aleksandra and the Orlovs to be revived?" Kent asked.

"I think that if they get their money, this will end. It is a lesson they are giving anyone who may, like Alexei, try to take drugs without paying, no matter that the shipment is lost. So, if Brennan doesn't interfere with the payment, everyone should be okay. Aleksandra would be safe, and Maddie is Brennan's responsibility," O replied.

"I've a thought: What if the ransom is traced and steps are taken by the authorities to retrieve it? It's a large amount, and they might be motivated to go after it, especially if it might lead to those behind the kidnappings, those in superior positions to Rojas," Albin said.

"Good point. I'll work that into my conversation with Brennan," Kent said. "We certainly don't want that to happen. Let them have their money.

"And there's something else bothering me about this, O. Had you and Oko discussed the presence of the cherry picker and the linesmen that showed up in front of the house since this started, but before Matteo and his crew arrived?"

"Thanks for the reminder, Kent. That wasn't your crew, was it, Matteo?" O inquired.

"No, and this is the first I'm hearing about it."

"In both cases, they were gone before we could challenge them, and in both cases, the Public Works Department for the municipality, as well as specific utilities, disavowed all knowledge of any such personnel scheduled to work in this area. We don't know what they were really doing, and we don't know who authorized them to be here. If we're the good guys in this, then I can only conclude they are, or were sent by, the bad guys. But to what end?" Albin asked.

"Maxim might have attempted to do something on his own prior to contracting Matteo," O suggested. "He's well-meaning, but he fiddles around, and things tend to get messed up when he does. Case in point: directing Matteo to consider

Horus' work here as a separate operation, instead of part of an overall protection scheme. Now that Grisha is gone, I presume I'm somewhat more out of the loop."

"Speaking of which, I know that Aleksandra has been told that Grisha has died, but it's not otherwise generally known. Why the silence, O?" asked Kent.

"It may be because any such upheaval may further complicate this matter with *El Viruñas*. Or it may be something more to do with the tangle of business interests the Orlovs have. I don't know. While it seems very odd to me too, it does provide some degree of consistency in which we can now operate."

"Well, it's good that Grigori Orlov okayed payment of the ransom before he died. At least that's available," Matteo declared.

O merely smiled.

CHAPTER 42
LIZARD BRAIN

"Rashid, have you been able to narrow down the search area at all?" Brennan asked.

"Somewhat. We've been scouring every bit of video collected that showed the victim, Maddie Birch, being forced into a black Jeep Grand Wagoneer with darkly tinted windows. There wasn't much, just a few security cameras in the area and fewer people. On a hunch, I had the team go over everything we have regarding the previous victim, Charles Ponzi, a.k.a. Smith, as well. They haven't found anything yet, but they haven't gone over all of what we now have available.

"We've now got a licence number for the Jeep SUV that picked up the second victim, Birch: FRF8538."

"Stolen vehicle or just a stolen plate?" Brennan asked.

"Not really. And this is where it gets weird. We visited the owner of the licence plate. He lives up north of here, just south of Muskoka, in a little town called Gkinaa."

"Never heard of it," Brennan commented.

"Neither had I. Seems the area is becoming a summer destination. There's a small lake, Gkide,, and with lots of the more popular lake sites in the area already developed, this community's become popular with tourists as well, so there's always strangers about."

"I hear ya; go on."

"Well, the owner of the licence plate, Bernie Concha, does have a black Jeep Grand Wagoneer with darkly tinted windows and it was sitting in his driveway, bearing the licence plate we matched. We were getting ready to impound the vehicle for forensics, but the owner had clear evidence that he and his vehicle were at Lake Gkide at the same time as Maddie Birch was being kidnapped in Toronto. He's in real estate and was hosting some picnic at the lake that day, just a casual thing for his staff—a small group of people, but all witnesses to the presence of his vehicle. The licence plate used in Toronto must have been modified somehow."

"You have photos of the two Jeep SUVs? I'd like to see the shot of the back-end."

Rashid sorted through the file and provided Brennan with two photos.

"And what about the vehicle at the lake?" Brennan asked.

"You've got a photo of each of the two vehicles," Rashid pointed out.

"Yes, but not at the same time, not even close. Tell me you have one of the vehicle at the lake, while it was actually *at* the lake."

With a blank expression on his face, Rashid looked at Brennan. "I'll get back to the witnesses. Hopefully, they've not erased photos, and perhaps they've even put more online. I'll find one and get back to you."

"You do that, Rashid, you do that." Brennan sighed as he reached for his coffee. It proved to be cold. He sighed yet again.

"It didn't take long once the right people got the message," Matteo crowed, pleased that his old Interpol connections had paid off. He was in the war room, as they had begun to call the Gillespies' basement room with the big round table, and with him were O, Albin, and Kent.

"Yes, I spoke with the detective inspector to confirm that the ransom would be paid, and shortly after that, he got back to me with news that the instructions had been sent to Sandra's phone, from Maddie's. It was Maddie's voice, and he says it sounded like she was reading a script," O explained.

"Other than that, how did she sound?" Kent asked.

"He didn't really comment on that, so I guess she's not falling apart or sounding unusually stressed or drugged, which is what particularly concerned me."

"Must be a strong young woman," interjected Albin. "I can't for the life of me figure out how either of them—Sandra or Maddie—could have anything much to do with this Smith character. I just don't get it."

"I have several nieces about their age, and it's not that uncommon, Albin. I don't know why either, but then again, I don't understand their taste in music or fashion either," Matteo explained. "It must be very difficult for parents, waiting for their daughters to grow beyond that stage, hoping they avoid coming to some harm."

"Come to think of it, I guess I saw something similar in our youngest military recruits as well; it just wasn't so blatant. Or perhaps I just saw things differently back then."

"So, where's the drop?" Kent asked, making air quotes with his fingers.

"There's no 'drop.' There are four transfers, so ten million euros each. Each of the four is to a different account, so I suspect each follows a different electronic route. When they gain control of the funds, Maddie's release location will be revealed," O explained.

"I understand there being no cash drop for such a large amount, but I rather expected cryptocurrency to be some part of this. Shows how little I know," Kent commented. "Where do you think the transfers will go?"

"Well, if I were transferring the funds like that, I'd consider Armenia, Guatemala, Macedonia, Paraguay, and the Philippines. No, scratch that, the Philippines report to the Americans under FATCA, and I don't think *El Viruñas* will want to chance it, especially with the Philippines' version of a war on drugs. They might find it easiest to deal with the Spanish-speaking countries in South America and narrow the field to Guatemala and Paraguay. Another country they might consider would be Armenia, given recent drug involvement out of that country," Matteo explained. "They might pass the funds through Macedonia as well, but I don't think they'd stay there."

"It doesn't matter, and we shouldn't waste time on it; it's distracting us," Albin said, rising from his chair. "We shouldn't be concerned about the money. We've got to stay focused on protecting Sandra and Maddie. *El Viruñas* can keep the ransom—sorry, but it's not even a ransom so much as payment of Orlov's debt to *El Viruñas*—and Brennan can deal with those responsible for Maddie's abduction and Smith's death. Sandra and Maddie—that's it."

"Albin's right. We've got to focus," agreed O. "Where do we think they've got Maddie? Brennan mentioned that they were looking into some leads that led them into cottage country up north of us, some place called Gkinaa near a Lake Gkide."

"I don't know either of those places," Kent admitted after considering what he knew of the rugged region north of Toronto and its collection of small lakes and rocky outcroppings. "I've got nothing to offer. The only area I'm at all familiar with is around Lake Rosseau; these names don't ring a bell for me. Can you display a map of the area on the screen for us, O?"

O provided the map, and Kent continued. "Okay, there's Lake Gkide and a short distance away is Gkinaa," he said, pointing to the two locations. "Anything else in the area?"

"This might be a dead end, which means we should be concentrating on Sandra and making sure that nothing happens to her."

"I disagree, O. Their only concern is the money, and they'll be getting that without any interference. They don't know that Orlov is dead, so they have every reason to assume that there'd be hell to pay should anything happen to Sandra, if not Maddie," Matteo explained. "The son's death was an accident in all likelihood, but any harm to Sandra would be seen as intentional."

"Look here," Albin said, pointing to an area on the map between Toronto and the region which included Gkinaa and Lake Gkide. "Isn't this where that big amusement park is? They have concerts up there. I had a mechanic from the dealership come out this morning and tend to some minor things on the Mercedes. He's a young chap and was all excited about some concert he's planning to attend up there on Saturday. A popular band, according to him— because I sure wouldn't know—called Lizard Brain from the US or UK. I don't remember. Anyway, it's a big deal. He paid a fortune for the tickets. Hell, if he's any indication, there'll be lots of crazy fans going wild—a techno Woodstock. If they release Maddie inside such a massive crowd, that would work to their advantage, wouldn't it?"

"We might not be able to figure out where she is now, but we could help ensure that she's found promptly after being released," Kent proposed, eager to become more involved.

"That's great information, Albin. Matteo and I don't have your insight on that, but it certainly seems plausible.

"And Kent, that would be a *no* on our further involvement," O emphasized. "We'll pass along that information to Brennan and let him handle it. You're well-intentioned, Kent, but I think we'd just get in the way and might possibly get some innocent person hurt, or worse."

The conversation was becoming unnecessarily long, and Brennan was becoming irritated. "Like I've already said, I'm going to need to cancel my appointment with you. No, I can't reschedule at this time, *Mr. McKelvie.* Some things are far more important than my retirement. We'll need to have that talk about finances at some later date." *If at all,* thought Brennan as he disconnected from the call. Brennan wasn't at all impressed with the pressure he was receiving from Murray McKelvie, the financial advisor. He fingered the cheap business card in his hand, then ripped it in half and tossed it into the wastebasket just as his appointment entered his office through the open door.

"Yes, Mr. Birch, come in and take a seat."

The man now seated opposite Brennan looked considerably older than he had the last time they'd met, the day after his daughter was abducted.

"My wife . . . she's under doctor's care, so she couldn't come," explained Mr. Birch, though no explanation was necessary.

"I understand," Brennan replied. "Well, I have some good news for you to share with your wife."

"You've got Maddie?" he asked, tearing up.

"No, not that good, I'm afraid, but we're getting there."

"No, I knew it couldn't be that good. That would be perfect. Nothing's perfect, except Maddie," Birch jabbered. Brennan had noticed the habit when last they met and gave him some time to collect his thoughts.

"What is it?" Birch asked, having composed himself once again.

"We have instructions for the payment of a ransom for the release of Maddie with the guarantee that she is unharmed."

"How much?" Birch asked, with the tone of someone making an inconsequential purchase and quite prepared to whip out his credit card. Clearly, the amount—whatever it was—would be far less than the value he placed on his daughter.

"Don't worry about the amount of the payment. Someone else has offered to pay it."

"That's wonderful, but I believe in paying my debts, even if I need to take out a second mortgage on the house. I've had some financial success, but it's likely to take me some time to get it all together. Shouldn't take me too long; I already looked into it. I'm a partner in an investment dealership, so I've got some connections that'll hopefully make things go more quickly. So, how much? I can't let anyone else be out for a matter that is ultimately our responsibility; it seems unethical. But I am appreciative of their assistance. If they can access funds more quickly than I can, then perhaps they can pay the ransom, and I'll pay them back immediately, as soon as I can liquidate whatever is necessary—might take a while to find a buyer for the RV." Finally, Birch stopped jabbering and looked at Detective Inspector Brennan.

"The amount is just over fifty-three million Canadian dollars, Mr. Birch."

CHAPTER 43
JANUS

There was nothing Lucy could do to prevent whatever fire would impact their lives at some point in the future. She had discussed the painting with Kent, and while he was now aware of this ominous portent, they had agreed upon two things: they would seek to become more actively aware of the threat, and the information would not be shared with others. They just wouldn't understand. Then they discussed the matter a second time.

"What about O?" Kent asked. "He's likely to understand, given his past experience with one of your sleep-paintings. He sounded very open-minded about your ability."

"Or my curse. . . . Oh, ignore me; I'm just being dramatic now. Back to what we were discussing . . ." Lucy breathed in deeply and refocused. "Actually, I was wondering about O as well."

"He may want to remove Blomma from the island as a result, but the fire may occur at the estate, or any other place for that matter. All this indicates to me is that there will be a fire, but it doesn't provide further detail, absolutely nothing beyond that one simple, horrible fact," Kent said, summarizing their discussion.

"That's up to him and Blomma, if he chooses to tell her, I guess. If he tells her, then she could tell the others, and they could panic as surely as I'm feeling panic just talking about this snowballing," Lucy admitted.

"Would that really be so bad, Lucy? We're all adults. I'm finding myself changing my mind completely about this. Now I think they should be informed; then they can do as they wish to protect themselves. Ultimately, this is your decision since it's your painting," Kent reminded her.

"At the very least, it would guarantee that everyone exercises an awareness, not just you and I," Lucy concluded. "We sure did a one-eighty on that decision, didn't we?

"I'll gather everyone here and let them know right away. We're planning to go to the manor house and look for a keyhole that matches that barrel key. It'll either be an appropriate distraction, or they'll be so overwhelmed, they'll just retire to their rooms instead. I really wonder about Juliette more than either Blomma or Helen. Then again, both Albin and Elinor are with you while Helen's here with me. I'll feel her out and clarify with her that if she wishes to return to the estate, she should do so. I suspect O will merely view this as an additional challenge."

"I'll do the same here. No point in talking about it further. We'll know more as soon as we announce the situation."

"I think we're procrastinating, Kent, so I'm going to say bye right now and end this call. Loves." Just as she was disconnecting from the call, she could hear Kent sending his love in return. Her heart was comforted.

Lucy contacted O on the cabin cruiser and requested that he meet with everyone at the summer house. When she thought she'd provided sufficient time for him, she called out to gather Juliette, Helen, and Aleksandra in the great room. While they waited for O to join them, Lucy ran upstairs to fetch the two sleep-paintings. By the time she arrived back in the great room, O had arrived, Helen had made beverages available, and everyone's curiosity was heightened.

"I have something of some significance to share with you," Lucy began. "While I am doing this with you here, Kent is doing the same back at the estate with all our friends and associates but without these visual aids," she said, nodding toward the two paintings, turned backward and leaning against a table. "They get photos; you get the real thing." She turned the first sleep-painting so they could see it.

"You have all seen this on display in the upper gallery and know that I painted this in my sleep. We later discovered that it was a likeness to a portion of the manor house and significant in that it led to the discovery of a metal box containing important documents. I eventually remembered that as a young child I had been in this very spot, the spot depicted in the painting. The second sleep-painting, the one that's back at the estate, is also of something I personally experienced as a child.

"O is the owner of the third sleep-painting. Unlike the two I've mentioned already, this third one was not based on my personal experience of the event. The scene was prescient, though we didn't realize it at the time. Do you remember how you explained that, O?"

"Actually, I do because I felt strongly about it, and I still do. I think you have an ability, a sensitivity to read subtle indicators in people. Its like reading someone's tells in poker. You may not even be consciously aware of this ability, but I think your brain makes sense of it, and then one night, you sleep-paint to communicate the message as you've subconsciously interpreted it."

Lucy noticed that Helen looked tense and focused while Aleksandra appeared a bit confused. Juliette, on the other hand, seemed politely amused. It was to be expected.

"I sleep-painted again a couple days ago and completely wiped out all the work I'd done on the third painting for the Orlov triptych. The subject matter upset me deeply, and I wasn't sure what the best response might be. Should I keep it to myself, or share it with you? With everyone, or just some of you? After much thought and a couple of conversations with Kent, I've decided to tell everyone and share the painting. How you choose to respond is up to you. There is no particular response that I'm expecting, nor requiring from any of you. This is essentially an FYI situation."

She turned the painting so they could all see the subject matter and examine it more carefully if they wanted. There was an audible gasp from among them, though it was impossible to tell who might have been the source. Clearly, everyone was uncomfortable.

"If you wish to leave here, please do. And that includes you too, Helen. I'll understand. Remember, while this appears to predict a fire, we have no idea where this will occur, or who will be involved, or how it will happen. It could be merely a bonfire for all I know."

"We have stronger beverages, if you'd like something other than tea, coffee, and juice," Helen said. "I know it's rather early, but I don't give a rat's ass."

As they nursed their new beverages, they spoke to one another, discussing viewpoints and options. Ultimately, they became resolute.

"I think that Blomma and I should remain here but become more aware. Blomma, that is my advice, but I work for you, so if you think otherwise—"

"No, O, I agree. We don't know where this will occur. I'll be more careful and increase my awareness. No offence, Lucy, but we don't really even know *if* it will occur."

"No offence taken." Lucy smiled at Aleksandra.

"While I truly appreciate your words regarding my abandoning ship, Lucy, I'll be staying with you. This does tell us something, but it doesn't really inform us sufficiently, other than to be alert."

Lucy was pleased and grateful that Helen had chosen to remain.

"Well, I guess that leaves me, Lucy," Juliette began. "All due respect, but I can't say that I put any stock in prescience—yours or anyone else's. Therefore, I'll be staying. And increased awareness is a good thing, no matter the significance of these flames in your painting."

As Juliette concluded her announcement to stay, Lucy noticed that O and Helen were examining the modified third triptych panel rather carefully.

"See anything?" Lucy inquired.

"No, I don't. I was looking for some awen since there were many in the first two paintings, but I can't see any in this one," Helen replied before leaving to attend to lunch.

"I can't see anything other than flames either, Lucy," O declared. "However, in the painting I have, we didn't notice the message right away. The painting hung in my stateroom aboard the *Croesus* for months before Alice, the one who acted as your personal assistant that summer, noticed it. She just happened to see it, so it wasn't even me who noticed, though it had been hanging within my view for a rather long time."

"I don't know how your theory about tells relates to this painting, O. That would imply I've already met someone capable of doing such a thing. I can't imagine anyone I know setting fire to some place."

"Perhaps it's not intentional," suggested O. "Unfortunately, it's always clearer in hindsight."

"I'll hang this one in the upper hall," Lucy declared. "It'll serve as a reminder to be aware, and just maybe someone will see something in the painting, something that eludes us right now."

"Lunch?" Helen asked, looking at O.

"Yes, thank you."

In the end, O returned to his cabin cruiser to resume surveillance, and the three women left for a visit to the manor house, just as planned.

"I'm so very grateful to Kent and Albin for arranging to get some additional clothing and luggage for me in the short time I was with them," Juliette said. "I can't imagine making this trek with any of the shoes and clothing I brought with me from France."

"Yes, well, Kent is very organized and attentive to details, especially practicalities."

Aleksandra confidently led the little group, following the path toward the manor house. Juliette and Lucy trailed behind.

"So, I understand that you've never been able to identify the Janus in your old firm," Lucy said. "What happened that you felt your life was in danger at Interpol?"

Juliette shook her head in response. "How did you know about the Janus?"

"You'll remember that I was doing my own investigation about Gianni Sarto," Lucy said. "Well, someone helping me introduced me to that term, and Gracie provided me with a recording of one of your conversations with her. It didn't take long to figure out there was a problem child at Garner and Garner."

"Gracie was truly a force to be reckoned with. The little sneak!" Juliette shook her head and smiled, but her shoulders drooped with the weight of emotional baggage.

"Regarding Interpol, it's complicated, Lucy, and with all due respect—because I owe you and Kent a lot here—I really shouldn't talk about what I learned in the course of doing my job there. Generally speaking I am, or was, just a paper-pusher for Interpol, an analyst. However, far too often my theories were negated by events which were statistically highly improbable. My superior agreed with me that there seemed to be a mole. Then he was killed in the course of our work, and there didn't seem to be a reason for it. The method used indicated to me that it was not random; there was much complex planning involved to execute the attack. Too many things linked back to me as well, so consequently, here I am."

"Before I forget: did you bring the barrel key?" Lucy asked.

"Yes, right here." Juliette tapped a zippered pocket on her pants. "I wish I could figure out what the decoration on the bow is."

"We're here!" Aleksandra announced, "The cairn is just over in that direction, Juliette," she said, pointing toward the hillock nearby. "With all the big old trees, you can't see it from here though.

"What about the marine archeologists working on the boat wreck, Lucy? Is there any additional information?" Aleksandra asked as she picked her way through the dense shrubbery surrounding the old building.

"They tested the contents of the bottle and declared that it's an alcoholic beverage, derived from plums and very likely not commercially produced. They pegged it from about the same time period as the other things—1930s—though I don't recall how they determined that. Kent said that there was some evidence of human remains, but he didn't go into detail. We've just been so distracted by that damn painting of mine. Kent got that information over the phone, so I'm waiting for the final report."

"Well, this looks even worse than when I last saw it, though not by much," Juliette said, as they rounded the corner and got a better look at the stone structure.

Lucy smiled and opened the door to her past.

"Where do you want to start, Lucy?" Aleksandra asked, keen to look for keyholes.

They began in the living room, deemed the most likely place for such a cabinet. Though they found keyhole cabinets, all had been forced open previously, and none was a match to the key in Juliette's possession. The same was true in the dining room and the kitchen. They held on to hope as they turned to Gianni Sarto's library. Disintegrating tomes lined the shelves. There were books on chemistry, economics, geography, geology, politics, animal husbandry . . . There were numerous fiction titles for works in several languages, and the same was true for volumes of poetry.

Lucy hesitated, sighed, and wished she'd known the man. Juliette paused to consider Gianni's desk, its drawers left partially open after previous searches. The key didn't fit the locks on the drawer either, and she was disappointed for Lucy.

"Have you looked for hidden drawers?" asked Aleksandra. "I've seen lots of old desks—antiques from various countries—and it's surprising how many have been designed with hiding places."

"I knew that," Juliette mumbled to herself. "I should have remembered." Again, she paused, contemplating something. She shook her head and rejoined Aleksandra and Lucy in examining the desk.

Aleksandra explained, "Panels can slide, pop open when touched or activated in the right way, or they can be pulled open like a cupboard door or flipped up or down, depending upon how they're hinged. But after all these years, the mechanism might not work quite as well as it used to."

When they could find no hidden compartment in the old desk, they drew away from it and considered it at a distance. It had been a handsome desk in its day. Now, the leather affixed to the top of the desk had dried and seemed to have provided a food source to vermin. Rather than being a footed desk, it had a base with a toe kick.

"Let's take the drawers out—all of them," Juliette suggested. The drawers were removed, and one by one the empty spaces they left were examined further. "These middle drawers are no longer popular, I'm glad to say. I always found it awkward to deal with pulling out this shallow middle drawer while you're sitting at the desk. You end up working against yourself and struggling just to get at a pen or other small item."

"What about the toe kick?" Lucy asked. "It's recessed so it's not all that apparent, but that would work in favour of hiding something, wouldn't it?"

All three got down on their knees and began to crawl around the desk, testing the small panels recessed into the toe kick.

"I can't get a grip on anything, not even at the corner," Lucy said. "How about we flip this over to work on it. It's not a salvageable piece of furniture anyway. We can use it as kindling in a bonfire. . . . No, scratch that last idea."

Although the desk was oak, being three of them, they flipped it with little effort.

"Okay, so there appear to be boxes attached behind the front toe kicks, but I don't see any keyhole, Juliette," Lucy said, looking about the room.

"What are you looking for?" asked Aleksandra.

"There should be a shovel or an axe—that sort of thing— left around down here somewhere."

"I think I saw that stuff back in the kitchen, Lucy." And with that, Aleksandra left for the other room.

"Don't despair, Lucy, most people have a whole ring filled with zombie keys with no matching keyhole."

"No, I'm not really upset we haven't found the keyhole yet, Juliette. There's still the bedrooms and the extension out back, though I don't hold out much hope for the keyhole to be found there. It's a cabinet-type key, and a fancy one at that, so if it isn't out here, it's not to be found."

"I've got an idea, Lucy. I'll try something with the bow decoration when we return to the summer house."

Aleksandra returned with an array of tools, accumulated as a result of previous searches at the site. Lucy started with a chisel and hammer and separated a box from the toe-kick panel. It fell to the floor, landing on the underside of the desktop, and shattering the brittle boards of the box.

"Surely, there would have been a better way back in its day for this to have been accessed!" Juliette declared, laughing.

"I've managed to get the toe-kick panel on this other side to flip up. I'm not sticking my hand inside. I've had enough of the spiders here."

"No problem, Blomma," Lucy assured her. "I brought some work gloves with me this time. Going back to the empty box I just destroyed, I can see how the panel was hinged as well. The hinge is just too corroded to function. Okay, here it goes . . ."

Flashlight in hand, Lucy first confirmed that there was a large, flat metal box inside the desk's wooden one. It reminded her of a pizza box. Once she located a clasp on the front, much like the handle of a suitcase, she withdrew the item with ease.

"Oh, the box needs a key, but not the barrel key," she announced, just a tad disappointed. "I think that we should return the tools and complete the search for the right keyhole. We'll open the box when Helen can join us, up at the summer house.

Helen had spread a clean cloth over the table in preparation for the opening of the metal box. "How about I clean this box before we go knocking even more dirt around?" She wiped down the outside of the box with a thick cloth designed for such purposes and caught plenty of soot-like tarnish, the kind that covers metal objects with a tightly held black grime.

"May I have that cloth?" Juliette asked, leaving Helen somewhat perplexed as she handed it over to her. Juliette excused herself and returned to her room to pick up the additional items she needed. By the time she returned, Helen had been successful in forcing the lock on the metal box, and Lucy was beginning to remove the contents.

"We seem to have only documents here," Lucy announced. "Oh good, Juliette, you've brought the magnifying glass. We've found it helpful in the past to also take photographs of documents, since they are sometimes so difficult to read.

"Wills, four of them. That's odd. There are two for Gianni Sarto and two for Annie, but on one she's identified as Annie Hogan, and on the other she's Annie Sarto. They're all signed on the same date. Weird."

"It's certainly odd that each of them has two wills. That first box you found at the manor house back years ago contained their marriage certificate, so the Sarto wills make sense. I guess it's good that there's a will identifying Annie as a Hogan. It's like they knew there'd be some sort of trouble."

"You're right, Helen. We couldn't make out all the information, but just enough to confirm that they had been married. Oh, this wouldn't have become known to you, Juliette, but somehow their marriage was never entered into government records, or if it was, it was later removed. May I?" she asked, taking the magnifying glass in hand and examining the witness signatures on the wills.

"All the wills have been witnessed by the same two people: Darri Fournier and Connor Doyle. I don't really know about either of them, except that the name Connor has come up before. It's the name my great aunt used for the cat in her little book, and it's the name on the medallion found at the wreck Blomma discovered here, just before you arrived, Juliette."

"More to put into that display case you keep talking about, Lucy," Helen commented.

Aleksandra began to photograph the documents. "This is going to be my bedtime reading material," she declared. "If anyone else wants a copy, let me know and I'll send it to you. Lucy? Helen? Juliette? . . . Juliette?"

"Oh, sorry, yes, please. Sorry, I just got distracted by something I've been fiddling around with here. I used the tarnish-laden cloth Helen gave me to transfer the soot-like stuff onto the surface of the key, and with the darker shading it provided, I've managed to clarify the decoration on the bow of that barrel key. It's an image of Janus."

"Who's that?" Aleksandra asked. "Oh, oh, hold on, I remember; it's a Roman god with faces front and back. He's the god of . . . beginnings and passages, so he often appears carved above doorways. Right?"

That and more, thought Lucy and Juliette.

CHAPTER 44
LICENCE TO KIDNAP

Rashid grabbed the photos off the printer and hastened toward Brennan's office. After a quick nod of acknowledgement from Brennan, he opened the door as Brennan was completing a telephone call.

". . . great. Thanks, O," Brennan said before disconnecting from his call.

"Hung up on, eh?" Rashid said.

"Huh?"

"No, sorry, I just thought since you said, 'Oh' . . . it sounded like you'd wanted to continue and your party cut off. Sorry, not my business. Just an observation, and I shouldn't have said anything."

"Well, what have you got?"

"Here are the photos you asked for."

They arranged the collection of photos on an old computer table. There were three sets of photos of the suspect Jeep SUV taken at various angles and with various magnifications.

"Okay, so these are the photos of the vehicle that took Maddie. These are photos of the vehicle belonging to the real estate broker, Concha, and taken in his driveway. And these are the new ones we've located. They show a Jeep SUV the real estate broker says is his, taken while he and his employees were at Lake Gkide. So, this third set should match the driveway shots."

Brennan started to examine the photos carefully when the door to his office began to open.

"Here are some additional shots of the Jeep SUV for you," one of the junior investigators said, directing his comment to Rashid.

"Just keep them, we've enough here for now," Rashid replied.

"These are photos of the vehicle used in the abduction of Charles Ponzi, sir. I thought you'd want them as part of your comparison. They just came in."

Rashid took the photos from the investigator and added them to the array on the side table.

"Set four," he declared as he put them into position.

Brennan poured over the photos, going back and forth as he compared them with one another.

"Just as I thought," he said. "What do you see, Rashid?"

Uncertain, Rashid examined the photos. He went back and forth over them numerous times before he finally declared, "Well, the lake vehicle and the driveway vehicle bear different licence plate numbers, though they are very similar: FRF8358 at the lake, FRF8538 in the driveway."

"What are the chances that's just by chance, Rashid?"

"My guess is, pretty low. One or the other might have been requested as a vanity plate, perhaps their initials and lucky numbers." He made his way to the door and got the attention of one of his subordinates making his way to the break room, empty coffee cup in hand.

"Jake, look into these two licence plate numbers. They may be vanity plates, and we'll need everything available regarding the parties requesting them. Coffee can wait."

J. A. Gibbens

"It's clear to me that the licence number on the vehicle in the driveway is also on the vehicle involved in both abductions, so that's most likely our vehicle. We'll need to get forensics on that, but I don't want to spook the kidnappers, so hold off on it for now," Brennan explained. Then he returned to examining the photos.

"Now take a look at the vehicles themselves and see if you can detect any difference. The guy or his lawyer will claim that the licence plate on the vehicle involved in the abduction has been modified and just so happens to match that of his client. These aren't amateurs, Rashid. If they're using two vehicles as a smokescreen, the one in Concha's driveway will have been cleaned thoroughly. Real estate people tend to have their cars detailed regularly anyway."

Magnifying glasses in hand, Brennan and Rashid repeatedly examined the photos, concentrating on the minutiae of the vehicles themselves, but to no avail. The vehicles looked identical.

"Get the team to continue with the comparisons, Rashid, and look for any distinguishing characteristics. So far, these two Jeep SUVs appear identical to me, but we know they must be two different vehicles. There's got to be some difference we can identify.

"Another thing, Rashid, that Lizard Brain concert scheduled for Saturday, get the team out there as soon as possible and evaluate the place in terms of . . ." Brennan scratched his head and groaned in frustration. "Have them look it over as if they were a perp planning to deliver a kidnap victim. Hiding places, that sort of thing."

"Something you're not telling us?"

"Well Rashid, I've been considering some—shall we say— more creative theories, but I didn't want the rest of the team working outside our usual methodology, so no, I didn't share."

Rashid's left eyebrow arched, and he looked at Brennan.

"How do you think I found someone prepared to ante up a ransom of forty million euros for Maddie Birch?" Brennan remarked.

A short time later, Rashid stuck his head inside Brennan's office. "Update on that second plate number: a numbered company. We're working on getting details."

"We've found something on one of the vehicles," Rashid reported. "It's slight but real. I've also put an APB out on the second plate number. Nothing reported yet. It may be stored somewhere.

"All this information is being passed along to the OPP. Wanna tell me how you got them to let you take the lead on this?"

There was no answer, just a look from Brennan, as they moved to see what tech had managed to discover in the photos.

"You know how you get little nicks, dents, and scratches when you park at a grocery store? Well, the driveway car has a little dent in it that we can match on the abduction vehicle, in three sets of photos. I doubt the owner would have noticed it since it's on the passenger side, toward the back. It's difficult to see, so that in itself might not be sufficient," civilian tech Heather Walker, explained.

"Three?" queried Brennan.

"Yes, set one: the abduction of Maddie Birch, and set two: the driveway photograph, and set four: the abduction of Charles Ponzi. But, as I said, the dent is really hard to see on some of the photos."

"Argh," Brennan groaned as he brought his fist down heavily upon the desk, making Heather jump. "Sorry, about that, Heather."

She smiled. "I'm not finished yet, DI Brennan. There's been a rash of vandalism recently that may have provided something we can use. It involves the firing of mini projectiles at tires. They're like paintballs only very small. As with paintball, these projectiles come in various bright colours, but generally they're green. The vandals claim they're part of the green movement, and they target tires on SUVs.

We looked at the tires to see if anything might be stuck to them and *voilà*. The same tire in a couple photos shows a very small green mark, and it's easier to see than the dent. See here?" Heather pointed to the tire from photo set four and the same tire in photo set two.

"So, that directly links the car used in the abduction of Ponzi with the car in the driveway?"

"I'm not saying it's a lot, but yes, it's something more for you."

"Thanks, Heather," Rashid said as Brennan rushed off, back to his office to think. Rashid followed.

"So, Rashid, we've got two vehicles. We've got the real estate broker as a suspect, but clearly he's not a kidnapper, nor is it likely he's the person directing this whole thing. I'd really like to get forensics to crawl over that one vehicle. Unfortunately, I think we need to hold off on that until we've got Maddie. We'll continue searching for the second vehicle, but we can't tip our hand."

Rashid remained silent while Brennan paced and continued his rant.

"We still don't know where Maddie Birch is right now, or where she'll be released after the ransom is paid. And we don't have the person ultimately responsible for this either. The most important thing is to get Maddie Birch, alive, so that assessment of the concert venue is critical. The second important thing is to put together a good case against the real estate broker—what did you say his full name was?"

"Bernardo 'Bernie' Concha. Do you want to bring him in for questioning?"

"No, hold off on that for now. I don't want to give him a greater reason to be worried; it could complicate getting Maddie. They've likely cleaned the vehicle thoroughly and are confident we won't find anything incriminating; otherwise, Concha wouldn't be so cocky. If forensics could just find a drop of blood or a hair—anything for DNA once we seize the vehicle . . . We've got a phone tap, but I doubt there'll be any calls to the abductors.

"However, let the OPP know that he's a person of interest. I'd like to pick him up immediately after we get Maddie. We might be okay to do it as soon as the ransom has been transferred, but I can't take any chances. Priority is getting Maddie, then Concha."

"What about recovering the ransom? Do you want tech to try and set a trace? I don't know if that's readily doable, but they could give it a try, I guess."

"No, that's not on the agenda. Recovering the ransom is not a priority. Maddie and Concha are the focus. If we can get a few other fish, fine. Hooking a big one would be nice, but it's not necessary, especially since I suspect Concha's loss will be a significant blow to them after further investigation is carried out."

"Sounds like you've got retirement on your mind. Fishing?"

"Yeah maybe, Rashid, just maybe I can see this coming to an end."

"The signer on that plate registration is a lawyer acting on behalf of his client, so it looks like a dead end. He'll claim privilege," Rashid said, concluding his update for Brennan.

"Rashid," Brennan called out before the door closed behind the younger detective. "Based on everything we've collected so far concerning the real estate broker, get whatever warrants are necessary and see if that lawyer's name shows up on any document for him. I want to know if there's a link between that lawyer and Concha. And check where the lawyer's office is located. It's one thing if it's local, but it may be something else if he's in Toronto, I suspect. Tread carefully; we don't want Concha to know we consider him a suspect. I want him to think that he's convinced us that his vehicle's been in his possession at all times. And make sure that surveillance doesn't tip their hand by being too eager or getting sloppy. We've got a life on the line here."

CHAPTER 45

WORMS

As if they knew it was a special day, both Merlot and Bijou demonstrated a remarkably high level of exuberance at the arrival of dawn, much to Serge's dismay.

"*C'est bon*," he said, yawning and stretching as he sat up in bed. "You little ones do not understand. I was awake at two and again at four until five. The older you get, the more you sleep and the less I seem to."

His slippers were where he had left them—this was not always the case—though as he pushed his feet deeper along the vamp, he could detect moisture.

"Oh, perhaps you too were awake last night—and maybe slightly bored?"

Serge grabbed his robe, which was slung over a nearby chair and shrugged into it. He quickly ran a comb through his thick white hair before ushering the two spaniels out the door. They followed close behind as he carefully negotiated each step of the old, wooden grand staircase. This morning, the creaking was minimal—both his, and that of the staircase. When they reached the kitchen door to the side yard, he opened it and the spaniels ran for joy in the yard, sniffing to read the news left by nighttime creatures. Serge stood at the doorway and leaned against the doorframe, as he enjoyed watching his young charges cavort.

"And now you may have your breakfast," he announced, as Merlot and Bijou knocked into one another in their eagerness to re-enter the house.

While the dogs were occupied in the kitchen, Serge returned to the guest room to prepare himself for the day. He considered whether he should arrange to visit a barber, but where would he find one who would understand the texture of his hair and the requirements of length necessary to maintain his style?

Today, he would be seeing Yoichi. That part of his art collection—his and Jean-Pierre's—which had been brought to Toronto would be on display to the public for the first time today. Serge was nervous, and he was uncertain whether this was a good nervous or a bad nervous. He felt euphoric taking this step into the future and sharing the collection with other art lovers; however, he also experienced fear that he may be making a mistake. He was unable to shake the feeling of disappointment that lingered, knowing that he could not maintain the entire collection as Jean-Pierre might have preferred. The moment of every choice is a doorway of opportunity. This evening, he would toast both the past and the future with champagne, as was his custom.

He laid out his clothes to be worn for an afternoon spent with Yoichi and a second set to be worn for the evening. The Gillespies and his new friends wouldn't be in attendance at the event, but there would be another held for them once their current security concerns were resolved, and Lucy returned from the island. Serge wondered about the island, but having seen photos and experiencing perch and chips with coleslaw at Doyle's with Kent, he thought it might not be to his taste.

His immediate concern was in selecting appropriate apparel for this morning's walk in the conservation area with Merlot and Bijou. The weather had turned cooler, and while this suited him, the frequent changes in temperature were significant and difficult to plan for.

Eventually, he was ready to take on the day. With the spaniels' leashes in hand, he cautiously descended the stairway yet again. Eve and Cookie were already waiting in the foyer, accompanied by Merlot and Bijou.

"*Bon matin*, Eve, Cookie. I must apologize," Serge said. "I hadn't realized how much time had passed." He bent down to attach the leashes.

"*God morgon*, Serge, Merlot, Bijou. No need to apologize; Cookie and I arrived at this very spot just a moment ago. Some days one just becomes more easily distracted, even by little things. Perhaps Astrid is delayed as well. We shall see," Eve said, opening the front door then locking it behind them.

As they reached the gate, Astrid could be seen still on the approach, wearing a smile and a new hat. "*God morgon*, everyone, I must apologize for my tardiness this morning. I'd forgotten my hat."

"What happened to your old hat?" Eve asked. "I quite liked it."

"It seems that the wind liked it as well. It's probably somewhere in Hamilton by now." Astrid laughed.

"Well, your new one is very nice. Would you like to take Merlot's leash while we walk?" Serge offered the lead, and Astrid took it in hand.

They arrived at the Gillespies' gate just as Matteo was waiting to enter.

"Do you happen to know if that young man ever found Juliette, his Havanese?" Astrid asked him.

"No, I don't. I'd actually forgotten about that; we've been so busy with other things, so thanks for reminding me. Did you by any chance catch his name?"

"It may have been Spence. That was the licence plate on his vehicle. At least, I presume it was his vehicle. It was the only one in the conservation area parking lot at the time."

"Do you recall anything more about the vehicle?" asked Matteo.

"It was a white, but I'm uncertain whether they call such a thing a cube van or a panel truck. I'm not really interested in such things, so while I remember it, I don't have the vocabulary to tell you."

"Would you be able to identify it in a photo?"

"Oh yes, no problem doing that," Astrid declared.

Matteo thanked her, and the little group continued their walk with the dogs while he entered through the gate to discuss the matter with everyone in the war room.

"I remember Elinor telling me something about that request from Astrid to look for a missing dog," Kent said. "Elinor said it left her feeling uneasy. So, when it comes to weird occurrences, we now have three: the cherry picker, the linesmen, and the guy with, or rather without, the dog. The first two have been a dead end. Matteo, what do we know about the guy and the dog?"

"The vehicle may have been a white cube van or panel truck. Astrid says she can identify it if we show her a photo.

"The licence plate was SPENCE. The dog's name was Juliette, a very old Havanese. Then again, we only have the man's word that the name of the dog was Juliette. It might not even be his dog or his vehicle," Matteo explained.

"Which properties did he visit?" asked O.

Matteo became visibly uncomfortable and squirmed in his chair. As he spoke, his voice became increasingly dampened. "Well, the guy seemed harmless enough. The only property he entered was Eve's. That's how I came to know about the bridge you have over the stone wall between the two properties. Of course, now he knows too. To be accurate, it was Astrid who opened the gate. I just accompanied them."

Kent, O, and Albin were all disgusted with Matteo's breach of security protocols, and it clearly showed in their body language and facial expressions. Matteo was even more disgusted with himself, though at the time of the incident he had been blinded by the task he had set for himself regarding Kent Gillespie on behalf of his sister-in-law, Gina. He had vowed to never make such a mistake ever again—new mistakes, quite possibly, but not that one.

"This might be more directly related to another matter and not Aleksandra, Matteo. I'm sorry, but I'm not at liberty to discuss this other matter with you, but thanks for the information." With that, Kent excused himself and went to his office to place a more private call to Brennan.

"Mr. Gillespie, what have you got for me today?"

Kent outlined the situation as much as he could, requesting that Brennan share information about the owner of the vanity licence plate and the vehicle to which it belonged.

"Normally, I wouldn't do this, but what the hell, I haven't got much longer here. Okay, I've found a licence plate: S-P-E-N-C-E. It's supposed to be on a 2019 Chevrolet City Express van registered to Spencer Worms, which I guess explains why he's got his given name and not his surname on his vanity plate.

Now, I'm not going to give you the fella's address, but . . . after a little more searching here . . . I can tell you that he's a licensed private investigator. Now, that's all the information I'm prepared to give you, Mr. Gillespie, certainly not without a lot more detail coming my way from you."

Kent paused and gave the matter some thought. "Look, I'm not sure I should say more, but as Lucy and I have been entrusted with someone's safety, and you may have information I lack, I guess I'll need to trust that her identity isn't shared with anyone. Does the name Juliette Garner ring a bell for you?"

"Isn't she the lawyer from that old Toronto law firm, the woman who suddenly left Toronto, essentially disappeared some years back? There was talk, but then the whole matter quieted down."

"That's the one."

"Say no more, Kent. My but you folks do come up with some creative problems. Look, you've got my numbers. If you get into trouble taking care of the woman, give me a call day or night, okay? You don't want to be going through all the details with someone new to your situation. Meantime, I'll see what might be going on with Spencer Worms, just to keep him on my radar."

"Thank you, Detective Inspector. Do you have any news about our kidnappers?"

"Unfortunately, nothing I can share. But I thank you again for the heads up on that concert venue. This could be coming to an end on Saturday, Sunday at the latest, is my guess. Look, you have a good day."

Kent felt good about his decision to share a bit more information with Brennan, but now he had to tell Lucy, and he hoped she'd agree.

CHAPTER 46
HAPPY ANNIVERSARY

"Don't worry about Merlot and Bijou, Serge. Astrid will take good care of them for you today. You know, they could have just stayed here and kept Cookie company," Eve added.

"You have things to do at the Gillespies', Eve, and I've noticed that the three of them seem to get into more trouble when left on their own. This way, Astrid will keep an eye on the little ones, and they'll be busy investigating their new surroundings. I would take them with me today, but there is so much happening, so many people expected, and . . ."

Clearly, Serge would continue to worry and dither about his decision, so Eve offered no further comment. She watched as he slowly mounted the stairs and wondered at his reticence today.

Having freshened up, Serge began to root around in his possessions, looking for what he now required. Having secured those things, he looked about the room. His gaze fell upon the small breakfast table set between two chairs in the alcove overlooking the backyard and Lake Ontario off in the distance. The air was still and barely warm; it was lovely. He drew back the drapes then opened the window. The scent of lilacs met him, and he appreciated the gentleness of it all—and so would Jean-Pierre.

Serge took in hand the portrait of Jean-Pierre encased in a leather book frame and opened it. He lovingly stroked the image of the face before him, unaffected as it was by age these past years, then read the quote embossed on the page facing it.

> *Le temps est trop lent pour ceux qui attendent, trop rapide pour ceux qui ont peur, trop long pour ceux qui pleurent, trop court pour ceux qui se réjouissent, mais pour ceux qui aiment, le temps est éternité.*

Not only had the quote been one of Jean-Pierre's favourites, it had been the impetus for Serge to learn English. It was a quote by Henry Van Dyke: "Time is too slow for those who wait, too swift for those who fear, too long for those who grieve, too short for those who rejoice, but for those who love, time is eternity."

After setting the portrait upright on the little table, he added the two tea candles he had shown to Kent in Port L'Orté and positioned them with care. A small bouquet of flowers completed the arrangement. His hands trembled as he struck a match and lit the wick of each candle.

"To us upon our anniversary," he said softly.

Serge closed his eyes, took a breath, and said a silent prayer. When he opened his eyes again, they were moist with tears. The bittersweet moment was interrupted by a knock on his door and Eve's voice informing him that Yoichi had arrived to take him to Toronto, and to please remember to leave open the door to the room in order to get better airflow.

The spell broken, he quickly checked himself in the mirror, closed his overnight case, then flipped it open once again. He returned to the small table and picked up the book frame, placing it in the small suitcase before closing it and leaving the room with it to join Yoichi. *Jean-Pierre should be present at the gallery. Ultimately, this was his collection.*

CHAPTER 47

COOKIE'S VERY BAD DAY

The slam of an upstairs door startled Cookie, and she awakened from her long nap, alone, in the kitchen, and suddenly quite nervous. Not even her new little friends were there to distract or comfort her. She quenched her thirst and returned to her reverie, sufficiently confident that Eve would return, or so she hoped.

Weather conditions had changed, and a breeze was picking up. Clouds were beginning to roll in over the lake. Off in the distance, white caps could be seen forming on the water of Lake Ontario. The weather was unsettled, yet again.

In the guest room, the flame of Serge's tea candles wavered as they caught the breeze, and the curtains and drapery in various rooms began to billow. More doors slammed shut throughout the house. Each time, Cookie awakened, startled by the sound and on the lookout for Eve. Eventually, she moved into the kneehole of the kitchen desk, dragging her mat with her. There was nothing else to do but take another drink of water and sleep, so she did. And she waited for Eve to return.

From her deep sleep, Cookie was awakened yet again—this time by a series of odd sounds; it wasn't soothing like that of familiar footsteps, or the opening of the pantry door. In due course, sleep returned, as she continued to wait for Eve to return home.

The fire started slowly, causing the fabrics and wood to smoulder awhile before a breeze would enliven them and the blaze would erupt into hungry flames, which grew rapidly, spreading throughout the room, then eating their way through the door and into the hallway itself. The old Tudor was as nectar to the flames as they consumed everything in their path. They crackled and cackled and continued to grow, filling the space with their hot, gaseous presence. Without regard for beauty, for memories, or for intrinsic value, they laid waste upon Eve's possessions, her precious memorabilia of a long life, well-lived. They laid waste upon Albin's possessions, the mementos of his military career, collected over years and destroyed in moments. The guest room furnishings and linens were rapidly turned to ash by a devilish fire that seemed angry that Serge had so few belongings left behind. There were no beloved creatures in his room, no highly valued keepsakes, and not even many clothes. The fire seemed incensed by this, so it continued to satisfy its rapacious appetite elsewhere in the house, treating the very structure as kindling upon which to grow even larger.

Both the sounds and the smells were unusual. The smells interested Cookie yet couldn't lift her concern over the strange sounds. She whined and scratched at the door. She knew she shouldn't scratch at the door, but she no longer wanted to be in the kitchen. She scratched and scratched and knew she'd be admonished for it, but now she was in a panic. As much as she looked around the room, she could see no way out. Tendrils of dark smoke began to find their way into the kitchen. Alone and fearful, Cookie picked up her stuffed bunny, took refuge back in the kneehole, and buried her nose in the familiar scent of her mat.

The gym at the Gillespies' was far busier than usual. Eve had decided to join Kent, O, Albin, and Matteo for an exercise session.

"I really don't think you need to wear that boot cast anymore, Eve," Albin said.

"Thank you for your opinion, but it stays on. I don't want to re-injure my ankle; it's important to me, and I'm going to continue to be careful. Afraid I'll use my foot as a weapon against you?"

It wasn't so much the words Eve used, but more her tone, which was both unpleasant and unwarranted. Anyone but Eve could sense that Albin was wounded by it, and Kent wondered if he still had the ring he'd bought for her and if he still planned to propose.

Nevertheless, they had come together for a workout, so they carried on. They did some circuit training, then the men sparred, during which time Eve worked on her stretches and ballet barre routine. Preparing to perform some yoga poses on the mat, she eventually removed her boot and put it aside. She positioned herself carefully, and starting from a downward-facing dog, she brought her right leg up and into a down dog split and then achieved the king pigeon pose. In that position, she faced the wall of integrated LED polycarbonate panels but viewed the self-luminous installation upside-down. She was accustomed to seeing it as a source of light therapy, so she was startled when her eyes caught something quite different in the security display it now carried.

"Smoke!" Eve grunted as she moved quickly to come out of the pose and stand, her eyes all the while fixed on the screen. The men hadn't heard her. "Fire!" she called out, as she ran from the gym and into the tunnel to the pool house. But her call was lost amid the discordant sounds of the men, focused as they were on honing their technique and urging one another toward greater achievement.

Eve flew out through the pool house door, pausing barely long enough to open it first. She thundered across the pool deck and down its several tiers to ground level. From there, she ran into the wooded area and over the little bridge.

When she arrived at her home, it was engulfed in flames and all she could think of was Cookie, left alone in the kitchen. She had no time to regret having forgotten her key and her phone and her boot cast back at the gym. She acted without hesitation. Using her good right foot, she positioned the impact directly at the lock, and with all her might, she kicked at the locked door. The frame shattered, but the door failed to open, so she became a battering ram and threw her shoulder into the door, exploding through. Finally, the door conceded defeat, and the momentum carried her deep into the kitchen. Acrid smoke filled the room. She took but a single breath of the foul air while frantically searching for Cookie.

Meanwhile, Cookie cowered in the kneehole of the kitchen desk, uncertain about the new noises. The clattering of broken wood and the large form bursting into the room had frightened her. The smell of smoke made it impossible to verify who or what the creature might be.

Eve's absence from the gym had not been noticed immediately. The men had been distracted and somewhat boisterous. Albin noticed Eve's boot cast leaning against the wall and quickly came to the assumption that Eve had gone to change, perhaps use the toilette or the swim spa. Then O noticed the fire, visible in one of the images displayed on the wall.

Eve found herself on the kitchen floor, disoriented by the smoke. Her eyes burned, and she began to feel the effects of the foul air she had inhaled. She called out to Cookie, but there was no response. She struggled to check those places where Cookie frequently slept. As she approached the desk, Cookie's panicked whine became more audible. Eve called out to her. This time, Cookie abandoned the security of her mat and greeted Eve, nudging her with her wet nose. The fire's breath continued to diminish their strength as they slowly made their way through the debris, getting imperceptibly closer to the doorway itself. Suddenly Eve collapsed, and even Cookie's wet kisses couldn't revive her. Excitedly, Cookie took hold of Eve's clothing, biting down, and jerking Eve ever closer to the opening . . .

That was the scene the four men came upon. While Albin and O took over from Cookie and carried Eve a safe distance from her burning home, Kent ran to the gate to ensure that it was open for emergency vehicles, and Matteo contacted his men to secure the area, preventing curious on-lookers from entering. He was relieved to learn that they had already made the call to emergency services. The arrival of the first fire engine soon could be heard.

Unable to access the property through the main gate, Astrid entered through the Gillespies' gate and used the bridge. She arrived at the Tudor before the EMTs arrived.

"Are they all right?" Astrid asked O, as she made her way through the treed area concealing the bridge.

"Eve needs you," he answered, nodding toward where she lay on the grass, Cookie pressed close by her side.

Albin was bent down, his ear near her lips.

"I can't make out what she's trying to say," Albin said, concern and tears leaving behind a tracery in the soot marking his face.

"Here, let me try," Astrid replied, moving to position herself as Albin had done. She put her hand up, her palm facing Albin, to indicate a need for silence as she tried to understand what it was that Eve was trying to say. She listened intently.

"You're not Sidney Carton and you're not dying!" Astrid declared, sitting back up. "She's quoting the end of *A Tale of Two Cities*," she explained to a befuddled Albin, leaving him yet befuddled.

Cookie's eyes showed a degree of redness; she coughed then wandered off and vomited in the plantings. No one but Astrid seemed to take notice.

"Someone needs to take that dog to the vet for treatment, Albin. The EMTs can take care of Eve," Astrid said as she and Albin moved out of the way, and the EMTs began to deal with Eve.

"Kent, can you please get Cookie to the vet's on Tecumseh, at the intersection with Brock?" Albin asked, aware that it need not have been a question.

Cookie seemed somewhat lethargic, so Kent swept her up into his arms and carried her over the bridge and from there into Albin's Land Rover, which he had parked under the portico. His concern mounted when he noticed that, though emergency vehicles and personnel were generally positioned to the one side of the roadway, it remained impossible for him to exit in the usual manner.

He changed direction and drove instead toward Matteo's trailer at the far end of the cul-de-sac. Kent took one look at the conservation area and another at Cookie then switched into four-wheel-drive. He would follow the conservation trail up to the parking lot and exit onto a main thoroughfare directly from there. The way was bumpy, and there would be hell to pay from the municipality, but neither consideration impacted his resolve.

The EMTs had provided oxygen and water to Eve, and she said she was fine, though her ankle hurt—but not the one that she'd previously broken. It was the right one, the one she had used as a weapon against the door. She was now sitting up at the open tail-end of the emergency vehicle. They gave her the option of being taken to the hospital, but, Eve being Eve, she declined. Albin wasn't surprised. She rose from the gurney to allow them to leave, then she shocked everyone by collapsing in a heap upon the ground.

Eve was returned to the gurney and the oxygen was re-started while the EMTs checked her a second time. "Has she ever passed out like this before?" one asked.

Albin answered, "No."

"Yes." Astrid corrected him.

"Which is it?"

"I've been present upon two occasions when this has occurred," Astrid said, "though she didn't lose consciousness then, or if she did, it was momentary. I'd have her checked for a neurological problem."

Astrid noticed the EMT roll his eyes as he caught the attention of his workmate. Albin noticed as well.

"It might be a good idea to listen to Dr. Carlsson; she's a neurologist visiting from Sweden," he said. As he spoke, Albin looked at them sharply, imparting his concern. Then he glanced toward Astrid, as if to say: Don't contradict me on the details.

While the firefighters worked to contain the blaze, the emergency vehicle containing Eve departed for the hospital. Albin ran to the Gillespies'. When he noticed that his own vehicle was missing, he borrowed their Mercedes. The path cleared for the departing EMT vehicle remained available to him. His exit was quick and easy.

CHAPTER 48
COULD THE DAY GET ANY WORSE?

While the vet tended to Cookie, Kent took the opportunity to make some phone calls. His first call was to Astrid Carlsson; the second call was to Yoichi.

"Hi, Kent! What's up?" Yoichi said. The background hummed with with the muted sounds of a sedate crowd and the faint strains of chamber music.

"Yeah, hi . . . Yoichi, can you take this call some distance away from Serge?" he asked. His voice was solemn and the tone suggested the matter was serious.

"Sure, no problem. Just give me a moment to speak to my manager, and I'll go to my office."

He heard some mumbling as Yoichi informed her second-in-command.

"What's happened?" Yoichi asked. She was perched on the arm of the sofa in her office with her phone in her right hand and a glass of champagne in the other.

Kent began to outline what had happened at Eve's house . . . Yoichi put down her champagne and took a seat properly on the sofa while Kent advised her that Serge would be staying at the Carlssons' for the foreseeable future.

"Please don't mention anything to Serge right now. I'd like him to enjoy his evening with you. It's a special day for him."

"Yes, we heard. This is his anniversary. He brought a portrait of Jean-Pierre Allard with him. He still considers this Jean-Pierre's collection."

"I think this has been a good day for him, so I don't want to break the spell until we must."

"Have you phoned Lucy about the fire?"

"No, not yet. She'll want to know how Eve's doing, so I'll speak with Albin first and see if there's any news. I'll let you get back to the festivities."

"Kent," Yoichi interjected. "Serge told me about your meeting and Lucy's most recent sleep-painting. I guess that's now been resolved not too badly from the sound of it. Eve's house is presumably insured, and no one died, not even the dog."

"Looks that way."

Shortly after Kent's call ended, the vet emerged from the treatment room with news of Cookie.

"From your description of the fire, I'd say that Cookie was very lucky. She didn't suffer any burns to her face or muzzle, and if there is any thermal injury to her airways and lungs, it's likely to be very slight. With fires such as this kitchen fire, you would expect the smoke to contain a variety of chemical irritants, which can cause swelling and inflammation, but I've not detected anything significant along those lines, though her oxygen levels were rather low.

"You may have noticed that her eyes are quite red and irritated, so she's squinting. We've provided treatment, and it's now a matter of making her more comfortable by reducing the inflammation.

"What concerns me the most is that you say she appeared a bit weak, and you were advised that she had vomited. Her gums aren't the cherry red usually associated with carbon monoxide poisoning, but I've put her on oxygen because she is showing some of the symptoms. I'm optimistic that she didn't get much.

"We've taken blood samples for testing, and I'll let you know how that works out once the results are in. Or did you want me to phone Eve and Albin?"

"Eve's in hospital, and Albin's with her. Please contact me, if you wouldn't mind."

"The fire?"

Kent nodded.

"I hope it isn't a serious injury. Please convey my concern and best wishes to both Eve and Albin.

"Cookie should stay with us for about three days. We've installed an IV to keep her hydrated. Dogs tend not to want to drink water under these circumstances, oddly enough. Anyway, three days with oxygen and the IV, and there's an excellent chance that she'll be good to go home. You'll let the owners know?"

"I will. Thanks," Kent replied. "Oh, I must tell you that Cookie is a hero. She pulled Eve out of the house. Take good care of her."

"Of course." The vet smiled, and they shook hands before Kent departed.

"Albin, how's Eve doing?" Kent asked, fearing what the answer might be.

"We had a bit of excitement shortly after she arrived. We were waiting, and she decided to visit the toilet, but on her way there she fainted and collapsed to the floor, all tangled in the tubing for the IV and the oxygen. Once they got her back on the gurney, it didn't take long before they did more bloodwork and then whisked her off to Imaging. There's no additional information available yet. How's Cookie doing?"

"That's essentially what I was going to tell you about Cookie, except for the fainting part. She's getting pretty much the same treatment from the vet, but no imaging. She's expected to remain there for three days of IV hydration and oxygen. Vet thinks she'll be fine."

"Well, we haven't been advised of any timeline, and when we are, Eve will defy it anyway, so it doesn't much matter what their opinion is," Albin said, exasperated. "We're waiting on the results of the blood tests. Eve's gone off to Imaging, so I guess they're x-raying her sore ankle. She used her foot to break the lock from the doorframe. That was a thick, old oak door, and she shattered the thing. I really hope her ankle's not broken; she'll be devastated."

"I guess with Cookie being inside, she was highly motivated. Love will do that."

Albin saw Eve, a tangle of tubes dangling from an IV pack on one side and an oxygen tank on the other, being wheeled back to her room.

"So, how did things go?" Albin asked.

"Just pictures of my foot. I hope it's not broken. What have you heard about Cookie?"

Albin relayed the information as he had learned it from Kent.

Eve was relieved. "I'll go and visit her as soon as I can. Three days is a long time for her to miss us, Albin."

By the time the doctor arrived to present the results of the MRI, Eve was bound and determined she was going home. "Well, what is the news?"

"The news is good, Eve. It looks like you've just got a badly bruised foot. You can take ibuprofen for the pain. We looked for a hairline fracture, but found none, so your foot is good.

"I was going to have you stay with us for twenty-four hours at the very least so we could continue the IV and oxygen—"

"I'm feeling fine."

"Yes, that's what I was going to say. You haven't been coughing or displaying a shortness of breath. And you're certainly not hoarse. How about a headache?"

"I frequently get headaches, so that's not connected to this fire," explained Eve.

"Since when?" asked Albin.

"For the past several months—you just haven't been around, Albin."

"So, the headaches don't seem to be connected to the fire. Your eyes are a bit red, likely from the smoke, but the slight irritation should be soothed by some OTC eye drops. Your blood oxygen level—that's determined by this light probe we've attached to your finger—appears normal. I'd say you're good to go. I advise that you follow up with your family doctor."

As the doctor moved away from Eve to converse with one of the nurses, Albin asked, "Has she had a neurological assessment, Doctor? A friend visiting from Sweden, Dr. Carlsson, suggested to the EMTs at the scene of the fire that Eve needed such an assessment." No answer was forthcoming.

Eve's IV had already been removed, so she removed the pulse oximeter from her finger and the oxygen feed from her nose then headed for the wardrobe on the far side of the room in search of her clothing. She had just reached the doctor and nurse when she passed out yet again, her imposing frame ricocheting between a cabinet and an over-bed table on the way down. The force of the crash sent the tray table hurtling toward the doctor, striking him forcefully in the middle of the chest. Through the clatter of furniture, the thud of bodily impact could be heard clearly, as Eve ultimately made full contact with the floor.

Albin watched as a swarm of medical personnel collected around Eve yet again, and she was hoisted back upon the bed. In short order, she was poked and prodded, and the bed with Eve in it was wheeled out the door and back down the hallway to Imaging for a CT of her head.

"Eve just passed out again, Kent. I'm waiting for information. They were just going to release her. Told her to use OTC eyedrops and take ibuprofen—and now they're doing a CT on her head." Albin would have preferred to have been the one in the hospital bed in need of a CT. Clearly, it was difficult for him to see Eve in such a state.

"Well, they'll get to the bottom of this now, Albin; I'm confident." Kent lied.

"Do you want me to do some shopping for you, Albin?"

"Huh? . . . Shopping?" Then the reality of this mundane question hit home for Albin. "Right. We don't have anything but the clothes on our backs—and in Eve's case, not even that.

"I can't think straight to do it, Kent. I guess we need toiletries and clothing and footwear, but I don't know Eve's size for such things, not the exact numbers, you know. I'll check the labels on the stuff they removed when we arrived here and get back to you. Maybe Lucy will have a better idea. If not, we'll get something for her to wear immediately, and then she can do some shopping herself, even just online.

"I guess I should phone the insurance company. And I'll shop online for my—oh, I can't. Yes, I can. My wallet's back at your place though. It seems I drove your car here without my licence. Would you please drive up here with my wallet so I can make some online purchases, and we can switch vehicles? Sorry about all this."

"Albin, don't worry about it. It's no trouble at all. You and Eve have a lot on your plate right now, so whatever you need, just let us know, okay? I'll contact Astrid, and between her and Lucy, I'm confident they'll come up with something for Eve."

"Oh, I hadn't even given any thought to Serge—"

"Taken care of," Kent interjected. "He'll be staying at the Carlssons'. Yoichi says he had a small suitcase with him, so he has some stuff, though I don't know what exactly. We'll deal with it. Don't concern yourself in the least with Serge. He was always my responsibility, not yours.

"So, you'll send me whatever sizes are visible on the clothing Eve's got with her in the hospital, and we'll take it from there. Please keep me updated on things, okay? Remember: Serge is not your concern. I can't say that enough.

"What is left to you is to deal with the insurance and your own clothing needs, but if you need any help there, just let me know. I do have some connections.

"I'll try to contact Lucy again; it seems the weather is interfering, or she's off doing something and for some reason didn't take her phone. Anyway, I'll meet you at the hospital as soon as I can, and we can switch vehicles."

Shortly thereafter, having had a brief discussion with Astrid regarding Serge's clothing and toiletry deficit, Kent phoned Lucy again. As before, she did not pick up. Kent located Albin's wallet in the gym and advised O that he would be leaving in order to meet Albin at the hospital. Effectively, O was now in charge—of what was unclear.

Next door, the Tudor lay in smouldering ruin.

CHAPTER 49
INFORMATION OVERLOAD

"What have you got, Rashid?" Brennan asked as soon as his colleague cracked open the door.

"You wanted me to find out more about the signer on the vanity plate application. The lawyer's name is Langston Garner. He seems to have done this outside of his responsibilities at Garner and Garner—say, isn't that the law firm that had a partner disappear some years back? I always thought that sounded kinda hinky."

"Hinky? I thought that word went out of style even before cool did." Brennan mulled over the information Rashid had deposited onto his desk. "Thanks. Leave it with me. Anything else?"

"Nothing so far."

"Mr. Gillespie, what have you got for me?" Brennan said in answering Kent's phone call.

"Just some news from the neighbourhood. Our neighbour's house burned to the ground today. So far, there's no indication of cause."

"Fatalities? Injuries?"

"One injured; she's still in hospital, so I don't know much of anything. I just thought you should know."

"Which house was it, not the Carlssons'?"

"On our other side, the old Tudor."

"So, this might be one of those age-related problems?"

"Possibly, though I'm keeping an open mind about it. It'll be interesting once the fire prevention officer takes a look at it."

"I know Frank Gies quite well, and he's likely to be the one looking into it. I'll give him a call and fill him in on the few things I can, just to provide some context for his investigation. If it's arson, it'll be turned over to us to complete the investigation."

"How's the Maddie situation? The money's available, isn't it? You've received the instructions for the transfer of funds. Shouldn't it be over by now?"

"It will be, very soon. Tonight. I just hope that weather system that's heading here doesn't disrupt things for us. I hear tell it's expected to spawn tornadoes. We've had a few bad storms already this season. Bad at anytime, but worse tonight," Brennan said, his frustration with the situation building rapidly. "My guess is that Rojas wants to distance himself from wherever they've been keeping Maddie before he shares the information, or—"

"She's already dead."

"Yeah, we've got to consider that."

"Somehow, I don't think that's the situation, Detective Inspector—"

"Call me Pat; time I heard that more."

"Kent."

"Too soon. I haven't retired yet. Tell me why you're so confident she's not dead already."

"Rojas wants the money, and he's getting it. Actually, he's already got it, all of it. He has every reason to assume that Maddie is very important to the Orlovs, else why would they be willing to pay forty million euros for her release. Hell, the Orlovs are the ones who suggested doing this, so Maddie must be important to them, perhaps as important as Aleksandra. At least, that's what Rojas has every reason to think. And I don't think they want to renege on the deal by harming Maddie in case this escalates into a feud with a very wealthy and, therefore, very powerful man. At the very least, it might make it more difficult for them to continue to do business if they were constantly under attack by the Orlovs."

"Well, I must say that you make a good case for optimism, Kent. I hope you're right. The matter is now being handled by the OPP. We're reasonably certain that she'll be released in some manner at the concert venue tonight. My sense is that this delay may also have been a test to see if we'd try to trace the funds, which we haven't. Grigori Orlov is quite the man to let that money just go like that. I really expected he'd want us to try to trace it. Forty million euros. Incredible. I'll give you a call as soon as we have her."

"I think perhaps you should make that call to O rather than to me, Pat. Now that the Aleksandra situation is coming to an end—I hope—my mind is more occupied with my neighbours' problem."

If only Brennan knew how hard Aleksandra had to advocate before Grisha agreed to provide the funding for the ransom, thought Kent.

If only Kent himself knew the truth.

Epitaph

The showing of Jean-Pierre Allard's collection went well at the Song Gallery, and both Yoichi and Serge were optimistic that the auction to follow would be equally successful. Yoichi noticed that a red dot had been affixed to *The Siege of Sevastopol*, the painting by Dzhon Portnoy. When the last guest departed, she asked among the remaining staff members only to have Serge provide the answer.

"I marked it so it would be known that it will not enter the auction," he said.

"Oh, so you've decided to keep it? I thought you found it disturbing, Serge."

"Yes, I do, but you don't, do you?" Serge said. "Please accept this as my gift to you, Yoichi. I hope you never need to run from such flames or even those painted by our friend Lucy. I am eager to see this sleep-painting she has done. And she is so very worried that it is a portent of unspeakable danger. This I find very interesting indeed."

"Serge, thank you for the gift, but you do remember that I receive a percentage based on the selling price you achieve for every work we auction, don't you?"

"Yes, that is the business. This is the friendship," he said, redirecting his gaze from Yoichi to the Portnoy.

She was so moved by Serge's gesture, yet now she had to deliver the bad news and end the day on a sour note. "Come into my office, Serge, and we'll have a little talk and perhaps a bit more champagne before I drive you home."

They were both comfortably seated, drinks in hand. "You won't be staying with Eve and Albin tonight, Serge. Their house burned to the ground earlier today."

Shocked though he was, Serge seemed to take the news in stride. It was likely that in the course of his long life, he had already encountered other tragedies, beyond the loss of Jean-Pierre. He asked questions, and the discussion of practical

295

matters went well, or so Yoichi thought. Then Serge became silent; a sudden, deep, and heavy silence encased him. Yoichi thought rather little of it. The drive to the Carlssons' was particularly quiet, and Serge was formally polite as he was welcomed and consoled by Astrid, Lukas, and the spaniels.

Yoichi didn't stay to visit. It had been a long day, and there was much work left to be done. As she drove back toward the city centre and returned to her Queen's Quay apartment, she became increasingly troubled by Serge's ultimate reaction to the news of the fire.

Brennan didn't leave the office when it was quitting time. He'd asked his OPP counterpart on the case to please give him a call as things progressed. He didn't want to be unavailable, not for the resolution of the final case of his career. When the phone rang, he hadn't the slightest idea what time it was, and he wasn't even all that certain where he was—but just for a moment or two.

"Well, Brennan, seems you were right about the concert venue being the place the kidnap victim will be released. We're in position here, and we've had plenty of surveillance cameras collecting video for hours already, so ultimately we may have something to catch the perps. I'll contact you again when we've got her. The message wasn't all that specific, unfortunately. They said that she's 'under the spike.' Any ideas?"

"Not at the moment. Let me get back to you, okay?"

Brennan put a call into O and relayed the information he had received from the OPP.

"So, we were right about the concert venue. I'll call on Kent and Matteo and anyone else I can find. They might have some ideas. I'll let you know if we come up with something," O advised him.

"A spike?" Matteo said, making a face as if it would help his thought processes.

"I have no idea," Kent said as he slowly shook his head. He rubbed his hands over his face, stretched, and began to pace. "I'm drawing a complete blank. I have no recent experience of venues like that. They host all sorts of activities. From what I understand, they have waterslides and . . . I haven't attended a big concert since I was in my twenties. 'Spike' could refer to something that's always at that location or something specifically associated with the concert itself. I have no idea."

"A friend of mine from Lyon is involved in the music industry, concert tours and the like. I'll give her a call." Matteo located the number in his cellphone and placed the call. He left two messages indicating a matter of some urgency, and when she picked up on his third try, he quickly explained the situation and asked about the spike.

"Okay, just in case that's not it, what would be your second guess? Nothing else? You're sure? Merci, mon amie.

"Lina says that spike is the term which refers to a mark on the floor made with gaffer's tape or paint or even an inlay on the floor itself. She says there's always a centre spike, but sometimes there are also temporary spikes marking the location for specific instruments or risers—but the centre stage spike tends to be the one they reference most often when setting up the stage.

"It sounds like Maddie may be under the stage itself. They may have had her hidden in some carrying case and come into the area as roadies, probably toward the end of setup."

That was all they could come up with in such short notice, so O conveyed the information to Brennan, who passed it along to the OPP. Then they waited.

"I'm getting too old for this," Kent said. "There's nothing more we can do here. I'm going to bed; I'm drained. If Brennan calls back with any news, particularly if it's good news, give me a call."

O and Matteo stayed behind in the war room and drank copious quantities of coffee. "Have you ever considered taking on a partner or two?" O asked. He paused and looked at Matteo.

"Go on, I'm listening," Matteo replied.

"Clearly, you're not well-suited to certain aspects of running Horus Security, and you might benefit from a partnership, which permits you to focus on your strengths. I mean no disrespect. You yourself have mentioned specific strengths you possess and difficulties, which you find quite challenging to overcome. My brother and I are interested."

"I'll give it some thought," Matteo said, trying to keep in check his enthusiasm for the idea. "More coffee?"

The night dragged on, but eventually O received a telephone call from Brennan, and a smile spead across his face.

Ebo first called his brother, Oko, with the news, and then he placed a call to Kent.

"That's great news, Ebo. Did Oko say anything about their communication problems?" Kent said, pleased to be awakened by such good news.

"Not much, just that everything seems to be working now. He said something about a Rachitsky Tower Lucy showed him, and they concluded there was probably an electrical storm in the area."

"Yeah, that's a beta communications tower we're testing for an engineering team at the University of Toronto. It's got some glitches.

"Thanks for the call, Ebo. Now I've got a call to place. Good night—whatever's left of it."

Kent got comfortable for what he expected would be a rather lengthy conversation with Lucy. She picked up promptly.

"Oh good, the phones are working again," Lucy grunted sleepily. "Really nice to hear your voice."

"Yours too," Kent replied, though the quality of her voice was gravelly and spoke of sleep. "I guess I need to report the outage to the engineering team; they're not going to be happy. They need to figure something out so this doesn't happen again, but I guess that's obvious. It's just that it's horrible not being able to connect with you."

"What's up?" Lucy asked. "Something must be up for you to be phoning at this hour." The fog of sleep gradually cleared. "Maddie's been released. That's got to be it! Right?"

"You're right, Maddie's been released, and she's unharmed, but that's not actually why I've called. It's bad news, but not as bad as it might have been. . . . Eve's home burned to the ground today. There were no fatalities. She rushed into the burning house to get Cookie out of the kitchen, and then she passed out. By the time the rest of us arrived, Cookie was tugging on her and pulling her away from the fire.

"They're both okay, considering. Both are in hospital. Cookie will be at the vet hospital for three days, but I haven't heard when Eve will be released."

"How badly was she burned?"

"No, neither one was burned. Sorry, I should have made that clear. Eve was in the house for a very short time and suffered only minor smoke inhalation. They were planning to send her home, but she passed out several times, once rather dramatically according to Albin, so they're doing more tests. I haven't heard anything more from Albin. To be honest, I'm not even sure where he is.

"They've lost everything, Lucy. All their keepsakes: Albin's military stuff, Eve's mementos of her dance career, and whatever she had stashed away about Lars. It's all gone. The house is unsalvageable. I told Albin that we'll take care of putting together toiletries, clothing, and shoes for Eve, but we'll need to wait until he lets me know her situation. She has absolutely no clothes whatsoever. What she was wearing was just gym attire, and they removed that and got her into a hospital gown at some point. It was a mess anyway. Perhaps you and Astrid can arrange something for her."

"Oh sure, I'll talk to Astrid and we'll deal with it."

"I'll take care of Serge's clothing. He's staying at the Carlssons'. I phoned Yoichi and asked her to hold off telling Serge until after the gallery show was concluded. I guess he knows by now certainly, but I've not heard from him. Today will be busy. I thought it was good to keep Albin somewhat occupied with concerns about shopping—that and the insurance claim—but I'll be helping him put together what he needs. It was primarily to distract him while he waited for news about Eve."

"I guess that's the fire in the painting, right?" Lucy theorized.

"Sure looks that way. At least, it's over and we can all relax a bit—what am I saying, there's no relaxation to be had until Eve and Albin are settled."

"I wonder if Albin has been trying to phone Helen?"

"I haven't the slightest idea; he didn't mention anything to me. I suggest you just let her sleep. There's nothing she can do right now, and if Albin is sleeping, he shouldn't be disturbed. The poor chap was having a tough time of it when they said Eve could come home, let alone now that more testing is needed."

CHAPTER 50
IT'S OVER, ISN'T?

"Good morning, Elinor," Kent said as he took a seat at the breakfast table. "There's no longer any need for you to wear that blonde wig, unless you want to. Maddie was recovered unharmed last night, and I suspect that Sandra will be returning here shortly and then going home to resume her life. Thanks for being a decoy. It was definitely above and beyond the call of duty."

"I didn't do anything, Mr. Gillespie."

"I suspect you did, but then I don't have any proof of that. We had all sorts of contingencies addressed, and as long as things have worked out in a positive way, I pronounce it a success. Only hindsight will tell us what things were unnecessary, or where we might have done a better job."

"Good morning, indeed! I heard your proclamation of success, Kent," O declared, as he joined Kent at the breakfast table, "and I happily agree. I understand that Aleksandra will be returning sometime today, so I guess that means I'll be leaving here as well. I regret leaving you to deal with the other matter on your own, this woman who is staying at the island."

"There's no specific timeline on that matter, O, nothing specific at all, so I have no idea what's going on there. I guess we'll focus on that next. Then again, Albin and Eve need some help right now. Our other guest will just need to relax on the island for more of the summer."

"That doesn't sound so stressful now, does it?" O said, smiling.

When Kent's phone indicated a call, he left the company of O and Elinor and took the call on the pool deck. As the call drew to a close, he re-entered the house.

"Elinor, please arrange for pool maintenance and a general cleanup to get rid of all the soot and ash that's landed around here. Give Helen a call on that. I'll be at the Carlssons' if you need me."

Astrid met Kent at her gate. "Something is very wrong with Serge, Kent. If Leo were here, I'd ask him to speak with Serge, but he won't be returning for a few days, and I think Serge needs help now."

"How do you mean 'wrong,' Astrid? What's he said or done to indicate there's something wrong?"

"He's trying to hide it, but I know he's been weeping. The dogs know something is wrong. They're agitated, yet they won't leave his side. I ask him about it, but he speaks quietly and becomes incoherent and then upset, and there is more weeping, so he leaves and goes to his room. I only know that there is trouble."

Astrid indicated which guest suite had been assigned to Serge, and it was there Kent found Serge and the spaniels. The man appeared to have aged ten years overnight, and given Serge's actual age, that was significant—and dangerous.

Hoping his French hadn't deteriorated significantly due to disuse, Kent spoke to Serge in his mother tongue. "Serge," he softly said. "May I join you, Serge? You don't seem to be well. How do you feel?"

Serge appeared nearly catatonic, and Kent had an increased appreciation of the urgency Astrid expressed. He had never seen him in such a state, not even when his beloved Nôtre Dame Cathedral had burned before his eyes. He pulled up an ottoman and sat facing the elderly gentleman, then he gripped Serge's drooped shoulders with both hands. Kent's touch broke the spell that had bound Serge, and he began to sob uncontrollably. He leaned into Kent, who welcomed him into his arms, then Serge went quiet again. As he regained his composure, he sat upright in his chair and looked directly into Kent's eyes.

"I am responsible," he said. "It was my foolishness which has led to this great loss."

"What do you mean, Serge? Kent asked.

Serge punctuated his explanation with sighs, sobs, and incoherency. Kent listened attentively as Serge explained how he had set his little altar of remembrance in front of the open window in his room at Eve's Tudor and how he had lit the candles and, at the last minute, had snatched away Jean-Pierre's portrait, yet failed to extinguish the candles before exiting the room to meet Yoichi. Kent listened but said nothing.

"So, I am responsible for their great loss: their beautiful and treasured home, their personal collections, which tied them to their past, and all those more common, practical things which enable one to live in our world. I have, through my excessive focus on my personal past, taken from them all that they had which represented their past. This was so selfish, so arrogant of me. I am ashamed. I shall, of course, compensate them for their loss, but I cannot see how any compensation I might provide could possibly undo the damage I have inflicted upon them. I am so very sorry, Kent. And I hear that Eve is in hospital. And her darling Cookie is in hospital . . ." And Serge again went quiet.

"Serge, you are overwhelmed by all of this, as we all are. I understand your concern, but the candles were tealights and highly unlikely to have been a cause of the fire, even if you are correct to assume that you should have extinguished them. Why don't we wait to see what the fire prevention officer has to say about it?" Kent said, hoping that the cause might be related to the age of the house, as was Brennan's assumption, rather than to the age of the house guest.

"Let me make a few calls and see if we can get some information sooner rather than later, okay? You just take it easy and spend the time with Merlot and Bijou."

Kent left him sitting there—a forlorn figure hunched in a chair, his eyes cast downward. He had expected to be arranging for replacement clothing for Serge, but that now seemed far less important. Maintaining Serge's privacy, Kent chose not to share the details with Astrid. She didn't press him for information and instead watched as he made a series of telephone calls. When he'd concluded the final call and placed his phone in his pocket, he turned toward her and sported a sad smile.

"Care to accompany me to Serge's room?" he asked.

As before, Serge failed to answer Kent's knock. Undeterred, Kent slowly opened the door and peeked inside. Serge yet remained seated on the chair, ignoring the comfort that might have been afforded him by placing his feet on the ottoman. Again, Kent moved to take his seat on the ottoman, facing Serge. He touched Serge's hand to get his attention while Astrid stood just off to the side and watched.

"I have some good news to share with you, Serge," Kent began. He gave Serge's hand a little shake as if to wake him.

Serge focused his attention on Kent, and there was a glimmer of hope in his eyes, then it quickly faded.

"Eve is coming out of hospital today. She has been declared fully recovered from her experience in the fire. She does have a medical problem, which was only discovered as a result of this hospitalization, and it will require an extensive workup and surgery in the near future. But that's all separate from the matter of the fire itself. So all-in-all, that's the first bit of good news.

"I've spoken with the fire prevention officer himself, and while the report hasn't been filed yet, he says that it is quite clear that the fire was arson and that it was started in three separate rooms. Did you hear me, Serge? Three separate rooms. It wasn't your tealights. This is now a police investigation. The fire prevention officer's coming by the house later today to discuss the matter with Albin and Eve, and later, the police will be by to get our statements. You're most welcome to attend the fire prevention officer's briefing, Serge.

"When you feel up to it, we can talk about doing some shopping for clothes. Lukas wears very nice clothes, but his style and fit aren't particularly good for you," Kent explained, smiling tenderly at the elderly gentleman. "All of the people involved are safe—including you—and the loss of property is largely covered by insurance. This is perhaps reason enough to celebrate with a bit of champagne, I think."

"I heartily agree," Astrid said, and for the first time Serge noticed her standing nearby to Kent and smiling warmly.

"I thought I'd drop by and bid you *adieu*," Matteo said, as he entered the Gillespie residence. "Maxim has pulled the contract since he now feels that Aleksandra is no longer under threat. I agree with him."

"Join us, Matteo, there may be another case here for you," Kent replied, ushering him into the war room.

Matteo acknowledged Albin and O, then noticed the new, uniformed person in attendance. He moved to introduce himself and shake hands. "Matteo Gallo," he said, "Horus Security."

"Matteo, this is the fire prevention officer, Frank Gies. Officer Gies, you were going to present your findings."

"Yes, Kent. This is informal, you understand; however, the full report won't be contradicting anything I say here today.

"I have photographs to support our findings, if you wish to see them. It's quite clear that at least three incendiary devices were used in the upper-storey rooms across the back of the residence. There is no evidence that they were electronic in nature, nor that they were hidden in any bureau or similar. It rather reminded me of the way a Molotov cocktail is thrown, so the location of the start of the resulting fire is random. However, this wasn't a Molotov cocktail; there's no indication of gasoline or alcohol being used as an accelerant. This wasn't a burning rag in a bottle that was hurled through the window. Since this was definitely arson, it will be investigated further by the police.

"We didn't locate an entry point for an intruder, though that isn't surprising, given the extent of the fire. There was no evidence of a break-in detected, and in my interview with Eve, she states categorically that the kitchen door was secured, necessitating that she break into her own house to free the dog. She didn't look elsewhere, but we were able to confirm that the front door was also secured.

"I understand you have surveillance video available. That'll confirm the *when* of the event. This fire spread rapidly, due to the composition and age of the residence. The wood was dry, and there was plenty of it. Think of it as a bonfire. The wind was picking up about that time too, so that fanned the flames.

"Detective Inspector Brennan has put forward some theories concerning a *why*, but nothing specific. He proposes that this was a deliberate attack of arson and very likely not one by vandals or anyone who we might peg as a pyromaniac. If, as he suggests, this is a deliberate attack with deep roots, you folks need to keep your guard up and your surveillance cameras functioning. You might consider placing fire extinguishers in each of the above-ground rooms, in case a similar technique is used here. Mind you, this place wouldn't go up as quickly, given the materials I've seen. I've also noticed you've got a fire suppressant system in place as well, Kent, although it's very well hidden.

"Pat, I mean Detective Inspector Brennan, says you're good at brainstorming ideas, so I'm asking you, how would you go about starting a fire on the upper floor of that house, in three different rooms without entering the structure itself?"

"A football player with a really good arm. And I don't mean soccer, Matteo," Albin suggested.

"There'd need to be some significant momentum behind the projectile to get it through a screen if the window was open, or through the glass in the event the window was closed," Gies said. "Perhaps your football player could throw a wad of something—"

"Wadsworth," said Kent, "Henry Wadsworth Longfellow."

"Who?" Matteo and O asked in unison.

"American poet, 'I shot an arrow into the air . . .' He used an arrow," exclaimed Kent. "Given the speed of the arrow, it would likely still be accelerating in the distance between the ground and the window, so even though the payload wasn't a great mass, the arrow would have sufficient force to penetrate the screening, or even the glass. I don't think Eve ever got around to retrofitting with triple glazing. And wooden arrows would just burn along with most other things. It would still take a lot of skill, given the awkwardness of dealing with the load, but I think it's possible."

"I've seen some impressive archery, and I agree with Kent," Matteo offered. "He could fire off a series of them in rapid succession; all he really needs is for one to work."

"You've seen such archery tricks? With weighted loads?" asked O.

"Yes, it was a test of being able to adjust one's aim to accommodate the unbalanced load. My old partner was a highly-skilled competitor, and on occasion I'd attend to support him. I could contact him for a list of fellow competitors who possibly have such a skill. I don't know how popular such an activity is, or if it is merely a regional sport. As a sport, they use any of the four types of bows: recurve, longbow, compound, and crossbow. In this case, I'd say a small, collapsible crossbow with a short, wooden bolt would work well."

"Perhaps I should interview him to better understand how this might be done," Gies said.

"He works through Interpol's Paris office, in France," Matteo clarified when it seemed that Gies might get confused with Paris, Ontario.

"Maybe not then," Gies said, chuckling. "Pretty unlikely that someone in France will have insight regarding a house fire in Canada, so let's hold off on that. We're still waiting on the completion of chemical analysis to identify the accelerant; it's got to be something other than gasoline. Sometimes, when an arsonist is particularly motivated, they'll hedge their bet and use a combination. Pat sure was right about the creative thinking you do."

"Might it be possible to fire a giant match as one would an arrow?" O asked. "A phosphorous tip would require only a bit of heat, possibly from friction as on a match box. It becomes a simple question of engineering, doesn't it?" O sketched his concept on a whiteboard as he spoke. "Perhaps a device behind the tip that generates sufficient friction to ignite phosphorous located behind it, further along the wooden shaft. It might work."

"Interesting. You've given me some food for thought, gentlemen," Gies said. "Now, let's take a look at the video you have from your surveillance cameras. I know that the police will request it, but I'd really like to view it to help verify the timeline."

O activated the system for playback of the surveillance video they had for the day of the fire. They advanced rapidly through the first portion of the recording, then slowed it down and paid more careful attention once there was evidence that the fire had started.

"What's that?" asked Albin. "There's someone in the wooded area, just before you see Eve approach the bridge into her property." The recording was replayed to confirm what Albin had noticed.

As they continued to watch the video, they realized just how much time had passed before they followed Eve outside and across the bridge. There was uncomfortable silence.

"There . . . again . . . ," Albin said, pointing out each time the intruder became visible. "We wouldn't have noticed him because our attention was on Eve and the fire, which by this time you could hear and smell."

"I'll need to switch cameras," O said, and the view changed to one focused on the house, taken by a camera set in one of the trees. Someone carrying something—a bow, perhaps—could be seen entering the pool house.

"How would he know to enter by the pool house?" Matteo asked.

"I think the skylights mounted in the deck give away the presence of the tunnel," Kent said. "Perhaps there was drone surveillance at some point that we missed. He seems resourceful."

"Where did he go?" Gies interjected.

"We don't have a camera in the tunnel that connects the pool house to the gym here in the basement, but there is a good view of the gym from this camera." O switched feeds, and again they located the intruder. He wasn't masked, but by chance he hadn't looked into the camera. "No problem, let me slow this down and enlarge it. Concentrate on his reflection in the mirrors. There's bound to be one that's informative. Here, this shot. Let me enlarge this and reverse it to correct for the mirror image."

"O, can you clean that up and send it to the LED wall in the gym?" Matteo asked.

"Sure, but why? This is big enough, isn't it?" O replied.

"This is even bigger than you think it is. It deserves to be on the wall," Matteo said emphatically.

"You may be right, Matteo," Kent added.

They left the confines of the war room and entered the gym. Kent activated the LED wall and Officer Gies was suitably impressed. After a short wait, a clear photo of the intruder appeared on the wall. All eyes were on the intruder; then they shifted questioningly to Matteo. He was silent until a moment later when they were joined by O.

"Gentlemen," Matteo began, "I give you Luc Anouilh, my former partner and now Interpol section head in charge of the France-east, including Paris. This is the archery expert I was telling you about. He is also a member of one of our great families; they are all powerful and influential members of the judiciary and law enforcement. *Merde.*"

CHAPTER 51

REVELATIONS

"I hope communications are still functioning," Kent said in conversation with Albin as they entered Kent's office on the main floor. The others had returned to the war room to wait. There was little reason other than curiosity for Officer Gies to have remained. He claimed it was to meet with newly-appointed Detective Sergeant Rashid Darwish, who was collecting statements regarding the fire and currently speaking with Eve, Astrid, and Serge elsewhere in the house. A busy morning was rapidly turning into a busy afternoon.

Kent placed a call to Lucy on L'Orté Island and, after providing her with an update, made a second call to Juliette. They quickly dispensed with pleasantries, and Kent delivered the bombshell of information.

"You've heard that our neighbour's house burned to the ground?"

"Yes, Lucy and Helen were discussing it."

"It was very likely part of an attempt to get to you, Juliette."

"I don't get the connection."

"Here's your connection: Luc Anouilh. He's the arsonist. And after he set the fires next door, he entered our house while we were busy with Eve and her dog. Elinor was in the panic room at the time and didn't even know he was here."

"I find that hard to believe. You must be wrong, Kent."

"We caught him on the security recording, Juliette. It's him; there's no doubt. Do you want to leave the island and face things here, now that you know who is involved, or would you prefer to remain where you are?"

"Well, O left a short time ago with Blomma, who I now understand is actually Aleksandra Orlov, so the cabin cruiser has left the island. The wind is picking up here, and there's talk of another storm brewing. Lucy says the last one knocked out communications awhile, and we don't know how severe this one may be. I'm not big on helicopters at the best of times, Kent, let alone in such weather. I don't know that they'd even want to chance it. The short of it is that I'll stay here and return to Toronto tomorrow, assuming the weather is better by then.

"What precisely did Luc do while he was in your house?"

"It appears he was just looking around, likely to find some evidence of your presence. We'd taken steps to make it very difficult for anyone to find Aleksandra, and I think you've benefitted from those precautions as well. We traced him through the house and saw just how close we came to discovering him ourselves upon occasion when we returned here. But we were focused on the fire next door—which is what I think was the whole point of the fire. Some good people lost everything, just because Luc Anouilh needed a distraction."

"But he was alone?" Juliette asked incredulously. "I can't for the life of me—"

"Nor can I. Seems this wasn't merely business for him; it was personal. We've both had committed enemies after us, Juliette. Sometimes they appear to act outside of logic. A sort of operational myopia, perhaps?

"Okay, so you're staying where you are," Kent concluded, adding, "I'd like your permission—or a really good explanation for why I shouldn't discuss this in more detail with the authorities here, Juliette. Matteo Gallo is also with us; he was working for Maxim Orlov on an additional protection detail for Aleksandra. He's seen the video on Luc, and I'd like to let him know more about what's going on regarding you."

"I guess," Juliette said, the tone of her voice tentative. "I'll trust your judgement on this, Kent. I worked with Luc for many years and never suspected him, so clearly my judgement is flawed. At some point, Interpol will need to be notified."

"I'd suggest leaving that for the police authorities here and for Matteo, who can liaise with all parties. For today, you continue to stay safe on the island. I think the three of you should be able to manage quite well. We'll talk again tomorrow and, if you want, arrange then for your return to Toronto."

O piloted the cabin cruiser toward Port L'Orté and docked at Doyle's. While he waited for the owner to tally his account, Aleksandra took a seat inside the restaurant portion of the old waterfront complex, enjoying her freedom.

The large screen television behind the bar carried the news of the day and featured a story about a cat that was friends with a mouse. Also behind the bar, the owner's son, Darrin, was busy topping up supplies for another hectic day. Having noticed Aleksandra, the young man tidied himself, then grabbed a pen and order pad.

"Hi, I haven't seen you around here before. What can I get for you?"

"Just strong black tea, please. And do you have any jam?"

"So, tea and toast, is it?"

"No, thanks, just the tea and jam. I use it to sweeten my tea," Aleksandra explained.

"That's it?"

"I'm just waiting for someone. Perhaps he'll order something more. He's with the owner, Mr. Doyle, I guess, paying for a boat rental."

"Ah, there's no 'Mr. Doyle,' not for a very long time anyway. My great-grandfather built the first bar and decided to name it after a good friend of his who had gone missing years before, a bit of local lore, I guess. Over the years, the Fourniers have continued to develop the site, and everyone has come to know the marina, the hotel, and the restaurant as 'Doyle's.' I guess that's how it'll stay."

When Aleksandra's order was brought to her table, she stirred a large spoonful of strawberry jam into the strong black tea and paid little attention to the television until the next segment began.

The captioning identified her as "kidnapping victim, Maddie Birch," and Aleksandra wondered for how long she would be identified in those terms, and how she might now view herself. Maddie, appearing alert and focused, was seated at a table with her parents. A uniformed OPP officer sat beside Mr. Birch. Aleksandra thought Maddie seemed wound a bit tightly, but that was understandable. She wondered why Detective Inspector Brennan wasn't at the table with them. She took a sip of her beverage and continued to watch the news report.

"We had no choice but to suspend the concert while officers explored under the staging in order to recover Maddie. We are grateful to those in attendance and to the members of Lizard Brain for their cooperation," the OPP officer explained in answer to a question from one of the journalists in attendance.

The lead singer and the lead guitarist for Lizard Brain suddenly appeared, and cameras centred on them rather than those at the table. They walked over to Maddie and handed her an envelop, explaining that inside there were four tickets to their next concert and vouchers for food, travel, and accommodation. Maddie graciously accepted, and she received hugs and kisses from the two band members.

The presence of the celebrities appeared to derail the press conference. They failed to interview Maddie and no mention was made of the ransom payment. Aleksandra was pleased, but she suspected that Maxim wouldn't be. The news programming continued, but little of the reporting was news to Aleksandra. The announcer droned on . . .

"In business news today, the death of billionaire Grigori Orlov. Orlov, eighty, was reported to have died on board his yacht, *Croesus*, near the French city of Nice. Rumours abound that a power struggle is rapidly developing between his two surviving sons: Maxim and Ilya. We'll have to watch how that plays out.

"Markets were down in the materials sector today; mining stocks took a beating . . . "

Through no fault of his own, Patrick Brennan had arrived late to the press conference. His tardiness wasn't noted. He'd not been invited. Brennan had found it difficult to gain entry to the press conference since he was now officially retired. He hadn't realized that his retirement had been fast-tracked, and there was no grey area—he was either a cop, or he wasn't one. But he had every intention of being present to look Mr. Birch and Maddie in the eye and bask in success. So Patrick

Brennan finagled his way in, though he arrived late. He took great pleasure in ending his long career in this manner, even in the absence of the recognition it richly deserved. *Recognition— never received it, never would,* he reasoned.

As the press conference came to its awkward end, Brennan watched as Mr. Birch whispered something to Maddie, and all three members of the family rose from their seats. Intending to disappear into the crowd before one of the uniforms accosted him, he nevertheless stopped when he heard someone call out his name. It was Mr. Birch.

"Detective Inspector Brennan, I'd very much like Maddie to meet you, sir."

"It's just Brennan now, Pat Brennan, Mr. Birch. I've been retired."

"Well congratulations to you, and all the best on your next adventure. Please, call me George," he said, extending his hand.

Brennan and George shared a firm handshake, then Mrs. Birch offered her hand. "And I'm Marge; it's so nice to see you again. . . ." Mrs. Birch rambled on, just as her husband tended to do, as Brennan was duly thanked by Maddie's happy parents.

"So, I guess you and some friends will be off to enjoy a Lizard Brain concert somewhere—that should be quite the experience," Brennan said, directing his comment to Maddie.

"After being stuck under the stage during part of their concert, I never want to hear Lizard Brain again," Maddie said, adamantly. "I think I'll look into how the tickets might be used to raise some money for victim support—maybe a lottery or an auction."

Brennan smiled, and Mr. Birch outlined to Maddie and her mother how Pat had been instrumental in her release.

"My dad says the ransom was paid by someone else, and he said it was forty million euros. I looked it up, and that's over fifty million Canadian dollars, Inspector. That's got to be wrong; I mean, that's just crazy."

"No, your father's correct, as are you. If you want further information about the payment of the ransom, you might talk to your friend, Aleksandra Orlov."

"Sandra Orlov? She's not really a friend; I mean I know her, but we just kinda had the same ex—"

"Trust me—she's your friend," Brennan said, emphasizing "friend" and holding Maddie's gaze until he saw a greater level of understanding take root.

"So, Pat, how are you going to be spending your retirement?" Mrs. Birch asked, perplexed by her daughter's stunned look and sudden inability to hold a conversation.

"Some fishing, I guess, though I really haven't even sorted out my pension yet. That's somewhat a priority, or so I've been told."

Mr. Birch removed a business card from his wallet and handed it to Brennan. "Give me a call, and I'll take you through the process if you want, Pat. Even later today if you have time. Please, it would be my pleasure. And, by the way, I'll be writing a letter or two about this. You haven't received the recognition you deserve. Maddie being home is your doing."

The foursome left the press conference: Maddie and Mrs. Birch led the way, followed by Pat and his new friend, George.

"I am fine, Lucy," Eve claimed. "Don't you worry about me. Albin does enough worrying for everyone. The doctors say this is a straightforward operation, and in no time at all, I should be well recovered from the surgery and be my young self. Well, they said 'old self,' but I like my version better. Albin and I are staying in Helen and Elinor's apartment at your house, so we are very comfortable.

"You should take precautions today, Lucy. I've been watching a lot of television in between repeating myself to doctors, the fire people, and the police. The weather reports are all talking about some terrible storm that's expected to hit your area and may have tornadoes and many such things that I don't understand, but they all sound bad, and some sound even worse!"

"Don't worry about us either, Eve. They said all that about the storm we had yesterday, yet all it did was mess up our telephones awhile. Ultimately, it was just another electrical storm—typical weather on Lake Erie. We haven't had rain, and I bet we won't get any this time either."

"I don't think we got much of it around here, not Lake Ontario. The wind had picked up a bit at the time of the fire . . . " Eve trailed off and while Lucy wasn't certain where her thoughts had pulled her, she let Eve bide her time and choose where to take the conversation.

"I'll send you my sizes. I really appreciate you and Astrid arranging something for me to coordinate a new wardrobe. Many of the things I had were too big, but if my weight loss is connected to my problem, then after the surgery, I should return to my normal weight. Maybe I shouldn't buy anything other than what I really need to get by until then. But I don't yet know the timeline involved, though they've mentioned three weeks. One test depends upon the previous one, I guess."

"So, what exactly did the doctor say?"

"Well, when I fainted at the house, they blamed the smoke and excitement. I don't know what they blamed the fainting on when the EMTs were here, but I don't think anyone was too concerned. Then, when I fainted for the first time at the hospital, they said it was because I'd gotten up from the gurney too rapidly, and because I'm tall, my blood pressure plummeted. I think they finally took notice when I crashed into everything just after they said I could go home. Apparently, the doctor developed quite a bruise as a result.

"They did some scans of my head, like Astrid had suggested to the EMTs. They already knew my blood sugar was low, which is why I'd been given juice. When they looked at the CT scan of my head, they discovered a tumour on my pituitary gland. They call it an adenoma and say it's benign, though I don't see how they can tell at this stage. They will perform surgery through my nose as soon as they have all the measurements. I'm told this isn't something that needs to be rushed; it just needs to be done reasonably soon. For a few weeks, I am taking some hormones that are supposed to help me feel better. Actually, I do already. Maybe it's just knowing there was a reason for how I was feeling before and what was happening to me. I thought it was all in my head—and I was right!

"They—not the doctors, but Albin and some firemen, I guess—located two of the safes from the house. The locking mechanisms were damaged by the heat, but I'm happy to say that Albin got into them somehow.

"Cookie is doing well. She was happy to see us. I'll visit her once a day, and Albin has promised to visit twice. She'll be home with us very soon."

"You sound good, Eve. I'm glad. You'd tell me if you were feeling down or were unwell, wouldn't you?"

"I think you would figure it out before I could even tell you, Lucy.

"You know, Lucy, it's not particularly nice to be featured like this in one of your paintings. But perhaps it was time for me to turn the page and move on with my life. This fire was the push I needed. You didn't ask what was in the safes that was so important, Lucy."

"I thought it was none of my business."

"If you're going to be a witness at our wedding, it certainly is.

"Albin and I had separately bought a ring for each other some time ago. I did not know about his, and he did not know about mine. However, we had not taken it that one extra step of asking the question. We have now taken care of that, and Euphrosyne Vighild Ek and Albin Tyrchniewicz will be exchanging vows and rings in a small civil ceremony to be held as soon as possible."

Having dropped that bombshell, Eve added, "I appreciate your call, but I think I need some sleep now."

There were some parting comments, and they disconnected, leaving Lucy happily flabbergasted.

CHAPTER 52
SEEING THINGS

Two days earlier . . .

The man Langston knew only as Calogero seemed as intent upon bringing down Juliette as Langston did himself. He was impressed that Calogero sought to involve himself in the task, rather than to consign the job to an underling. He learned that Calogero had commissioned his own surveillance of the Gillespie estate, which supported information Langston had obtained later from Spencer, and it was determined that Juliette was most assuredly connected with that location.

But while Langston agreed that it appeared she had been there, he wasn't convinced that she yet remained there. He was willing to stake everything on her being on L'Orté Island. They agreed to disagree.

When Calogero exited their meeting, Langston immediately placed a call to Spencer to see what information he might be able to collect about Juliette and whatever and whoever might be at L'Orté Island.

As soon as he had made arrangements to have Preston cover for him at the office, Langston left for Port L'Orté to survey the situation there and learn as much as possible about the Gillespies, the island, and its current visitors. Information compiled by Spencer would give him a head start, he pre-dicted. Langston was well-versed in the history of the small watercraft, which were popular on the lakes of Ontario, and the lore of the mahogany runabouts favoured by early cottag-ers. This provided him with plenty of material with which to begin discussions with locals and visitors to the area, and he expected that by the second day, he'd have collected sufficient information. The overnight accommodation was a bit rustic for his tastes, but the discomfort was a small investment with the promise of a great return.

This morning . . .

Langston was taking a leisurely breakfast at Doyle's when a cabin cruiser docked and a strapping black man, broad-shouldered, and in the company of a young, blonde female, emerged. His mere presence commanded attention and intimi-dated Langston. While the female entered Doyle's restaurant, Langston watched through the window as the man entered the boat rental office. Quickly Langston exited the dining area and followed the man, ostensibly to arrange for the rental of a boat. While the man arranged for payment of his rental, Langston overheard mention of Gillespie and island and knew his luck was turning.

"Will the ladies continue to need delivery of fresh produce?" inquired the owner, Mr. Fournier.

"I don't really know. Probably. You should give them a call before you make any changes to your agreement. There's one less now, so it might just be a matter of quantity," O replied.

Langston thought himself rather clever. As soon as the man departed, he ramped up the subterfuge. "Did he just return that cabin cruiser?"

"Yep," Fournier answered.

"I'll take it."

"You want to know the rate first?"

"No, I trust it's the going rate, and you won't gouge me. Besides, it's perfect, and I don't want anyone else to claim it while I'm dithering about it."

"I've got to clean it up a bit for you."

"No need. Just refuel it for me, and it'll be good to go. My wife will clean it up even if you do, so it'd be a waste of your time, my man. She brings her own cleaning supplies and fresh linens, so don't bother. What can I say? The woman's a bit fastidious—okay, nuts is a better word." He chuckled at the scenario he'd created, failing to notice that Fournier hadn't joined in.

"Well, okay. If you're sure, it's fine with me," Fournier said, reaching for a checklist affixed to a clipboard hanging from a hook on the wall.

The exchange went back and forth awhile. Fournier went down his checklist, verifying that Langston knew how to handle the boat, what safety equipment was available, and how the marine GPS worked. When finally Fournier appeared satisfied, the deal was struck, and Langston provided a cash deposit along with identification in the form of a driver's licence.

"Okay, everything seems to be in order, Mr. Martin," Fournier said, matching the photo on the licence with the man standing in front of him. He handed Langston the completed paperwork. Langston attempted to hurry Fournier along, but Fournier seemed intent on providing even more advice. Langston's annoyance became clearly visible on his face as Fournier continued.

"There's a storm headed this way, so I expect you back here before things get too rough out there. Don't go losing my boat, ya hear! It's up to you to tie her up at the dock and get the tarpaulin covering in place. That's all in the contract, in case you're wondering. Had my lawyer take care of that."

Langston wasn't wondering; he just wanted to get out of the office already, grab a few supplies, and leave for L'Orté Island. Eventually, Fournier released him from his hell of minutiae.

He placed a final telephone call to Calogero.

"How did it go?" Langston inquired.

"I cleared the house and took a good look; there's no evidence that she's there. You're at the island, I take it?"

"Yes, well, I'm at the port nearby, but I've got a boat, and I know where I'm going. Friendly yokels are amazingly chatty."

"*Les crétins*," offered Calogero. "Perhaps I should drive down and join you."

"No, there's a storm coming in, and I want to finish this before it hits. I can't wait for you." Langston ended the call. He didn't want or need Calogero. He already had Spence. This was always as he saw Juliette's end coming, just the two of them—Spence didn't count. He didn't expect there to be any significant challenge presented by the women left on the island; at least the imposing, brawny man was gone.

The vessel was of adequate dimensions and weight to deal with the waves, even as they increased in size and became markedly larger toward the end of their trip to the island. The pitching of the boat caused Spencer to heave overboard, and that disgusted Langston.

He noted that there was dockage on one side of the island and rocks and debris on the other. A large stone house was visible through the vegetation on the rocky side, and he remembered that one of the yokels had spoken of an old manor house. An odd tower structure could be seen on a rocky promontory toward the north end of the island. The beacon acted much like that of a lighthouse, and Langston decided that the panels and dishes he saw were likely a solar array powering its light source. Through the tree covering, he could just make out the sharp angles of a modern structure, the house itself.

The storm was coming up faster than Langston had anticipated, but as yet the clouds did not appear to be heavy with rain. It was, however, darker than expected for that hour of the day. Waves crashed against the dock, and trees began their dance, their branches and leaves agitated by the increasingly strong gusts. Langston approached the dock area, cutting the engine as early as possible and tying the rental at the outermost point of the floating wooden structure. Spencer remained useless.

Langston took hold of his equipment and checked again that his gun, another gift from the friends of Calogero, was loaded. This would be the first time he'd ever had occasion to use it, and he found himself somewhat excited by the prospect.

"You brought a gun!" Spencer hissed. "Why? You said this was information gathering. I don't need that shit Langston. I could lose everything, you pompous ass." It would have sounded forceful, as Spencer intended, had he not still been feeling queasy. He clung to the bottom of the boat, ignored by Langston.

Exiting the boat proved a challenge for Langston as the waves moved the dock and boat, seemingly in opposite directions. Once on the dock, he staggered and stumbled and swayed while the dock increasingly pitched and rolled. When he finally reached solid ground, he found a well-worn path and followed it to the house, a modern multi-storey structure with plenty of glass. Some rooms were already brightened by artificial lighting to compensate for the early arrival of darkness. He watched and looked for a point of entry.

Inside the residence, the occupants adjusted to the rather sudden departure of their young guest and her bodyguard. Helen had returned Aleksandra's bedroom to an unoccupied status, cleaning and airing drawers and cupboards, stripping the bed, and removing the linens. Toiletries and cleaning products were returned to a central storage area. Juliette was occupied in trying to be helpful, but providing her with specific tasks was more work for Helen than carrying out the task herself proved to be. So, Juliette wandered about the house, listlessly trying to find something to occupy herself. Eventually, she found herself outside Lucy's bedroom door.

"Lucy," she called out, giving the door another gentle knock in case the first had been too light a tap.

Inside her studio, Lucy had heard both the initial tap and now Juliette's second attempt to get her attention. Emotionally exhausted though she was, she finally chose to answer her door.

"I'm sorry to disturb you, but I feel so useless; what can I do to help?" Juliette asked.

Lucy sighed, then softened toward the intrusion. "Okay, how about you remove that sleep-painting from the wall and bring it to the studio? I'll put the previous one back up." Lucy fetched the painting of the manor house and crossed Juliette in the hallway as she delivered the painting of flames to the studio. Lucy joined her shortly after.

"Will you be completing the third canvas for the Orlovs?"

"I don't have the slightest idea, Juliette. I haven't heard from Agafya, Aleksandra's grandmother. I thought I'd just wait until after the funeral and give them time to get things settled. I think that Aleksandra and her uncle Maxim—and I presume O as well—have already left to be with Agafya. I'm not going to work on the third canvas until I hear from them."

"What are you planning to do with this painting of the fire?"

"That I don't know either. Probably put it into storage. I don't think my friend, Eve, will want it. It's really not an interesting painting."

"May I see it again before you put it away?" Juliette took the painting nearer to the windows to take one final look. . . .

"What's this?" Juliette asked.

"What's what?"

"Down here, near to the bottom and toward the left, where it's a bit darker . . ."

Upon closer examination, Lucy could just make out the awen that Helen and O had looking to find. The odd quality of the sunlight through the storm clouds had revealed the form and it now appeared quite distinctly.

"Would you please get Helen for me? I'm not too sure which room she may be in right now. Just bring her here, please." While Juliette went to fetch Helen, Lucy kept her eyes fixed on the awen, half-expecting it to fade from view.

Time seemed to pass slowly, but eventually the women returned. Helen joined her at the window to examine the painting.

"Maybe this one deserves a permanent home here, along with the manor house painting, Lucy," Helen said when Lucy pointed to the awen in the painting. Helen took the painting into her own hands and examined it at various angles in the available natural light, looking for additional awen. Juliette joined them, peering over Helen's shoulder.

"Don't look now," Helen said, her tone somber. "I mean it. Just continue to act as we have been. There's someone outside the house. I don't know who it is, but no one is expected, so I think we've got to assume the worst. Let's just wander over to the sofa with the painting and sit and figure this out."

After their planning meeting ended, Helen grabbed three sets of matching blue coveralls from the storage closet and distributed them. While they changed and found proper footwear, Lucy phoned Kent, but again, the storm was already interfering with cellphone service.

"Okay, we're on our own here." Lucy said. "We've got things to do like we talked about when Aleksandra and O were with us."

"Ultimately, we stay inside and take refuge in the panic room until we can get help, right?" Juliette said, seeking reassurance.

Helen nodded.

"There's a panic button built into the base of the Rachitsky Tower," Lucy said. "It activates an emergency signal of some sort. I'll go and activate it."

"No, let me," Helen replied.

"We're not arguing about this, Helen. Your job is to keep Juliette safe. You two are off to the panic room. That's final. Just make sure you have everything you need in there and that you've secured the outer part of the house as best you can. But do it quickly. I'll join you as soon as I can."

The women disappeared deeper into the house, but Langston was pleased that at least he had identified Juliette. She was the one garbed in blue, while another had been dressed in green, and a third was wearing a white shirt and black pants.

Helen returned to the storage room, unlocked the gun cabinet, and removed the shotgun, an M3020 Compact. She loaded it then re-locked both the cabinet and the storage room. Meanwhile Juliette collected up all the knives from the kitchen and took them with her into the panic room. There was no need to provide additional weapons for an intruder to turn against them.

Langston rounded the corner of the house just as a figure wearing blue quietly exited and made her way in the direction of the odd-looking tower. He fondled his Beretta then followed the figure at a distance.

After giving Juliette strict instructions to remain in the panic room, Helen decided to follow Lucy to the Rachitsky Tower. She reached the back door of the summer house just in time to see a hunched figure stumbling through the undergrowth. The figure appeared to be compensating for the force of the wind that was impeding progress along the rarely used path to the tower, though without much success.

As Lucy made her way ever closer to the tower, she sensed, then distinctly heard, the sound of someone following. *Helen,* she assumed, though she remained cautious and focused on the task at hand. Finally, she reached her destination. She located, then depressed the button that would relay an emergency signal to someone, some place. She wasn't too sure about the details. There was nothing to indicate whether her action had been successful. There was nothing more for her to do; she had done all she could. Lucy stepped back from the tower, ready to return to the house.

"Behind you!" Helen yelled.

Lucy turned to face her and saw the intruder.

Surprised, Langston turned his head toward Helen, leaving his body positioned at a ninety-degree angle between the two women, and for the first time, Helen saw that he was holding a Beretta pistol. As their eyes met, he seemed as surprised as she was. Here was a second woman dressed in blue, and she was yet another wrong woman. And this one had a shotgun.

"Drop the gun," Helen commanded.

He didn't have time to consider her demand.

Lucy saw the gun in his right hand in the same instant that Helen did. It triggered in her an immediate response, and she reacted as she had been trained by Albin and later by O. Acting with lightning speed, she took a single step toward Langston, and with her left hand she hooked his forearm near his wrist and pulled it toward herself while simultaneously striking his wrist forcefully with her right hand. The action effectively dislodged his weapon, and it went flying into the underbrush. She followed that with a powerful, adrenaline-infused palm strike to his right temple, knocking him to the ground. Thanks to her training and reflexes, it had all taken but a split-second.

At that moment she caught sight of a flash of blue. A form was rapidly moving within the vegetation and travelling in the direction of the manor house path. *Was Juliette being pursued by someone?* Lucy left her attacker on the ground and gave chase to the blue form.

Helen had taken a single step toward the disoriented Langston when Spencer suddenly appeared, crawling about within the shrubbery. She took no chance that he might find the Beretta. She aimed her shotgun at him and announced her intentions. He protested that he was just trying to secure the Beretta so Langston wouldn't get it. While Helen's attention was focused on Spencer, Langston found his legs, though not his Beretta. He bounded through the thicket after the blue forms that had caught his eye— away from Helen and her shotgun.

Uncertain what this second intruder's role was in the attack, Helen collected the Beretta and, pointing it at him, ordered him to move back down the path to the house. There she located tape and cord and managed to secure him, under threat of being shot—his choice: the Beretta or the shotgun.

When Helen went to check on Juliette and provide an update, she found the panic room empty. Juliette was gone. It was unclear when she had left and where she had gone. There was little Helen could do other than guard her prisoner.

But Helen could excel at intimidation. "Where is she?" she demanded, assuming a crazed expression.

"Where's who? I don't know who you're talking about. I came up to the house to make sure Langston didn't do anything stupid. I didn't know he had a gun. Honest!" Spencer continued to plead his case. "I thought we were coming here just to talk to you ladies. Honest!"

Lucy glanced backward and saw Langston struggling to gain on her. Though she had taken her eyes off Juliette for just a moment, when she returned her attention to the path ahead of her, Juliette's blue form had disappeared from view. Nevertheless, Lucy continued her race, luring Langston even farther from the summer house. She was more agile and more familiar with the territory, so he was unable to make ground on her. She veered off the path to the manor house, stumbling noisily as she followed a less worn path. Langston continued his relentless pursuit.

Behind Langston, and unknown to them both, Juliette now followed at a distance. Lucy continued her run toward the rock cliff, just beyond the glade where Aleksandra had discovered the cairn. The crashing of surf against the rocks below echoed through the trees. The wind had picked up, and leaves and twigs were being ripped from the trees and thrust toward the runners in a growing maelstrom. Juliette caught up to them in the glade. Flashes of lightning illuminated the horizon with increased frequency.

"Hey," she shouted, "I'm the one you want." She could feel the hairs on her neck and head prickle. The intruder stopped and turned toward her as the sky lit up again. "Langston," she said, identifying her cousin in the flash of white light. Disappointment swept over her.

"Bitch," he mouthed silently, menacingly, as he took a step toward her. She held her arms behind herself and her feet in a broad and stable stance against the wind. Defiantly, she held her ground, as if trying to stare him into oblivion.

Lucy stood at a distance from them, transfixed in the moment. Although she failed to hear the words spoken, it was evident that the communication between Langston and Juliette was both significant and ominous. The feeling was palpable. It was as if the air were electrically charged. There was a profound solemnity to the moment, and then the peace was shattered.

Langston ran toward Juliette, and the distance between them rapidly closed. Just as he lunged for her, she repositioned her right arm, revealing Helen's favourite chef's knife, and thrust it forward and up at an angle. He was impaled upon the six-inch blade. She may have given it a twist as she withdrew it. In that moment, he seemed surprised, unwilling to accept that he had underestimated her. Perhaps he was distracted by pain.

Amid sounds of buzzing and crackling, he stumbled backward, toward the ancient walnut tree at the edge of the glade. The bolt of lightning that hit was blinding, and the explosion of the walnut tree and the nearby cairn spoke to the phenomenal force of nature. Lucy and Juliette were knocked to the ground.

Somewhere in the middle of it all was Langston—past tense. The walnut tree and surrounding brush caught fire—as did the body of Langston Garner. The fire quickly spread. It was all Lucy and Juliette could do but pick themselves off the ground and run to escape the scorching red spires as the flames took on a life of their own.

They reached the fork in the trail but maintained their frantic pace. As the summer house came into view, the skies opened, and a welcome rain pelted down harder and heavier than at anytime Lucy could ever remember. It quenched the flames and washed away much fear and sadness, leaving a new calm in its wake.

Their running slowed, and they made their way back to the summer house in silence, save for the sound of water. Large drops continued to fall from the sky; water trickled from the branches above onto those below; water accumulated and formed rivulets on the uneven ground, and the surf continued to pound the shore. The winds gradually diminished even as the rain continued.

They were met at the summer house by an anxious Helen and a compliant Spencer. While Lucy went into the kitchen and put on the kettle for tea, Helen and Juliette ushered him into the suite previously occupied by Aleksandra and locked him inside the walk-in closet.

"Aw-w, c'mon, I'll be good," he entreated, but his whining was ignored.

"It's just until your transport arrives from the mainland," Helen explained.

"You'll survive until then, dear," Juliette added.

They locked the bedroom door, then Helen went to the kitchen to tend to the tea while Juliette and Lucy changed into dry clothes. The women convened a short time later in the great room.

"What were you doing, running toward the cliff, Lucy?" Juliette asked. "I was worried you'd forgotten it was there and would end up going over onto the rocks."

"Oh, I knew where I was. I thought if I could get him running fast enough and then divert to the side, he'd possibly continue straight through. We were lucky with the lightning. I've never seen anything like it. It's been so dry here that the whole glade went up in flames, Helen."

"I guess that was the fire in your painting. It wasn't Eve's house fire after all," Helen commented.

"Perhaps," Lucy answered. "Such a shame to have lost that old walnut tree. It's as if the sky's been storing up the rain this entire season, just to dump it on us now. I'm so very thankful for it.

"I looked out over the area when I was upstairs just now. The fire seems to be out; I couldn't see any hotspots. I think we can relax."

"I checked as well, and I agree with you," Juliette affirmed.

"What I'd like to know is why you didn't stay in the panic room, Juliette," Helen asked.

"Well, I left the panic room to grab a bunch of cookies, if you must know."

"Cookies." Helen rolled her eyes.

"Yeah, cookies," Juliette repeated. "I eat cookies when I'm nervous. I knew Lucy had gone out to that tower, and I suspected you had as well. I was planning to return to the panic room, but then I saw the guy we've got upstairs..."

"Says his name is Spence," Helen interjected.

"I saw Spence and thought I could help in case he gave you and Lucy any trouble. I think I may have been inspired by Serge and his attitude toward villains. Anyway, I went out the other door and found a path, but I guess it wasn't the one you'd taken. Once I got out there, with the wind moving the branches around and everything, I got spooked, so I started to run in the general direction of the tower. At that point, I could have sworn someone was running after me."

"That someone was probably me," Lucy said. "You certainly looked like you were running from someone. I just got a quick look at you, but that was my impression. That's why I left Helen to deal with Langston, and I ran after you."

"As soon as you took off, Lucy, Spence showed up, and as I was dealing with him, the other one, Langston, got up and took off after you. I couldn't stop him. I didn't want to shoot in case I'd hit you. It was hard to make out where exactly you were. I didn't know Juliette was out there too."

"I didn't see him behind me initially. I was just running after Juliette. I glanced backward at one point. I heard him or sensed him, I guess. Anyway, when I looked back in the direction you were going, you were gone, Juliette!

"I dropped off the trail near the fork in the path and hid behind the old oak tree. I needed to catch my breath and it was such a relief to finally know exactly where I was. You ran right by me, then I saw a man coming up after you. I didn't know at the time that it was Langston, not until that first flash of lightning in the glade."

Lucy and Juliette shared with Helen the details of their encounter with Langston and his death in the glade.

"It's really too bad about the old walnut tree," Lucy said, repeating herself.

"Speaking of walnut, Lucy, something's been in the back of my mind since you first mentioned that tree after the fire. May I please borrow the barrel key? I just might know where it belongs."

"How about some brandy in your tea?" Helen suggested while Lucy went off to fetch the barrel key with the Janus carved into its bow.

The three women sipped their tea with brandy, nibbled cookies, and periodically tried to connect with the mainland by phone. Eventually, they each nodded off where they sat.

Outside, the hotspots around the glade steamed, and the still air was damp and heavy with the smell of smoke. What remained of Langston's body rested near the cairn.

Once the storm ended, marine and air traffic resumed. Emergency services, responding to Lucy's distress call, arrived toward morning. Kent, Albin, and Matteo arrived by helicopter.

The Gillespies left the matter with the authorities. Having entrusted Helen and Albin to secure the premises, Lucy, Kent, Juliette, and Matteo returned to Toronto. Later that same day, Juliette invited them to accompany her to the offices of Garner & Garner.

Kyle Garner was called to the reception area, a request Sarah was loath to make.

"Juliette, you're back!" Kyle Garner said in greeting. His tone and facial expression were well practised. He was friendly, but guarded. Juliette introduced the three people who accompanied her, then moved toward Langston's office, the office that had once been hers.

"I'm sorry, you can't go in there. Mr. L has a client waiting for him," Sarah exclaimed, expecting that Kyle would act to prevent their entry.

"Actually, I'm taking this meeting," Preston Garner called out while rapidly approaching from his office at the end of the hall.

"Mr. L is no more, I'm afraid," Juliette stated flatly. Sarah was confused. Kyle had already been provided with certain facts, so while he remained taken aback by the bluntness of the statement, he permitted them to enter. Preston continued to protest the intrusion and appeared unaffected by the news concerning Langston, his father.

"Might you know the identity of the client, Sarah?" Kyle inquired.

"It's a Mr. Calogero," Sarah answered, stumbling over the pronunciation.

Juliette opened the door to the office and came face-to-face with her remaining nemesis. "Surprised to see me, Luc?

Langston will be missing your meeting. And you're going to be missing a lot of meetings, well into the distant future I should think."

While Kent phoned Detective Sergeant Rashid Darwish to request his presence, Matteo had the dubious pleasure of detaining his ex-partner, Luc Anouilh, AKA Calogero. As they waited for the Detective Sergeant, Juliette and Lucy began to examine Langston's old burled walnut desk.

"I remember this desk being in Langston's office since Grantham retired from the practice. This office used to be mine, but the furnishings are Langston's," Juliette explained.

Ultimately, they focused their attention on the marquetry panel over the kneehole, and Lucy discovered that it could be flipped downward, revealing a series of four, small, brass name-plates: Clarence Garner, Grantham Garner, Langston Garner, and Preston Garner—his career pronounced dead in his thirty-fourth year. In the middle, positioned between Clarence and Grantham, was a brass keyhole escutcheon constructed with a split cover depicting the Roman god Janus.

"There's no key for that," Preston said, seemingly uncertain whether he should remain or leave. Kyle told him to sit.

Juliette's excitement was apparent as she removed the barrel key from her purse and tried the lock. It was tricky. She paused, took a deep breath, and tried to position the old key yet again. This time, she heard the click as the lock released, and a cubby hole containing a metal box dropped down into the kneehole. Gingerly, she reached in and retrieved the box, placing it on the top of the desk.

After yet another deep breath to steady herself and calm her nerves, she opened the unlocked box to reveal a treasure trove of old documents, all signed by or referencing Clarence Garner, the first Garner Janus. The documents contained the names of individuals who were contacts for the Calogero crime syndicate throughout North America and Europe during the early to mid-1900s. Among those names, the one that stood out for Juliette was that of Judge Hugo Anouilh, the great-grandfather of Interpol special agent and chief of operations for France-east, Luc Anouilh. Matteo placed a call to Interpol.

CHAPTER 53
GHOSTS

As soon as the various teams of police and fire personnel, and one group of engineers from the University of Toronto, who thought this a good time to check on the Rachitsky Tower, completed their tasks and departed from L'Orté Island, Helen and Albin closed the summer house and returned to Toronto. They brought with them a little something for Lucy.

Helen and Albin gathered everyone in the Gillespie household and asked them to have a seat in front of the fireplace in the great room. The siblings appeared delighted by something. Helen was grinning.

"Helen, you look like a Cheshire cat. What's up?" Lucy asked while moving to take her seat.

Albin reached into the bag he carried and withdrew a parcel wrapped in layers of towelling. All eyes were on him as he removed the towelling to reveal a metal box, measuring about seven centimetres in height and resembling a tissue box. But this box had a lid and padlock. The metal bore the bluish blush of oxidation, and the soldered joints were dark with a heavy tarnish.

"One of the teams working at the glade found this. They said it had been hit by the lightning, likely the same strike that blew apart the cairn," Helen said, as she proudly and happily handed the metal box to Lucy. "And we didn't sneak a peek, so curiosity is killing me."

"The lock was fused," Albin explained, "so I cut it open with the tools I had. I hope you don't mind."

"If you hadn't, I'd be asking you to do that now. It was a good decision, Albin. Thanks." Lucy placed the box on the low table in front of her and examined the thermal discolouration of the metal. Aware that this might very well be the last box to be found at the site, the contents—whatever their nature—she already considered to be a treasure.

Inside, she found a single roll of parchment. "A scroll of some sort," she said. "I can just barely make out the writing on it. I'll probably need to send this to one of your U of T contacts, Kent, just to be sure I'm right, but I'll give it a try.

> "'On this day and in this place, I buried my dear friend, Giovanni Sarto, torn from us in his thirty-fourth year by Jozsef Szabo and Clarence Garner. His dear wife to be taken to St. Margaret's where his child will be welcomed into loving arms.'

"This next bit is written more forcefully. 'Curses be upon those who desire wealth and power above all.' It's signed by Connor Doyle and dated 1933. I think it's the twenty-first of October.

"Thank you, Connor," she whispered, "Thank you for giving my grandfather back to me." Lucy would arrange for Gianni and Annie to be reunited; there was no doubt in her mind about that. As she returned the parchment to the box, a single tear marked her cheek.

Grandaunt Gracie would have been pleased.

True love is like ghosts, which everyone talks about and few have seen.

— Francois de La Rochefoucauld

THE END

GLOSSARY

Antibes	French town on the Côte d'Azur, between Cannes and Nice
arraksboll	Swedish; *punsch cake pop bites*
asma	Italian; *asthma*
Aubry Prison	Fictional French prison near Limoges
avocat	French; a lawyer who is a member of the bar, works independent of the client
babushka	Russian; *grandmother*
Billy Bishop Airport	At the time of writing, there had been mention of permitting jet traffic at this airport in Toronto, but the landing of jets there may yet be a fiction
bon matin	French; *good morning*
chokladbiskvi	Swedish; *chocolate biscuit*

CT scan	A computerized tomography scan which combines a series of X-rays into a series of cross-sectional images
dedushka	Russian; *grandfather*
El Viruñas	Spanish; *the virus*; in Colombian folklore this is the equivalent of the devil; a fictional drug cartel
fika	Swedish; *coffee or coffee break*; used as both a verb and a noun
fouettés en tournant	French; *whipped turning*; a ballet move usually performed as a series in which the dancer turns on one foot while thrusting the other outward and inward at each revolution
Gkide	Nishnaabemwin; a fictional lake in Ontario
Gkinaa	Nishnaabemwin; a fictional town in Ontario
god morgon	Swedish; *good morning*
houlala	French, from Arabic; *wow*
hue	Pure pigment, usually in vibrant colours

Interpol	An international organization that facilitates worldwide police cooperation and crime control
J'ai besoin de champagne.	French; *I need champagne*
Janus	Roman god; fictional old mob term for their "special" lawyer, a community member not otherwise known to be their associate
juriste	French; a sub-class of lawyer who is not a member of the bar and is therefore considered unqualified, though possibly a legal scholar and expert on the law
kardemummabulle	Swedish; *cardamom bun*
Limoges	French city known for decorated porcelain
Lyon	French city near the confluence of Rhône and Saône Rivers
Mary Jane	An American term for a closed, low-cut shoe with a strap across the instep
Merci, mon ami	French; *Thank you, my friend*
merde	French; *shit*
Mnimi	fictional drug; Greek word for *memory*

MRI	Magnetic Resonance Imaging
OPP	Ontario Provincial Police
OTC	A reference to drugs sold without a prescription, over-the-counter
Port L'Orté	Fictional; small touristy town on the north shore of Lake Erie, a short distance due north of L'Orté Island
Port Myer	Fictional; previous name of Port L'Orté
postura	Italian; *posture*
punsch	Not to be confused with the generic term, "punch," this eighteenth century Swedish alcoholic beverage originated in Java and is a mixture of spirits (arrack, brandy or rum) with arrack tea, sugar and water
punschrulle	Swedish; *punsch roll*
Rachitsky Tower	Fictional communication tower design
Rufina	Russian; *red-haired woman;* Grigori's nickname for Lucy
schadenfreude	German; *malicious joy; celebrating another's misfortune*
tint	Pure pigment plus white produces delicate pastels

tone	Pure pigment plus grey reduces vibrancy and is generally more pleasing to the eye
shade	Pure pigment plus black darkens the colour
sotto voce	Italian; *said quietly, so as not to be overheard*
U of T	University of Toronto
ustrasana	Camel pose is a kneeling, back-bending yoga pose
zayka	Russian; *bunny*—used as a term of endearment

ABOUT THE AUTHOR

Author, artist, and "gym rat," J. A. Gibbens holds degrees in biology and chemistry from the University of Waterloo and in education from Queen's University. She has worked in the field of research and pathology, taught high school students for twelve years, and established a financial services business. She has written two other novels—*L'Orté Point* (2021) and *Cow on the Ice* (2022)—the first and second books of The Awen Chronicles. *Epitaph: Full Circle* is the final instalment of the trilogy.

J. A. Gibbens lives in Guelph Ontario, with her husband, and a woodchuck that lives under their deck.

REVIEWS

The Awen Chronicles, a trilogy
Book 1—*L'Orté Point*

"A complex, riveting thriller about shocking family secrets . . . Gibbens has crafted a gripping series opener with unpredictable yet believable twists and turns. The author skillfully mixes the dark doings of her unsavory characters with more lighthearted scenes between Lucy and her loved ones."

— *Kirkus Reviews*

Book 2—*Cow on the Ice: ko på isen*

"Gibbens once again delivers an engaging mystery, returning to the dynamic character of Lucy Gillespie with a whodunit that offers bigger twists and more compelling villains. Astrid and her friends Lilly and Juji are intriguing new players who bring a challenging new mystery into Lucy's life. The characters feel like real people, and the story that surrounds them is immersive and suspenseful throughout."

— *Kirkus Reviews*

Book 3—*Epitaph: Full Circle*

"Gibbens concludes her multigenerational family drama series with this eventful thriller . . . The tangles of the plot involving powerful, plotting lawyer Langston Garner and surprisingly adventurous architect Kent Gillespie branch elegantly through-out the narrative. The author throws herself into narrating this sprawling, complicated story with tremendous gusto and a sharp skill at drawing characters . . . A fizzy and fast-paced conclusion to a complicated family saga."

— *Kirkus Reviews*

Printed in the USA
CPSIA information can be obtained
at www.ICGtesting.com
LVHW051119290823
756579LV00001B/51